THE TELLING

THE TELLING

Jo Baker

Vintage Books

A Division of Penguin Random House LLC

New York

FIRST VINTAGE BOOKS EDITION, SEPTEMBER 2015

Copyright © 2008 by Jo Baker

The Library of Congress Cataloging-in-Publication Data
Baker, Jo.
The telling / Jo Baker. — First Vintage Books edition.
pages ; cm. — (Vintage original)
1. Haunted houses—Fiction. I. Title.
PR6102.A57T45 2015   823'.92—dc23   2015008304

Vintage Books Trade Paperback ISBN: 978-0-8041-7265-3
eBook ISBN: 978-0-8041-7234-9

www.vintagebooks.com

Printed in the United States of America
10 9 8 7 6 5 4 3 2 1

For Glenn
with thanks

The light was fading. I was pretty sure I was lost. The car wasn't used to that kind of driving and had started making a nasty whining sound on the bends. I hadn't reached the Hall yet, hadn't passed a house in miles. I pulled in at the side of the road, bumped up onto the grass, switched off the engine. There was a breeze, a bird singing; it was so quiet.

I rifled through the junk on the passenger seat for the directions, snapped them straight and peered at Dad's crabbed handwriting. The car ticked as it cooled. If I'd gone wrong, I couldn't see where. I'd come off the motorway at the right exit, taken that turn, passed the lake and the farm. The next landmark was listed as Storrs Hall, a grand old house with a tower, in woodland, off to the right of the road. The village would be shortly after that.

I slipped another chip of chewing gum into my mouth, crossed my fingers, and turned the key in the ignition. The engine started first time. Another ten or fifteen minutes, I told myself, pulling out onto the empty tarmac, bothered by the low-level whine from somewhere down and to the left. After that, I'd have to think of something else, find someone, ask for directions. But that was easier said than done: I hadn't seen a soul, hadn't even seen another car, since I left the motorway.

The tarmac spun on between stone walls and patches of hedge. Wide scrubby fields sloped up towards the sky; trees stood torn and twisted by the wind. A building blurred past. I glanced back in the mirror. A square-fronted house, its windows blank, and a vast stone barn standing in the blue twilight. It made me notice the dark. I flicked my headlights on.

The road ahead became a tunnel, and I hurtled down it far too fast. Any minute I would catch up with the sweep of my own headlights and blunder on into the darkness beyond. The road dipped into woodland. Branches broke the sky into a flickering craze. I eased my foot off the accelerator as the road swept in smooth bends downhill. Glimpsed in passing, a crenellated tower stood against the evening sky. Then flash of wrought-iron gates, a curve of gravel. The Hall: it must be, at last. I felt as if I'd been driving forever. Even so, I wasn't keen to arrive.

*

A terrace of stone cottages first, and then a crossroads. A shop, a pub, a school, a parish hall, none of them open. According to the directions, it was half a mile down the village street, towards the church. I made the turn, and drove on about half a mile, slowed to a residential-area crawl. And there it was.

The cottage stood elevated and set back from the street, six stone steps leading up to the front door. I pulled in at the side of the road. Whitewashed walls glowed in the twilight; four front windows reflected back the evening sky. It looked like a child's drawing of a cottage. I'd seen it in a photograph, but then it had stood flat against a blue-summer sky, and Mum had been sitting on the top step in jeans and a print blouse. Now it loomed solid, stony. I got out, took a lungful of clean, cold, wet air. Reading Room Cottage. The place they chose to be.

The front steps were worn into hollows and the handrail was skin-smooth. The clutch of keys weighed heavy in my hand, the old leather key fob pressing against my curved fingers, folding back on itself.

I turned the key until it clicked.

The door opened into the living room. I saw the faded blue sofa-bed, sagging in the middle, the arms worn shiny. Next to it, the smoked-glass coffee table from when I was a kid. Stuff that could be spared from home. Stuff that would do for summer holidays and Easter breaks, while they did the place up. Stuff that would do until they retired, until they lived here.

I went in and dropped my holdall. The carpet was flattened and tracked with grey. A breakfast bar corralled off a stark kitchen extension. To the right of it there was a staircase, modern, with separate planks whacked into the wall and a banister of cheap dowel and unsmoothed wood. The smell of the place hit me: a smell like forgotten Sunday dinners, damp, long emptiness.

I wanted to be home, stepping over toys, the flat smelling of coffee and baby and drying laundry.

I headed straight back out to fetch the rest of my stuff from the car; it seemed to have got much darker already, as if I'd blinked, and afterwards something of that internal darkness lingered. I opened the boot, lifted out Sainsbury's bags, and glanced up the village street.

The tarmac was slick as graphite in the moonlight; windows caught a gleam here and there. There were no lights on in any of the houses. And beyond the street, the darkness seemed deep, and somehow absolute. I knew that out there, the M6 was streaming with light and fumes, strip-lit service stations were selling coffee and cigarettes and travel sweets, that there were towns and cities and hospitals and people, teeming people; but it didn't quite seem possible, didn't quite seem real. Not beyond this blue-black night, a tree's bones, the call of some bird or other.

I shivered. I slammed the boot shut, scooped up the bags and scrambled up the steps. When I flicked on the light, a latticework of shadows scattered across the room. The lampshade was one that Mum had made in a craft class, out of string and glue and a now long-burst balloon. It was way off-centre. It gave the room an uneasy feeling, as if everything were slipping sideways, as if it were sinking.

I dumped my groceries and took my bag upstairs. Here and there I could see traces of something real and beautiful in the building. Smoke-stained stone, ancient wood. Clues to what they'd seen here, what they'd wanted to realize. They must have thought they had years to peel all this away; the stained carpets, the greyed woodchip, the varnished plywood. That they would be able to uncover something.

I glanced into one of the bedrooms. Two single beds lay draped with white candlewick. The curtains were thin and drooping. A dressing table, varnished thickly brown, stood underneath the window with a primrose-yellow kitchen chair pulled up to it. None of it was familiar, it must have belonged to the previous owner, and there was a smell, a faint lingering sourness that I couldn't identify. I pushed open another door: a box room, stacked full of boxes; shoeboxes, cardboard boxes, a tangle of wire coat hangers on the floor. An old brown suitcase trimmed with aluminium that I remembered from childhood airport carousels. Laundry bags full of books, carrier bags stuffed with objects wrapped in newspaper. I lifted out a papery bundle, weighed it in my hands, instinctively knowing the cool heaviness of it. I peeled back the paper: the pewter jug, for big bold flowers, for daffodils in springtime, long-stemmed roses in summer, dahlias in autumn. The sleek curve of the metal sucked the warmth from my hands. I could smell newsprint, and the jug's metallic tang. The room felt cold; it was as if the shadows had taken a step closer.

I could just go. I'd be home by midnight. The flat with its night-time smells of baby bath and milk; I'd sneak into Cate's room and kiss her head, her hair curling into sweaty ringlets, and pull the covers up over her shoulder, and slip down the corridor and out of my jeans and into bed beside Mark. He'd mutter something, not really wake; I'd listen to him breathe. The alarm would go at half past six, and we'd lurch awake, and I'd be there, where I shouldn't be, and that would make him right. Right about me, and about what should be done about me.

I pushed the final door.

As it swung slowly open my mobile rang.

I remember that moment, the sense of pause. Even though I was looking down into my bag, rifling for my phone, there was something about the space in front of me that brought back a memory of my Mum's jewellery box, with its interior padding of pink baize; a memory of picking through her bits and scraps of jewellery, laying them out on her counterpane. The room felt absorbent, somehow, containing, as if it would take in sound and light and warmth and hold it.

My hand closed around the phone. Mark calling. I flipped it open, stabbed at the buttons with a thumb, the other hand reaching around the doorjamb to fumble for a light switch. The room seemed spacious and high, a reservoir of dark. The call connected.

"Hey there," I said.

"Hey. How is it?"

My hand brushed the inner wall.

"Y'know," I said.

"Oh."

I could hear the shift in tone. I should have been more careful.

"Doesn't matter," I said. "Get it sorted, get home. That's what we said. I knew it wasn't going to be pretty."

"You're just tired after the drive, Rache. You'll feel better in the morning."

After sleeping here, in one of those sagging beds, absorbing the sour smell and the damp into my clothes and hair, waking in the morning to walk the worn grey tracks across the carpet? I could feel myself contract, like a touched snail: I couldn't face it. At the same moment the back of my hand brushed against a light-cord.

I caught it, and tugged. The light came on. I saw the bookcase. I went towards it.

I was opening my mouth, and drawing a breath to tell Mark, when the phone bleeped, and went dead. I glanced at it; connection failed. I slipped it into the back pocket of my jeans.

The bookcase was massive. Maybe eight feet tall and five feet wide. It was completely empty. It stood in the middle of the gable wall, the ceiling sloping away to either side; it was the only point in the room high enough to accommodate its size. It must have been built to fit. In all her talk of this place, she hadn't once mentioned the bookcase. She'd been keen to discuss her growing list of books for retirement-reading, the books she hadn't had time for in her thirty years of teaching; the books she'd worn to shreds in rehearsing them for A levels. Living here, she'd binge-read, she'd gorge on these books; that was why the place had seemed so fitting, with its unusual name. She'd talked about all that, and their plans for renovation and refurbishment, but she never once mentioned the bookcase. The wood was dark and old, and there was something about its crafting, the way its parts were shaped and finished and fitted together that gave it an almost archaeological feel. No lines were ruler-straight, no edges precision-angled: it was as though the wood had been split along its fault-lines, smoothed and considered and pieced together in the only way the grain would naturally allow. I laid my hand on a shelf. It was silky, ridged with veins, and my own pulse beat back at me.

Behind the bookcase, I could see the gable wall was bare unplastered stone. Underneath, the floor was uncarpeted. It must have stood where it had been built. The whole house had morphed and changed around it, covered itself in woodchip and magnolia and varnish, but this had remained here, darkening with the years. A kind of gentle heaviness descended on me, like thick fog. It was as if I had been waiting to feel like this, as if I had just been holding it off till I reached this moment, this room. I thought, I can stay here, if I just stay here it will be all right.

I noticed the rest of the room bit by bit, in a tired way: the bare worn wood of the boards, the last blue evening light spilling in through the window beside me, onto the varnished surface of a dressing table. Over to the left, in the back wall of the house, a door stood open: the bathroom, on the top floor of the extension, directly above the kitchen. The light was soft through the window that overlooked the street; it caught on the dark blue satin quilt on the bed underneath, silvering the bulge of each pocket of down. The wardrobe door stood open: clothes hung darkly inside. I walked over to it and pushed the door shut; empty coat hangers chimed against each other.

✳

I lit the fire and emptied out the bags of food that I'd brought with me. I ate straight from the packets; breadsticks, hummus. I swigged wine from half-remembered petrol-station tumblers. I checked my phone. There was a signal, so I phoned Mark.

"It just went completely dead," he said.

"Yeah, the signal went."

"You didn't call me back."

"He-llo? Calling you back now?"

"It's been ages. I thought you'd fallen through the floorboards."

"You would have heard the crash."

There was a smile in his voice. "You over your wobbles, then? You okay?"

"I'm fine. I'm tired, like you said; it's a hell of a drive. And I miss you both."

The smell of woodsmoke, the taint of garlic and wine, and a feeling that was like nostalgia, but not quite: it was all somehow unexpectedly familiar.

"We'll be up to see you at the weekend, take back the first load. Don't kill yourself over it, Rachel, you've got plenty of time."

"A fortnight. There's not that much to do, really."

"You can always come home early. But take your time. Don't overdo it."

"How's Cate?" I asked.

"She's brilliant. She keeps telling me 'Mummy back soon,' like she's trying to reassure me. Mum bought her a new toy lion; she keeps shaking it and pretending to growl and you have to be scared."

"That's great," I said, my throat thick. "That's really great."

"Yep," he said. "Don't you worry. Just you get the stuff sorted, and take care of yourself. We're doing fine."

I couldn't settle after that. I had one of Mum's comfort reading books—*Pride and Prejudice*—but even with that I couldn't get comfortable. The top of the breakfast bar was only slightly wider than the base; my legs were twisted around to one side. I fished around for a toehold, glanced down, saw that the bottom of the breakfast bar was formed out of the old back wall of the house; where I was sitting had originally been the garden. The wall was a good two feet thick, made of great big undressed stones. It looked like a tree stump; rooted in the earth, organic, cut abruptly off.

I felt it for the first time then. A faint electrical hum in the room. The fridge, perhaps. The cooker. The TV.

I turned a page and took another sip of wine. It was sour and dusty on the tongue. The hum continued, and I ignored it, but it soon became intrusive, irritating. I slipped off the stool and crossed the kitchen to check the fridge. I switched it off at the socket, and there was a kind of wet, settling rattle, but the hum didn't change. I switched it back on again. The cooker was off at the wall. The little portable TV was off, no standby light glowing. I was puzzled. I stood a moment, breath held. The hum was still there: if anything, it had grown. It wasn't even a noise as such; it was a tingling, an agitation; it teased the hairs up on the backs of my arms. I switched off the downstairs lights. In the sudden dark, my eyes swam with coloured amoebic plaques. I stood and listened. The room seemed to soften in the darkness. The fire's glow took on a new intensity, and I was aware again of the old smell of the place; of damp and someone else's cooking and the faint sour greenish smell. It was not a scent I associated with my parents. It must, like the carpets, the wallpaper, and half the furniture, come from the time before, from someone else.

I brushed my hands down my arms, rubbed at them.

The wiring must be dodgy. Or someone was vacuuming in a nearby house. Or it was internal; post-motorway tinnitus. It could be anything, really. The fridge clicked into gear; it hummed a slightly different note, as if in confirmation.

The fire had crumbled down to glowing coals. I dropped on another log and put the fireguard on. I left the lower floor in darkness. It felt quieter up in the Reading Room. Gentler somehow, more welcoming.

*

I wasn't really asleep. I was conscious of the space beside me on the mattress, the dint in the flocking where my ankle pressed, the give of the springs beneath left hip and shoulder. I was listening to the darkness. Amazing, just the distance of it. Here and there, a splash of sound. A fox's bark—I recognized that—and a bird's cry, and the sheep in the field behind the house calling back and forth across the dark. And then just as I was drifting off to sleep, there was a screech so loud and sudden that it startled me bolt awake, and I was staring around the room in darkness, my heart going like a train. I reached for the bedside lamp, but it wasn't there, of course; it was back at the flat. I lay in the bed just looking into the black, and there was nothing: no movement, no further sound, and my heart began to slow and settle. I got up out of bed and went to switch on the light. The bookcase stood solid and dark and stacked full of shadows.

An owl, perhaps; or something killed by an owl, up in the fields behind the house.

*

Daylight. There was a sense of weight beside me in the bed; if I just reached out a hand, Mark would be there. Cate down the corridor in her little room: a mutter; she's about to wake. The day teetering on its brink, ticking towards the shriek of the alarm. The race of it all ahead of me; a battle with breakfast and with the pushchair and bus, and Cate's clinging at the childminder's, and then work; and the books dragged home from work, and lugging Cate onto the bus and she'd be tired and starting a cold, and holding me responsible. Feeding her, and bathing her, and putting her to bed, and feeding us, and getting on with the marking or reports or lesson plans, and an exhausted slump in front of the TV, watching the news with the sound turned down, ice shearing into the waves, blood in the dust. Hurtling, unstoppable change. Night, and bleached sleeplessness. Hours staring into the dark.

There was no alarm clock. The space in the bed was cool and empty. The house was silent. I didn't have to be awake, not yet.

*

I spent the morning wiping dead flies from windowsills and fingerprints from doors. I dragged the old upright vacuum out of the kitchen broom-cupboard and did all the carpets. I found a rusting cylinder of Vim under the sink and scoured the baked-on meat juices from the inside of the cooker. I cleaned the bathroom. I opened all the windows. The house smelt clean; of vacuuming and Vim and wet spring air. It needed doing, it all needed doing. I wasn't wasting time.

There was no means of making coffee in the house. No cafetière, no percolator, not even one of those filter efforts you balance on top of a jug. So I made coffee in the teapot and brought it, with a cup and a tea-strainer, back upstairs. I was going to go into the box room. I was going to go in with my cup of coffee and start sorting through the stuff, unfurling packages, assessing their contents, putting them in one of three piles, destined for home, Oxfam, or the bin. But instead, I found myself standing at the Reading Room window, looking out at the garden, at the nodding daffodils, the bare branches of a tree trembling in the wind. At the end of the garden stood an electricity substation; it was surrounded with green chain-link fence. On its pebbledashed wall was a sign showing, in silhouette, a man falling over backwards, a lightning bolt embedded in his chest. Beyond it was a farm, though it didn't look as if it was still in use; there was no sign of animals. The outbuildings were all painted pastel blue.

All I could think was: this is an ending. The beginning was lost; the first peeling of the helix from its twin, the first bulge and split of cells: there is no way back to that from here.

THE DAFFODILS WERE BRIGHT YELLOW AND THE DAMSON tree was in milky blossom. It was a fresh spring day and the sky was tumbling with clouds. I'd sat at the window in my Sunday dress, staring out across at Agnes's house, nothing moving, till it seemed like everything—flowers, tree, Agnes's four windows and brown front door—were all painted on the glass, and not real at all. It was like looking at the windows in the church, of St. Hilda and St. John, too deeply coloured, too neat, too calm to be anything like real.

My work lay beside me on the flags, a book was neglected in my lap. I had my shawl wrapped tightly around me; it was cold away from the fire. No one came, and no one left, and I shivered in the draught, and Mam scolded me for mooning about and wasting the day. The light began to fade.

She left for the evening milking, and the boys were playing out somewhere, and Sally was at the Forsters' for her tea, and the house was empty.

I had wanted to stay with Agnes, but they wouldn't let me. I'd asked her mam to let me know when it was over, and she had said she would send me word the first chance that she got. What good did I think I'd do anyway, my mam wanted to know. Hanging about, getting in the way? I'd only scare myself, and be put off ever marrying, and end up an old maid. But it seemed to me that it would be better to be with her, to know how things went with her, however badly they were going, than remain in ignorance for so long.

Dad would be back soon. Once he was back, and given his tea, I would just slip across the street and gently knock, and if someone answered I'd ask after Agnes, and if no one answered then I would just come home, and no one need know I'd been, and I'd be no worse off than I was now.

I had the kettle hot on the stove, the teapot standing with the tea spooned in, the canister with its picture of a Chinaman and a lion put back on the dresser. The bread and the cheese were cut, and a clean cloth laid over them. There was nothing more to do. I leaned against the table, chewed a fingernail. Of my mam's confinements that I could remember, none had taken as long as this.

My father's cap came bobbing slowly along the far side of the garden wall. I poked up the fire, got the kettle steaming. He scraped his way up the steps, and came in. His cheeks were flushed: he brought a pool of cool spring air with him, and the smell of his work, of horse and tobacco and beer. He was in one of those slow, philosophical moods that he gets into when he's had a drink or two. He saw the steaming kettle and the tea things set out on the table, and shook his head, as if it were some fancy of mine to make him his tea, but he was prepared to humour me and play along with it. Then he saw my book lying on the windowsill, saw the work half done and lying on the floor, and his mood turned sharply.

"If you're going to waste your time reading that old nonsense again," he said, his breath sweet with malt.

"It's Sunday, and it's *Pilgrim's Progress*, which is a fine book for Sunday," I said quickly. "And it's better than many ways of spending the Lord's Day."

He gave me a look, sat down in his chair, and kept himself bolt upright in a poor imitation of sobriety. I made the tea and I gave him his bread and cheese. I left him to pour his own cup and slipped out to stand on our top step, and look over to Agnes's house. No candles lit there, as yet.

It was a lovely soft evening, a little way off dark. The sheep were calling up in the back field, and someone was chopping logs up at Goss House. A curlew flew overhead, giving its shrill repeating cry. I went down the front steps, crossed the road, the loose stones crunching loud underfoot. I peered through the front window, but couldn't see anyone. I rested my ear to the front door. I heard nothing but the beat of my own heart. I thought that she had died. That she lay cold and dead upstairs. That they could not bring themselves to tell me. I lifted the latch; the door creaked open, and I stepped inside, onto Agnes's clean-sanded kitchen floor.

The room was stuffy; I could smell something sweet and rich and spiced. There were figures slumped at the kitchen table. I moved closer in the gloom and saw that it was Mrs. Skelton and Agnes's mam, and that they were sleeping, their heads resting on folded arms. In the middle of the table was a half-eaten batch-cake, the crumbs scattered like grain, whole raisins lying plump on the scrubbed deal tabletop; the scent sweetened the air. Agnes had made the cake for eating after the baby came, moving slowly, bending red-faced at the stove, with her belly vast and in the way. Between then and now was last night, and the walking up her garden, as far as the apple tree, and back. She had paused when the pains came, her eyes screwing tight, and her mouth opening. She whispered to me, so that the women wouldn't hear, "I can't do this, I can't do this," and I hissed back to her, "Yes you can, of course you can, it will be all right," because I was thinking, everybody that walks the earth is born, it happens every day. Then her breathing changed, and her eyes went distant and glossy, as if she were looking inward; she did not look like Agnes anymore, and the women had brought her upstairs and sent me home, and I began to be afraid for her. But it was over now, because there were cake crumbs and tea-stained cups. This was not a scene of mourning, these women sleeping with their heads on their arms, the smell of spice, the huff and whistle of their breath: she had lived through it. They had been too tired, too exhausted by their labours, to think of telling me.

I slipped past them and went up to Agnes's room; the room she has had since she was married. Agnes was lying in the bed, sleeping, the covers pulled tight over her. Her face had the same pulled-tight quality as the sheets. Her hair lay in a thick dark braid over her shoulder and down over the quilt. The room smelt of blood, but there was no blood to be seen. She looked so completely done-in, so pale and wan. I came closer and saw the baby; it was tucked in the crook of her arm. It was red, dry-looking, its eyes pinched shut. Its head was a strange shape, bulged and squashed. It didn't look like her.

I wanted to touch her, but I couldn't bring myself to do it.

I heard the stairs creak and lifted my sleeve to my face to blot away the wet. Her mam appeared and came over to me, moving quietly in stockinged feet. She stood beside me. Her face was a maze of wrinkles; she smelt of tobacco and bad teeth.

"A boy," she said. "We're calling him William Stephen, same as his father."

The words whistled through the gaps in her teeth. She went on talking, the sound hissing and wet, and there was a constriction in my throat, and my nose felt raw inside.

"I said to her last night, it's taking that long it's bound to be a boy," she said. "Girls are that much easier, God grant her a girl next time."

"I'd best go."

I turned to shift past her, and she was in front of me a moment, her hair combed into a dry white parting, her shawl greasy and threadbare, her skin creasing happily. She'd seen it all before, of course, seen how much worse it can be. She had ten children that I knew of, and she had delivered all her six daughters' babies. She turned to leave, and I followed her out towards the landing.

There was a pail tucked out of the way behind the door. I'd passed it unnoticed on the way in. It was full of blood-soaked rags. The blood was crimson. On the floor next to it was a folded blanket: it had been folded to hide the worst, but I could see the corner of what must have been a huge bloodstain. I looked back at Agnes lying white against the white sheets. I could hear the stroke of the older woman's stockinged feet on the stair treads. I turned again and went after her, the weave of her grey plaits pinned up like a rush basket on the back of her head. Halfway down the stairs she stopped, and looked up at me as if out of a hole.

"If you've got any old linen spare, can you bring it over, and any lye you've got made up?"

I nodded, my face feeling cold and numb. Agnes and I had shredded old sheets and shifts and shirts until we were covered in thread and lint and Agnes had laughed and said it looked like it had snowed indoors.

I managed to speak. "Is it often this bad?"

Agnes's mam shrugged. "Every time is different."

She turned to go on down the stairs, as if this was my question answered. I stood there, feeling cold. I had said that it would be all right.

I could hear the women moving around in the kitchen, and low voices: Mrs. Skelton was awake and they were talking softly. I heard the clunk of stove-iron and clink of china as they made tea. I went down the stairs and straight outdoors. I needed air.

Outside a fine soft rain was falling. I pushed my hair back, tucked my shawl over my head and lifted my face to the clouded sky. I tried to pray. I tried to thank God for her safe delivery, but my prayers melted in the rain. I leaned there against the doorjamb and I cried selfish tears. I couldn't do without her.

I heard the racket of clogs on the wash-house lane, voices; it could be my mam back with the other hands from Storrs Farm. I wiped my palms across my cheeks and ran for home.

I came in and started talking brightly to Dad, saying how Agnes had had a boy, that they were calling it William Stephen and what was the point giving a child the exact same name as its dad, he'd only get pet names all his life so you might as well think of something new to start with. I had my shawl off and was marching over to the fire to get the kettle on again so that it was hot for when Mam came in, and then I saw him.

He'd been sitting in Mam's chair. He was getting to his feet. He was dark-clothed and tall; a good span taller than my father. Tall as the Reverend, though lean, and his clothes seemed more like a working man's. I don't know what it was about his features—the dark eyes, the strong nose and heavy brows, the clean-shaven lip and chin—but something just kept me looking at him. As if his face were a puzzle, and I couldn't work it out.

Then I realized what it was. I'd never seen him before. I couldn't remember the last time I'd come across someone that I had never seen before.

"Ah, Lizzy," my father said, "this is Mr. Moore."

I nodded. "Good evening."

He dipped his head, returned the greeting. His voice was strangely accented; he was not a local man. I reached up to smooth my hair and became suddenly conscious of my hands, of how chapped and rough they were, calloused as an old hedger's. I tucked them behind my back. I'd never, not until that moment, thought of my hands as anything but cold or sore or deft or fumbling. I don't think I'd ever thought about my hair at all. I couldn't

think what to say. My father leaned back in his seat, grinning.
Mr. Moore didn't say anything, just looked at me, and didn't
smile. The silence continued. I began to think he was expecting
something from me. He was in working clothes, but his stature
and carriage were that of a gentleman. Was he waiting for me to
curtsey? I glanced back at Dad. He nodded at me, his lips pursed.
I turned to Mr. Moore, looked him in the eye, and curtseyed. He
held my gaze, watching as I bent one knee, wobbled, scraped my
clog toe along the flags and dipped my head stiffly. I have never
made a graceful curtsey in my life. For a moment, his face was
sober, his brows knotted. Then he laughed, his face breaking up
into creases.

"You mistake me," he said.

I felt my cheeks colour. "So it seems."

He stopped laughing then. My face burned.

Dad made a clumsy joke about the refinements of the establishment, and I turned away, and went to tidy up my work, and clear
the leftovers of his tea, and all the time I was blushing, fiercely
conscious of myself, of how ungainly and uncouth I must seem. I
slipped upstairs, and washed my face in yesterday's water. I loosened my hair, gave it forty strokes, plaited it and pinned it up
again. I looked at my hands, the yellowed calluses on the palms,
the nails stained dark and rough. I soaked them in the water and
scrubbed at them. I heard Mam come in downstairs. I heard her
greeting. She called Mr. Moore by name, which was a surprise to
me. I looked at my hands. Pinker, a little softer, still badly stained,
the nails worn dull with work. I went downstairs to help Mam get
the supper.

Mam and I were at the table. She was spooning tea from the

canister. One for each of us. One for the pot. One for Mr. Moore. So he was staying for supper. Over at the fireside, Dad was talking to him. Mam was telling me what else needed to be done that evening and what was to be done tomorrow when I rose. I nodded, trying to keep my attention on her, and not let it drift towards the fireside. Every so often, Mr. Moore glanced over. I kept my attention on the loaf and the neat portioning of slices. One for each of us. One for him.

Then Mr. Moore spoke, and Mam's words faded out of my thoughts, and all I could do was listen to him. Dad must have asked him about the towns and cities to the south, because he was giving an account of them. Leeds, he said, was like a midden, filthy, all of a fester, a summer's heat would suffice to make it burst into flames. Manchester was a tinderbox: any reckless hand might strike the spark. People were arming themselves, he said; in towns and villages all over the country, he'd seen arms hanging over the fireplaces in the poorest houses.

His voice, his manner and what he said: it reminded me of something, but I couldn't quite remember what.

"Everybody's spirits are down," Dad said. "The bad seasons and these unchristian taxes. People don't like going hungry."

Mr. Moore half shook his head. "When an employer says there is a slump in trade, and makes a reduction in wages, a man who already works every hour he can to watch his wife and children starve must feel the injustice of his circumstances as keenly as he feels brute hunger. What can he do? He can't take his labour elsewhere, since if one employer makes a reduction, the others follow. They are reducing wages now, all across the region. And if there is a slump, then by God but the mill-owners are doing well out of it. Oversby's building his new Hall on the strength of the current crisis."

I realized that I was staring at him. His words and the manner of his speaking made me stare.

"They do well, the Oversbys," my father said, seeming to think they were in complete agreement. "That's a fine new house they're building up at Storrs. A man needs a little land, a little seed-money, if he's to make anything of himself."

Mr. Moore said nothing for a moment. He inclined his head, and when he spoke, it was quietly, almost too calmly. "You know my position, a joiner on the new hall, and you know I need the work as much as the next man. But every peg I hammer home seems like a coffin nail to me."

He was still as a rock, the whole of his body, but for his hands; they did not cease moving. He pressed his fingertips together; his fingers slid and meshed and separated. These slight motions seemed to be connected with what he said, as if he felt the distress in his own body and could not be at ease; as if his hands were eager to be at other work. His thumb rested for a moment between his lips, his teeth teasing at the skin beside the nail. I noticed my own hand was at my mouth, my own knuckle resting in the wet between my lips. I dropped my hand and looked away.

"I take the money that could be used to pay his workers decent wages, and you will take it from me, and that is how we must live, and so all our hands are stained with this guilt, however little we intend it. We cannot be free of it."

I knew what he reminded me of. Years ago, when we were girls, a preacher had come to give witness to the Lord from a tree-stump on the green. Our mams had forbidden us to go, so me and Agnes sneaked up through the field behind the green, huddled down behind the wall among the buttercups and wild carrot and long grass, and listened to the preacher's great strong voice, his passionate words. We scared ourselves witless with what we heard about the Elect and Grace and the Second Coming and the End of Days. I felt it again, the same blend of fear and guilt, a sense of the coming apocalypse; and with it a new feeling that I couldn't name. I was vexed at being laughed at, but there was more to it than that. The kettle began to rattle and boil, and I remembered the tea. I had to go to the stove, right between Mr. Moore and my dad, and bend to get the kettle. They paused in their talk a moment, and I was all too conscious of myself and of the way my cheeks flushed in the heat from the fire.

Ted and John bundled in, red-cheeked and full of buttoned-down laughter. Mam sent me to the larder for preserves, though it was Lent, and there were only a half-dozen stone jars left on the shelves. Then Sally came in, looking prim and pretty. She had been up at the schoolhouse sewing with Mrs. Forster. The younger ones took their supper to their stools and sat to eat, and I kept company with Mam, standing at the table to eat our bread and apple-jelly, while the men sat by the fire and ate theirs. Sally wanted to know about the baby and wanted to tell me about the dress Mrs. Forster was making, but I didn't want to talk, didn't want to listen to her, didn't want to think about the blood and the baby, and all the time she talked I couldn't hear what Mr. Moore was saying. My mam was now too tired for conversation, she just leaned against the table, and sipped at her tea, and ate her bread and jelly as if it were almost too much of a bother for her to do it. We cleaned up the plates and put them away, and still

Mr. Moore lingered there, listening to my father, who now was talking about the Enclosure. I didn't like it when Dad got talking about the Enclosure. It seemed so long ago now, and there was nothing to be done about it, and it made him nasty to reflect on it, and I could not imagine what kept Mr. Moore there listening to him, when he could have been off home hours before. He couldn't have known the trouble he was courting.

I'd go up to my room and read and get myself out of the way. There was a little light left: I could get a few pages read at least before Sally came up and started wittering about bonnet trimmings or the baby. It didn't cross my mind that I'd be remarked on, either in my going or my being gone. I had my hand on the stair-rail, my foot on the first tread, and my new chapbook about Robinson Crusoe under my arm, when Dad called out after me, asking where I was off to.

I turned and went back to him, bent to give him a kiss on his cheek, and said goodnight. The hem of my skirt brushed against Mr. Moore's booted feet, and I caught his scent for the first time: the smell of cut wood. There was wood dust in his hair.

"You're not up there anymore," Dad said.

I looked at him, not comprehending.

"You're down here. You and Sally. You'll be good and warm with the fire."

"You mean sleeping?" I asked.

"Of course I mean sleeping."

"But—"

Ted laughed. Only then did it dawn on me what was going on. Mr. Moore was lodging with us. He was to have our room; mine and Sally's room, and we were to sleep downstairs. There'd been talk of a lodger for a while, but nothing had been done, and I'd thought the idea had been forgotten. I looked down at the floor, the rag rug, the ash on the hearthstone. I will sleep like Cinderella tonight, I thought, and every night until he's gone, and I will not have a moment's peace or solitude until he goes. In the corner of my eye, I could see Mr. Moore looking down at his hands, his right index finger bent and pressed down hard with the thumb of the same hand, so that the fingertip nearly touched his palm. The knuckle cracked, he looked up, and our eyes met. His eyes were brown and clear as peat-water. He looked a little ill at ease.

"Go and get what you need down from your room, and put it in the chest," Mam said, "and then Mr. Moore can go up when he wants to."

My eyes left his. I turned away. I went up to our room, and fetched bedding and clothes and brought them down and put them in the chest, and then went back for the books I had up there, and rearranged the crocks on the dresser to make space for them, and moved aside the Bible and the prayer book, and pushed my *Pilgrim's Progress* and my chapbooks in beside them, and all the while the pair of them were sitting there at the fire, my father smiling and watching me as I made the arrangements. Mr. Moore didn't look around at me, which was good, because I could not have easily met his eye.

It was pitch dark by the time Sally and I had got the bedding spread out and undressed and laid ourselves down to sleep. The fire was a low smoulder. I was beginning to drift into sleep, thinking that another night, when I was not so tired, I'd stir up the flames a bit, put a few sticks on, and I'd be able to read in the firelight, and it wouldn't be so bad. It was good just to be lying

down, and I didn't really feel the hardness of the floor, and my
eyes were closing, and I was thinking how Agnes hadn't seen the
new chapbook yet, that I'd take it over and read to her in bed
tomorrow evening, and when she was well enough, she'd sit in her
kitchen, and I'd do her cleaning or some baking for her.

"Are you never going to get married?"

I opened my eyes. "What?"

"You were nineteen last birthday," Sally said.

"I know how old I am."

She took a noisy breath. "I was thinking what with Agnes having the baby now, you would be thinking of it, you could marry
Thomas and move out and have babies of your own."

"You'll wear yourself out, thinking like that."

She rolled onto her side, pulling the blankets with her. "You
could have your own room then too, though I suppose you'd have
to share it with Thomas."

"Leave off, will you?"

She sniffed indignantly. "It isn't just me."

I leaned up on an elbow, looked over at her. "What do you
mean?"

"Oh nothing."

I prodded her. She yelped in protest. I said, "Tell me; you'll
have no rest till you do."

She rolled back over and looked me in the eye. I remember
her eyes, dark and glossy, catching the firelight, and her smooth
young skin glowing pale. "Our mam was saying that we're too
crowded here, I heard her say it. And Dad agreed."

"They should have thought about that before they invited that
man in. There's just him taking up a whole room to himself while

us two have to sleep down here, and that's just daft, it makes no sense at all."

Sally shrugged and heaved herself over again; "He could hardly have the boys' room, it's too small, and you wouldn't wish this on our mam at her age."

Just as I was about to ask whether she knew if he'd be stopping long, she said, her back still turned to me, "I'm to be apprenticed soon, you know, Mrs. Forster is arranging it for me."

"Who to?"

"Mrs. Forster's milliner at Settle; one of the girls is leaving to set up for herself, and when she does, I'm to be indentured in her place."

I rolled onto my back, lay there with the blanket pulled up to my chin. "What did our mam say?"

"It's clean work, and I'll be mixing with a better sort of people. She's glad."

Time passed in silence, and the church clock chimed ten.

"Good for you," I said.

Sally muttered something, but her breath was coming softer, and I knew that she was almost asleep. The blanket scratched against my chin. I turned, tugged at the covers, and saw that there was light overhead, sieved by the boards, slipping down between them, hair-thin, golden. He was awake up there, up in our old room. He had a candle burning. He sat in light.

It was barely a town at all. Just a motorway exit, a railway station, a grimy, busy crossroads with traffic thundering through. Dirty great lorries and 4x4s and car after car after car. No one stopped. I waited at the traffic lights, looking down the curved slope of the high street. A greengrocer's, an off-licence, a post office, a couple of charity shops, and three estate agents.

I parked outside the train station. It was practically derelict. Dusty windows gave onto dim empty rooms. Rails curved off north and south towards their vanishing points.

I carried a plastic bag of paperbacks, another of coat hangers, and one with her jumpers in it, lifted from the wardrobe, still just ever so faintly scented with her perfume.

I phoned Mark as I walked up the street, all the bags clutched in one hand. The signal was fine. He spoke discreetly, in that at-work kind of way. I asked how Cate was doing; he said that she was fine. His mum was going to pick her up from the childminder, and he'd drop around to get her after work. This was all as we'd agreed. I couldn't mention the noise in the night, the electric hum, the way it made my skin prickle. Or how little I had managed to do, so far, by way of sorting out the house. Cate was an ache in my throat, a flash of panic at the empty space at my feet. The bag-handles cut into my palms, but I had nothing to push, no one to carry, to hold. It made me uneasy.

The conversation didn't go well. The wind blew my words away; Mark was distracted by his email. After a few minutes, we gave up and said goodbye. I was slipping the phone into a pocket as I passed a shop window: deep in the pale interior, a woman bent her head to paperwork and the phone, a sheet of silk-blonde hair screening her face, a perfect nail skimming a line of text as she read. A shift in focus, and I caught my own reflection on the window: pale, eyes shadowed, that line between the brows that didn't used to be there.

I pushed into the first charity shop I came to, the bell jangling. It smelt of old clothes, instant coffee and other people's perfume. I put the bags down on the counter. A woman in her sixties, her face deep-lined with smoke, came out from the back room. She thanked me and went to gather the bags to her. "Just these two," I found myself saying, keeping hold of the bag with the jumpers in and retreating. They'd absorb the old-clothes and other-people smell. I couldn't leave them.

There was a bookshop just across the street; an independent

one. I crossed in a gap in the traffic, clutching my bag. The window was dusty, the display sparse. Dead flies desiccated on the window-shelf and local history books bleached and buckled in the spring sun. I was here to shed possessions, not acquire them. But there was no harm in looking.

The place had that breathy, fusty kind of quality that libraries used to have, before they were full of computers. A sandy-haired man sat behind the counter, his head down, reading. I poked around in the local history section for a while, flicking through contents pages, dipping in and out of articles. There were books on local industries, local farming practices, maritime history, educational institutions. I skimmed chapters in the final one and read the index, thinking that I might find something there about the Reading Room, but there was nothing.

At the back of the shop there was a flight of stairs. Sunlight poured down them and the carpet was worn to hessian fibres. A sign had been balanced on the lintel: Second-hand Books. I went up.

The smell of old books: musty, skin-like, of the attic. The room was lined with tight-packed shelves and in the centre a table was heaped with books. A real jumble: *Teach Yourself to Knit*, *Socialism New and Old*, *The Odyssey*. A door stood open into another room. I went through. There were shelves on all four walls, bookcases dividing the space into bays and booths and alleyways.

I wandered through the narrow spaces in an acquisitive daze. I picked up books, examined bindings, checked prices, weighed volumes in my hand. The rooms were dim and soothing and felt private and quiet as a pine wood. The carpets swirled green and gold and red. I had picked up a craft book and was looking at a very seventies illustration of a woman making a wicker basket, when someone sniffed close by, making me start. In the space between the top of some French paperbacks and the bottom of the shelf above, I saw a fold of denim and a blunt-fingered hand. I'd thought myself alone.

I ducked through the next doorway, into a corridor lined with shelves. It ended on a small room where the floor was almost entirely covered with boxes of sheet music, slitheringly overfull. There was a second, narrower, flight of stairs with books stacked on every tread. I made my way up, was soon half-hypnotized by the repeating labyrinth of corridors and rooms, the same layout as the floor below, but with sloping ceilings and different patterns on the patchwork carpets. I found myself standing in an attic, white sunlight through a low window, a wedge of shelved wall packed solid with books, with a sense that this was something I'd once dreamed. The heavy red book seemed to nudge itself into my grip like a dog pushing its muzzle into a hand; blunt, mute, accepted instinctively. I took it downstairs with me.

The sun was shafting down the stairwell, so that I came down it in a stream of golden dust-motes. At the cash desk, the bookseller grunted and took my stack off me. A shiver of guilty self-consciousness ran through me: this was not what I was supposed to be doing. The bookseller flopped open the cover and checked the pencil-written price, keyed the figures into the till and set the book to one side. I tilted my head to look at the handsome old Everyman edition of Bunyan's *Pilgrim's Progress*, with a design of leaves and an armour-suited pilgrim on the front. When the bookseller lifted the cover to check the price, I read, upside down, an inscription in browning copperplate: *Prize for Holy Scripture*, but I couldn't see the name beneath. The next book was a shabby tan-leather *Robinson Crusoe*, the edges rough where they'd been cut, and blotched and dark with age. *A History of the Lune Valley*, its porcelain-blue dust jacket worn white at the edges. The big red book was called *History of the Chartist Movement*. I couldn't remember why I'd thought it was a good idea.

*

I was climbing the stairs to the Reading Room, to go and put the books on the bookcase. I held them in my hands, shuffling and reshuffling them as I climbed, so that one was on the top, and now another. I was ignoring my unease, indulging instead the rare pleasure of acquisition, the beauty of the books, tracing the embossing of the leather, lifting an opened volume to inhale the skin-scent of the pages. And then there was a voice.

A young woman's voice, speaking softly, urgently. I lowered the book and closed it. Not so much words as a suggestion of speech, like the burn a sparkler leaves behind when traced through the air. Then a pause, as if someone were replying, but the voice was too low for me to hear. I must have left the window open; there must be people out in the street. But there hadn't been anyone on the street when I came in; no one at all. I pushed the door open, my books crushed to my chest. The room was silent. Both windows were shut; they gave a greyish, muted light. I set the books down on a shelf, went to look out of the window. The street was empty.

The moment didn't linger in my thoughts; when I turned away from the window I caught sight of the books, and they looked so right on the bookshelf, as if they'd always been there, that I felt an inarticulate urge to do more, to somehow soften the starkness of the place. I took the pewter jug from the box room, brought it downstairs and set it by the kitchen sink. I wandered down the garden, picking daffodils. The grass was long, rank, tangling around my feet. Shrubs sprouted gangling stems. Last summer's dead heads wizened on the rose bushes.

The daffodils glowed yellow on the windowsill. The air was fresh with their scent. I sat, legs stretched out along the worn blue sofa, and in the back of my mind was the thought that I should be scouring a Yellow Pages, calling charities to see which of them would collect a second-hand sofa, a pair of grotty single beds, and somewhere beneath my breastbone was an ache of Sunday evening homework-guilt: I should be getting on with this. I should be sorting things out. Instead, I was leafing through the local history book for a mention of this place. Not even reading, really: looking at the photographs.

Farm workers, straight out of D. H. Lawrence; all beards and rolled shirtsleeves, squinting in the sun; a flat expanse of field behind them, and a heap of bleaching hay: *Haytiming, Caton, 1911.* Just up the road from here. A massive horse with a floppy fringe, a boy in knee britches and bare feet at its halter, standing next to a moustached man in a stained apron, hands-on-hips; behind them, a dark low lintel and the white flare of a captured flame: *The forge at Bentham, 1908.* The next image was a sketch, not a photograph. In pen-and-ink. A woman sat on a stool by an open hearth. In her lap was a bristling palisade of sticks, like an unfinished bird's nest. *Basket-making*, the caption read, *Lancashire, 1840s.*

I heard a dog bark. A motorbike burned up a distant road, and was gone. The quiet settled again, and seemed even deeper. I turned back through the chapters to take a glance at the essay on basket-making. After a while, I flicked back to look at the drawing again and came upon a photograph that I hadn't seen before. An old man, his head as bald as an egg, squinted in the light, the lines radiating from the corners of his eyes. He was sitting on some stone steps, a half-made basket clasped between his knees. He sat on the third step up, and there were six. Handrail to the left, a glimpse of flower-border and the bottom of the door. This house. It certainly looked like it; but there was no mention of it, no evidence in the caption. *George Williams*, the caption read. *Last of the Lune Valley Basket-weavers.*

I gave up on the local history book and picked up the *History of the Chartist Movement.* It was a sour thing: a contemporary account by a member of the organization, full of grievances and the sense of failure. It was a facsimile edition, reproducing the nineteenth-century type, which was cramped and difficult to read. There was mention of a trial at Lancaster, which wasn't far, it was where I'd left the motorway, but there was no mention of Reading Rooms, and Lancaster wasn't close enough to seem relevant. I slapped the book shut and set it down.

I felt it. A teetering, pregnant silence as if a breath had been drawn, and someone was about to speak. I looked up, glanced around the room. The daffodils on the windowsill, the grey paths across the floor, the silky ashes in the grate; it was all absolutely ordinary. The view from the window, grey sky and green fields. As I turned my head to look, I felt slow, as if moving through water. The air was thickening; if I lifted up a finger, and ran it through the air in front of me, it would leave a ripple. But it was too much to move a finger. I couldn't move a finger. Each breath was a conscious effort.

I must have sat like that for just a minute, maybe less, waiting. Nothing happened. No one spoke. My skin teased itself into goose bumps.

And then I sneezed, and a sheep coughed in the field, a great barking, rasping cough, as if it were taking the piss out of me.

Idiot.

What would Mark say? I swung my legs off the sofa, got up and went over to the window. He'd have me down the road in an instant, have me in the queue to see the peeled man. I looked out at the garden, the intensity of its green, its lushness. I saw what I had seen before, but failed to take account of until that moment. Down at the end of the garden: the electricity substation.

Double idiot.

On the corner of Kirkside Road, our road, there's an olive-green metal cabinet, pressed up against the low wall, the privet hedge behind swelling up and around it. I don't know exactly what it is: electric wiring or telephone cables, perhaps. Occasionally I've seen a guy there in overalls, he'd have the doors open, the cabinet spilling wires. Sometimes, passing by, I've heard the electricity hum inside, like a dozen violins playing the same chord. The substation must have been similar, only bigger, grander, more expansive. An orchestral strings section thrumming out a single chord. Electricity: that's what the hum was, that was the strangeness in the air. Nothing more than that.

*

I took myself out for a walk, the way I might have taken Cate out for a walk. I had to organize myself into jumper, jacket, boots, and practically drag myself out of the door. I'd get some fresh air and some exercise, and then I'd get stuck in to the work: unwrap everything, take everything out of the boxes, bags, suitcases, heap it into piles, begin triage. I could get it done in a day or two, once I'd got started.

I stalled at the top step. I felt so obvious, so conspicuous, the street a clean sweep in both directions. To my left, the ground rose, the street ducking out of sight down the other side, towards the church. The road was a cul-de-sac; I knew from the directions. To the right, the street flattened for a while, and then curved and climbed towards the crossroads where it was lost from sight behind the bulk of a converted barn. There was about a quarter of a mile between my cottage and the barn, and in all that space there were only four houses, standing in wide pools of garden. In between, fields reached right up to the edge of the street; sheep grazed and lambs stood around in gangs, like teenagers. There were no pavements, no white or yellow lines, no hard boundaries at all. Grass nibbled and cracked at the edge of the tarmac. Hedges were bony and holed, fence posts had been strung with invisible wire. The only solid lines were the dry-stone walls edging some of the gardens and fields, so ancient that they seemed more like an accident of geology than anything man-made. It made me feel exposed, and somehow porous, as if I were too vulnerable to face the air. At home, I'd head for the park, the canal, the open spaces, but where do you go when everywhere is open space?

The nearest house was a cottage just across the street, a little further down the hill: low sleepy-looking windows and an ancient front door, a flagged front path with daffodils growing in the borders. There was something weird about the light: the daffodils' colour seemed almost phosphorescent. To the right of the cottage there was a gate; a track of bare stones and mud was worn into the grass beyond. A yellow arrow glowed on the gatepost, pointing upwards and away across the field: a footpath, a direction to follow. Somewhere to go.

The gate had fallen off its hinges and been tied in place with wire and twine. I dragged it open far enough to slip past, and then I was out in this great green field, the track sloping away in front of me, the valley opening out ahead; copses, hedges, grass, the woods and hills rising up beyond, and on one of them, a solitary cottage silhouetted against the pale sky. I made my way down the track. To my left there was an ancient hedge, half dead, half wildly sprouting, patched with wire. The leaves weren't out yet, but everything was green: green algae on tree trunks, slim green saplings, green reeds in the ditch, rich green moss in mounds on the bank. It felt like my eyes were being bathed, as if they were being re-educated in colour. After a lifetime of London's yellow-brick and red-brick, tarmac and concrete, its odd pool and splash of green, my eyes were now learning to work in negative.

At the bottom of the hill there was a small wood. I could hear the sound of running water. The path forked in front of me. To the right it passed a tumbledown building and climbed an open field; at the top of the hill I could see trees, and the tower of Storrs Hall. Straight ahead, there was a stile, another yellow arrow hammered to the post, pointing diagonally across the wide meadow beyond. I followed the arrow. It felt better, having my route decided for me.

In the meadow, the ground was sodden underfoot. Pools of standing water reflected back the slaty sky. The air was cool and damp and there was a smell of cow dung, and grass, and something peppery that I couldn't identify. The next field was thick with thistle, nettle and dock; a narrow path traced its way through the waist-high weeds. I lifted my hands and rested them on my head to avoid the stings. I came to the riverbank and stood looking down at the tumbling water. It was thick and full, the colour of black tea. I could see rounded pebbles on the riverbed. My boots were soaking; there was mud on the hems of my jeans; nettle-stings had penetrated the denim and left a trace of bitter heat behind a knee. A bird flapped overhead, I looked up to watch its flight. It was so large and slow that I couldn't quite believe it. It settled under the far bank, at the river's edge, and stared down into the water. A heron, I think.

I don't know if it was the blank whiteness of the sky, or the intensity of the space, or the emptiness, but by the time I came to the woodland, I felt so choked and miserable that I knew I had to talk to Mark. I'd have to be cheery with him, and it might just stick, and last beyond the ending of the call. I was climbing a steep wooded slope, through this low-growing broad-leafed plant, the whole place reeking incongruously of garlic. The air was still, the signal strong; it was as if he were standing right beside me.

"What's up? You all right?"

"Fine. A bit breathless. Out for a walk. Is everything okay your end?"

"Everything is okay, and was okay, and will be okay. Car seat correctly fitted and used. Mum insists no chocolate buttons were administered. How are you getting on?"

I came to the top of the hill, the edge of the woods. I looked out across the valley, at the motionless livestock and good grazing, at a curve of river and a bridge, at the wooded hills and moors rising beyond. It had started to rain while I was under the trees, the white sky settling into grey, and everything was becoming muffled with drizzle, and seemed empty, really empty.

"I miss you," I risked.

"I miss you too, and Cate misses you; she's right here, do you want to talk to her?"

He was at home: I hadn't realized. I'd imagined him at his desk, paper cups and Post-it notes, the glow of a computer screen and the smell of printing and the line that lingers between his eyebrows. Suddenly it was briefcase in the hall, rolled shirtsleeves and the faint hair on the back of his arms, and the end-of-day lines at the corners of his eyes and half a dozen reports to write for the morning. Things had changed so much; he had changed so much: he was trying so hard. I glanced at my wrist. It was bare. I had left my watch somewhere.

"What day is it today?"

"What? Tuesday."

"Already."

"Mum said she's fine to lend me the car, so we'll definitely be up to see you at the weekend. Maybe you can come home with us, drive in convoy. If you're done by then. Do you want to speak to Cate?"

I could hear in his voice the cool echo of the bathroom, and Cate babbling in the background. Bath-time.

Her absence was suddenly catastrophic. I could almost smell her. Her hair, musty and appley. She'd stand between my knees as I knelt to undress her, arms up as I pulled her vest over her head, and her belly round and firm and smooth as a peeled boiled egg.

"No." I was surprised by my own urgency. "No."

"She's just here."

"I don't want to—don't want to unsettle her."

We talked for a while, and I could hear her high little voice in the background, and she had half of Mark's attention, and we spoke uselessly, it was impossible to talk. I said goodbye; he hesitated.

"Do you think you'll—you don't really seem—"

"It's slow going."

"Of course it is. It's a lot for anyone to face."

There was just a shade too much emphasis on *anyone*. We both retreated carefully from the moment and its implications, knowing we had got too close. We talked brightly about nothing for a bit, and then we said goodbye.

I stood looking at the grey and green of the landscape, the smell of garlic in my mouth, the drizzle cool on my skin, thinking about the tender places that we can't bear to touch. He used to give me Sunday mornings, when she was still tiny. He would bundle Cate into her snuggle suit, bump her down the front steps in her pushchair, and give me two hours of quiet in the flat. Chill out, he'd say. Have a sleep. Read a book. Do nothing for a while. Footsteps on the floor above, muted voices from downstairs, but otherwise, quiet. Heaps of folded laundry and Mark's work files on the dresser. My head throbbing on the pillow, my eyes dry with sleeplessness. The clock ticking away the minutes of Mark pushing Cate through the park, their noses pink, stopping at the café, Mark ordering a coffee for himself and giving Cate her bottle. Me lying rigidly awake. I'd get out of bed. I'd start by putting away the laundry. Then the washing up. Then I'd be cleaning the kitchen surfaces, the table, rubbing fingermarks off the doors, wiping down the skirting boards. They'd come back, and I'd be down on my hands and knees dabbing at milk-spots on the carpet. I got this from my mum, I know. She could never do nothing. She just couldn't be still.

I had to get back. I had to get back to the house. I had to get started.

The rain hung in the air, a thick and saturating mist. My jeans were wet through, the mud walking up the inside of the ankles and wedging into the seams; my jacket was sodden and leaking. I needed waterproofs. I needed, and this is a phrase I never thought I would ever catch myself even thinking, I needed an anorak. I trudged on through the fields, collar turned, head down, miserable.

Cows stood motionless, trees dripped, grass bent under the weight of water droplets. To my left, a thick hedge and beyond that an expanse of open field; ahead, a steep hill, the river cutting close to its base, and then woodland. But no sign of the village.

I'd missed a fork in the path. At some point the path had split, and instead of heading back the way I'd come, across the flood-pooled meadow to the bottom of the track, I'd kept straight on, along the riverbank. Useless townie that I was, the first time there wasn't a garish yellow arrow to point the way, I'd got lost.

I pushed the wet hair off my face. I turned around and looked back, taking stock.

Behind me, the flat land seemed to stretch for miles, the footpath trailing off into blank meadow. Drizzle, patches of white-lit sky, heavier clouds bundling up the valley. I could go back and try to find the path; or I could go on, hope that this path would get me somewhere useful. I turned around again, glanced along its snaking line into the woods. How could that be useful?

My eye caught on something. On the top of the hill, high up, between the leafless branches, I caught sight of a chunk of slated roof, and what looked like a bellcote. The village church, at the end of the village street. From the church, it should be just a brisk walk up the street to the cottage, dry clothes, coffee. And it looked like the path was a back way to the church. I wiped the drizzle off my face and headed on into the woods.

It was dark under the trees. The ground was thick with that broad-leafed glossy plant; again, the scent of garlic: I began to think it must be a wild variety. At first the path was wide and straight, but it was soon twisting between briars and fallen trees, heading away from the river and up the hill, which suited me fine. I was doing okay. Even though the light was fading, I felt confident, competent and in control. I was steaming up the flank of the hill, damp, breathless, beginning to sweat.

I'd soon lost sight of the river; the trees grew thick; the undergrowth was a tangle of bare shrubs, briars and creepers. Heading uphill at an angle, my feet slithered out sideways from beneath me on the loose rich earth. I was no longer sure if I was on a path, or just following a coincidence of gaps between tree trunks, bushes, bramble patches. Now I was scrambling, pulling myself up by low-hanging branches, grabbing at roots, heaving myself over banks and landslips with my hands pressed into the crumbling earth; it smelt rich and dark and ripe. Birds were twittering and calling in the bare wicker of branches. I was hot with the climb and shivery with the soaking. My jacket was tight and awkward and wet, my jeans clinging. All notion of a path had gone and it was getting towards dark. I was conscious of my heartbeat. I should have turned back earlier, while it was still relatively easy to retrace my steps. The woods were quieter now; no birds, just my own huffing and scrabbling. Rain dripped in heavy clots from the branches above. It couldn't be much further. I dragged myself up, grabbing at tree roots. I made my way around a holly bush, and up over a rise. At last I was on flat ground.

There was a wall, and a narrow wrought-iron gate. Beyond, in the fading light, as if in a woodland clearing, stood the church. It was low and damp-streaked. It looked ancient. Gravestones leaned at angles. On the left of the church, there was some kind of earthwork, a grassy mound that looked far older even than the church. I came up to the gate; it was wired shut. I shivered. The damp pressed through my jacket to my skin.

The rain had stopped. I leaned on the gate, let my head hang forward. I was so out of shape; I took a minute there, just letting my heart slow, my breath calm.

There was a smell; a sweet and warm and fetid smell. I felt the uneasy softness beneath my feet. I glanced down, saw the heap of browned grass-clippings, dead flowers; points and curls of funereal nylon ribbon stuck out between the layers of rot. I was standing on the lower slopes; towards the top of the heap lay a balding funeral wreath of moss and wire, with three creamy plastic roses still attached to it. Undegradable, too familiar, lying there forever. A heave of panic: I had to get away. I hitched myself up onto a lower rung, swung myself over the gate.

I dropped down into the graveyard. I felt something. A movement in the corner of my vision. I swung around.

The worn faces of the gravestones stared back at me, blotched with damp. I could smell the earth on my clothes and hands, the rot, the wet wool of my jacket.

No one there.

Of course there was no one there.

I glanced around again, unsure, my skin hard with goose pimples. There were just headstones, then the churchyard wall, with trees beyond. It was a bird, probably; the wind in the trees.

COMING OUT FROM THE DIM CHURCH, INTO THE SUN, I felt changed. The breeze picked up my bonnet ribbons, stirred my shawl and skirts. After the torment and darkness of Good Friday, today was suddenly all light and life and air, the stone rolled from the tomb, the shroud shrugged aside. The yellow daffodils, the river silver in the valley below, the blackbird singing his heart out from the top of the Bowkers' headstone, it all seemed new, as if I'd never seen any of it before, as if I too were born again, dragged out of bloody darkness into light. Agnes was safely delivered and getting stronger every day; I would have her back to me, churched and full of talk and laughing, before the daffodils had died.

Sally shoved past me, her friend Ruth following tight after. The younger ones were pushing out of the congregation and haring off around the side of the church, to the pace-egging on the mound. I took Dad's arm and Mam took his other and we went to watch.

Children were scrambling to the top of the mound, hooting and calling, and the Reverend Wolfenden climbed up to join them, in his black clothes looking like a rook against the blue sky.

I scanned the crowds, searching for him. I caught sight of him standing a little way off, his back to me; I caught a breath. Then he turned, leaning down to listen to one of the older Webster girls, and I saw that it wasn't Mr. Moore. It was just David Airey, back from Claughton for the holiday, besieged by the spinsters of the parish. He spoke a word privately to Rebecca Brown, making her blush and laugh; and I realized I should have known that it wasn't Mr. Moore when I'd seen him so crowded about with women. In all the time Mr. Moore had been with us, from Lent to Easter, I'd never once seen him in the company of women. Mr. Moore worked, and he ate, and he sat up in his room till late with a candle burning, and whenever we passed each other, he'd just nod, and slip past, with the barest of civilities. He often had a book with him, but I'd never had a chance so far to see what it was. And now I thought of it, in all these weeks, from Lent to Easter, not once had he walked to church with us; he was hardly likely to join us today. He was a Methodist, no doubt; or a Catholic. Something of the shine went off the day.

The pace-egging started. The children came forward in turn to where the Reverend stood, to roll their decorated eggs down the side of the mound. The eggs were dyed pink and yellow and green, stuck with petals or bits from the scrap-basket, inked with patterns. They rolled and bumped down the grass, and settled against tussocks or in hollows. Some made it to the foot of the mound and rolled out onto the smoother slope of the grass below. I stood with my father, my arm still hooked through his, but after a while, he unlinked our arms so that he could fiddle with his coat button, and when the button was corrected, he didn't offer me his arm again. I craned my neck to look for Sally, to see how she was getting on. She had a duck egg; I'd boiled it for her, carefully, so that it wouldn't crack. She'd kissed me, said that this year she was bound to win, her egg was so big and strong and beautiful. I watched her come forward and throw. She lobbed it high; it hit the ground, and bounced, and bounced again, then hit a stone, and stopped dead. She tossed her head, gave a laugh, and walked away. I felt a rush of tenderness for her. When the contest was concluded, and Gilbert Mason had taken the prize, I went to find Sally's egg. It had not smashed, not really; the force of her throw had crushed it against the stone. Fragments of shell were still held together by the silky skin inside, but the white flesh beneath it was crushed and broken into pieces. Ted came bouncing up and begged it off me: he'd already eaten his. I knew Sally would want nothing to do with it now. I gave it to him, and he walked away, peeling it and biting into the flesh.

I saw Thomas. He saw me too and smiled. I looked away, hoping he would think I hadn't noticed him. But he made his way towards me, threading between dark Sunday coats and Sunday hats and fresh Sunday dresses. He was there, rosy, eager, asking how the pace-egging had gone for us. I smiled for him.

"Did Sally roll this year?" he asked. "Or is she too much the lady now?"

"She did. The last time, I reckon."

He nodded, and smiled broadly. The sun was glowing through his ears, making them pink. I could smell his smell; warm, grassy, of the byre. He asked if I was going on the walk, and I nodded, and he asked if he could walk with us, and I said I supposed so, and I glanced over at my mam, but she was talking to Aunty Sue.

*

It was the usual Easter way, down the Glebe and across the hay meadow, through Thrush Gill woods and down the slope to the parish marker, where we would spread rugs and eat our dinner. My brothers and sister raced ahead with the other children, playing games of tig across the open spaces, dogs barking and leaping around them. Now and then they'd start a hare, and the dogs would turn on a pin and go flying after it. We'd watch the chase across the hillside, watch each dog in turn slow and then wheel around and turn back, knowing themselves outrun, returning to the children's games.

I carried the basket. Thomas was at my side. I'd lost sight of my mam and dad in the crowd. By Bainsbeck I had given in to Thomas's persuasion, and surrendered the basket to him. After this, he did not seem to feel the need for further talk. When I glanced around at him, he was striding along through the grass, leaving the worn-bare path to me, and there was a smile on his face like a sunbeam, brilliant, painful to look at.

I spread the family rug with the others, and Thomas helped,

bending to tug the cloth straight and flat. Aunty Sue and Agnes's mam were looking at us, and speaking low between themselves, and when they saw me notice, they smiled little sly smiles, and I looked away. Sally was down at the water's edge, skimming stones with Ruth. Mr. Forster was going over to join them, clambering down the bank in his tight black clothes to get to the shilloe.

Thomas settled himself down on our family blanket. I stood watching as Mr. Forster said something to Sally and her friend, then bent and fished up a stone. He planted his feet wide apart, crouched, swung his hand back to show how to turn, how to flick the wrist around to give the stone the necessary spin. Even from that distance I could see the girls wilt under his instruction. He loosed his stone and straightened up to watch it skip across the water. I counted ten. Mr. Forster had taught me to count, but my father had taught me to skim stones. I used to be good at it. Once in a while, I'd get a bit of slate to curl across the river without seeming to bounce at all, as if the water became, for just that moment, a sheet of rippling silk, but that was when I was a girl and there were long summer evenings down at the river with my dad. Skimming stones is one of the things you grow out of, if you grow up to be a woman.

I watched the girls have another few throws, watched them pick through the shilloe looking for skimmers, watched Mr. Forster crouch again to demonstrate the necessary swing. The girls' hearts were no longer in it; it was clear they were only waiting for him to leave. When he did, clambering up the bank, wiping his hands on a handkerchief, beaming at his wife, they pulled off their clogs and stockings, hitched up their skirts and waded into the water, bending over, arms in deep to turn over stones, looking for bullheads and caddis-houses and eels; I would have been doing it too, if I'd been twelve years old.

On the walk back through the woods, the leaves on the beeches were so new that the sunlight streamed right through them. Thomas was beside me again, my mam following behind trying to keep my dad upright and steady. The younger ones were trampling the garlic, making it stink. Ahead and behind and all around me, I knew everyone, I knew the weave of their shawls, the wear of their clogs and the way they tied their hair, and whose breath was particularly foul and which of the men would try and get a hand up your skirt if they got half a chance, and I knew that Thomas, with his easy smile and his red ears and his gentle ways, was as good a man as any there, and that he didn't have a single quality that I didn't know, and that he was decent, and that I couldn't, I really couldn't ever think of marrying him. But as I was thinking this, he was speaking, and what he said seemed to chime with my thoughts, so I looked around at him, and felt for the first time that day warm and well-disposed towards him, because after all, none of it was his fault.

"That bit of land," he was saying, "down near the ford, I planted it with willows just last year. There's a fine crop coming on; it'll make some good whitework. My father says the money's all in the supply these days, he's making twenty pound a year on the raw willow and it'll not be long before I'm making twenty pound myself, and that'd be on top of the cow money."

"That's good," I said. "You're doing well."

He nodded, and we went on walking, him at my side, and as we walked he shifted the basket so that it hung from his arm and brushed against my hip, a bridge across the space between us. "How's work at the vicarage?" he asked.

"It's not too bad, I'm well used to it."

I knew what would come. I knew it was like something spoiling in his belly and that he could never quite be at ease until he'd rid himself of it. I couldn't let him speak, not here, now, with my mam and dad following just behind and the whole village around us. His face went red. I felt my own face redden. I looked away.

"Do you remember," he said, "that day at school, I couldn't say my lesson and I got a thrashing from Forster?"

"That's a long time ago now, that's years ago." There was a tightness in my throat, making my voice strange, but Thomas didn't notice anything.

"He said I'd get another thrashing too if I didn't know it by the next day, and I tried and tried but I couldn't learn it, nothing was going in, and you met me at the hay barn after school, and the two of us sat there till it was dark, going over and over the lesson."

"I remember."

"You must have missed your tea that night; I'll bet you got into trouble with your mam."

"No more than usual."

"The next day, when Forster had me stand up in front of the school and say the lesson, I could say the whole thing without stumbling once, because you'd helped me, and because I knew you were there, in the schoolroom, and were wishing me well."

"It's so long ago now, I don't really—"

Thomas cut me short. "Not so long that I couldn't tell you every word of that lesson now if you wanted me to, and that was

more than Forster could ever do, he could hardly hammer anything into me at all. I'm not quick like you, nothing else has really
stuck, but for that one lesson."

I walked on in silence at his side, and he said, "Lizzy?" and I
looked up at him, and he looked down at me, and he must have
read the unhappiness on my face, because his expression changed,
and it seemed as if for a moment all awkwardness was gone, and
there was something else there, something sore and grown up and
strong. A moment passed.

"This isn't one of your father's baskets, is it?" he asked, and I
laughed, because my dad's baskets were a byword in the village,
thrown together in half an hour, looking like a jackdaw's nest,
and rarely lasting beyond the job that they'd been made for. This
one was as neat as a lady's braids.

"I made it," I said.

"It's very good."

After that we walked on side by side in silence, and after a
while he handed the empty basket back to me, and we went on
like that, and then some of the lads came up and he fell into talk
with them, and then joined them, striding long-legged back to the
village, to the public house, and soon he was far ahead and out of
sight among the crowd, and I walked on alone.

The last time it happened, I'd found myself standing in the canned goods aisle, holding a tin of chickpeas, my trolley already half-full of all the usual weekly stuff, Cate in the child-seat mouthing at a bit of baguette. Nothing led up to that moment, no intentions spooled out ahead of me. I just said something cheerful to Cate, and put the tin in the trolley, and pushed it on, around the end of the aisle, into the next: pasta, oils, and vinegars. I got on with the shopping. I paid, drove home, unpacked the groceries, fed Cate her lunch of avocado mush and all the time I was searching for one moment. One clear moment's memory of before, before the chickpeas in Sainsbury's and the doughy gummed bit of baguette, and Cate's drooled-on fist and perfect thoughtful clear wet eyes. I found an image of me at the kitchen table, drinking coffee, staring out of the window at the squirrels as they raided downstairs' bird table. But it was from the outside; I could see myself sitting there, hunched over one of our blue mugs, my head turned to look out of the window, and I don't know if it was true. But while I was filling my trolley with the usual stuff, and turning up where I needed to be, and doing the things that needed doing, and finding my way home again— so long as Cate was happy and thriving—there seemed no need to talk about it, no need for anyone to know about the dark space. The blanks I couldn't fill in.

This time I surfaced looking at the bookcase, thinking how the wood grain seemed almost rippled, like sand where the tide has pulled away. I had no notion of what led up to that moment, or what should follow next. I was aware of the pressing need to pee, and grasping on to this sensation as if it were a rope that would haul me up, I was on my feet and heading for the bathroom, and pushing at the bathroom door.

I sat, my head in my hands, and peed for ages. I washed my hands and the soap was veined with grey. I ran a bath. The tap coughed, spluttered, poured scalding water. I tipped Mum's Radox into the water, swirled it with a hand. There was a dead spider plant on the windowsill. The papery transparency of the leaves was beautiful. I picked one off and rolled it between my fingertips. The room filled with steam, the window veiled itself in condensation. I sat down on the edge of the bath to take off my boots. I shivered; a deep muscular shiver, my teeth gritted together. There was a trail of dried mud across the bathroom floor. I remembered the drizzle. The scramble through the woods.

Getting back. I looked down at my feet: same boots. Same jeans stuck with dry mud. Same jumper.

"Jesus."

I'd not dealt with these basic, animal needs. I'd not noticed my own discomfort. Perched on the bath's edge, steam rising around me, I bit at the skin beside a thumbnail, tearing away a tiny strip, leaving the flesh bright and oozing. My whole body was clenched tight with cold and fear. What was happening to me?

The bath was so hot that my nerves misfired, and for a moment the water seemed cold, almost freezing. I eased myself warily into it, onto my knees, and my skin flushed up, almost scalded. I slid my legs out from underneath me to sit, wincing at the heat, and then slowly, carefully I lay down, sweat salty on my upper lip, and it was almost painful.

My scar looked awful in the water. It flushed up bright pink, bulged at the right side, where the join is not quite right. The water cooled, and I lay on, till it was the temperature of blood. I could only feel its heat by stirring it, by bending a leg, by lifting a hand, by shifting myself higher and then sinking lower in the water. The air was colder than the water. I couldn't bring myself to get out.

If something's broken, you fix it. If it's torn, you stitch it up. But you always know the mend is there, ready to tear again. You can feel its rawness.

*

I dressed in clean dry clothes and sat down on the bed, my back against the wall, the street window to my side. I was looking at my hands. I felt too fatigued and apathetic to do much else.

The skin was dry and cracked from housework and the weather and the bathwater and neglect. It had already thinned across the backs, tendons rising to the surface like rock through eroding soil. I pinched it; it didn't spring, it seeped back into place. My hands have become my mother's hands.

The stack of bags and boxes in the next room. The daffodils fading in the pewter jug downstairs. The soap by the sink worn to a sliver by cupped palms, cracked and hardened by disuse. It all needed sorting, dealing with, finishing. But first I had to claw my way back towards the beginning, to find a place to start.

I remembered that Saturday morning, in Waterstone's. I was pushing Cate through towards the Children's section. The woman was standing in Crime Fiction, her quarter-profile to me as I came up the central aisle. Her hair was dark and curly and salted with grey and she was slim as a hound, dressed in navy blue, a brown leather bag hanging at her hip, and she was looking down at a book, reading the blurb on the back cover. It was a moment of brilliant instinctive happiness. Mum. I wheeled the pushchair around, headed straight for her. I was going to grab her arm, shake her, scold her. Look, I was going to say, Look at your granddaughter. Look how beautiful she is. But when I touched her, and she turned and looked at me, her face was strange, bird-like, blue-eyed, nothing like Mum: it winded me. I stammered an apology, wheeled the pushchair away; I had to get out of her curious gaze, away from anyone who might have seen. At the back, near the Children's section, I stopped the pushchair abruptly; I ducked down to kiss Cate, and told her she was my lovely girl, and we wheeled off towards the picture books and I bought her more than we could really afford.

Mum had been dead just over a year by then. She died on the fourteenth of December. In the days between her death and her funeral, I carried my belly like a medicine ball around the Christmas-rush shops, trying on coats. I didn't have a decent one to wear to the funeral; my parka was the only thing that would fit over the bump. Nothing fitted, nothing seemed right, anything that was nearly okay was also vastly expensive. I'd come home heavy and sore, my feet and ankles swollen, and Mark would put my feet up on the sofa, and stroke them, and tell me to give up on it. People understood, no one would think twice about it, I should wear whatever felt comfortable. I'll go in tracky bottoms then, I said, and slippers, would that make him happy? Better that than make myself ill, he said. Better that than harm the baby. I told him to fuck off. He said that my mum wouldn't have minded what I wore anyway, and certainly wouldn't have wanted me unhappy over it. I cried. He held me, and after a while I felt better. It worked, him doing that. He must have forgotten how easy it was.

The day before the funeral, Dad brought me the coat, still wrapped in its wardrobe polythene. Empire line, double-breasted, slate-grey wool. There's a photograph somewhere of her wearing it; she can't be more than twenty-four. It's snowing; she's laughing; shoulders up, hands raised to cup the falling flakes. Dad handed it to me and waited for me to put it on, so I put it on, and his face crumpled and I put my arms around him in the slate-grey sleeves and his face rested on the collar. It was an uneasy moment. She got it when she was pregnant with you, he said. I let go of him, and slid it off my shoulders. It was a little tight, with the extra pregnancy-flesh. I said I didn't want to spoil it.

We drove Lucy to the crematorium, via the airport to pick up her boyfriend from the Paris flight. They'd be heading back together on the Sunday; she'd been back and forth almost every week during Mum's final illness. We'd left too much time and got to the crematorium early. Outside, I shifted and swayed in my good boots as my heels sank into the gravel. The smell of the coat was neutral, dry cleaning and wardrobe lavender, and I felt dragged to the earth by the weight of the baby inside me. Dad arrived with Aunty Val and Uncle Peter. Val squeezed me, saying that she didn't know what to say. I kept saying, it's okay, it's okay, it's okay, my hand pressed to her back, feeling the padded nylon of her coat, the painful press of her breasts against mine. There was the smell of someone else's burning in the air; hints of ashes catching in my throat. I saw Lucy, her face buried in Louis's coat collar, her body slim and straight and dark against the grey of his coat. Dad's face was bleached. Mark was standing silent nearby, his blue eyes the only colour I remember in that day. He stretched out a hand for me to grab, to pull me to him like a tired swimmer through resisting water. Then I was walking into the crematorium beside him, our hands clasped dry and cold together, the bulge of my belly making me feel grotesque and embarrassed. I was wearing Mum's coat, unable to catch the scent of her, unable to feel anything at all. Her coffin lay at the top of the aisle, the lid screwed into place. We sat in the pew, and I felt pinned down by gravity, as if I might never get to my feet again. Dad got up to speak, his voice thin; Lucy choked on the poem she had chosen, and I just sat there, swollen and heavy, and didn't say a word. They'd said that it was fine; no one minded if I didn't want to speak. People understood. Later, when the coffin rolled off into the darkness and the flames, I remember feeling an uneasy kind of relief. That we were not burning my mother's body, but burning the sickness out of her.

Later, Dad had us share out Mum's jewellery, me and Lucy. She lifted off the rosewood lid, and turn by turn we picked out the pieces from their cushions of pink baize. We laid them out on the counterpane: the charm bracelet that had fascinated us when we were little; the locket with a picture of her father in uniform; an embroidered bronze swimming badge that neither of us could remember winning; earrings and brooches; pendants and beads, dating from her grandmother to last Christmas. I looked up at Lucy, at her clear skin, her greyish eyes pink with tears. I can't do this, I said, and she shook her head; me neither. We put everything back, neater than she left it. We sat on the counterpane and talked about Dad, and how Dad would cope, what we between us could do for Dad. And then Lucy went back to Paris, and Dad went back to work, and then Cate arrived, and I just got on with it.

All the time I'd been scrubbing baby bottles clean, sterilizing them, washing my hands again and again till the skin cracked; all the time I'd been boiling kettles, letting them cool, filling the bottles, counting scoops of formula, one for every fluid ounce of water, and losing count, and staring down at the powdery surface of the liquid, and pouring the formula into the sink in a rage at my own incompetence, and scrubbing the unused bottles, putting them back into the sterilizer, and starting again; all the time I'd been wearing sunglasses on cloudy days, pushing the pram around the park, the scar pressing itself against my jeans; all the time, this house had stood, gathering desiccated flies, the air dry-

ing in the sunshine, the spider plant dying in the bathroom. The
soap splitting into cracks. The lampshade gathering dust on its
bones. The static growing. Waiting.

There was movement outside. The shock was almost physical. An elderly woman came out of the front door of the cottage
across the street. Until that moment I hadn't seen a soul. I wiped
my cheeks with my fingers and turned to watch her.

She had a bucket in her hand. She had that old-lady stooped
carefulness. She set the bucket to one side of the step, then knelt
down, took a scrubbing brush from the bucket and knocked it
against the side. The curve of her back to the street, she rocked
back and forth as if in prayer, the flesh-coloured soles of her slippers vulnerable and tender. She dipped her brush into the bucket,
tapped it, and started scrubbing again, this time with tiny circular
movements, as if cleaning a large tooth, the action making her
jiggle on her haunches as she worked. Then she got up stiffly, and
emptied the bucket into a road drain, and the suds spilled back
onto the tarmac like spat toothpaste. She was wearing a navy cardigan, a knee-length skirt. She looked up, and looked straight up
at the window where I sat. She raised a hand and waved.

Not to me.

I knew it. I knew she wasn't waving to me. There was someone
else in the room. Standing just over to my right, just out of my
line of sight. I could feel it in my flesh. A young woman, younger
than me, needing to be noticed. If I just turned my head a fraction,
she'd be there.

I glanced around.

Sun blared through the far window. The door onto the landing stood ajar, and a dim strip of space beyond. No one. I

got up from the bed. The mattress creaked, eased itself back into shape. I stood there in the sunshine, breath held. Listened. Nothing.

I moved over to the bookcase, set a hand on the upright. I had an image of myself as a child, clinging to the side of a swimming pool, children's shouts bouncing off the surface of the water, water glittering, and Mum in up to her chest, hair in soaking ringlets, smiling encouragement, outstretched fingertips just out of reach.

The room was filled with empty, dusty sunshine. Prickling silence.

I drew a breath; I could have sworn to it: the silence shifted. As if another breath had been drawn, as if someone anticipated me and was about to speak. My body fizzed with adrenaline. I let go of the bookcase, took a step into the sunshine. I don't quite know how, but the air seemed to change, to soften, to lose its charge. There really was nothing. I pressed my eyes with the heels of my hands, ground at them. I glanced back out of the window. The street was empty: the old woman had gone and the suds had trickled away. I had to know what she had seen. If she had seen what I had felt.

I ran down the stairs and walked straight out of the house, letting the door slam behind me. I crossed the street to the cottage. The door knocker was a curled brass fist, cold and smooth and solid in my hand. I knocked and stepped back off the doorstep. I had left footprints behind in the damp.

I heard footsteps approaching and fixed a smile on my face. The door opened. I didn't know what I was going to say. It was stupid coming over: I should have thought it through. How could

I ask? The old woman opened the door, smiling. Then her expression faltered. She looked at me, studying my features, her brows pinching.

"Hi," I said uneasily. "I'm Rachel; I'm the Clarkes' daughter."

"Is your mum with you?"

"No," I said.

"It must have been you then," she pulled a self-deprecating face. "My eyes aren't so good anymore. I'm Jean, Jean Davies. Come on in. I'll make some tea."

She turned away, expecting me to follow. I went in across the blue- and blood-coloured lino tiles, into the dark hall. I'd have to face it, again. The telling.

WILLIAM STEPHEN WORE THE FAMILY CHRISTENING GOWN, and howled when the water dripped onto his head, a sure sign of the Devil leaving him. I stood as godmother, and swore to renounce the Devil and all his works. There was a jar of bluebells on the windowsill above the font. The Reverend was solemn, handled the baby with uneasy care, and when I took the hot squalling bundle from him, he smiled at me, relieved, and for that moment, it seemed almost as if all distinction of rank had disappeared and we were not master and servant, nor pastor and parishioner, but God's children, standing together and equal before our Father to welcome this new, howling Christian child into His family. I smiled back at the Reverend, and took the baby in the crook of my arm, the white gown dangling in soft folds, his little body struggling, his face red and furious. I dipped my head to talk to the child, to comfort him.

Agnes had her head covered with a light lace scarf, which had been her grandmother's. She looked pretty, though still pale and tired.

"He's a fine strong lad. He'll be a credit to you," the Reverend said, when the service was over. Agnes's cheeks flushed dog-rose pink. It was a pleasure to see it; it seemed a sure sign of her full return to health.

*

It was maybe a fortnight after the christening. It was a beautiful May evening; the sky was deepening blue and there was birdsong from the garden. Agnes had the baby lying in the curve of her arm as she sat, his head turned into her bodice and his nose pressed against the cloth. He was starting to be pretty. The room smelt of his milkiness. I read the story to Agnes, keeping my voice low so as not to disturb the child, and Agnes smiled as I read, but the baby stirred, and mewed, and she lifted him and set him against her shoulder, rocking back and forth, back and forth, crooning to him, and he just went on crying. I stopped reading.

"Is there anything I can do?"

She shook her head, and laid him down in her lap. She unbuttoned her dress, and her breast inside was hard-looking, streaked with blue, and the nipple was welling drops of pale bluish milk. I looked down at my hands. She tucked the baby inside her clothes, and he began to suck. She arranged her shawl over herself and the child. I looked up again at her and smiled, but she was smiling down at her son.

"Shall I read on?" I asked.

She shook her head, and did not look up. I thought I should say something about little William Stephen, but could think of nothing to say that I hadn't said already, and so we just sat there in silence, the only sound being that of the baby's sucking and swallowing and the fire crumbling into coals. She looked up at me, her face pinched.

"Does it hurt?" I asked.

She shook her head. "Sometimes. A little."

I nodded.

When I bent to kiss her goodbye, she thanked me for my company, and the way she spoke, thin and breathy, mouthing the words at me rather than saying them, seemed to me to be the meaning of it all, and how everything would be from now, nothing left for me in her but the husk, the weightless chaff of words.

The evening was full of birdsong and May blossom. I walked down the coffin lane, the mud hard and dry underfoot. I came to the salmon pool and sat down underneath the hornbeam tree. A heron stood at the far bank, staring down into the water for the flicker of fish. I heard the church clock strike the quarter-hour. An otter slipped out of the water at my feet, saw me sitting there, looked at me with its wet eyes, and turned in one smooth movement to slip back into the water, as soundlessly as if it were formed entirely of that element.

I got back around the three-quarter bell, expecting to be scolded for my lateness, but the house was quiet, and the kitchen was cool and dim. Dad was asleep in his chair, with his head thrown back and his mouth open, the fire crumbling into ashes at his feet. I put some sticks on the fire and lit a rush-light. I drew a chair over to the windowsill and set the candlestick on the chair arm to have the best of both lights. I got down my *Pilgrim's Progress*.

Dad started to snore. The smell of old mutton fat from the rush-light was strong and unpleasant; I could have taken a dipped candle but it would have caused more trouble than it was worth. I turned a page. My eyes followed the lines of print. I shook the cobwebs from my head and tried to pay attention, but it wasn't working; I couldn't get through the words and into the world beyond. I was stuck there, in the darkening kitchen, with my father sleeping drunkenly in the chair; I was not walking the close-clipped grass at Christian's side, setting out with him on his journey from Destruction to the Eternal City. All I could think was, Agnes is gone from me. It was right, and proper, and it made me feel that I would choke.

I let the book fall closed, and held it at the flyleaf. I looked at my name written there in Mr. Forster's hand, my name, my prize for Scripture, the date of my leaving school. I'd been an idiot all this time. Since I first heard that there was going to be a baby, I'd thought somehow that it would be just like a doll that we could play with when we wished, and leave aside when we chose to.

I wanted more than anything just to lay my head down and close my eyes and be alone, but there was Dad there, snoring out drink fumes, and there would be others home before long; the house was always either full or threatening to be full. Sally had had the right idea, to go and be prenticed. At nineteen, I was too old, and I didn't need to ask to know that there wasn't money for it, with the boys sent out, and Sally to be indentured now. To get away meant to go as a live-in servant in another village or in one of the towns, it meant millwork in the city, or it meant getting married.

The clock struck ten. The rush-light was burning low, sputtering. I licked my fingertips and pinched out the light. I levered off my clogs and carried them upstairs. I was going to lie down on the boys' bed. I would stay there till they got home and turned me out.

On the landing, light slipped out under Mr. Moore's door, pooling on the bare boards. I could smell the honey-scent of beeswax. A chair creaked. There was a breath, like a sigh. He moved: I heard the scrape of the chair on the floor. I shrank back into the darkness, but then the light was gone, pinched out. I heard the rustle of tugged covers, the creak of the bed. I leaned against the wall, pressing my head back into the rough stone and let a breath go shakily.

He had my room, he had my bed, he had beeswax candles and I had stinking rush-lights and was begrudged them. He passed me in the house as if I were a ghost. He was the stranger, but he had made me a stranger here.

I crept into the boys' dark, untidy bedroom and lay down in my clothes. The pillow was musty and sour. My old bed was just a single course of stones away. Mr. Moore lay, so to speak, within arm's reach of me. I turned and curled around, tugging the covers close, then twisted back again. My thoughts softened, started to drift, and in the darkness I was in my old room, and Mr. Moore was in my bed, and I was standing over him, watching him sleep, and his eyes flicked open, and he looked up at me.

Ted woke me in the cold dark, shaking me by the shoulder. I heaved myself out of bed. The landing was dark and Mr. Moore's door shut. The house was silent as I went downstairs. Dad had gone and Sally was asleep on the rug. I lay down beside her, and listened to her breathe. I couldn't sleep. The images of my dream would not be shaken clear: Mr. Moore lying in my bed, looking up at me.

I must have drifted off eventually, because the five o'clock bell woke me cold and sore on the hearthrug. I washed my face and hands and neck, struggled into my clothes and clogs, drank some cold tea, ate some bread, and left the house as the sun was rising. The sky was salmon-pink with little wisps of golden cloud. I turned my back to it, headed down the village street, towards the vicarage.

I have never liked the way the vicarage looks at me, its big sash windows somehow blank, whatever the weather, whatever the light. Crunching up the gravel drive, through the dark yew trees and underneath the willows, I could feel the dim glass blink at me through the gaps in the shrubbery, making me feel guilty, making me feel ashamed, as if it were wrong for me to walk the same drive that was crushed by horses' hooves and carriage wheels, by the slender soles of ladies' shoes. I ducked around the side of the house, and in through the servants' entrance. The smell of mice in the scullery was terrible; as usual there was no sign of the cat; Petra was too well-fed to consider catching vermin. I undid my clogs and put on my work slippers. My apron fastened in a careful bow, I straightened my cap in the vague coppery reflection of a milk pan.

We beat the bedroom carpets that day: it's a nasty job. When they're rolled up, carpets slip out of your grip, they slump and loll and are a trial on the stairs, and there is nothing to get hold of. Maggie was at the top end, staggering and sweating by the time she got to the half-landing, and I was at the bottom, stepping uneasily backwards down the stairs and taking most of the weight. The carpet drooped heavily between us. Mrs. Wolfenden watched from the landing, not because we needed watching; we'd been in the household longer than she had. Maggie and I had to bite our tongues all the way from the bedroom to the scullery. It was only once we'd heaved the carpet out into the yard that we were free to mutter and gripe, though the freedom was short-lived. We slung the carpet over the rope, and started beating, and then there was no more opportunity for complaint; talk meant getting a mouthful of dust.

*

The boys were playing in the street when Thomas came. I heard them shout to him and heard the scuffle and laughter when he joined in the game. I'd washed my face and hair, and the rest of me at the washstand in my parents' room, stripped to my shift, while Sally leaned against the inside of the door to keep anyone from coming in, talking about Mrs. Forster's new bonnet as I scrubbed off the carpet-dust and perspiration and mumbled my replies. Sally left her post to help me rinse my hair, pouring the water for me, making me catch my breath at the cold, at the rill she let run down the back of my neck and on between my shoulder blades. After, as we tidied away the tea things, I could feel the faint dampness of my braids against my head, the scent of sage and rosemary, the crispness of fresh clothes, the cool tautness of my skin. It was pleasant to feel so clean.

But now that I heard Thomas about to come in it seemed an awkwardness; he might notice, he might say something. I stacked plates, then wiped the table, trying to cover my confusion, knowing Sally wouldn't miss it, because she misses nothing. There were other voices too; men's voices, kept too low to distinguish the speakers. Then the door opened and Dad came in, his cap pushed back. Thomas followed him, took off his cap, nodded to me and Sally, said good evening. Then Mr. Moore came in. He said nothing. I noticed that he looked at me, and that his eyes lingered a moment too long. He took off his hat, and went over to the dresser, and stood considering my books.

"All right, young Williams?" Dad said.

"My dad'll be up shortly," Thomas replied. "The Huttons and Mr. Gorst are coming too, from down our end of the village. Once they're done for the evening."

Dad brushed down his jacket front, drew himself up a little taller. "That'll do rightly, lad."

"We should be getting on," Mr. Moore observed.

Dad agreed effusively and gestured Mr. Moore towards the stairs. Thomas seemed suddenly very conscious of himself. I caught a glance of his, there was a pinkish flush to his forehead. He followed the two older men up the stairs, and I just stood there, holding a dish and a teacloth in my hands. I heard them move around above me: they were in my room.

"Come on," Sally said, "or we'll be here till suppertime."

She finished clearing the tea things, and I poured the hot water from the kettle into the tub and washed up the crocks. I listened to the movement and the ongoing exchange of conversation upstairs but I couldn't catch the words. It seemed to be Dad's voice mainly. When Mr. Moore spoke, it would cause flurries of agreement from my dad; Thomas didn't seem to say anything at all. Sally set down a dried dish, and waited for the next, and she looked at me as if to say, Of course *I* know what's going on; so there was no way under heaven that I would actually ask her. The chimes began for half-eight, and I handed her the last tea plate, and she dried it, and put it down on the stack, and I went out of the back door with the tub and slopped the water onto the herb patch. I took a pinch of melissa, and rubbed it between my fingers, then tucked it into my bodice for the scent. I came back in, dangling the tub from one hand, as Mr. Gorst was coming in the front door, tobacco trailing after him, and behind him came Joe Stott and then the Hutton boys. Sally and I said good evening, and they nodded politely, and went upstairs, to our old bedroom. My face began to burn. The door had barely closed on them when there was a knock; I opened it and there was Mr. Bibby, his nose red as a rosehip, and Mr. Jack and his son from up Locka way, smelling of sheep, and then old Jimmy Williams, Thomas's dad, with his hands still black from the byre; all of them coming in with red cheeks and a cloud of evening cool air, going past us with a nod and up the stairs, and joining the crowd in our old bedroom. The press of weight on the boards above us, the low rumble of voices, were like a gathering storm.

Then Thomas came back down, and lifted the two fireside chairs.

"It's a pity you can't come, Lizzy," he said, sidling back past us. "It'd be just your kind of thing."

"Indeed."

"I'll tell you all about it afterwards."

"I wouldn't want to trouble you."

"It would be no trouble at all," he said, his cheeks reddening. Then he went upstairs, the chair backs tucked up under his arms, the seats hanging like panniers at his sides, and we were left with a blank expanse of cold stone floor, a rag rug, and the boys' creepy-stools.

When Mam came in, Sally and I were sitting back to back, on the rug, working on our baskets, and I was envying the Wolfendens their carpets. She sat down with us, beside the stove, leaning against the wall. I got up and fetched a blanket, folded it and slipped it between her and the bare stone, to make her more comfortable. She didn't comment on what was going on, and I wouldn't ask, not in front of Sally, who already knew. At first, there was just the weight and restlessness of the men on the boards above our heads, the general grumble of voices, and the creak and tap of the willow as we worked it. Then Mr. Moore began to speak and all the other voices fell silent. Sitting there below, half drunk with tiredness, it seemed not so much a sound as an absence of sound, as though a dark space was opening up above our heads. I couldn't make out the words.

My mam was nodding with sleep. Sally was leaning heavily against me; I thought she was drowsing too; there was no sound from her of work. I set down my basket and pressed the heels of my hands into my eyes, smelling the willow on my skin.

"I am sick to death of this green wood," Sally said, making me jump.

Mam's head sprang up. "What?"

Then Sally said the same thing again, and they got to talking, and there was no hope of hearing anything distinct from above. At ten o'clock the men came down, and Thomas brought the chairs with him, and he stood there while we swallowed yawns and rubbed at our faces. He made some comment about things being very interesting, and making a person think, and he was dying for me to ask him about what had taken place upstairs, but I wouldn't. I wanted rid of him, of them all. I just needed to sleep. Sally yawned; a big natural unsmothered yawn, like a dog, not caring who saw. Thomas finally noticed that he was keeping us from rest and said goodnight.

Sally and I made our bed up on the rug, and lay down. She fell instantly and deeply asleep, and began to snore.

A light continued on upstairs; it filtered down between the floorboards. I lay awake, looking up at it, my eyes gritty with fatigue. Dad knew, and Mam knew, and Sally knew, and Thomas knew, and everybody knew what was going on, everybody but me. It was not a pleasant feeling, to be alone in the dark.

I turned on my side, drew the blankets up to my chin. Mr. Moore could not stay forever. The work would finish, and he would go on somewhere else, and we would have our room again.

*

I must have drifted through work that morning, half asleep; I don't remember much of it, but then hardly any of it requires me

to think, and so is easily forgotten. I was polishing the copper
pans in the kitchen, watching the image of my face spilling back
and forth over the curve of the milk pan like grain tipped from
palm to palm, when I realized Mrs. Briggs was speaking to me.
I looked over at her. She was frowning, her hands on her hips.
Her hands were white with flour; scraps of dough were stuck to
them and peeling off onto the flags, as though she were suffering
from some awful malaise of the skin. She seemed more puzzled
than cross.

"Don't you hear me talking to you? You're wanted in the
morning room. Wash your hands before you go."

The door into the morning room stood open. Soft southern
light fell through high windows, so that the room seemed full
of misty sunshine. Mrs. Wolfenden had had this room fitted out
for her particular use. Papered walls, delicate furnishings; a sofa
in a golden brocade, a carpet in a creamy shade that just sucks
in the dirt; all seemed to gather up and hold the morning light,
as if in a golden cup. Mrs. Wolfenden sat on the sofa with her
sewing. Wearing a yellowish poplin, her fair hair scorched into
ringlets, it seemed as though she had dressed herself to suit the
room, or that the room had been dressed to complement her
beauty. Both might, now I came to think of it, indeed have been
the case.

I came in softly in my slippers. Reverend Wolfenden was
standing with his back to me and his hands clasped behind him.
He was gazing out of the high windows across the lawns, towards
the orchard. Mrs. Wolfenden looked up and saw me. She smiled
faintly, and glanced at her husband.

Mrs. Briggs had reported me, I knew it. I'd been tired and stupid these past weeks, having had insufficient and shallow sleep. I would have explained to her, I would have tried harder, if she'd but spoken to me first. Now, I stood to have my wages docked and a black mark set against my name. I'd seen others lose their positions for not much more than that. Nothing was forgotten or forgiven here.

Noticing some movement, or sensing his wife's glance, Reverend Wolfenden turned around. He moved stiffly, buttoned up in his waistcoat, his chin held high over his starched collar. I bobbed an awkward curtsey to him.

"Ah," he said, "Lizzy."

"Sir."

"You have a lodger at your house," he said.

Surprise made my look sharpen; I remember noticing that his skin was raw from the razor, and already bloomed with blue. "Yes, sir."

The Reverend tilted his head to one side. "One Mr. Moore," he said.

"Yes, sir."

"I believe he is a joiner in Oversby's employ."

"I understand that is the case, sir."

I felt a strange uneasiness of spirits. The Reverend continued looking at me thoughtfully, and didn't speak. He pinched his lower lip between his forefinger and his thumb, squeezing it into a damp red bulge, then let it go.

"He has been holding meetings in your home."

My unease deepened. Was this blameworthy? The Reverend's expression gave no hint.

"Just one meeting," I said. "Last night, in fact, and that's all. I didn't know anything about it."

Reverend Wolfenden looked at his wife, and she put her work aside, and stood up and came over to me. Her hair caught the light, looked golden as angels' hair. She took my hand in her ungloved hand.

"We have always been good to you, Lizzy."

Her hand was cool and soft, and mine felt hard and dry and sore, and I couldn't catch her meaning. I had done the work, I had worn the slippers they insisted on so that I went about quietly, and I had curtseyed as required, and they had paid me, and I had never thought that there could be more to it than that. They gave me a half-day on a Friday once a month so I could help my mam with the washing, but I'd never felt particularly grateful for that. Mrs. Wolfenden didn't say anything more, but just looked at me, her pale eyes earnest and on a level with mine. This was far worse, far more unsettling than any scolding could have been. At the same time, I felt flattered by the cool touch of her hand, and by the Reverend's keen attention; I had never felt so noticed, so taken account of before.

They were waiting for me to reply; there was just the clock ticking on the mantel, and the sound of their breath, hers light and shallow over her stays, his heaving in and out through his nostrils. I said, though I wasn't really sure that I meant it, and by that point wasn't even sure what question I was replying to: "Yes, madam."

"Well then, you will not mind if Mr. Wolfenden asks something of you in return."

I looked up from her soft young face, her light curls, and back to him tall and red-cheeked by the window.

"No," I said.

Reverend Wolfenden nodded. "Good girl. It is just this, and it is not too much to ask a good Christian girl. Be watchful. Be watchful of Mr. Moore, and tell me what you see."

Mrs. Davies gestured me into the sitting room, and left me there, while she went out to the kitchen. I could hear the rush of water into the kettle and the clatter of crockery. I sat down gingerly in a sunken armchair, which, with its twin and a beige sofa, formed a corral around a big old box of a TV. I found myself looking at the crocheted doily draped over the top of the box, the way it hung down over the screen like a fringe. A glass vase stood on it, holding a single fake rose. Plastic dewdrops caught the light and refracted it. I sat there, aware of the rumble of the kettle, the clink of china, the soft murmur of the old woman talking to herself as she made the tea, and I watched the chip of light in the plastic dewdrop, its pink and green facets, and I felt as though I was going slowly out of focus; as if, when she came back into the room, she would find me fading, faint, dispersing into the surrounding air.

She came in with a tray, placed it on top of the nest of tables, and began extracting the smallest table from underneath. She was solid and awkward and flustered, and I was half rising to help her, but was too slow, and sank back as she shuffled out the table and whisked it over to my side. She handed me a cup and saucer with a smile. The cup was patterned with poppies and wheat-ears. The tea was grey and milky and a clot of milk-fat floated on the top. I wanted to be back in the Reading Room. It was almost panic: if I was going to disappear, it had to be there, where I could lose myself completely and no one would even notice I was gone. I glanced up at the window, but the lower half was shrouded in creamy net curtains, and I couldn't see out.

She sat down with an old-person's huff of breath, fidgeted with cardigan buttons and then with the metal watch strap that was pinching her skin. She glanced up and offered me a smile.

"How are your mum and dad?" she asked.

Her skin had the soft translucency of age; her lips smudged and bluing, her cheeks traced with broken capillaries. She knew something was up; I could tell she'd noticed there was something wrong with me. It has a smell, I think: like diabetes, kidney disease, or cancer. I found myself suddenly aware of another scent in the air, raw and cool and dusty-sweet: icing. She'd been icing a cake.

"You must have been wondering," I ventured. "The place standing empty so long."

"I saw you pottering around." Her voice was biscuity and soft. "I thought you were your mum. I was going to come over and say hello."

There was a pause. She sipped her tea, gently expectant.

"She got ill," I said.

"Oh."

She set down her teacup.

"Not long after they bought the cottage. They came back a couple of times, after the diagnosis, but I guess she didn't have the energy to do much."

She didn't ask. She shifted forward on her seat, stretched out a hand.

"It's over a year ago now, since she died." I spoke quickly, knowing whatever I said the words were bubbles, fragile, weightless, bursting in midair between us. "Dad's not been back. He couldn't face it. I'm packing up and putting it on the market for him."

"Oh, my poor love," she said, and shuffled forward again, her thin hand extended towards me. I didn't take it. I smiled, my eyes open wide to accommodate the wet.

"It seems lovely around here—I haven't seen much, but what I have is really beautiful."

"It is." She retreated, put her cup down on the table and looked away. "Really. Some lovely walks. But it's awfully quiet nowadays. A dormitory, really."

"It's so quiet I can hear the electricity in the house. Do you get that over here, a kind of humming sound, you can barely hear it? I was thinking it must be the substation."

"No," she said. "Or at least, not so I've noticed. I don't recall

Margaret mentioning it either. Perhaps there's a fault in your wiring. You should have it checked."

"Margaret?"

"Margaret Hutton. She lived there before your parents bought it."

She smiled, revealing her neat ceramic caps. There was a pause. She looked down at her hands, lifted her right hand, turned it over and ran a fingertip from wrist to knuckle. The silence stretched like chewing gum. I was reminded of myself, just a short while earlier, studying my hands like that.

"It'd been a labourer's cottage before they bought it; part of the Storrs Estate. It'll say on your deeds." I noticed then the colour of her eyes, a soft clear tea-brown. The lower lids fell loose and looked sore and pink. "I just hope I can afford to go to as good a place as she did."

I thought she was joking. I thought this was a camel-through-the-eye-of-the-needle reference. I thought of the old lady whose slippers had worn the tracks into the carpet, whose Sunday dinners still lingered in those rooms; there was nothing ghostly about her presence: it was all very real.

"I thought the less money you had the better?"

"It certainly doesn't help, it seems. Her boy Jack had to sell up just to pay the fees."

"Fees?"

"It's a good place, but it's not cheap. The home."

"Ah."

"She's been in the home four years now. Up at Storrs. You'll have seen it, the old hall, the big house with the tower. Jack's her eldest, he runs the farm now; his wife Sandra told me that when he goes to visit his mum she doesn't even know who he is."

"That's really sad," I said.

She looked at me in a precise, thoughtful way. Then she told me what had happened.

It was about six years ago. It was windy, February, the middle of the night, and she was woken by someone shouting in the street outside. It sounded like a woman's voice, calling for someone, calling out a name, but she couldn't be sure whose name it was, it was too windy to hear properly. She had woken her husband Edward, and they'd gone out to see what was going on. It was Margaret Hutton out in the street, in her nightdress, blue with cold, the wind whipping her hair across her face. They asked her what she was doing, and she said Charlie had gone out earlier to pick the blackcurrants, and he hadn't come back. She was barefoot; her feet cold and muddy on the dark wet tarmac. She said she'd looked all over the garden, but she couldn't find him, she was still looking, could they help her. And that was how it began.

"How what began?"

"Well, her decline, really."

"She didn't find him?"

"Picking blackcurrants in February?" she shook her head. "And anyway Charlie, well, he'd been gone a while by then. She was a widow, had been for the best part of a decade."

"Oh," I said. "Oh."

"Me and Edward, we said to ourselves that she'd just been dreaming, sleepwalking or what have you, but I think we already knew that there was more to it than that. She seemed to come around somehow, and had a bit of a cry, and we sat with her a while, and then I put her to bed. It was just the start of it, really.

It's a cruel illness; what it does to you is cruel. We'd just find her, I don't know, straying. She'd be talking about people and we'd have no idea what she was on about. Names we'd never heard; even Jack could make no sense of it. It got so she couldn't really be left alone. She just kept on drifting off into her own little world, and couldn't cope with this one anymore."

I felt the words come out clumsy, overladen: "She must have been quite elderly by this time?"

She smiled. "These things are relative! She was only in her mid-sixties, when she went into the home. But she'd been ill for years and years. People get good at hiding it, apparently. They can hide it for years."

The words seemed to fall slowly, as through water, catching and reflecting gleams of light. *They can hide it for years.* I could feel the hairs on my arms rise up and press against the inside of my sleeves.

"It seems callous even to admit it, but it scared me. To lose all sense of yourself, like that." She shook her head, smiled. It was an unhappy smile. I watched the intricacies of the shifts in her skin, the neat ceramic teeth and the gold towards the back, the retreating gums. "You're right; it's really sad."

She sipped her tea. I lifted my cup in thoughtless echo, sipped, swallowed hard to get past the catch in my throat. I watched her hand set the cup on its saucer; I watched the press of the handle into the skin, the bulge of flesh around her wedding ring. Mum's hands were frail and white, translucent, like the bones of fishes, bunched to lift off the loosened rings, to set them down on Dad's broad palm for safekeeping. Her lips pale, her eyes big as saucers and bulging as a newborn's.

She was looking at me with a friendly, faintly puzzled expression. I cleared my throat and blinked.

"The cottage. Mum loved it. I got some local history books, but I can't find out anything about it. The Reading Room, I mean. Who lived there back then."

She shook her head. "I don't know anything, I'm afraid. I'm a relative newcomer: only been here twenty years! If anyone knows, Margaret will. Born and bred in the village. You should see if you can talk to her."

"But I thought—"

"When she's having a good day, she can be as lucid as you or me."

For a half-second I was tempted to make a joke. I could have dragged the fear out into the open, mocked it, made it ridiculous, made it shrink. I just nodded.

"If not, then there's always Pauline; Pauline Boyd. She's a newcomer like me, but local history is a bit of a hobby for her. She'd be happy to meet up and talk, I'm sure."

"I'll do that, if I have the time." The words made me glance at my wrist. It was bare still. I had no idea what I'd done with my watch.

Mrs. Davies glanced at her narrow gold watch. "It's a quarter past four," she said.

"Thank you."

But I didn't know what day of the week it was. I wanted to talk to Mark, urgently; the fear was like a grey worm in my chest; I could feel it moving, mouthing blindly; but I had to do normal, do cheerful for Mark. I knew what he would say if he caught a whiff of this. I should come home straight away. I should go and see the peeled man. And I couldn't do that. Not again, not now.

"Thank you," I said. "Thank you for the tea."

"Drop in again anytime. And I'll mention you to Pauline."

I heaved myself out of my seat, leaving my tea half-drunk.

Back in the cottage, I grabbed my phone off the breakfast bar and turned it over in my hands. Could I call him? Could I get away with it? I saw the screen; it was blank: the phone was dead. Decision made, for the time being. I took it upstairs to where I'd left the charger, in the dressing-table drawer. I plugged it in at the socket between the dresser and the bookcase, and left it on a low shelf to charge.

IT WAS ONE OF THOSE BRIGHT WINDY DAYS YOU SOMETIMES get even in late May, the kind that make you feel more awake than usual; a good drying day.

I went straight from my morning's work to help with the washing, passing home and Agnes's house to go down the wash-house lane, my clogs clattering over the loose round stones as I went. The clotheslines, looped from post to post across the slope, were almost full; the white linen was brilliant against the green grass and blue sky; dark britches and jackets danced like drunkards. The breeze made sheets billow, shirts fill and flap, made chemises belly out like sails. At a glance, it looked like the Naval Fleet had run aground on our patch of green, and the village was having a party in its honour.

Aunty Sue and Aunty Edith were outside the wash-house, at the mangles. They dipped and rose with the handles' turn, muscles proud on their bare arms, sweat patching their bodices. Sue glanced up and saw me.

"Your mam's in there, she'll know what's most needed."

It was steamy and hot inside, full of the sour smells of soap and sweat and the bitter tang of lye. Mam was tired and flushed, standing at a tub and pounding something dark with her paddle. When she saw me she rested the paddle against the side of the tub, stepped down, wiped her face, and went outside, without saying a word. I got up onto the step, took up the hand-polished haft and stirred the clothes through the murky water, swirling them around and slapping at them, pressing them down and mashing them against the bottom. Considering them done, I heaved them out with tongs and slopped them into a basket, hefted the dripping basket up and carried it outside. My mam was sitting on the stone bench by the door flapping at her face, her top buttons undone and her shift stuck to her skin.

"That's the last of the washing," she said. "You'll need to get the dry things down."

So I took an empty basket on my hip and made my way up the slope towards the lines. The drying laundry stirred in the breeze. I walked the billowing halls between the lines, and felt hidden from everything, and alone. I could see nothing but white linen, green grass below, blue sky above. I lifted shifts to touch the seams to my cheek for dampness, scooped up the trailing ends of sheets to test their coolness, breathed in the cold sweet smell of linen on the line. I unpinned what was dry, put the pins in my apron pocket, bundled up the washing and laid it in my basket. My hands felt dry and papery from the clean cold linen. I moved on through the white corridors, and into the dark, where britches and dresses danced around me, still wet from the tubs.

Someone began to sing. Aunty Edith: I could hear her, faint but clear, a lovely voice, sweet and full. It was a song from a new ballad sheet that had been doing the rounds lately.

> *In Liverpool town is my delight,*
> *and in that lives many beauties bright,*

The other women joined her, swelling the sound.

> *but the one I loved did me disdain,*
> *so I fixed my mind on the raging main.*

I'd reached the top of the slope, the last clothesline. My basket was heaped and overflowing with linen, and the clothes pegged out up here were still sodden. I hitched the basket more tightly onto my hip, turned and climbed the lane for home, feeling the press of the slope in my calves and thighs. I opened the gate one-handed, eased myself and my basket through the gap, and fastened the latch behind me. The women's voices were still ringing out from the bottom of the hill.

> *I left my ma, I left my pa,*
> *I turned my eye to the fixed star,*
> *'Neath sun and moon, through howling gale,*

Then I noticed the cart. It was standing outside our house. The tailgate was down and the carter was trying to unload a box. He'd got hold of a strap, and was tugging at it, pulling it towards him; the box lurched heavily. I tucked the basket tight into my waist, and strode across the street towards him.

"That's not for us," I said. "You've got the wrong house."

The carter dragged the box off the cart and into his arms. He peered around the side of it to look at me. He was a small man, I'd seen him every so often bringing parcels for the Wolfendens or the Forsters.

"I was told to deliver this here."

His face was all red with the strain and the weight of the box.

"We're not expecting anything; you've got the wrong house."

He took a couple of staggering steps backwards, turned, and dumped the box down on our front wall.

"Well," he said, "you're in luck, then."

"Don't you dare," I said.

He brushed his hands together, shook his head, smiled. "Too late."

The box crushed the little creeping thyme plant that grows in the wall; I could smell its fragrance.

"We are not going to pay you for that, you know."

He tugged his jacket straight. "It's paid for in advance."

Dad. What had he done? "Listen," I said, "whatever he told you, we can't afford—"

The carter spoke over me, his complacency infuriating: "It's no fault of mine if your husband doesn't reckon up every expense with you."

He heaved himself up onto the seat, and flicked the reins.

The horse took a step forward, and the slack went out of the harnessing; the wheels began to turn, and I was left standing there, mystified, watching as the cart pulled away up the village street, looking at the back of the carter's greasy hat and his narrow shoulders in mouse-coloured fustian. Then I noticed the words scrawled across the top of the box in wide chalk letters. *Robert Moore, Esquire.*

I felt a sudden flush of self-consciousness. The words of that conversation were like moths around my head. *Us.* I'd said. *We.* The carter had said *husband.* Mr. Moore. I was back in that half-sleeping dream of the dark room; I was standing over him, bending to him; his arm was curling around me, drawing me down towards him. The dark warmth.

My hand had risen to my lips; I snatched it away. I looked at the box on our front wall, scrawled with Mr. Moore's name. This must have been what the Reverend meant, when he asked me to be watchful, and tell him what I saw.

I'd bring the box up to his room.

I couldn't carry everything at once. I ran in with my basket, shook out the shirts and shifts and sheets and pillowslips and draped them on the clothes horse, the dolly and the chairs, to let them air; three families' stuff all muddled together; we'd sort it out afterwards. The carter had been struggling with the box, but he was a slight little person; it shouldn't be too difficult to shift. I was straightening up and pushing my loose hair back, and turning to go out again, and there, at the foot of the stairs, in waistcoat and shirtsleeves, his shirt open at the neck so that I could see a dip where throat and chest met, was Robert Moore.

"It's you," I said.

He bowed his head in acquiescence.

"I didn't think there was anybody home."

"A half-day's holiday," he said.

"There's a package for you; it's outside. I was going to bring it in."

I turned towards the door. My other shift, worn shamefully thin, looking grey as cobwebs to me now, was hanging over the back of a chair. My face began to heat. I lifted the latch and stepped out into the sunshine. He followed me out and down the steps. My clogs were hard on the stone slabs: he went quietly, leather-shod. I was very conscious of him, of his bodily presence, his warmth and his breathing; if I turned, he'd be just two steps away, two steps above; my face would be level with the middle button of his shirt.

And then I realized. He'd been sitting up in my old room, waiting for his package, waiting for the carter to arrive. He'd have sat on the bed, with his back against the wall, and kept his eye on the street through the front window. You could see a good way up the village from there. You can also see the top of the wash-house lane. It was a favourite spot of mine, when it was my room; I'd sit with a book in my lap, looking out whenever movement caught my attention. If the casement is open, you can hear every word that passes in the street. I glanced back, up; the casement was open.

He'd seen everything. He'd heard everything. He'd watched me daydream afterwards.

I reached the foot of the steps; I couldn't face him; I just kept walking. I crossed the street and unlatched the gate, slipped through and fastened it again and did not so much as glance over to where he stood. If I could but have looked up then, and waved, and called out my farewells, it would have been smoothed over, but I was mortified. I ducked back down the track, the breeze cool on my hot cheeks, the sun making the grass shine silkily, past the white linen snapping in the breeze, towards the women's figures dark at the bottom of the hill, and my only thought was that he must think me such a fool.

The voices were ringing out like bells from another parish, now clear and bright, now interrupted by the wind.

> And where'er—
> —Afric to Americay—
> —I'd rather—
> —my love, my love—

They hadn't even finished the song. When I came to the foot of the track, my mam lifted her head from the mangling.

"Where's your basket, honey?"

I pressed my hands to my cheeks, shook my head. I'd left it back at the house.

"You're a mooncalf," she said, but not unkindly. "A right mooncalf."

*

When he came into the room, my stomach swooped as if I were falling, but he just nodded and said good evening to us all, the whole family. He took his seat, and Mam gave him his tea. I took my plate and cup and went over to the windowsill. I perched there, looking out at the garden, at a blackbird hopping through the herb patch, turning the earth with his yellow beak.

He set his empty cup down on the hearth; I heard the chink of china on slate, and my gaze flicked across to watch his dark hand retreat from the white china and return to the arm of the chair. Mam noticed he was done, and called across to him to ask him if he would take another cup.

"Thank you," he said. "I will."

"Lizzy, give us a hand here."

I left my place at the window to fetch the pot. It was heavy and hot; it took two hands to carry it, one cupping the belly with a folded cloth, the other grasping the handle. I was aware of the sound of my skirts rustling at my legs, the press of garters against my thighs, the way the blood rose to my face as I stood in front of him. He was looking at me. His eyes were dark flowers, pitch-black at the centre, the irises traced with peat-coloured petals. He lifted his cup and I poured the tea. There was a fan of creases across the ball of his thumb, and a scar ran down the back of it. I found myself looking at the scar, at its precise whiteness. I forgot my awkwardness, forgot myself, studying the narrow white line, its dip into the flesh, the way the skin puckered at the edges. Afterwards it was in this way that I remembered him, these little details; the darkness of skin, the way it creased, that scar, his eyes.

"Thank you," he said.

The cup was over full, the tea was welling to the brim. I dipped the pot back quickly, splashing tea onto the floor, and onto my hand, scalding; I shook it off without thinking and drops flicked onto his shirt. I watched the brown liquid seep into the weave of the cloth.

"I'm sorry—"

"Are you hurt?"

"I'm so sorry."

"But are you hurt?" He set down his cup and stretched out his hand. "Show me."

I shook my head, trying to manage the pot, to right its balance. "It's fine. My skin's like leather."

He took the pot from my hands. Mam was speaking at the same time, saying that she didn't know what was wrong with me lately, I'd lost any sense that I'd been born with, what was I thinking, getting clothes mucky on a washday. He set the pot down on the hearth, and took hold of my wrist, and drew my hand towards him, making me take a little awkward step closer to him. He looked at my hand; at the calluses from housework; at the scratches, scars and scabs from basket-making, the stains from preparing vegetables, cleaning copper pans, blacking boots and fireplaces. He turned it over, examined the cracks between the fingers, where the flesh is geranium-pink, that come from the cold, from scullery and laundry work. His fingers pressed strong and warm into my flesh. Then he let go.

"No harm done," he said.

Mam ducked in between us with a rag and dabbed at Mr. Moore's shirt. I went back to the table. I stood with my sister. I lifted my spoon and pushed the pudding around on the plate. My mam was still leaning over him, dabbing, talking. He said little, and calmly. I could feel my cheeks burning. Sally looked strangely at me. For once, I did not give a tinker's damn what she might notice, or what she would find to say about it.

He went upstairs not long after and we tidied away the things.

The boys went out and Dad took himself to a corner with a newspaper, a half worn-out rag of a thing that must have done the rounds of a dozen households already. Mam had me stoke up the stove, and get the irons out of the cupboard. I stirred myself and set the irons to heat.

We dragged the chairs and stools out of the way, brought the table across to the fireside. We sorted the linen. Sally took her unfinished basket and sat herself down on the far side of the kitchen, at a distance from the heat. There's not enough room or irons for more than two of us to work at once. Mam lifted an iron from the hearth and spat onto its polished base. The spittle sizzled and was gone. She nodded at me. I picked up another iron and we began to work.

The room grew hot and damp, the windows misting; there was no sound but the crumble of wood as it burned, the creak and tap of the basket-making, the hush of irons on linen. From time to time my dad turned a page, shook the paper straight. My hair fell in tangles around my face, my shoulders ached, my nose itched. I rubbed at it with the back of a hand.

"Would you read to us, Dad?"

He glanced up at me, frowned thoughtfully, and went back to his silent reading.

The first knock was a jolt to me; I'd been lulled into such a stupor, a fug of repetition. Lift an iron, chase it around the creases and folds of a shift or shirt, fold the clothing, change the iron, take another item from the heap and start again. Mam flinched too; she glanced at Dad, who didn't move. She set her iron on the hearth and went to the door. Mr. Gorst stood on the doorstep; behind him his two boys. It had started to rain; a fine light drizzle.

Dad rose from his chair, folded his paper and welcomed them in. Mr. Gorst took off his cap, shook it, flicking the drops of rain into the street. His boys followed him indoors. Mam closed her eyes, breathed carefully. She left the door a fraction open, came back to the hearth, lifted an iron, and smoothed out the last creases from a chemise. She folded it, set it on the pile, picked up another. She pursed her lips, said nothing.

They came from further off, this time: Mr. Woods and his oldest boy from Broomfield, and the Mackereths from out at Docker, the Blacows from High Carr, and the Tysons from Cawood. They brought cool air, the sweet musty smell of cattle and the sour smell of clothes that had been long worn and got damp.

We had our sleeves rolled at the heat. The room was full of steam and the smell of scorched cloth. We were dripping with sweat. Sally was hunched like a goblin in a dark corner, working on her basket and muttering to herself. We were in no state to receive a soul, much less half the men of the parish.

I was dipping down to change irons. There was a knock on the open door, a quick quiet tap that pushed the door a little further back. I heard Thomas say good evening to my mam. I stayed down, my skin scorching, my eyelashes sticking together as I blinked at the fire's heat.

"Lizzy," Mam said. "Lizzy. Get up. Thomas is here."

I had to stand up, and wipe my sore hands on my apron, and push my hair off my forehead, and smile, and say that I had not heard him come in. He offered me his big pink hand; I was expected to shake it. It was as ridiculous to be shaking hands with Thomas as it would be to shake hands with Ted or John. I glanced at Mam; she nodded at me, urging me on. I lifted my hand to be shaken. It was worn, sore with the iron, and a little scalded with the tea. Thomas's hand when it closed around mine was cold and hard; he squeezed my hand tight. Mam would have left me crouching at the hearth, let Thomas come in and go upstairs without acknowledgement, if she hadn't been vexed beyond patience at finding her washday made a public spectacle.

We were still sitting up when the ten o'clock bell rang out. The linen was folded and put away; the fire had died down, and we had opened a window to let out the fug of heat. We were as dumb as moles, fatigued beyond complaint. We sat on the rug, and passed a jar of goose fat back and forth, digging out a lump and rubbing it into our hands. Sally had finished one basket, started another, and abandoned it. It now lay like a jackdaw's nest under the dark window.

Above us, the creak and rumble of the meeting went on, and I suppose we listened to that, or rather listened for a change in it, for any sign that it was nearing an end. I was glad of the silence between us, the mute passing of the jar felt like something from when I was a child. The day had done me in. I held only one clear thought in my head: I had to sleep. If they did not leave soon, I would lay my head down on the rug, and close my eyes, and not care if half the county were to troop past and see me lying oblivious on the floor.

At the half-hour bells, the noise from above altered; furniture scraped on the boards, and clog soles clattered and thumped, and the voices became separate and distinct as the door opened overhead, and the men began to spill down the stairs, their faces cast into sharp shadows by the rush-lights. Mam waited until the

last of them was out of the door, and then, shrunken with weari-
ness, she climbed the stairs to her room, and went to bed. Sally
and I stumbled out of our clothes and heaped our bedding on
the floor.

Sally breathed quietly, her head pillowed on her arm. Hair-
thin threads of light slipped here and there between the boards
above. My mouth kept on opening, but I didn't speak out loud.
Her breath was coming deeper, slower; she was drifting further
into sleep. I could see blank spaces on the ceiling where no light
penetrated. I picked out the pattern of our old room: our bed,
the blue and white rag rug in front of the fireplace, the chest, the
washstand, and another black shape that for a moment I could
not identify: the box. I licked the tea-scald, the blisters from the
iron. Mam's patience was not inexhaustible. What if she were to
hear what the Reverend Wolfenden had asked of me? And why,
after all, could he possibly need to burn so many candles? Why
did he need the light so late?

*

Morning sun did not reach this side of the house; in the dim
light the leather of the Reverend's chair seemed to glow; the deep
swirling walnut of the desk had a soft bluish sheen, like silk. The
books, lining the walls, were bound in warm tan leather; here
and there the gold lettering caught a little light, so that it seemed
that tiny candles gleamed and flickered all about the room. I had
always liked dusting in there. Before that day, dusting had been
the only reason for me to be there.

The carpet gave under my slippered feet, like moss. The Reverend's brow creased as I spoke, his chin drawn back into his neck,

so that the folds of flesh stood out over his collar. As I told him what I knew, he drew his chin further back; if he continued like this, I thought, he might disappear into his own skin; the rolls of loose flesh would close around his face, like water. When I had finished, he thrust his chin back out again.

"You had no indication of the contents?"

"No, sir."

The Reverend nodded, pressed his lips tight in thought. "And Mr. Moore did not speak of it to you?"

"Sir, I am not in his confidence."

The Reverend nodded again, and did not seem to notice how the colour rose to my cheeks.

"You must make an effort to become so. Find out what was in the box, and when you know, come and tell me."

"Sir—" My voice failed; I cleared my throat. "Sir, I was able to tell you this only because half the parish could have told you; the box was delivered in full public view. As for anything else, I am at a loss, sir, I don't know how I could go about it. He is a man who one does not easily approach."

The Reverend's look was assessing, but did not seem unkind to me; it was a long moment before he spoke.

"Very well," he said. "I understand. If you leave early this afternoon, you will find him absent; he's hardly likely to have another holiday so soon. You shall find out for me what is in that box. Then when I summon you again, you shall tell me what you have learned."

He said this as if it were a simple instruction such as any employer might give, such as clean the stair carpet, or straighten your cap.

"Is it right, sir? To do such a thing? I shall have to go into his room."

"It is not only right, it is essential."

"What if he is there?"

"Then I must speak to Mr. Oversby about keeping him more fully occupied. If you are not fortunate today, you may leave early again tomorrow. If he is there tomorrow, then you may leave early the day after; you may go every day until you get the opportunity to make a close examination of that box."

I nodded. He still looked at me, expecting something more.

"Thank you, sir," I said, but I did not feel at all thankful. Mr. Moore, when he arrived, he'd talked of weapons, of people arming themselves, of cities on the verge of conflagration. That was Lent, and now it was just past Whitsun, and Sunday just gone was Trinity Sunday, and he was holding meetings in our house, and had had a box delivered to our front door, and the Reverend had demanded to know what was in the box. I recalled the dark flowers of Mr. Moore's eyes, his words, the press of his fingertips into my hand. The first warning of tears stung my eyes.

"Can I ask, sir, what he has done?"

"It is not so much what he has done," the Reverend said, "but what he intends to do."

This seemed all the answer I would get. I thought myself dismissed; I curtseyed and turned to go. I heard the Reverend draw breath to speak again; I turned back. He stared at me so determinedly that I knew he must have found it hard to look at me at all.

"I can trust you, can I not, to keep this between ourselves?"

"You can, sir."

"I have your word on that?"

"You do."

I turned away, and left the library. My slippers trod soft on the wooden floor of the hall. It seemed to me as though I walked a narrow path indeed; a moment's loss of balance, a single misstep, would send me reeling into the abyss. This was more grave, more strange a circumstance than I had imagined. The Reverend should not have asked me for my word, a servant's word; he should not have needed to.

To be out in the open light and fresh air and without anything to carry, going to fetch nothing, expecting to carry nothing back, was stranger still. It was as if a gust of wind might lift me and carry me away, like a dandelion seed or the fluff of old-man's-beard. Circumstances had changed so profoundly, so swiftly, that I could no longer be sure of the earth beneath my feet.

I shut the door carelessly behind me, pulled off my clogs and dropped them on the stone flags, trying to make as much warning noise as possible. The house gave no sound back: it seemed empty. Upstairs, I stood and listened, breath held, at his door. Nothing. I knocked, hopelessly. *Be there*, I was thinking. *No matter that you would think me a fool, be there and save me from doing this. Save me from knowing.*

There was no answer. I knocked again, louder. Still nothing. I lifted the latch, my hand trembling. I slipped into the room.

My room. The patchwork curtains hanging from the windows, just as ever. The same china-blue and white rug on the floor beside the bed; sun streaming in through the windows as it always had, the boards that warm rich honey-colour beneath my feet. But a bag lay on the floor, slumped, dark, unfamiliar, with the smell of worn leather and smoke about it. There was a man's jacket slung over the back of my old chair. And on the far side of the room, sitting just where its shadow had been last night, was the box.

The straps hung loose like dogs' tongues, the lid was flung back, and the contents were spilled out onto the floor. Books. My heart softened with relief, and then with pleasure. I had crossed the room, knelt down, and picked up the first volume that came to hand before I could even think about it. The book was a creamy block of sewn pages, unbound. I leafed through it and weighed it in my hand. It was not a rifle, or a pistol, or gunpowder, or a sword. It was a book, unbound, innocent and naked as a newborn baby.

It was as though all the treasures of Spain had been flung up from the seas to land on my old bedroom floor. I lifted book after book from the box. There were works by men called Thomas Paine, Homer, William Shakespeare, Charles Lyell; some were familiar to me from the vicarage library, some I did not recognize at all; but I could tell the Reverend about this without fear. They were just books; books the two men had in common; whatever the Reverend's suspicions of Mr. Moore, they must be dispersed by this. And if there was no guilty secret here, then there was no need to hasten back to the vicarage with the news. I settled myself down on the floor, took up a volume, and opened it.

THE LIFE AND
STRANGE SURPRIZING
ADVENTURES OF
ROBINSON CRUSOE,

OF YORK, MARINER:
who lived Eight and Twenty Years, all
alone in an un-inhabited Island on the
Coast of AMERICA, near the
Mouth of the Great River of
OROONOQUE,
Having been cast on Shore by Shipwreck,
wherein all the Men perished but himself.
WITH
An Account of how he was at last as strangely
deliver'd by PYRATES

Written by Himself.

I closed it, looked at the cover, turned it around. It was embossed in black on the tan leather: *Robinson Crusoe.* The same name as my chapbook, the same story briefly told; but it could not be the same. My chapbook was barely thirty pages, and this was hundreds. I opened it again, flicked through titles and blank pages till I reached the start of the story.

I was still there, lying on the floor, leaning on my elbow on the rug, utterly lost in the book, the sun hot on my head, the sand soft under me, the call of strange birds, turtles clawing up the beach, when I heard the front door slam. I dropped the book and fled to the boys' room. I thumped at pillows, shook out covers, folded clothes and slammed the chest shut, making as much noise as possible. Then I came downstairs, trying to look unconcerned, but it was only Sally, lolling in Mam's chair like a moppet.

"I am done for," she said.

I made her tea, and she drank it, and looked at me over the rim of the white cup. "You're home early," she observed.

I just shrugged. "I'm something of a favourite with the Wolfendens," I said. "They gave me a half holiday."

*

Mr. Moore came home late, his face lined with fatigue and damp with sweat, his skin stuck with wood dust. Mr. Oversby had kept him busy, and worked him hard, it seemed. He went straight upstairs, and my heart quickened with anxiety: I had left without thinking, without tidying, without putting the books away.

When he came down, there was nothing to suggest that he had noticed anything amiss. His skin was shiny with washing, and his hair curling wet; he brought a book with him and took his customary seat. He did not speak, and did not seem either particularly to notice or ignore me, just sat at the hearth and read until it was time for tea. He ate his tea with us, and afterwards Mam went off to the evening milking, and Sally went to sew with Mrs. Forster, and the boys went out to play, and Dad hadn't come home anyway, he must have been on an evening's work at the public, and so we were alone in the house, me and Mr. Moore.

I took up my basketwork, and sat by the window for the light. He stayed in his seat by the low smoulder of the kitchen fire. It was quiet, just the creak and tap of my work, the soft sounds of our breathing, the turning of his page. Once he gave a little huff of laughter, making me start and look at him, at the dark curls on his bent head; he was so lost in his reading that he did not seem to have noticed that he'd made any sound. I wanted to ask him what it was; I wanted to ask him about *Robinson Crusoe*; I wanted to confess what Reverend Wolfenden had asked me to do, and laugh with him about the strangeness of it all. I kept glancing up at him, my lips opening on the words, but not daring to speak. The willow creaked as I wove it. He turned a page, let a breath go. There was no other noise.

The bell struck for the quarter hour. Shortly after that, he closed the book and heaved himself out of the seat. I watched him stand, watched the creases in his dark woollen waistcoat unfold; I watched him pass, the unknown book still clamped in his hand. His movements were fatigued and stiff. My hands fell still, the basket a palisade of sticks in my lap; I listened to every creak of the stairs, every footfall overhead, thinking I'd seen the last of him for the evening, and regretting it.

The footsteps went on; he had not settled to anything. I heard him moving about, as if traversing the room from the bed to box and back again. Then the footsteps crossed the room briskly, the door was opened, and he was out on the landing again, crossing it, coming back downstairs. My chest seemed somehow to compress, as if there was a knot at my breastbone, and it was being tugged, pulled tight like corset strings. He came down and crossed back to his seat.

He had a traveller's writing desk with him; a fold-out gentleman's set in rosewood; the Reverend had one not unlike it. He carried a book too; a wide cloth-bound ledger, red in colour, the kind that accounts are kept in. He held it clamped against the bottom of the writing set. A box of books, a writing set: I hadn't been so misled when I curtseyed to him. He settled back down in his chair, arranged his things, and began to fold paper for a letter. The desk lay open on his lap; his long legs stretched out across the rag rug. Though the writing desk was good, well made and expensive-looking, the ink bottle was a clay one, roughly made, and the glaze was blemished with thumbprint smears and unsmoothed edges. It occurred to me that he had most probably acquired the writing desk second-hand, it being brought within his means by the loss of its glass or china bottle. After such an expense, a clay ink bottle must have seemed perfectly sufficient, and was probably all he could afford.

There was better light, more space and solitude upstairs: why would he bring his things down here to write?

He took up his pen, examined it, trimmed it, examined it again. He dipped it, eased the excess ink off against the ink-pot's rim, and began to write. I observed his craft closely while my hands were at their own work on the basket. I shifted it around in my lap, bent the withy to the curve of the frame, levered it in and out through the uprights, tamped it down to fit snug against the layer before, all the time watching the strange progress of his hand across the page. The pen's plume wove and wobbled, his hand shifted a fraction further, traced another pattern, shunted on again. He paused to dip the pen. Mr. Moore's face was in shadow; he leaned back from the writing slope, peered down at the page.

I wanted to tell him that he might have my place at the window, where he might see what he was doing. He finished the letter with a flourish. I opened my lips and he glanced up at me. His dark eyes caught the firelight. I lost my nerve, looked down at the basket and didn't speak.

He lifted the shaker, scattered sand onto his page, then leaned the sheet towards the hearth. The grains showered into the flame, making it spark and sputter. He folded the paper, smoothed it flat, and bent to light a spill at the fire. I watched him light his sealing wax, watched the wax drip onto the white folded page, and pool there, like blood. My hands had fallen still.

"Would you like to see the stamp?" he asked.

The way he was sitting, his eyes were shadowed, his face half-lit by embers, half-lit by the evening window. The moment, with the redness and flickering shadows, and the pale blue light from outside, had an unearthly quality to it; it did not seem to belong to this world. His fingertips were stained black with ink.

"I've seen stamps," I said. "The Reverend has stamps. I take the family's letters to the post if Mr. Fowler's occupied."

"Yes, of course."

He put the letter to one side, and took up the ledger from where he'd left it on the floor. I pressed my lips together, looking away and feeling foolish. He was writing in the ledger, leaning back, peering down at the words as he formed them, seeming to be utterly occupied by the movement of his pen. I could have said yes. I could have just said yes. If I had, then instead of sitting in silence while he wrote and thought me discourteous and cold, I would be standing at his side, bending my head to look at the dainty image in his hand; I could have reached out to draw it nearer, and our hands might have touched again. I turned the basket in my lap and tugged sharply at the withy, wrenching it through the stakes. The wood creaked and splintered on the curve. I muttered inwardly, undid the last few weaves, my cheeks burning. I cut the withy short, behind the splintering, and wove the stray end in. I started it off again.

We continued without speaking. His feet were stretched out on the rug: the leather soles of his boots were patched, well mended, and the mends themselves were worn and needing repair. How far must he have come, to wear his boots into such holes, to wear the patches thin? He was leaning back still further than before, putting more distance between himself and the work as the light faded. He peered down at his hand, at the pen as it moved in its pattern of tiny shiverings, forward shifts.

"Isn't it driving you out of your wits?" I said.

He looked up. His brow was creased into a headache frown.

"I mean, not having enough light to see what you're about."

"My eyes aren't what they were."

"You'd be better here."

I dropped my tools into the half-made basket, gathering it to me as I rose. He shook his head and gestured with an inky hand for me to sit back down.

"I don't need the light," I said. "If someone but thought to put the tools into my hands, I'd be making baskets in my sleep."

I didn't know what devil had got into me. I lifted the basket; I remember particularly the green sappy smell of willow, and the cool smooth feel of the exposed split surface of the withies, the bulk and slight weight of the basket in my arms. I went over to him, waited for him to rise.

He stood up. He lifted the writing set with him. The pen was clutched against the board, the ledger and letter and loose papers sliding against each other.

"It's very kind of you," he said.

He carried his things over to the windowsill, and took my seat, and said nothing more. The evening light brought out the blue of the stone floor, the iron sheen of his dark hair. It had only been a tone, an inflection to the voice, but it filled me with indignation. He was mocking me, I knew it. There was a sufficiency of irritations and vexations in my life, without him mocking me.

I sat down where he'd been sitting, my feet on the rag rug where his had been. The wooden rungs of the high-back chair were smooth; they held me upright, supporting me, so that I could lean back and feel some relief from my stays. I felt somehow taller, sitting there in my mam's chair; less of a child.

He was setting his writing slope to rights. He wiped and dipped his pen, touching the nib against the rounded rim of the ink pot.

"You're a joiner, on the new house up at Storrs," I said.

He looked up, nodded. It was only afterwards that I learned that he was Master Carpenter, and was in charge of seven men, and saw the grandness of the house that was built, and the staircase that flowed like a stream, like birdsong, and realized the meanness of Reverend Wolfenden's mind in calling him a joiner. The ledger lay open on the windowsill while he arranged his writing things. I could see that the left-hand page was half-full, covered with densely written words; not dotted with numbers, dashes, single words, the rows and columns of income and expense, as one would expect. His eye caught the direction of my sight. He slid the ledger off the windowsill, drew it onto his writing slope, so that it was inclined towards him, away from me, and I could no longer see it.

"You're a domestic, I believe," he said.

"At the vicarage."

Could I say that I had been cleaning in his room, that *Robinson Crusoe* had fallen open when I was dusting; I had not meant to pry, there had been no intention at all, just accident? But then why would I need to dust the contents of a newly delivered box?

"There are books about the house. Whose are they?" He glanced across towards the dresser: Fox's *Martyrs*, *Pilgrim's Progress*, *Saints' Rest*, the family Bible.

"I like to read."

"Of course you do."

He smiled, but the smile did not reach his eyes. He closed the ledger and set it down upon the floor. He wiped the last drops of ink from his pen, stoppered the ink pot and closed the writing set. He put it down on top of the ledger.

"So the abridged *Robinson Crusoe*, that's yours, and the ballad sheet, and the tale of Jack the Giant Killer? They belong to you?"

My chapbooks. His air was calm, but I knew he must hold them in contempt. A man with books like that, with so many; of course he must hold my few slight things in contempt.

"There are others," I said, "but they're lent out, and the *Pilgrim's Progress* was my school prize. Fox's *Martyrs* and *Saints' Rest* were my grandfather's, but he's dead."

Mr. Moore nodded, but didn't comment.

"No doubt you think them foolish," I said.

"Of course not, no."

"Then why are you smiling?"

It was a faint flicker of a smile; it plucked the flesh up at one corner of his lips. It irritated me.

"It's strong meat, all those martyrs and saints and pilgrims, that's all. And the chapbooks; well, you may as well eat sugar straight from the bowl."

"What do you mean?"

"Just that I fear such a diet would upset even the soundest of constitutions."

"I suppose you'd tell me I have no constitution at all for reading?"

"Indeed no, I wouldn't dream of saying such a thing."

I was conscious that my hands were motionless, the fingers curling into fists, the knuckles pressing in at the sides of the basket. I was angry, like a child whose toy is snatched away in the middle of a game. If he understood the difficulty of acquiring the few books that I possessed; if he knew how hard I had to beg my mam to get a few pennies back from my wages; if he could see the magic-lantern-show I saw when I began to read; if he could have understood what a rich treasure it seemed to me, that box of books lying upstairs, overflowing with mysteries; if he could have glimpsed a fraction of how much this meant to me, then he would not have chosen the company of men like Thomas and my father over me, and he would not mock me now.

"I don't like being laughed at," I said.

"No, of course not." There was a pause. My face was hot. "Did you think that I was laughing at you?"

I shook my head. He regarded me with a level gaze, and I did my best to return it.

"It wasn't my intention—" he went on; and he drew a breath as if to say something more. After a moment, he nodded. "I'll leave you in peace," he said.

He bent to gather his things. He stood up. I wanted to say something, to protest, but the words would not come. He ducked his head to pass under the low lintel, and climbed the stairs. I was left alone. My work lay neglected a long while.

*

The library bell jangled, but it was not my duty to answer the library bell. I had a rag and sand and was scouring burned sugar and fruit off a baking pan; Mrs. Briggs would have been more careful if she'd had to clean her pans herself. I was thinking of Mr. Crusoe, I was thinking of Mr. Moore; I was muttering to myself, chagrined, at the memory of our parting. There was someone at the scullery door. I glanced over my shoulder. Mrs. Briggs leaned against the doorjamb, her round face creased and red with the heat of the kitchen. There were damp patches on her frock. She looked at me suspiciously for a moment, her lips bunched.

"You're to lay a fire in the library."

I nodded, set down the pan and rag.

"You, in particular, he asked for. Maggie went up, but he sent her back to ask for you."

I wiped my hands on my apron. "I'm good at it," I lied. "The way I lay a fire, it lights easy, straight away, every time."

"But it's roasting out."

I shrugged. "It's easy to get chilled, if all you do is sit."

I carried up a coalscuttle and kindling, and knocked on the library door.

The Reverend was sitting in his wing-backed leather chair, a closed book in his hand, his thumb stuck in and squeezed between the pages to mark his place. The same binding as all the other ones; they arrived like that from his bookseller. I bobbed a curtsey to him, then knelt to lay the fire, and he sat and watched me, and let me work, until I had set the last of the coals upon the wood.

"Don't light it," he said.

I sat back on my heels.

"Well, my child?"

I looked around at him. I don't quite know what it was that did it, whether it was the dirt on my hard hands while his hands, holding his book, were soft and white as Mrs. Briggs's dough; or if it was that I was kneeling on the floor while he sat in comfort in a leather chair; or if it was because he'd set me about a pointless task, or that he'd used a contrivance to get me there which would not fool a child and would only serve to set the women downstairs against me; I don't know if it was one of these, or all; but whatever caused it, the feeling was new and unexpected: I wouldn't have thought it possible to feel angry like that towards a clergyman.

"Did you find out what was in the box?" he asked.

I brushed my hands together, but it did not brush the coal dust off them, it just rubbed it deeper in.

"Well?"

I could have told the truth then, and gone back to the scullery, and worn my nails to the quick scouring baking pans, and my part in it would have been over, and whatever happened as a result of what I said would not have been my fault, since I was only doing what my pastor asked of me. But, instead, I lied.

"No."

The Reverend's lips narrowed to a line. "And why not?"

"He was in the house, he kept to his room; I did not get the opportunity."

"Then why did you not return to your work?"

"I thought it best to wait, in case he left." It was as though I stood outside my body, and watched myself there, kneeling by the unlit fire, lying like a heathen. "I didn't want to disappoint you."

"Good girl."

All he had to do to discover my deceit, was to enquire of Mr. Greaves, the Oversbys' overseer, what work Mr. Moore had done that day. I was too far in the lie to retreat from it now; the practicalities concerned me, not the stain on my soul. I didn't even blush. I shifted the coalscuttle to one side.

"I'll leave that for you should you need it, sir, and matches," I said, as if it were all the same to me, setting unnecessary fires, spying on the lodger; all just services performed to ensure the Reverend's comfort.

"Very well," he said distractedly. "Very well."

He set his book down on the desk, and steepled his fingers against his upper lip.

I stood up from the fireside. I tucked my coal-dirtied hands beneath my apron.

"Do you wish me to go again today?"

He glanced at me, preoccupied. He meshed his hands together, and held them against his upper lip a moment, as if praying. Then his hands fell to his lap, and lay there, soft and white against the black cloth of his britches.

"I do not think I ask too much of you," he said, "but before I ask more, you should know what you are dealing with, what manner of viper it is that has crept into your nest. I am informed of Mr. Moore." He took a breath, sucking it in through parted teeth. "He is an agitator, a democrat, a Chartist. That much is known, and I hope soon to know more; but if you were to discover any-thing, anything at all—" His voice had grown passionate; he was leaning forward from his seat. He stopped, and seemed to correct and calm himself, leaning back, reaching up a hand to touch the linen at his throat. "You will have noticed that he does not attend church. I have it from Mr. Brakes that he is not part of the Wes-leyan congregation either. As a good Christian girl," he said, "it is your duty to watch him, with all modesty and discretion, and to report your discoveries to me."

I could say it. I could defend him with just a few words. What-ever his faith, whatever Chartist or an agitator or democrat might mean, I could reveal Mr. Moore to be a decent and educated man, a man whose interest in books was not very far divergent from the Reverend's own.

"You will do this for me, yes?" the Reverend asked.

"Of course, sir."

"If he is there, come straight back. Don't waste your time waiting."

*

I took *Robinson Crusoe*, and I lay down on the bed, my head on the pillow, my body stretched out in the dip left there by his body, my stockinged feet on the heaped bedding at the foot; the pillow smelt of wood dust. As I lay there reading, a sweet comfort descended upon me; the book grew too heavy for my hands, and my eyelids too heavy to keep open. I kept blinking; the weight of the book made it teeter towards my face. I thought I'd just close my eyes for a few minutes. I laid the book down on the bed beside me and curled around on one side. The pillow was cool beneath my cheek, the scent was pleasant. I closed my eyes; I must have slept, or nearly slept; I dreamed. It seemed to me that Mr. Moore was there, in the room with me, his jacket off, shirtsleeves rolled, his collar unbuttoned, and that there was nothing wrong or strange or frightening about it, that I was dozing in the bed, and he was half undressed, and we were alone together. He sat down on the edge of the bed. He said something.

The church clock: a quarter bell; what hour I didn't know. The words of the dream slipped away like smoke. The room was empty, glaring with sun, and I was sick and foggy with untimely sleep. I heaved myself out of bed, shoved the book back with the others.

I ran out the back way, through the stinks of midden and the pigsty and the privy and out the field gate. I cut through the fields, hoping to go unnoticed. There was a breeze; the long grass whispered. My mind was elsewhere, caught in the dream: the hint of words, the ghost of a touch. I was angry at myself, at what I'd wasted: my last chance.

I reached the back wall of the vicarage garden and unhooked the gate. I waded up through the long grass of the orchard. The kitchen garden was thick with greens: asparagus, pea and bean-stalks; the air full of the scent of growth and fresh-dug earth. As I crossed the stable yard the grey mare flared her nostrils at me and huffed. Perhaps the Reverend would not call for me again that day. Perhaps no one would have noticed I was gone. If I told him some urgent order of Mrs. Briggs's, some kitchen emergency had detained me at the vicarage, then he would be obliged to send me again. And I would be deeper in the deception. Was it worth it, for an hour's holiday, another chance to read?

I reached the kitchen yard, the scullery door. Maggie had left the family's boots in the hallway for me to clean. I sat on the stone bench underneath the scullery window, and polished the boots till they shone, setting them in neat pairs on the ground at my feet. I turned over possibilities in my mind, but could think of no contrivance that would not readily be discovered. The church clock chimed two. I had been gone from the kitchen nearly three hours. It could not escape Mrs. Briggs's notice.

I carried in the boots, and left them for Maggie to take up, and changed back into my slippers. I went into the kitchen without washing, hands smudged with bootblack, to give the air of time spent busily at outdoor tasks. As it happened, Mrs. Briggs was occupied with the roast, and didn't pay me any heed. I spent the remaining hours of my working day labouring furiously at whatever I was set to, jumping at shadows, alert to every jangle of the bells. Mrs. Briggs didn't speak to me until much later, when dinner had been served and eaten and she had a moment's pause. I was scouring roasting pans, and she came to smoke a pipe at the scullery door.

"He got his fire, then?" Her cheeks were red as rhubarb, her face shiny from the long day's cooking.

"I laid it for him, but then he changed his mind."

She nodded, the pipe-stem clamped between her teeth. "Funny that."

"Yes," I said. "Funny."

Everything was changed since that morning. I had lied, and read, and slept, and dreamed, and lied again, and everything was different because of it.

*

They had been setting up the games for days. Sheep had wandered among the booths and stalls, scratched their heads on the posts of the wrestling ring. That evening, work done, women walked down with baskets of refreshments, tea services, urns. I could hear people passing; their voices, their clogs clattering on the stones. The house was empty. I was in a fireside chair, with my *Pilgrim's Progress*.

I had read that book a hundred times; the title page was as familiar as the gate across the way: I'd slip past it every day without even considering it. Now, as I looked at it, I saw it as if for the first time, as something fresh, and unknown: I saw the words as what they were, and not as an opening, a gateway to something else.

THE

PILGRIM'S PROGRESS
from this world to that
Which is to come
delivered under the similitude of a dream.

Similitude: I had read the book a hundred times, and I had never noticed that; but now I worried at it as a dog worries at a rat. *Delivered under the similitude of a dream.* I turned the page, to the *Author's Apology For His Book.* I'd tried reading it before, but had found it dull, and had given up, and turned forward to the story, and since then I had always started where the story itself began, with Christian. But now I read the apology word by word, carefully. It made me uneasy.

Read my fancies, I read. *They will stick like burs.*

Similitude. Fancies. I was beginning to see the book in a new light; the experience was uncomfortable, and vexing to the eyes.

The front door opened, a pillow of evening air touched my face, and Mr. Moore was coming in backwards, his jacket off, in waistcoat and shirtsleeves. A slow blush rose up my throat. Mr. Moore cradled the end of a sheaf of planking, holding it low. He backed into the room, hoisting the weight up to his hip, as someone outside lifted the other end high, onto a shoulder, to clear the steps.

His arms were bare, the hair there caught the sunlight, and was gold. I stood up. He noticed me and nodded.

"Good evening," I said.

He turned his attention back to the work. I set my book down on the windowsill, but did not know whether to stay or leave, stand or sit. The wood moved back into the room, bringing Sammy Tate, the lad from Storrs Farm, up the steps and into the house, shifting his end of the wood down from shoulder to hip. Dad followed after, came and stood in front of the fireplace, his hands pressed into the small of his back, his elbows wide, and said that it was a fine bit of timber that Mr. Moore had there, and that it must be worth a good deal, and that Mr. Moore would make a grand job of it no doubt. Dad was in the way; I could see that he was in the way; Sammy would have to pass too close to him, if Mr. Moore was to get his end of the timber past the kitchen table, but Dad didn't seem to notice it himself. He just kept on nodding sagely, talking, and it was only when Sammy moved around right in front of him that he finally shifted himself to go across the room and stand at the foot of the stairs, taking up station there to admire and comment. He didn't seem to notice the brevity of

Mr. Moore's answers, or the obstacle he formed as they edged the wood up into the stairwell.

"Dad—"

He swung around to look at me, his expression blank. My book was lying on the windowsill. I moved in front of it.

"What?"

I could think of nothing to say. All of them were looking at me.

"What?" He looked at me a moment more, and I remembered a time when I was very young, when he had carried me in his arms through the big barley field, up above the hay meadow, where Mr. Oversby now keeps his sheep, and the barley was as green as anything could be, and seemed to stretch endlessly, and the sky was wide and blue above, and at my cheek my dad's shirt was soft red wool. I remembered the green barley, the blue sky, the red shirt, and feeling safe and happy and proud. He'd said, *Your father's barley is the finest barley in the whole field.*

"Sitting idle," he said. "Can't you do something useful, for once in your life?"

My eyes turned to Mr. Moore; he was watching me. It can't have been more than a moment; I was vividly conscious of every inch of my frame, from the sore patch on the back of my left heel where my clog rubs, to the pull of my hair at the nape of my neck where it's twisted into a braid, and the sheen on my nose, and the dry soreness of my hands. I put my hands in my apron pocket. My cheeks burned.

Then Mr. Moore said, "Come on, Sam, let's be at it. You go at the top."

They moved with brisk purposefulness. They swapped places. Sam went backwards up the stairs, guiding the planks, and Mr. Moore took the weight, and directed his attention upwards.

My dad followed Mr. Moore upstairs. I heard shuffling and scraping and the brief, low sounds of Mr. Moore's instructions, the ongoing roll of my dad's talk. I sat down and lifted my book again. Up above, they were sorting and arranging the wood. Then there was silence as chalk marks were made, plumb lines tried. The certain sound of wood on wood: a chisel struck with a mallet. Another patch of scuffling movement. A few gentle taps; pegs being hammered home, perhaps. I knew what he was doing; I didn't need to be told. He was making bookshelves; bookshelves for his books.

When the three of them came down to swallow a cup of tea and eat some bread and cheese, he brought the smell of carpentry; of wood, beeswax, and linseed oil. Mr. Moore went back to his work; Sammy Tate went home. Dad stayed downstairs and shook out a ragged paper. I dithered about, tidying things away. Then Thomas called for me.

He stood on the top step, his face red, his eyes flickering from the step to my face and then beyond me into the house, then back to the step again. His sister Martha smiled up encouragingly from the street. She had her arm linked through her husband Gerard's arm; he was gazing down the village street, his mind on the shot-put or the wrestling. Thomas cleared his throat.

"Would you like to come to the sports with us?" he said.

My dad yelled from his seat to know what was going on, so I told him Thomas was there, and Thomas called past me to my dad and said he wanted to take me down to the sports. Dad told me I was to go and get my bonnet on. It was easier to go than to argue with all that.

I walked down to the water meadow with Thomas and his sister and her husband, trying not to care what it might look like. I talked to Martha. Thomas walked silently at my side in his Sunday coat. I noticed the way his long legs swung his clogs out ahead of him, like plumb lines. His trousers were too short for him, and showed the cuff of his clogs, an inch of worsted wool sock.

They came from all directions; along the riverside paths from Newton and Hornby, down the hill from Docker and Storrs, wading through the ford from Melling and Wrayton, gathering on the water meadow to walk among the stalls and games and wait the start of the sports.

When Mr. Aitken announced that the wrestling was to begin, the men crowded close to the roped-off circle, almost screening it from view; Martha and I climbed the bank to watch from a suitable distance with the other women. A Gressingham man won the first bout. Then Thomas was in the ring, stripped to the waist, being slapped on the back, having his hand shaken, looking very ill at ease. I glanced over at Martha: she smiled at me. Thomas looked disastrously vulnerable; his blue-white skin, the dark scattering of hair across his chest, the pink-brown darkness of his face and neck and hands. He looked somehow more than naked: he looked as if he'd been skinned. His opponent pushed in through the crowds. I recognized him as one of the Huddlestones from Cawood: a big square meaty man in his middle years; I didn't see his face. Mr. Aitken dropped his arm, and the bout began. I glanced at Martha again: her smile was uneasy. I had been brought here, to be shown this.

"I'm sorry," I said. "Excuse me."

I turned away, and picked my way down the bank, passing through the crowds; I walked along the hedgerows, looking at the speedwell, the stitchwort and lady's mantle, and trying not to think of Martha's look, so full of anticipation and anxiety, and not about the fight. I stayed away till the noise and shouting had died down.

Thomas found me later. There was blood on his neck; his ear had been torn. It made me shudder to look at it. He brought me to the tea tent, and sat me down at a quieter end of one of the long benches, and fetched me a cup of tea. It was noisy in there, and airless. He had to shout to speak to me: he'd won his bout, he was going to be in the second round. I could smell the sourness of his body. He was red with awkward pride. I said I was pleased for him, and that I was tired, and was thinking about going home soon. He seemed to falter a moment, and there was a look about him again, almost angry, not sure if he'd been given cause to be. Then he gathered himself, and said that he would walk back with me.

"There's no need," I said. "You'll miss the bout."

"Doesn't matter."

I looked down at my hands resting on the white tablecloth. Two dozen different conversations were continuing loudly and close by, competing with the rattle and hiss of tea making, the sounds of eating and drinking. The air was full of steam and sweat and the smell of boiled ham and teacakes and canvas and crushed grass. Pinpricks of light sheered in where the canvas had been holed, like stars; I remember thinking, stars are holes in the sky, where the light of heaven breaks through. I remember thinking of Thomas's red-brown face and hands, the blue-white of his body, that scatter of dark hair. Mr. Aitken leaned in through the open flap of the doorway, and called out that the second round of wrestling would be starting shortly, and I looked up and gave Thomas a quick smile.

"Go on," I said. "Good luck."

"Lizzy," he said.

"I'm just so tired," I shook my head, and the way he looked at me made me begin to hope that he understood me more fully than I was able to say. I got up, and he sat there still at the trestle-table, and let me go. I slipped out of the tent and away from the crowds, the noise. I left the water meadow, and passed through the gate into the hay meadow. The ground was dry and hard, the evening air whisked with swallows. I could hear the shouts of the men behind me as the wrestling began again, and the calls of the birds in the hedgerows, the rustling of small creatures. I climbed up the wash-house lane, my face cooling in the evening air.

I slipped off my clogs and bonnet in the dark empty kitchen. I remember the feeling; it was as if all sensation was suspended. I remember thinking, I'll not worry about this now; I'll worry about it afterwards. There had been a light burning in the upstairs room; a light to read by as the daylight faded. I picked up my chapbook, my *Pilgrim's Progress*, and I climbed the stairs.

The door stood ajar. My fingers pressed against the pale wood. The door swung softly open. I saw the bookcase. He had already shelved his books, stacked newspapers and journals on a low shelf. I crossed the room and rested my hand on the wood. Soft-napped, with a cool iron hardness underneath, it seemed like something formed by nature, not by man. I lifted my hand away, and there was wood dust on my fingertips. It made my skin prickle.

"It's beautiful," I said, as I turned around to where he was.

He was sitting at a table on the far side of the room; the door had screened him as I came in. The table and chairs were new to the household; he must have brought them in that evening. A wax candle was dripping in one of our pewter candlesticks. A book lay open in front of him. The room smelt of oak and beeswax, and was warm with the glow of candlelight. His dark eyes caught a gleam.

"You made this," I said.

He didn't speak, he just looked back at me.

"It's beautiful," I said again.

He cleared his throat. "Thank you."

He stood up, pushing his chair back from the table and came over to me, his leather soles quiet on the wooden floor.

I said it again, and shook my head; "But you *made* this."

"Yes. But you make things all the time; you never stop."

"It's not the same. I make the tea and make baskets and I make things clean and neat, but none of it lasts, not beyond the use of it; it gets eaten, it gets dirty, if it's a basket it gets sold and I start all over again." I shook my head again. "But this, this is different. There used to be nothing there, and now there's something. And it looks as though it could stand here forever."

He smiled, but I turned to watch my fingertip slip across the smoothness of the wood. It was a strange feeling, the softness of the surface, the iron hardness beneath. I heard his breath as he drew it.

"There's no such thing as forever," he said. "What are you doing here?"

I was suddenly aware of myself, standing there, uninvited, with wood dust on my fingers. If ever there were cause for him to mock me, this was it, but his expression was serious and sober. He gestured to the chapbook tucked under my arm, my *Pilgrim's Progress*.

"Have you brought something for me to see?"

His voice was barely above a breath. Someone could come home at any moment, and find me alone with him, at night, in his room; I had not considered this. It made me feel more nervous to realize that he had.

"I wanted to ask you," I said, and it all came pouring out, without pause for reflection. "I wanted to know. My chapbook of Robinson Crusoe, and your book about the same man. I don't understand at all. They're the same thing, but not quite, and the book is so much bigger, has so much more of the island in it, more words, more thinking. I looked at my *Pilgrim's Progress* again—" I felt my voice thicken with the beginning of ridiculous, foolish tears. "I looked at it again; I thought I knew it back-to-front, but I read the title properly, I read the *Apology* properly for the first time ever. It seems, it seems that both books, the *Progress* and the Crusoe book: I don't think they're true."

He reached out, and for a moment I thought he was going to touch me, to just rest a hand on my waist, but instead he took hold of the *Progress*, which I was holding pressed with the chapbook between my arm and my side. I loosened my grip, let the book slip away and took the chapbook in my own hand. His practised fingers opened the book's cover and leafed through the pages.

"'Read my fancies,'" I said, craning my head to look at the words. "It says *fancies*. And similitude; I think that means a pretence, a deceit, doesn't it?"

He pressed his lips together, tilted his head. "Also counterpart, where one thing seems an echo of another; as in music, where a melody returns again in the same piece, and is familiar, but not the same, is perhaps rendered in different instruments, in a different key."

He set the book down on an empty shelf, reached up and took down his *Robinson Crusoe*. He handed it to me. "Would you read the title page for me, Elizabeth?"

My name on his lips. It startled me, made me glance at him. He nodded to the book, waiting for me to read, so I opened it, turned the leaves, found the title page, and I read it to myself.

"So who's Mr. Defoe?" I asked. "What's he got to do with it?"

"Mr. Defoe," Mr. Moore said, "wrote the book."

"He isn't mentioned in the chapbook," I said, lifting it up. "Why does it say that Robinson wrote it?"

"It's a device," Mr. Moore said, "a convention. There was no Mr. Crusoe, at least, not in the way you might have imagined. There was a sailor, one Alexander Selkirk, who was shipwrecked in the South Seas. Defoe based the book on his travails. May I?"

He took the chapbook from my hand. He examined the cover, the woodcut of Robinson with his goatskin umbrella.

"So it's not true," I said. "None of it was true?"

"It's fiction. So is your *Pilgrim's Progress*. Did you really think there was a city called Destruction?" His tone was kind. I didn't mind it.

"For all I know," I said, "there might be half a dozen."

He smiled; there was something very pleasant about his face when he smiled; his brows seemed to clear, his eyes to soften, and I found myself wondering about the young man that he had been; if at nineteen, at twenty, his brow would have been always unfurrowed, his gaze as open and clear as that. He handed the chapbook to me and went back to his seat. He touched the book that he had been reading, gentling the page flat.

I hesitated, watching him, then went over to the table, and stood there, not knowing what to say. The chair beside him scraped back from the table; he had pushed it out with a foot. He glanced up at me, the candle burning clear and warm, the open pages of his book creamy gold between us. He nodded towards the seat.

"I only know what I learned at school," I said.

"I doubt it," he said. "Sit down."

I slid onto the chair.

"What did they teach you?" he asked.

"To read the Gospels. I've always read everything the way I was taught, as if it were gospel truth. I never knew that books could lie."

For a moment he did not reply, and the words seemed to hang in the air like a bell-chime, unanswered, and I thought of what Reverend Wolfenden had said, about Mr. Moore being neither of the church or of the chapel, and being a Chartist and an agitator and a viper.

I leaned forward. "Will you tell me, please, will you explain? I mean, tell me the nature of what I have read. What is truth, and what is lies, and what pretence?"

In the candlelight his eyes were dark and wet and peaty, and his skin lined and tired and weather-worn. He looked at me, leaning back. Then he grinned, shook his head.

"That's a good question," he said.

"Is it?"

"It's practically unanswerable."

"How can it be?"

"Well truth and lies and pretence; it's a question about how we can understand the world. And there are so many ways of understanding the world. There's natural science and that's an attempt to describe the physical world as it is, ever since Aristotle and the crab; but how can you describe the world as is when you only have your partial and imperfect senses to guide you, and an imprecise and mutable language to express what you have seen, and a mind that may not, after all, be adequate to the task? And then there's history and that has all the attendant problems of science but with the complicating coda that it describes the world as it *was* not as it *is*, and there's politics, which is describing the world as it could or ought to be or ought not to be, and is driven by faction more than anything else. And then there's philosophy, which some would say is the only way we can understand anything, but leads, I have found, more to an understanding that nothing can be perfectly known in this imperfect world, which is how I feel about science, if you remember. But you've been reading fiction, which, it seems to me, when run through as it is in both books with a strong vein of religion, is an attempt to pretend that it can."

I shook my head to clear it. "What can what?"

"Sorry. That something can indeed be perfectly understood in this imperfect world."

I was dazed with it. I felt as though I had walked into a haber-dasher's shop, like the one that I had once seen into when I was a girl, and we were taken to Lancaster for a fair. But instead of just peering in the window and admiring the ribbons, I was stepping through the door, passing the drawers of buttons and hooks, the rails of laces and braids; going further in, moving between bolts of glowing velvet and swathes of brocade, bemused and almost gawping with delight.

"What do you do here, when you have the meetings? Do you talk to them like this?"

"You don't know what the meetings are for?"

"No one told me."

He raised his eyebrows.

"Really," I said. "I didn't even know the room was to be let until the evening you arrived."

There was a moment's silence. His expression was muted somehow, but when he spoke, he spoke briskly.

"I'm setting up a reading room," he said. "With your father's permission, of course; he adds a little to my lodgings bill for the increased wear and tear and inconvenience. I have my books and papers to lend, and others bring theirs to exchange. Sometimes I talk on a subject. Others will take their turn later; we will have talks on natural science, history, geography, when the men feel easy with the idea." He paused again. "No one told you?"

"No."

He nodded. "You must resent me."

"No—"

"I didn't fully understand the nature of the arrangement when

I agreed it with your father. I think of you at night, sometimes; sleeping on the floor. I mean, are you sufficiently comfortable?"

I glanced up at him; his gaze was turned towards his book, as if he were half-reading a line there.

"Perfectly."

"You are young, I suppose. You sleep soundly."

"I'm nineteen," I said, my cheeks burning.

He nodded, though I had not meant it in agreement. There was a silence, and it seemed strangely coloured, as if the situation had rendered the words unpredictably powerful. I retraced our steps, looking for a moment that I could return to, a point before words became slippery and stronger than they'd seemed.

"Everyone that comes, they must bring books to exchange?" I asked. I knew my father didn't; I suspected that Thomas couldn't, unless he borrowed them off someone else beforehand.

"Many of them do," Mr. Moore said, his voice sounding deliberately lighter. "There are some books that everybody has, that are not worth exchanging, such as the *Progress*. We have put together a subscription for the *Penny Cyclopaedia*."

I'd walked that road with Christian so many times, and I'd always thought it was a solitary journey, but there'd been a horde of us, all the old farmers and cowmen and ostlers that came to the meetings: everyone had the *Pilgrim's Progress*.

"Can I come?" I asked. I knew even as I spoke what his answer would be.

"If a woman were to arrange something—to find a place—it's not for me to do; there would be complaints, inquiries, noise; I am trying to avoid noise."

He closed his book over, pushed it to one side. His hands lay loosely curled on the tabletop. I could see that fine white scar down the back of his thumb.

"There is no one to do it."

"Any woman who came to our meetings would be—"

"I would come."

His hand lay a finger's breadth from mine; I could just lift a finger, and touch his skin.

"Do you want this, then? Do you really want it so much?"

I looked up at his face, his eyes shadowed, his skin warm in the candlelight.

"I'd give anything," I said, not knowing that the words were there until I'd said them.

He smiled. "That won't be necessary."

I lifted the coffee cup and took a mouthful. The coffee was cold, greasy, more smell than taste. I could feel there was something else, something soft but solid; it brushed the roof of my mouth. I opened my lips and let the liquid fall back into the cup. A brown ring of coffee-residue stained the cup, a faint scum edged the liquid. A disc of grey-green mould floated on the surface. My stomach heaved and I pushed the cup away.

I was sitting at the dressing table. Outside, the sky was grey with evening. It had been raining. The garden looked sodden and dejected. A brown bird hopped through the ragged grass, jabbed at something, then flew away. The fields beyond were deepening green as the light faded.

The room was dim and chill. The bookcase loomed nearby. She was there. My skin, my entire body, bristled into goose pimples. There was a breath, light as a moth, on my neck.

I was on my feet, swinging around to look behind me. The chair toppled, crashed onto the floor. The air flinched, the shadows took a step back. I searched the room, the hair standing on the nape of my neck. The bed was rumpled with my sleep. The bookcase was stuffed with shadows. The bathroom door stood ajar and the bathroom window was open on birdsong. A hint of breeze; it had touched my neck.

For a moment, I had no idea of who I was.

*

"I've been calling and calling."

"I'm sorry, really; I've just been up to my eyes in it. I lost track."

My hands were shaking and I was sweating. The peeled man, and those little blue lozenge-shaped pills that taste sweet and faintly chalky on the tongue, that melt into the veins and make you warm with the faith that everything will be fine, everything will be just fine. No more fear. No more dark spaces. I could soften at the edges, melt, ooze into the world.

"And there's no signal," I said. "No signal in the room."

"You must be nearly done."

"How's Cate?"

"She's fine. Look, we'll see you at the weekend."

I couldn't grasp his meaning; he went on.

"Whatever's left, we'll just get a houseclearer in. You must have gone through all the, you know, important stuff, by now. We'll have you home by teatime Sunday."

A flood of panic. "When," I asked. "When are you getting here?"

"I'll come straight from work, pick up Cate. She'll sleep in the car."

"Tomorrow?" I guessed.

"Yep," he said. "Friday."

Suddenly the days had names again, and ticked like bombs.

*

I picked my way through the box room, began to sort out the things. The aluminium clasps of the suitcase were stiff and oxidized. Inside were men's jeans, sweaters, T-shirts, all well-worn and faded. Dad's old holiday and weekend stuff: I couldn't see him wanting it now. I set it to one side for the charity shop, then dragged a carrier bag towards me. It was full of photographs. Framed photographs, loose photographs, wallets straight from the developers, the contents still not sorted into albums. I crushed the bag closed, pushed it away. Couldn't face it.

I opened a box: Mum's books. Austen, the Brontës, George Eliot, Dickens, Tolstoy: her comfort reading, books to sink into and disappear for days. My first instinct was to take the box through to the other room and unload the books onto the shelves, as she must have intended to, as she would have if she'd had the energy or time. I was supposed to be packing up, though, not unpacking: this was an ending, not the new beginning she'd anticipated. I folded the top of the box back together.

Moments like those have me wishing for the pills. I take the pills, and I don't find myself back there, climbing the worn linoleum stairs, the sunlight warm through high windows, conscious of the heaviness of my legs, the round hardness of my belly, the nausea. The pills close off the door to the ward, keep me away from her bed by the window, the freesias drooping on the locker, the drip's quiet occasional mutter, the drain-tube snaking from inside her gown, streaked with dark fluids, with the body's weeping. I forget the paleness of her smiling lips, the darkness of her eyes, the dry coolness of her drip-punctured hand as it held mine.

You look a bit tired, she said. I said, So do you. I bent to kiss her, my face full and heavy with tears. I wanted to tell her about the two pink dots on the test-stick that morning, the final confirmation of what I had been suspecting for weeks. I wanted to give her the secret, hand it over like a gift, tiny and exquisite. Her delight would be a kind of prism: it would split this bald fact into an array of brilliant potentialities, make it seem at once wonderful and real. Instead, I drew up a chair, and sat down, and asked about the wound, the drip, the pain. She answered quietly. I peeled her an orange, the zest spurting up into the air like tiny fireworks, and fed it to her piece by piece. I watched the careful precision of her fingers' grasp, the slow consumption of each segment, the way the flesh had fallen from her cheeks, and I knew without even thinking that this was not the time to tell. Once she was home and convalescing, when this thing was over and done with and the tests had come back clear: that would be the time to tell her, that would be the time to enjoy her delight in this. We'd hunt out old knitting patterns, hoarded angel tops and matinée jackets.

With the blue pills, I can almost believe it had happened, that we had sat on their bed, the case pulled down from the top of the wardrobe, the thick dust wiped carefully off. Her dark hands lifting out baby blankets, bootees, bonnets trimmed with broderie anglaise, her eyes soft with memory, and with gentle wonder at the swift flight of time. Still, even now, that image seems almost a memory, almost more real than the reality.

It's too tempting. The blue softening of the pills is just too tempting. I could have a handful of them on Monday; all I had to do was make the appointment, ask.

I heaved myself up off the floor and was out of the box room and downstairs, opening drawers, grabbing handfuls of utensils, cutlery, dropping them into a carrier bag to sling into the car, anything to be busy, to be occupied, to feel capable. Then I stopped: there was no point packing the kitchen stuff up yet. We'd be needing it over the weekend. But I had to keep busy, had to do something, had to get things into some kind of order before they came.

The fridge smelt bad. The unwrapped end of a block of cheddar had gone translucent and started to crack. I lifted the milk carton and shook it gently. The milk was solid. I'd have to go into town.

*

I walked into the first estate agent's I came upon. The blonde woman with the beautiful nails. She gave me a seller's pack, a sheaf of leaflets on similar properties, her card, and a lovely smile. A seller's market at the moment, she said. Lots of families looking: property of that kind often went well above the asking price. She seemed quite excited. I stuffed the papers into my bag and slipped her card into my wallet; it all felt rather unseemly. I thanked her and said I'd be in touch.

A youngish man was at the counter of the charity shop. They didn't deal with furniture, he said, but he gave me a card for an organization that did. A few quid to take it away, then they renovate it and sell it on; skills training for the long-term unemployed, cheap furniture for those in real need of it. I said that it seemed really worthwhile, and I'd definitely give them a call. I put the card in my wallet. I gave him a smile. It was Friday. There was no point calling anybody now.

I hadn't planned to go to the bookshop.

I was climbing the stairs into the dusty light, passing framed prints and maps. I was walking the hushed aisles, picking up books when I should have been trying to get rid of the ones I already had. I bought an old blue-bound collected Milton, a battered *The Flora and Fauna of the British Isles*, and an old book on geology, the cover burgundy and faded gold, the frontispiece an engraving of a classical temple. It was built high on rocks; the sea had risen to lap at its columns and receded again; had left bitemarks in the stone.

I went to the supermarket. I was hopeless at it. I had forgotten how to do it. I glazed over at the vegetable section: flowpacks of sweet peppers, pillow-packs of salad leaves, punnets of mushrooms, strawberries, blueberries, sealed plastic packs of chives, basil, rosemary, chillies, sage. Oranges, bananas, papayas, mangos, avocados, persimmons. Golden Delicious and Macintosh, Williams and Conference. Anya, Charlotte, King Edward. Organic, basic, or Fair Trade. I felt dazed with choice, befuddled by the shades and nuances of distinction. And I was thinking of the seasons, of the true distance from one harvest to the next. I took stuff and dropped it into the trolley; I had to get something.

I was in the bread section, gazing blankly at a wall of loaves; seeded and unseeded, wholemeal and wheat-free and white and white-but-wholegrain, and sandwich loaves and toaster-loaves; when I remembered avocados for Cate. Had to wheel the trolley around and go all the way back through the store for them. Always going back to that, to avocados.

Her little toothless gums munching away like a tortoise's, me scraping the bowl to spoon the last of the creamy green mush into her mouth. Taking the bowl to the sink and washing it, and then dropping it into sterilizing fluid, and looking out across the garden below, the garden that belonged to the flat downstairs. That dry ache in my nose and throat. Washing the plastic spoon. My daughter seven months old, sitting in her highchair babbling, slapping the tray, avocado on her vest. My hands pressed down onto the countertop, my shoulders high and shaking. I was going to dry my eyes, and blow my nose, and turn around to Cate with a smile, and say she was a good girl, she was my lovely girl, and we'd get her zipped up in her suit, and out and around the park, she'd like that, wouldn't she? I was going to get on with it, I was going to be fine, and I wasn't going to inflict any of my misery on her. But I heard his key in the lock, and the door opening, and he was coming down the hall, and was at the kitchen door, and it wasn't his time yet, he wasn't due for hours, but Cate crowed with delight to see him, and I turned from the sink, trying hard to be bright, but red-eyed and puffy with tears, and feeling terrible, feeling guilty, as if he'd caught me bingeing, caught me stoned or drunk alone in charge of our child. He leaned against the end of the work surface. He stuffed his hands in his pockets. He looked at me; he had paled, as if nauseous. I didn't know it was like this, he said. How long has it been like this. And he didn't hold me. And that was just before the talks, and more talks, and more tears, and him forgetting how easy it was to hold me and stop me crying. And the phone call that brought me to the peeled man.

*

They arrived late Friday evening, the headlights sweeping down the village street, the engine noise a tear through the silence. I went out onto the steps; the stars prickled above. The street was cool and quiet; there was a soft leafy smell, the odd birdcall in the dark. The car—his mum's, a silver Mazda—had pulled up at the grass verge. He got out.

He was creased and tired from driving. He was still in his work clothes, a grey-blue shirt, faintly striped suit trousers, the jacket hanging in the back of the car. I came down the steps in bare feet. The stone was granular beneath them; grit pressed into my soles. My skin felt strange in the evening air. I'd showered. I'd washed my hair. I'd put on a little make-up. I was ignoring the static hum in the air. I was trying to do normal.

I went to him and put my arms around his neck. He reached around me and pulled me close. The warmth of his body against mine. I had forgotten it.

"Hi," I said.

"Hello." He mumbled it into my hair.

Cate was sleeping in the back seat. Her face was turned away, so that all I could see was the smooth curve of a cheek and dark curls of hair. She was wearing her stripy pyjamas; her strawberry-patterned blanket was rumpled, half kicked off. Mark ducked past me to open the back door, leaned and fumbled with the car seat. He lifted her out, and she curled up in reflex, whimpered. He handed her to me, and I took her. She was heavy, limp, and hot. She'd grown. She whimpered again, nuzzled into my shoulder. Her smell: musty, appley; milky and ammoniac. I rested my cheek against her head, stood there just a moment, turning slightly from side to side, soothing her, a haziness coming over everything.

"C'mon," Mark said, a hand pressed on the small of my back, steering me. I carried her up the steps and indoors. I sank into a chair and leaned back to let her lie against me. Her warmth and weight and scent, the soft puck of her lips unsticking. In the hospital, newborn, curled and pink, her bald head squashed into a mitre, she had lain on my chest, her ear resting on my heart. She had weighed almost nothing, breathed butterfly breaths, radiated heat. Her ear on my heartbeat, me counting her breaths; we were keeping tabs on each other, me and Cate; we were making sure.

I was becoming drowsy with her sleep.

Mark carried in the travel cot. I gestured for him to take it upstairs.

"Room on the left," I breathed. "There should be space."

He nodded, took it upstairs. I heard him up there, in the twin bedroom, setting it up. He came back down and slipped his arms around her. I let her weight be lifted from me, blinked the haze and dampness from my eyes.

Normal. Normal normal normal.

I got up and went into the kitchen. I opened a bottle of wine, made a sandwich for Mark. Goat's cheese, vine tomatoes, rocket. Poppy-seeded bread.

He sat on the sofa and I sat on the hearthstone, watching him. The room smelt of woodsmoke, vacuuming, good tomatoes.

I liked that shirt on him. He was absentmindedly biting at his sandwich as he looked around the room. He swallowed, and his Adam's apple rolled down his throat and back up again. I could have got up, and gone over to him, and sunk down in his lap, and nudged my cheek in to rest against his throat, and breathed in the warm musky end-of-day scent of him. He looked back at me, pulled a sadly comical sympathetic face.

"Not fun," he said.

"The estate agent says this kind of property is really shifting," I said deliberately. I heard the breath hiss in between my teeth. "You should have seen it when I got here. I've taken loads of stuff to Oxfam."

"You've got someone coming for the furniture?"

"Yep." I stood up, walked past him, into the kitchen, started wiping up the crumbs. "There's this great charity. It's all under control."

*

Cate woke us in the night, wailing at the unfamiliar dark. Mark had lunged out of bed before I'd even really surfaced. I could hear them from across the landing; his shush, shush, shush, her wet retreating gasps and sighs as she settled back to sleep.

I didn't sleep again. The dark was pixellated, swimming, like a television screen when the sound's turned down and the signal's gone. On Sunday, with the car crammed with Mum and Dad's stuff, I'd be following the rump of the silver Mazda down the M6, and the cottage would settle into bright dusty emptiness again. I lay watching the shadows in the bookcase shrink, its shape become definite as the room filled with morning light. The air seemed to seethe, to swarm like bees. I turned to look at Mark, his face soft with sleep. How could he sleep, how could anyone sleep through this?

It was bright full day and I had been lying awake for hours when he stirred and reached for me. I huddled close, lay with my cheek pressed to the warm cotton of his T-shirt, my bare leg slipped between his legs. I felt him breathe. No alarm clock, no sound from Cate. No hurtling rush towards the day. The scent of his skin, warm and sleepy. He shifted onto his side, his arm laid loosely over me, and I looked at him, his long lashes, the grey shadows underneath his eyes, the still-faint lines at their corners. The slight fall of flesh towards the pillow, his skin loosening already with the years. He used to be such a boy. I leaned up and kissed him on the lips. I retreated, but his arm squeezed tighter and held me there. He kissed me back. We shifted together, pressed close, him waking into the kiss, me forgetting the static, forgetting the room, forgetting that Cate was just across the landing; I was lost in the tender wet of inner lip, the graze of a tooth that made me push harder against him, kiss him harder.

The way his nails grazed my ribs made me stretch. My hand cupped his hipbone, where it surfaces to press against the skin. His fingertips scraped across my belly, slid down to my underwear, then underneath. His fingertips dipped into me, and the kiss ended, and his face was pressed into my neck, and he was murmuring something I couldn't hear. Then the heel of his hand pressed down onto my lower belly. It pushed against the scar. I went still and was back in it; beyond being touched. I was crouched at the side of the bed, gripping the cold metal frame, a strap around my belly just where the contractions are, and I'm desperate to move it because if I move it it will hurt slightly less, but every time I touch it she shoves my hand away, resettles the strap back over the crushing pain. There's a phrase from a poem I've half-forgotten, it's going around and around in my head, and I know it's not the right words but I can't shake the real ones clear:

> *just the worst time of the year*
> *for a baby, and such a cold baby*

The baby's heartbeat stutters on the monitor, it stammers almost to a halt, kicks up again. And the midwife, who I've never met before, says You have to let yourself give birth, you have to give yourself over to it, you have to give yourself completely, and I know what she means; she means, You won't let this child be born. I want my mum, I really want my mum. And I am failing. Failing before I've even begun.

"Mark," I said.

"Dad-ee!"

"Shit."

"I'll go."

His hand slipped out from my underwear. I rolled out of bed.

"You make the coffee," I said. "You'll have to use the teapot."

Cate was straining for the door, leaning against the side of the travel cot, her face pink, yelling for her daddy. Her face softened when she saw me and she reached her arms up for me to lift her. I swung her up and set her on my hip; she glued herself to me. I carried her through, her nappy damp against my arm.

We got back into bed. She settled into the dip between us,

made staccato observations, pointing at the bookcase, the window, tracing the blue mountains and valleys of the bedspread with her hands, tapping on my arm when she felt my attention was drifting. Her hand on my arm was pale, plump, almost luminous. Mark brought up two mugs of coffee, and Cate's blue spouted cup half-filled with milk. We sat in bed, propped up against the headboard; me, Cate, and Mark, facing out across the room at the bookcase. Mark hadn't commented on it, seemed hardly to have noticed it. Cate's nose was squashed against the lid of her cup. I could hear her muffled breathing, her sucking and swallowing.

"So what's the plan?" Mark said.

Sleep had crushed his hair on one side, pressed it upwards against his skull. He smiled, showing the lines around his slate-blue eyes. The T-shirt was loose and sagging at the throat, exposing an edge of collar bone, and honey-coloured skin. He'd had that T-shirt from before I'd known him. I remembered it when it was still day-wear; it was part of the happy acquisition of detail, part of coming to know the stuff that made up who he was. I remembered it from sex in the hallway, pulled up urgently so I could press myself against his skin.

"The plan?"

I reached over the side of the bed, put my coffee cup down on the floor; Cate clambered onto me, crushed my left breast with an elbow. I straightened up and shifted her to sit upright on my lap. Her toes looked cold. I cupped them in my hands to warm them.

"We should do something, go somewhere," he said. "We don't often get the chance, not as a family."

"The Park," Cate said grandly, and grinned up at me.

THE TELLING · 147

"There's no park here, sweetheart." My eyes unaccountably filled with tears. I ran my fingers up her ribs, digging gently, tickling. "No parks, just fields."

"But there's bound to be something," Mark said.

Cate laughed at my touch. A big wet open-mouthed laugh. She wriggled and clamped her arms to her sides, but made no attempt to get away.

"Whatever you want to do," I said. "We'll do whatever you want to do."

I stopped tickling her, ran my hands over her hair, brushing it off her face. Her curls were tangled, ratty at the ends; they'd never been cut. She leaned her head away, complained, climbed out of my arms and onto her daddy.

*

It was a cool grey day; no threat of rain or hint of sunshine. We drove to an open farm, about five miles from the village. Mark had spotted the brown tourist signs the previous night. We took his mother's car. He drove and I looked out of the window. High hedges blurred inches from my face; a tattered white carrier bag whisked past; a sudden gateway gave onto a glimpse of green field, green-yellow moorland rising up towards the sky, scabs of exposed white stone. Then the blur of hedgerow again, a sliver hubcap, a crushed blue beer can.

The place was busy with parents and small children. They clotted at open barn doors, disappeared down alleyways and around the sides of buildings, lingered around the dog-pen, pressing up against the chicken wire to stare into the dark kennel at the back. There was a couple there with two young boys. The adults wore light Gore-Tex jackets and all-terrain walking shoes; the father carried a neat little rucksack. Their children, two solid boys in clean wellingtons and matching blue anoraks, peered solemnly into the darkness of the kennel. I held Cate on one hip, her skirt riding up, her little patent shoes dangling mud onto my jeans. Mark was in his suit jacket, talking about the Arctic Monkeys. My Converse were worn so thin that I could feel every pit and pebble, every ridge in the concrete. We are children, I thought; we will never be grown up.

Cate struggled; I let her down. She ran ahead, her little legs fat in their stripy tights, and we followed her. Mark caught my hand, and held it.

Piglets skittered through the yard like women in high heels. A horse leaned its head over a stable door and blew through its nose. I scooped Cate up to show her the horse's silky muzzle, grasping her with one arm around her belly, the other under her bottom. The warm comforting smell of stables, of ammonia and horse. Mark leaned beside us, arms folded across his chest, watching us.

"They've got pony rides," he said. "Shetland ponies."

"If you fancy it, love," I said, "you go right ahead."

Mark laughed. There was just a glance, but I caught it, saw its appraising edge. I set Cate down on her feet again, and we followed her along the rippled concrete pathways between the barns and sheds. Huddles formed at doorways, broke apart, families moving off along their separate trajectories. We leaned on a barrier to watch the piglets suckle, the sows like great fleshy feeding stations, lying on their sides, motionless but for the roll of an eyeball, the flap of an ear. A box of yellow chicks basked under light bulbs. In a barn, lambs butted at their mothers' udders, a calf stood uneasily on slender legs; the cow kept her head down, turned away. Blood and membrane and mucus hung from her back end. Cate pointed, frowned wisely, didn't know what to say.

"Let's see what else there is," I suggested.

Back in the main yard, Cate tottered over to the kennels. The Gore-Tex family had gone. She hunkered down to peer in, her pinafore dress lifting up, her backside sticking out. We followed her, crouched at her side to look in through the wire mesh. In the darkness of the kennel, a collie lay on newspaper. Her belly was turned towards us; puppies squirmed over each other to get at her teats. The dog looked back at us, her eyes wide and wet with anxiety.

We bought Cate a Mini Milk in the café and coffee for ourselves. I forgot to get napkins; Mark went back for them, tucked one into Cate's pinafore, mopped her chin with another. Afterwards, Mark swooped her out of the highchair, set her down on the floor, and hitched up her tights. They must have been sagging all morning, by now the crotch was down around her knees. He straightened up, didn't look at me; I think he must have been waiting for me to do it.

*

Cate was sleeping in the next room. I sat on the floor, staring at the heap of my parents' possessions, with an almost superstitious unwillingness to do anything, even to move. I could hear Mark downstairs, rattling around in the kitchen, opening and shutting drawers and cupboards, unable to find something. I felt a thin bright thread of resentment at his sending me up here. Dinner in half an hour, he'd said maybe fifteen minutes ago. I mustered the will to lean forward and drag a shoebox towards me. I lifted the lid and took out one of the paper-wrapped bundles. I peeled away the paper. The things inside were slim, heavy for their size; they clinked together. Underneath the newspaper there was dark blue tissue paper, still sealed with shop-counter Sellotape. I picked at it; the paper tore and I pulled the rest away. A pair of blue-and-white ceramic candlesticks. I turned them over; the green Oxfam label was still stuck to the base of one of them; I had an image of her in the High Street, cheeks flushed, swinging into the Oxfam shop with a bleep of the bell, to buy ethically sourced candlesticks for her country cottage. Such small domestic victories made her disproportionately happy. The next package I unwrapped was lighter, but in the same deep blue tissue paper. A pair of creamy beeswax candles; I raised them to my nose, but they'd lost their scent with time. I brought them and the candlesticks downstairs. I set them on the mantelpiece.

Mark had his back to me, grating Parmesan. He didn't seem to notice, didn't comment on the candles. We ate pasta and tomato sauce. That night we slept curled on our sides, our backs to each other.

*

Their bags were packed, the travel cot folded; it had all been transferred out to the car. I had my clothes and books to pack up. I had to bundle up the crockery, the china, start bringing whatever we were keeping down from the box room and out to the cars. Start slinging the rest into the bin.

"I'll get Cate out from under your feet," he said. "We'll go up to the shop and buy a paper. Give you a chance for a last look around."

He kissed me on the cheek, then he scooped her up, and they were gone.

I'd forgotten that there was a shop. I just stood in the living room, looking at the pewter jug of limp daffodils, the shiny patches on the sofa arms, the grey trails across the carpet, alert for a hint of static, but there was nothing. Birdsong. Cate's high twittering voice as they walked away up the village street. Nothing more.

I brought down the brown suitcase and the shoebox. I put them in the boot of Mark's car. I heaved the clothes out of the wardrobe and laid them on the bed. I threw the Radox and the soap into the bin. I sat down on the edge of the bath. I fished the soap out again, turned it over and over in my hands, looking at the crevasses and canyons, the grey streaks through the yellow, feeling the palm-smoothed shape. I set it back on the edge of the basin. I went downstairs and started on lunch.

They came back. Cate was all fresh air and smiles; Mark glanced around the room, taking it all in: the candlesticks, the jug, the nothing-very-much-achieved between his going and his coming back. He looked at me, an enquiring crease to his brows. I avoided it, focusing hard on making sandwiches.

Cate was pushing her toy car around on the living-room floor. It beeped and flashed as she scooted it across the carpet. She made a wet brumming sound with her lips. Suddenly the air was bubbling with electricity. My arms were rough with goose bumps.

"Don't you feel that?" I asked Mark.

Mark was leaning thoughtfully against the breakfast bar; he watched me pluck the stalk from a tomato.

"What? Is it too noisy? Shall I get her a quieter toy?"

I shook my head. "It's all right."

"So," he said carefully, "it's not done, is it?"

I glanced up at him. I could feel the press of the tomato flesh between my fingers. It felt uneasy, faintly unclean.

"Not nearly," he added.

"Mark—"

He shook his head and closed his eyes. He let a breath go.

"It's not been easy," I said.

"I don't know why you even—no one asked you to."

"Dad, though; he's not great—"

"And you are?"

"It wouldn't have done him any good."

"But you're in such robust psychological health."

"That's not fair."

"We could have done this together, in a weekend. Left Cate with my mum. We could have *paid* someone."

"Someone had to go through it all."

"And it had to be you."

"It had to be *someone*."

"No," he said, "it had to be *you*."

There was a silence.

"Are you going to explain that?" I asked him.

"You've got this attitude; it's like this past few years, for you, they've been an endurance test, and you're having the most godawful time, but you won't let yourself give up; you have to win, you have to get through. You won't stop and you won't ask for help. Fuck. You won't *let* anyone help."

Of course I couldn't give up; how could I give up, what was the good in giving up?

"I'm coping," I said.

Then he said, quite simply, "No, you're not."

The peeled man, his blue trace of arteries, his deep red veins, the grey maze of his brain. I shook my head. "I'm fine. I don't need help. I just need to get this sorted."

"Right," Mark said, his tone ironically light. "I see. So. What happens now?"

I didn't speak. My throat was too constricted.

"Nothing happens now?"

"I'll stay," I whispered.

"Stay?" he repeated, louder, an edge to his voice.

"Just another couple of days. That's all it'll take. Honest."

His face was cold, closed. I didn't blame him.

"We did say. At first. We did say a fortnight."

He looked at me a moment longer, eyebrows raised, on the verge of speaking. Then he pushed himself upright, away from the breakfast bar. "Right. Okay. Fine."

He crossed the room and lifted Cate. He held her with one arm, his hand gripping around a plump thigh. Her toy car was falling out of her hands. She wailed at the loss; Mark caught the toy one-handed and gave it back to her. He grabbed a bag with his free hand. My heart tugged towards them.

"Love—"

He turned around and looked at me. It must have been a long time since I said that word, in that way, if it could make him look at me like that. If I could have gone to him then, it might have been enough. But we were stalled there, too much space between us. His expression hardened and he shook his head. He left.

I felt sick. I walked along the grey track in the carpet to the front door. I went down the steps, and stood at the bottom; I watched Mark lean into the back of the car to strap Cate into her seat.

I came closer, looked in through the gap between the doorframe and the car.

"I'm sorry."

He tugged at Cate's straps. She craned her head around to look past him, to look at me. I smiled for her. He straightened up and went around to the driver's door. I stuffed my hands into the back pockets of my jeans, and raised my eyebrows at him, trying to smile. He gave half a nod, a slight upward movement of the chin. He didn't kiss me goodbye and I didn't get to kiss Cate.

He slid into the car, slammed the door and started the engine. He swung the car around and burned off up the village street, leaving me with the smell of petrol fumes, a scattering of gravel, and a grey ache in my chest. The awfulness of it all.

IF EVE HAD FOUND THE FRUIT NOT TO HER TASTE, AND spat it out, it would still have been too late. Long before she realized her bodily self, her poor forked and vulnerable nakedness, and could not bear to feel like that alone; long before her teeth met in the dripping sweetness of the fruit, before she listened to the serpent Satan, before she opened her new eyes to blink at the sunlight and the man that she was made for, before the moment Adam's rib was torn from his side and formed with God's deft thumbprints, she was already hurtling to damnation; and us, all of us, falling along with her, as unstoppable as rain; because the crime is in the thought that comes before the act, the crime is in the need that comes before the thought, the crime is in the nature of the being and so must be in her maker, who creates her knowing she must fall, and damns her for being as he made her.

I could not help myself, no more than she. I was made like this.

The church bell was tolling for the morning service; its heavy impatient clang shuddered up the village street, swelling the house with hurry, vexing the spirit. Mam was hooked into her best dress, her bonnet on; she had John by the collar and was brushing at his hair. Dad was already in the street in his dark Sunday jacket, and Sally was halfway down the steps towards him; he swiped his arm through the air at her, hurrying her down. Hair combed and braided, dress neat, shawl pinned, bonnet on, I leaned against the windowsill, and kept quiet.

Mam released John; he bolted for the door. She set the brush down on the dresser, turned to speak to me, to gather me up into the general flurry and fluster. I let my eyelids sink. I frowned slightly, raised a hand to my brow.

"Oh Good Lord, no." She hurried over, pressed a hand to my forehead. "What feels wrong?"

"My head."

"Are you hot?"

"A little."

"Do you feel sick?"

I nodded.

"Sit down."

She fetched liquorice root from the pantry. I slipped it into the side of my mouth and crushed it between my back teeth. The sap oozed onto the side of my tongue, strong and numbing.

"Keep warm," she said. "We'll be back after communion. Will you be all right?"

I nodded feebly and swallowed liquorice juice. The church bell tolled. She strode over to the door, Sunday-skirts swishing, then glanced back at me. Her expression, so concerned and tender, made me blink guiltily. She smiled, making her cheeks plump up; she looked pretty. Usually we skim past each other, going from paid-work through housework to piecework, barely glancing at each other, our attention demanded by the boys, by Sally, by Dad's needs, by meals and baking and laundry and cleaning up afterwards. I couldn't remember the last time we'd looked each other in the eye, not for more than the briefest of moments; I couldn't remember the last time we'd spoken of anything other than immediate concerns. I smiled back at her, the liquorice root a bulge of pulped fibres in my cheek. She closed the door behind them; I listened to their voices and footsteps retreat. Then I got up and spat the liquorice into the fire.

*

The room was full of sunlight, smelling of wood and ink. He had his pen in his hand, and the red-bound ledger was splayed out in front of him on the desk; he was reading over something he had written, his brow furrowed with thought or poor eyesight. His waistcoat was unbuttoned. He wore no collar, even though it was a Sunday. I tapped gently on the doorjamb. He saw me.

"Come in," he said, and started to button up his waistcoat. The church bell tolled. The air quivered with its sound. I came in.

"No church today?" he asked.

"I was hoping I might read."

"Help yourself."

He gestured towards the bookcase with an ink-stained hand,

his attention already returning to his work. I went over to the shelves. I was looking for *Robinson Crusoe*, and at the same time I was thinking I shouldn't waste my time on *Robinson Crusoe*, since there were so many others there to try, and time was short, and who knew when another chance would present itself again, and then the thought occurred to me for the first time, that he must know that I had been in his room, uninvited, and that I had read his *Robinson Crusoe* without permission. The titles and names blurred: I couldn't distinguish the books beyond their bindings, the leather and board and cloth. In my mind I was playing out again the conversation of the other night, from his taking *Pilgrim's Progress*, to our hands lying on the table a finger's breadth apart, and him saying that I may come back when I could, and choose any book I wished. All that time, he had known what I had done.

His chair scraped back on the boards; he came over to join me at the bookcase, his shoulder just level with my cheek, his arm at my side. He reached out and rested his fingertips on the spine of a large blue book. His arm was dark, his sleeve rolled back. The bell tolled out again, fainter still.

"I don't know what you'd like," he said. I glanced at him, the underside of his jaw and a trace of the morning's beard. "There's Fielding, and Richardson," he said. "Recently acquired, and maybe neither are strictly speaking Sunday reading. There's Milton, and there's Dante, which might be more appropriate. Homer; he was a pagan, but the translator is, as far as I know at least, a model Christian, and if your only chance to read is Sunday, then I'd say you should get what you can, while you can, and not worry too much about it."

His hand moved back and forth across the shelves as he spoke, lighting on a book here and there, brushing over others.

"So," he said. "Is that all right?"

I nodded, swallowed: "Yes." The word came out strangely.

"I'll leave you to decide."

He returned to the table. I ran a hand along the spines, bumping from one book to the next. I dug my fingertips into a gap and levered out a volume. It was bound in fine maroon leather, embossed with gilt. I had no idea what it was: Fielding or Milton or whatever else he had spoken of. I had been too flustered, too absorbed in my own reflections, too much looking at his hand, to consider where it paused, or what he said.

The church bell gave its final, dying toll. The service was beginning. I turned from the bookcase, the volume heavy in my hands. He didn't look up; again, he pushed a chair back from the table with a booted foot; it was his only invitation to sit down. I sat.

My feet tucked in under my seat, my skirts tucked in around my feet, very conscious of my rough hands, I opened the book cover, smoothed the page flat. As I began to read, my thoughts were edged with the gentle scratch of his quill.

The book was the *Principles of Geology*, by Charles Lyell, BA, MA, Oxon., and it seemed almost impossible to me, and yet there was no way under heaven that I would even consider returning it to the shelf unattempted.

Just inside the cover there was an engraving of a strange and ruinous building. There were pillars at the front, and a shallow-pitched roof on top. I sat looking at the picture for some time, at the worn and pitted stone of the pillars, the slender trees behind the building, the sharp rocks underneath. It was beautiful.

"It's a temple."

I glanced up.

"A pagan temple. Those are water marks on the pillars. It was built on dry land, of course. But the water rose all the way to lap at the pillars, and stayed there long enough to wear away the marble, then shrank back to the foot of those rocks."

"I don't understand."

"The book explains."

I tried to read; I got some of the words: I couldn't vouch for the meaning, not the whole of it: I felt as if I were grasping fragments, as if seeing some wide valley from the far side of a thick-laid hedge; glimpsing it through the gaps. I struggled my way into it. My finger followed the lines, my lips formed the letters. Sometimes the sense was clear as a raindrop, making me smile. Difficulties became like stones in mid-stream; I slid around them, flowed over them; they remained, but I did not let them check my progress. There was no time to waste.

I read about great sores in the land that spewed forth ash and molten rock, devastating the country for miles around. I read about the rock cooling, and hardening, and being worn away by sea and wind and rain and frost. I read about the warm shallow seas alive with creatures, tiny and delicate as lace, that died, and sank down to the seabed, and laid their bones and shells and scales there like snow. I read about the land rising and the seas drying, and the ground covering itself with plants, that flourished and grew, and then died and fell, and fallen, rotted into the earth. I read about the ice that came and pushed across the land, scraping away the earth, revealing the stone beneath. The stone that had once been innumerable drifting creatures at the bottom of a shallow sea, and then was covered with earth and plants, and then with ice, and now is bare as bone, cracked with ancient frost and worn with ancient water, right up on the roof of the world, up on the tops, the moors, the fells.

He had spoken. I raised my head. He was looking at me, his dark eyes. I had no notion of how long he had been watching me.

"Lyell," he said, "an interesting choice—"

There were creases at the corners of his eyes. He was talking. I had to gather my wits and direct them to what he was saying. It was about the book, but I'd missed something: I couldn't make out what he was asking me. I shook my head.

"Just, that it seems to have caught you." He leaned back in his chair, his face softening with that smile. "Go on, tell me. What do you think?"

My thoughts were formless, but in that moment his expression made him seem almost young, almost an equal, and I began to feel as if I knew him. I spoke, and as I spoke the thoughts came together, like butter out of churning milk.

"There are two kinds of stone around here. There's limestone, which can be burned, and the ashes spread on the fields to help the crops, and unburned it's used on the roads, which is what makes the roads so white; you get that from the tops, from the fells and crags. There's also sandstone; it's golden; the houses are built out of that—it's a lowland stone, a valley stone. I read here, the white stone, limestone, is made out of the bodies and bones of ancient sea creatures, and that sandstone is compounded sand, and that the sand itself was once solid rock, but was worn down by an ancient sea, which must have been just here, right here where we sit now. And it just seems extraordinary to me, that there should be so much time, that a fish can turn into a stone, and rock can turn into sand and then turn back into rock, and that we all march the roads every day, and spread lime on the fields, and sit in our homes, and we never think beyond our brief lives, and don't consider the nature of things, but just the use we can put them to."

The creases deepened at the corners of his eyes.

I took a breath. "I mean, I'm sorry. I don't know what I think of it. I'm sorry." I pushed back my chair and was on my feet to go. "I'll leave you in peace, I should be—"

"No." He put a hand on my arm, and I looked down at it, resting there on the holland sleeve, and felt the warmth and heaviness of it. "Stay."

My heart, I think, must have held itself still. I sank back down onto my chair.

"Go on," he said.

But his hand was still on my arm. I wouldn't look at it again, the dark skin, the creases around his knuckles like knots in wood. I couldn't speak sense: there was no sense in me to speak. He lifted his hand away, but the touch, the sense of weight lingered, as if flesh has a memory of its own, independent from the mind.

"I don't know that I can," I said. "It's just. I'd never thought like this before. I'd never thought about what lay beneath, about the bones of the earth; I'd never seen time like this, beyond the turn of the seasons and day and night and the chiming of the church clock. All I ever knew about land was that some of it was good and some of it was less good, and some of it was bad, and that we all had a share of it, good and bad, before the Enclosure, you know my father after a drink, he's told you all about that."

He dipped his head slightly. "Enclosure is widespread, and well known."

"Oh?"

"It happened all over the country; it's still happening, it'll happen everywhere."

"I remember the barley," I said. "There was nothing quite so beautiful as that field in early summer."

"I think we forget, you know, that this world is not young; that it can't drink up our filth and poison forever, and still be beautiful."

"What do you mean?" I was leaning forward, the book set aside, my eyes fixed on him.

He pulled a face, as if in discomfort. "You don't know the cities. The manufacturing towns. You haven't seen. A child there might grow up and grow old and die without ever seeing clearly the blue sky, or the stars, the moon; the sun is reduced to a bloody glare. The smoke and dust are such that the trees die, the flowers die; there are no birds."

"That's terrible," I said. "It sounds like Hell."

"And no sin required to enter," he said, "unless you count poverty a sin."

"I saw your shoes," I said. "The way they're mended: I thought, you must have been halfway around the world to wear your boots into holes like that."

There was a silence; I'd said something wrong, but I didn't know how to retreat from it.

"I've been to London," he said eventually, and then, "You'd like London."

The words seemed to gather, swell, like a drop of water on a leaf, suspended for a moment before falling. He'd thought of me. He'd thought of what I might like.

"Other places, too. I've been through the West Country," he went on, "lived for a time in a town called Sherborne; dead really, and its deadness near did for me. I've spent time in Cheltenham, Northampton, Leeds, Bolton, Birmingham, Sunderland, Aberdeen and Edinburgh and Glasgow and Dumfries."

The names as he spoke them were like a litany to me, beautiful, conjuring inexplicit wonders. I'd never been beyond the boundaries of the valley; had only been as far as Lancaster in one direction, Kirkby Lonsdale in the other.

"And you didn't settle anywhere? What made you keep on moving?"

"Circumstance," he said.

I nodded, as if I understood exactly what he meant by that. "And the Enclosures are happening everywhere?"

"The whole country will be enclosed eventually, since there's profit in it."

"I barely remember, but Mam says it broke his heart, he used to work so hard on his strips, he had the best crops of anyone."

"Your father isn't alone; there was a great deal lost when the commons were enclosed. Independence, and mutual aid, and community. Many people were heartbroken."

"Dad's found consolation, though."

"The drink, you mean?"

"That, and complaint. Between them they seem to offer him some comfort."

Mr. Moore laughed. It made me feel somehow satisfied. I went on.

"I think sometimes it does better to just get on with what you have, rather than dwell on what you've lost. Perhaps it's hard to believe that change happens, that it can and will happen, and is happening all around us, all the time. I mean, not like the seasons, which always come around again the same, maybe worse or better but much the same, but bigger than that."

I looked down at my hands, folded there on the table, and I started to tell him something I had never told anyone before, not because I kept it purposefully secret, but because I hadn't had anyone to tell it to.

"A while back, the cat caught a shrew. The boys were watching her toss it about out behind the house; you know what cats are like, and boys. I got it off them, but didn't know what to do with it: there was no helping it, there was only stopping further cruelty. The fur was brushed the wrong way and there was a seep of blood at its throat. I stood there out the back of the house with it lying in my hand, so absolutely tiny, alive, weighing nothing. It was last summer; I remember the ground was packed hard beneath my feet; the midden had that summer-stink, I was trying to think where I could leave it and neither the cat nor the boys would get at it again, and its heart was hammering away, tiny and fast, and it was hot as a coal in my hand, and there was this shift, and I saw myself differently; I was a giant, all sluggish and vast and cold, and this creature was hot and vital and more alive, even in those moments of its death, than I would ever be. Shrews live just a few short months; what seems but a season to us is to them their whole existence. I just thought, how wonderful must be the sun's warmth, the scent of pollen, the colours of a beetle's shell, how every moment must extend to a day's duration, and every part of that moment be filled with experience we are unable even to notice. It seemed to me that we drag ourselves through years and years and years, and never feel anything as minutely, as exquisitely as that."

The church bell tolled out. A single bell, sounding the same whether it begins or ends a service, whether it is ushering in a new Christian to the congregation, or ushering out the dead. The sound seemed to make the air itself shudder.

"And yet," I said, "and yet, now I know about the stone, it's as if we flicker into life, and out again, like candle flames."

There was a moment's silence. I was still caught up in my thoughts.

"You're nineteen," he said. "You told me the other night."

I shook my head to clear it. "Yes. Nineteen."

"And only had a church-school education."

I nodded and looked down at Lyell's book. The deep slow movement of stone; its accretions and abrasions, its sudden shudders. The shallow sea full of drifting creatures. The images seemed to cluster, to press against some invisible barrier. The bell tolled again, and though the sound dispersed, it felt like the air still quivered in the room, as if the lime-washed limestone walls contained and amplified the effect. The barrier cracked, splintered; meaning flooded through the gaps. I understood.

"Where did you get the book?" I asked.

"I bought it from a dealer."

Reverend Wolfenden would be stalking down the aisle to the church door.

"And where did the dealer get it from?"

"It belonged to some gentleman's library that was broken up after he died; see the initials?" He reached over, closed the book, shifted it around to show me the spine. "D.F.C.? They're his."

The bell tolled again; the air in the room seemed almost to hum with resonance. The congregation would be on its feet, shuffling into the aisles. The Reverend would stand at the open doorway, ready to shake a hand, to nod, to give a word of caution or approval. The cold waters of knowledge stifled me; I found it hard to breathe.

"I shouldn't have read it. You knew what was in it; you shouldn't have let me."

He leaned back, looked at me a long moment.

"You should take this in no way as an insult," he said, "but you're talking bobbins. Think about what you've just said. It's no business of mine to dictate to you what you can and cannot read. What are books *for*?"

The bell tolled out again; the room was full of it, my head was full of it. My thoughts had slipped their moorings and were dragged away. The congregation would be gathering at the church door; there would be polite Sunday talk. My mother would be approaching the Reverend's station, dropping him a curtsey. He, his hands clasped in front of him, twisting his neck above his starched white collar, would crane his head down to her and say, Where is your elder daughter? Where is Lizzy?

"What were you reading, when I came in?" I asked.

He glanced down at the open ledger. "It's something I am writing."

"May I read it?"

"I don't think so. It's my own account—unfinished, private—"

He began to smile, realizing what he said.

"You dictate that it's not for me to read, then," I said.

"Because it's not very good, because I'd be ashamed to show you, not—"

The bell tolled out once more. With the Reverend leaning so close, Mam would have to take a half-step backwards before she began to explain, her face reddening as if at a guilty conscience, as if she had known all along that I was skiving. In the conflict and muddle of my thoughts, one thing was clear and still: however much I might want it—the books, the peace, the conversation, the man in this room—I couldn't have it.

"This book," I said, pushing it across the table towards him. "Lyell's book, it's wrong."

He folded his arms, leaned back in his chair. "I don't know what you mean."

"I think you do."

"Wrong factually, or wrong morally?" He held up a palm to stop me. "Bear in mind you've only got the first volume there; don't judge too hastily, you can't be sure what else he had to say."

"I regret reading even this."

"I certainly didn't recommend it—"

"It's heresy."

"That's a bit strong." He leaned back in his seat, folded his arms. He seemed to be enjoying himself considerably. It made me furious.

"It doesn't fit with the Good Book, with the Creation," I snapped.

The church bell tolled again; the distance between one ring and the next had grown; the sexton would be letting the rope slip between his palms; letting the bell rock itself back to stillness.

"Forgive me, it's been a long time since I read Lyell, but as I recall, he shies away from the more radical implications of his theories. He never claims that the Bible is actually in *error*."

"There is no call to laugh at me, Mr. Moore."

He leaned forward, regarded me with what seemed like honesty. "I assure you, I am not laughing."

"Anyway. There is no need for him to make such a claim. His argument is there throughout, running through everything like a bad thread. There is no place for Eden in this book."

Mr. Moore inclined his head, seemed about to speak, but didn't. It seemed to me that his calm demeanour barely covered a profound amusement.

"What if you are to God as that shrew was to you," he said. "What seems countless aeons to us might seem just seven days to Him? So Genesis is not contradicted, just considered on a different scale. Would that work?"

I stood up, my chair scraping back; "The Lord is not a housemaid, sir, and I am not a shrew."

He laughed outright; he shook his head and laughed. I thought, he'll stop me, he'll stop me leaving. He'll say something that will explain it all, that will make this yawning darkness close up again and everything seem safe again: God will be reaffirmed in His heaven and all will still be all right with the world. His hand will rest warm upon my arm again, and we will be reconciled; we will be friends, because we were, I thought, beginning to be friends. But he didn't stop me. I was already at the door, a hand to the latch, before he spoke again.

"What then," he said, "what then if I suggested that God, and Eden and the Testaments new and old, were all stories, were ways of understanding the world, but not like philosophy or history or science, but like the stories we tell children at bedtime, to reassure them in the dark."

I paused at the threshold and turned to look at him. He was leaning away from the table, his chair balanced on its back legs. He was frowning slightly, but seemed to be in perfect good humour.

"*Stories?*"

"You know the kind of thing: the baby was found under the gooseberry bush, your grandmother was very tired and went to sleep. Stories you tell children so as to keep them from the fear and blood and pain and the realization that some things are unknown and unknowable, and that we are all going to die."

"You are saying that the Word of God is an old wives' tale?"

"I just think we need to grow up. Mankind will never be adult, be responsible, while we still expect our Father to come and dispense justice, to punish the naughty children and hand out peppermints to the good."

His words bruised my soul. "But Jesus said—"

"How do you know? Did he tell you? Did he write it down? Hand me the Bible from the shelf. Let's see the Gospel According to Jesus, shall we?"

"I can't defend my faith as I would like; I haven't the education. But I'll pray for you."

He put his hands behind his head and grinned.

"You said at school they taught you to read the Gospels as gospel truth. So no one ever taught you to think; they just taught you to accept. And yet there you were the other night, marching into my room with your forehead like a thundercloud, thinking away. And here you are again, battling with it, furious with me, so cross at what I've said. I don't care if you never agree with me; I really don't. Nineteen and a housemaid." He shook his head.

I wanted to go over to him and shove him; to send his chair flying over backwards. It'd do him good, I thought, to fall. And with the fury, there was an ache deep in my chest, almost like grief. My mother and father would be walking up the village street, arms linked, united for the walk home. The boys would have raced off ahead with their pals. Sally would be trailing along with Ruth, Sunday frocks swishing around their feet, Sunday bonnets concealing their whispered confidences. This was over.

"Tell me this," I said. "I need to know. Do you believe in anything?"

"Of course," he said.

"What, then?"

"That there is nothing else but this, the material world in which we live. That we must love one another. That we must die."

My skin stood up in goose flesh, and the air seemed to hum again, as if after a bell, but the bell had ceased chiming some time ago, and my people would be at the door at any moment. Mr. Moore held my gaze, his brown eyes steady, honest, but a little wet, as if he had brought himself close to tears.

"God bless you," I said.

He inclined his head.

I left him. I made my way down the stairs, clutching tightly to the rail. I sank down into Mam's chair. It was as though all

172 · Jo Baker

my life I had been looking down into a safe and familiar pool, and now a sudden shift had shown me that it was not a pool but limitless, and I was looking not down, but up, into vast blue sky, into space dizzying in its emptiness.

They were home; I could hear them outside, on the steps. Mam was saying something to John, and John was whining back at her; and then Dad shouted at him, and probably raised a hand; the door opened, John dodged in, around the table, and darted upstairs. Dad followed, bellowing after him, then Mam and Ted, and Sally trailed in last of all.

Everything seemed to shrink into the distance. I leaned my head back against the chair, closed my eyes. I would be sick; I knew I would be sick. My mam's cool calloused palm was on my forehead.

"Poor love."

I swallowed, didn't speak.

"Go and lie down."

I opened my eyes; her spider's-web cheeks, the weather-dark skin, the creases at her eyes and lips, all caught up in concern. I loved her for this gentleness.

"Our bed," she said, and made to hook an arm under my arm. "Come on."

I shook my head and pressed my eyes tightly shut. For once, the last thing that I wanted was to be alone with my thoughts. She let me stay there, in her chair, and busied herself with the dinner. After a while, she brought me a cup of mint tea, soothing to the nerves.

He came down for his dinner. I could not look at him.

Mam excused me, saying I was poorly, and I could feel his eyes on me a long moment. I would not look at him. He retired to his room after dinner; he did not come down again.

> *In the beginning God created the Heavens, and the Earth.*
> *And the Earth was without form, and void, and Darkness*
> *was upon the face of the deep: and the Spirit of God*
> *moved upon the face of the waters.*
> *And God said, Let there be light: and there was light.*

Light spilled down through the gaps in the ceiling. I crooked my arm over my eyes, and listened to Sally breathe. The Spirit of God moved upon the waters. Warm shallow waters full of tiny drifting creatures, swimming with fishes and the rocks crusting with mussels and caddises. Water that ground and pounded at the rock seabed, and crumbled it to sand.

No; it was lifeless water, dark water, empty water, until verses twenty and twenty-one.

> *And God said, Let the waters bring forth abundantly the*
> *moving creature that hath life, and fowl that may fly*
> *about the earth in the open firmament of heaven.*
> *And God created great whales, and every living creature that*
> *moveth which the waters brought forth abundantly after*
> *their kind, and every winged fowl after his kind: and God*
> *saw that it was good.*

So fast, in a blink, with just a word.

Mr. Moore was up there, his face as still as stone, leaning over his book, his hand raised to support his head, his fingers splayed in the dark curls of his hair. The ink on his fingertips. Writing. Writing his book.

*

Monday morning. The vicarage kitchen was white with flour, full of the warm yeasty smell of breadmaking. I had my sleeves rolled and was kneading dough on the deal table, under Mrs. Briggs's close scrutiny. I knew I would be called to account that day; the Reverend would send for me. My thoughts twisted like a wool-scrap on a twig. I leaned my body into the work, pressed and folded and pressed again the warm fleshy dough. If only I had told the truth when the truth was simple and safe; if only I had told the Reverend about the books when I had yet to see what temptation into error they contained. My arm was haunted by the pressure of his hand; I would almost have thought to see its print upon my bare flesh. My thoughts were haunted by the echoes of his words; they fell into the rhythm of my work. He had denied God, he walked alone in darkness; he needed guidance; he needed the Reverend's help. But would the Reverend really help a man he had called a viper? And yet, and yet, I kept returning to what he had professed, without hope of redemption or reward: *we must love one another.* Every time I tried to think ahead, I could see my rough hand extended to knock on the library door, I could hear the Reverend's voice calling me in, I could see the door swinging slowly open, and me moving silently into the room; I could see the books glinting with gold, and the Reverend sitting in his chair, his waistcoat stretched into creases, and I could see his lips parting to form the words of his first question, but after that, nothing: images tumbled into confusion, thoughts would

not come clear. I could not see myself speaking; I could not begin
to think what I would say.

It happened, as I knew it must. The bell rang above our heads,
making me jump. Mrs. Briggs said, "Scrape that slather off your
hands, get washed."

"Can't Maggie go?"

"And have her come back straight away saying it's you they're
wanting? And don't answer back."

*

There were green willow boughs in the hearth: no pretence even
that a fire was to be lit. The day was warm and the room full of
golden sunlight. He was standing at the open window, basking
in the warmth. I had knocked and he had told me to come in: he
knew that I was there. I came to a halt in the middle of the carpet.
I was conscious of the tick of the library clock, the warm blaze of
sunshine on my face, I didn't know what I would say.

The window gave onto shrubbery-patched lawns, the boundary wall, the fields beyond swept up towards the pale blue sky.
The grass was long and heavy-headed; the wind moved it in silky
ripples. A breath of outside air came in, sweet, smelling of grass
and earth. I found myself thinking of the temple in Lyell's book,
the water at the base of the rocks, the water rising to eat at the
temple's pillars, the water retreating to lap again at the rocks. The
lives lived in that duration. The ignorant change and continuity
of the material world.

The Reverend turned from the window, and crossed the room
to his seat, looking like a crow in his black clothes. He sat down
and folded his hands over his stomach.

"Child?"

I bobbed a clumsy little curtsey, and said nothing. My head was like a jar of flies; I didn't dare open my mouth.

"You were absent from communion on Sunday."

I forced myself to speak. "I was poorly, Reverend: my mother will have told you."

"And yet you are well enough to work today."

"I must work, sir; the money is needed."

"And you must worship! It is folly to put material needs before the spiritual. Consider the life beyond! Consider the lily of the field, consider the story of Martha, if you will, did she not find that—"

I looked down at my slippered feet pressed into the thick velvety plush of the carpet; my eyes followed the methodical, intricate patterning of red and ivory and green. I didn't need to hear the story of Martha again. I was waiting for the words to form themselves in my head, words that could explain Mr. Moore and not at the same time condemn him, words that would secure assistance for me in my confusion and yet not harm him further in the Reverend's sight. I was glad, at least, that the worry of anticipation was over; while the Reverend talked, the clock on the mantelpiece ticked away the moments of the interview, and I was glad of that too, since the longer the Reverend talked, the less I would be required to: he could not keep me there forever.

Mr. Moore had said that there was no such thing as forever. He carried the scent of oak about with him, and that made me think of oak apples that are not fruit at all, but galls, perfectly round and smooth; grown by a little creature out of the flesh of the tree, to be its comfort and retreat. I was thinking of what

Mr. Moore had said, his articles of faith, and that he didn't care
if I never agreed with him. I was thinking of Eve in the garden,
expressly forbidden to taste the fruit, and created with all her
faults by the same God who caused the tree to grow there, within
her easy reach. I felt as though some time ago, I had been handed
something exquisite, and dangerous, and prone to harm, and that
I had not noticed it, not really, not recognized its true value till
that moment.

I raised my eyes and looked at Reverend Wolfenden. He sat
with his legs crossed and his hands folded on the dark bulge of
his waistcoat. His mouth was moving, his lips forming the words
of the story, but I still didn't listen, I watched instead the way
the flesh of his throat folded over his collar and wobbled as he
spoke, and I was thinking, I did a good job on that collar, coming to me all grimed and shiny with dirt, and there it is now,
white as the proverbial lily of the field. And the other clothes,
the underthings, coming to us sweat-patched and soiled, to be
scraped and rubbed and soaked in lye and hung out for the night
air to bleach, to make clean enough for a gentleman to wear,
though it was a gentleman that dirtied them in the first place. And
the chamberpot I whisked out from under his bed every morning, and what swam in it that I tried not to look at and not to
catch the smell of as I carried it out to the privy and slopped it
down into the pit. Easy to be fresh as the lily, easy to sit there in
spotless white linen and tell a story about the sinfulness of letting
work distract you from spiritual matters, easy to devote yourself
to cleanliness and Godliness when there's always someone else to
do the dirty work, to do your cleaning, to slop out your dung
for you.

The sing-song tone of his voice shifted; the story must be ending. I gathered my attention and fixed it on his words.

"Because whatever you may know, it is your duty to inform me. You understand that, don't you, child, that as your pastor, as the man charged with your spiritual security, you must tell me whatever you know, however slight, that might represent a threat to your wellbeing, your family's, and that of the wider parish."

The silence stretched. Reverend Wolfenden looked at me with his pale grey eyes. He said, "Child? On your soul, child. You must tell me what you know."

"I am at a loss to know, sir, why you are so concerned with Mr. Moore."

The Reverend's eyes sharpened. His hands slowly separated; he took hold of the arms of his chair. He did not speak. I watched his eyebrows raise, pushing his forehead into folds.

"I mean, sir, that I am sure you know more than I do. No one tells me anything."

"What," Reverend Wolfenden said, "do you actually know?"

I couldn't tell the Reverend about the box without suggestion of my own laxity: if I had discovered it, why had I not come straight to him with the information? And better, perhaps, that the Reverend believed the box brim-full of gunpowder than packed with books like Lyell's. But the meetings, they were public; whatever went on there went on openly. Anything I could say about that could be heard from any quarter, should the Reverend but ask.

My mouth was dry. I had to say something. I said what seemed most safe to say. "They have meetings. They exchange books; it is for the education and betterment of the men. They hold debates."

His pale eyes glittered. He leaned forward.

"What manner of debates?"

"I don't know, sir. Being a, being a female, women are not allowed, so, I think it must be a great addition to the parish if—"

He waved away my words. We lumbered towards disaster. "What books does he possess?"

There was a moment's awful silence.

"I don't know."

He looked at me narrowly, studying my face. I felt certain he would see my guilt, my knowledge, as immediately as God had known of Eve's.

"No," he said. "Perhaps you don't."

My heart lifted, exultant. There was silence. I watched him, alert, on my nerves. His grey eyes with their pink tracery of veins, his pale hands, the reddish hair growing on their backs. I blinked, a tiny moment of darkness, and all the while he kept his eyes on me.

"Sir, as I said, I can only tell you what I know, I wouldn't like to risk a guess on such a grave matter."

The Reverend rubbed his hands together, palm-on-palm, with a papery kind of sound.

"And who goes to these meetings?"

"I don't know."

When he spoke again, it made me flinch: "Of course you know. You live there."

"It's just, people come once and never come again. Some come once or twice: but I am always so tired, sometimes I'm half asleep."

He said, "Tell me who comes."

His eyes did not leave my face. My mouth was so dry. I felt that we teetered on the brink of something, of some awful precipice.

"One man," he said. "Tell me the name of one man who comes."

My eyes slid away from his, across the room towards the mantel, where the clock sat, with its cool china face and prickly gold casing, with its arms spread wide and low like a man driving cattle, and I caught sight of my face in the mirror behind it, the pale oval of my skin and the dark smudges of my eyes, and I got that odd feeling you get when you happen once in a while to see your own image; the way it's familiar and strange at the same time; an uneasy kind of a feeling, of being caught unawares, of being caught staring.

I looked back towards the Reverend. "Thomas Williams, sir. Thomas Williams of Brunt Hill Cottage."

Reverend Wolfenden let his eyes fall shut. He nodded. "You may go about your work."

*

The kitchen was a hell of baking. I wove my way through the noise and swelter and out into the cool dimness of the hallway. I took off my slippers, levered on my clogs and exchanged my maid's cap for my shawl. If she noticed, let Mrs. Briggs think this just another of my mysterious errands. Let her just ask Reverend Wolfenden; let her challenge him with the misuse of the maids.

I stole out of the scullery door, around the side of the house, and down the drive. I risked being seen from any of those dark glassy windows, but this was the quickest way to get to him. The gravel crunched underfoot. The willows caught the breeze and whispered to themselves. I walked briskly, head up, as if I had every right to be walking down the drive on a sunny June morning. My facility for deceit was surprising to me.

*

I'd got as far as the gate at the far side of the low meadow when I saw him coming up from the beck, a bundle of green willow-wands on his shoulder, his head bent, and when he looked up as he approached the gate, he saw me, and I saw his face change from the closed-off look of animal thoughtlessness, to an expression of concern and uneasy pleasure. I opened the gate for him, then fastened it after, turning and walking at his side, back towards the village, and a soft rain began to fall, wetting the air, wetting the long grass, so my skirt grew heavy with it, and it stood out in droplets on the fibres of his jacket. I drew my shawl over my head and held it pinched at my chin. I searched for words. He seemed content to walk in silence. We came to the brow of the hill, and I knew I would be in sight of the vicarage again in a moment.

"Thomas."

He stopped. The rain fell onto my face as I looked up at him, catching on my lashes, wetting my skin, so that I could see the drops glittering in the corners of my sight.

"The Reverend might want to talk to you sometime soon."

"Why d'you say that?"

I felt cool and calm as I said it. "He was asking me about the meetings, and since I don't know anything about them, I told him to ask you."

Thomas let the weight fall from his shoulder, set the bundle down on the ground. His face showed his feelings: surprise, pleasure, uncertainty. Just as I had felt when Mr. Moore had spoken my name, when he'd said that I'd like London, Thomas was unsettled to find that he'd been thought of.

"I never talked to you about what goes on there, Lizzy."

"I know."

"You never asked me about it."

"It didn't seem my place."

"You hardly talk to me at all unless you have to."

"I'm sorry."

I wiped the rain from my face. He nodded, as if there were some new understanding between us. I looked away, out across the long grass laced with raindrops.

"What do you talk about?"

"There's plenty that just goes right over my head."

"Then what makes you keep going back?"

"I want to learn." He blinked then, and looked away. "Then it won't go over my head anymore."

"So you need him. You need Mr. Moore."

Our eyes met. He didn't say anything. At the time I took the look in his eyes to be one of assent; I am not so certain now.

"We need him too," I said, feeling the press of a toe against a too-tight clog, the thin-worn rub of old darning at a heel; with each breath my belly and ribs pushed against the constraint of my stays. My skirts hung heavy with the rain. A raindrop hung blurred on an eyelash. "We need the money he brings in."

Thomas didn't reply. Words floated in the silence between us like moths; words that could be said, words of affection, words about money, about its relative scarcity and plenty, and arrangements that could be made to balance this out. Nothing was said.

He let out a breath, and he bent down and picked up his bundle. He shouldered it.

"All right, then," he said. I felt that I could trust him.

*

When I got home, Sally had gone. I'd known that she would go, but I had not thought that it would be so soon, and had not realized how complete would be her removal. Her Sunday clothes were gone from the press, and she had taken two chapbooks and a ballad that weren't really hers, even her cup was gone from the dresser. I should have been there to help her pack, to tell her she was welcome to the books, to carry her parcels for her up to the crossroads, and wait with her for the coach. I had occupied myself otherwise, and not well, and had not said goodbye to a much-loved only sister.

I found her doll that night, lying limp and grimy, one button-eye hanging on a thread, when I opened the press to get out my bedding. It had been mine before it was hers; now she had given it back to me. It seemed like a message; at twelve years old she was a woman grown up and gone out into the world, and I was still a child at home. It may not have been meant as such; she couldn't have brought it with her, not to her work, and perhaps she had just not known what else to do with it, had not thought it good enough to pass on to another child, or thought it mine to dispense with, to throw on the midden or the fire. She might have thought our mam was not the kind to keep a daughter's doll, but Mam is soft enough, if circumstances allow.

That night, for the first time since Sally was an infant, since she was weaned and put into my bed, I lay down alone. I missed her. I slept shallowly, troubled by dreams. I dreamed I was wading through a shallow sea, and the sea stretched forever, and the sky was blue, and the sea was blue, and I waded with my skirts bunched up in my hands, and all around my legs tiny fishes fed, picking off scales of skin like the minnows do in the river; painlessly, slightly ticklish. I was happy, walking through the water and letting the fishes feed off my skin, but as I walked the sea grew shallower and shallower and the fishes began to die, drifting away from me and down into the bottom of the sea, and I knew I had poisoned them, that they were dying from my contagion. I tried to run, but the water was too thick and heavy, and I couldn't get away from them; they mouthed off flakes of skin, and they gulped them down, and they died in their multitudes, and the reason the water was thick was that it was now dead fishes, slippery and heavy around my legs, and ahead, a mountain rose up into the sky, and ash tumbled out of it, and fire, and smoke filled the skies, making it dark, and something was coming towards me out of the darkness, and I didn't know what it was, but I knew I had to keep on going, on into the darkness and the heat.

I was feeling sick; that kind of low-level nausea that you barely notice till you swallow your saliva and your stomach lurches. The sky was too bright; it made me squint. A man stood outside a house: Willow Cottage. He was cleaning his car, an orange-red Volvo estate. He watched me pass as he soaped the roof with a sponge. I shoved my hands deep in my pockets and nodded at him. He was in his fifties, losing his hair. He didn't quite nod back. There was money in my pocket; a satisfying clump of coins. I was going to the shop. Bread. Cheese. Tea. I raised my hands to push the hair from my face, and there was a shake to them, and my hair felt damp and greasy against my skin. Then the air was suddenly dim, cool, as if I'd stepped into the shadow of a large building. I glanced around. It was just a glance; the ordinary blank face of a bungalow stared back at me. Then the grey rough-cast surface of the walls seemed to begin to melt, to slip and ooze away and reveal natural stone beneath. I blinked, and there were just grey walls and plate-glass windows and sunshine. The man straightened up from his car-washing, stared towards me. I turned and headed on up the street. On the right, on the end wall of a house, a bricked-up window seemed to shimmer with old glass; I glanced over, but the gable wall of the cottage was blank, just an outline of stone lintel, sill and upright, and infill where the window had once been. I could feel the hair pricking on the nape of my neck. As I passed, the converted barn seemed to sprout sun-bleached wooden shutters; to leak drifts of hay onto the road. When I looked it straight on, there was a 4x4 in the drive, net curtains in the downstairs windows. I turned away, and the garden seemed to melt back into pasture, to scatter itself with pale flowers. A water pump stood against the far end wall of the barn. As I came closer, I knew, I could hear, I could feel in the prickling of my skin, the faint whispering of women's voices. I reached the corner, made myself glance around it, almost expecting to see her there, a young woman standing with a water jar on her hip, head cocked to listen to the evening gossip; the frown line between her brows, the shawl tucked over her head.

The pump stood with its back against the wall, its mechanism locked solid with thick black paint. A black bin-bag leaned against a green recycling box, and the tarmac had cracked to let a tuft of grass through. No one there.

I pressed my fingers and thumb onto my eyes, pushed at them, trying to gather myself. I glanced back to see if I was still watched, but the man had gone. Somehow this made me even more uneasy. Then my phone went off, making me jump. I fumbled in my back pocket and flipped it open. My hands were shaking. Mark.

His voice was brittle. "I've been calling and calling. All I ever get is Call Failed."

I unpeeled my lips. I couldn't remember the last time that I'd spoken. "The signal's dodgy."

"Are you okay?" His tone had shifted, softened. "Honey. Rache. Are you okay?"

The breath on my skin. The prickling air. The figure almost there in the corner of my eye. The way the houses had seemed to melt into something older. The way I disappeared. I couldn't risk naming it; I couldn't risk naming it to him. Then something moved, over to the right: my heart kicked; I glanced around. A blackbird, tilting his head to look at me.

"Nothing," I said, not remembering the question.

"Come home. Sweetheart, come home."

The blackbird's eye was black and glossy, rimmed with orange. What did it see with the eye that looked the other way? In human vision, only a tiny proportion is direct, exact: the rest is filled in with the broad brushstrokes of the mind. So we see the mind's constructions, not what is really there.

"Sweetheart?" Mark said it so gently; it made my nose prickle. "You're allowed to find this difficult, you know. It's allowed. You're allowed to break down."

The blackbird turned its head again. I looked away.

"Okay," I said, and sat down on the grass verge. "Okay then. I give up."

The phone cupped to my ear, I listened to Mark's plans, the underswell of relief, the edging forward of my recovery. In a week, give or take, depending on appointments, I'd be sitting on Dr. Cowan's vinyl chair, the words squeezing out of me in ugly clots, part request, part defence, part apology. I'd be talking to Dr. Cowan, but I'd be looking at the peeled man. The peeled man had watched it all, and didn't judge. He'd observed the first blood pressure test, the dip of test-strip into the vial of urine, the taking of bloods; he'd seen the press of professionally cool fingers on my healing scar. His eyes bulging from the sockets, teeth bared in a lipless grin, he'd watched the same hand scrawl the prescription for those sweet blue pills. The peeled man knew everything. He knew the fury of a severed nerve, the touch-shy tenderness of inner flesh; he knew it in the dark meat of his heart, the dull ivory of his bones. And as I spoke to Dr. Cowan, the peeled man and I would eye each other, and Dr. Cowan would look at me, weighing me up, and when I'd finished talking he would caution me, and when he'd finished cautioning me, he'd reach for his prescription pad, and I would watch his pen scratch the words that conjured up those benzodiazepines, diamond-shaped, in the crease of my palm, sweet on my tongue, and the warm chemical certainty, the melting, the sense that everything would be fine.

I wanted Cate. I wanted Cate. It already felt too much like goodbye.

"Can I talk to her?"

"Tomorrow. She's at my mum's. You can see her yourself tomorrow. Get a good night's sleep, then tomorrow just sling your stuff into the car and come home. Bring whatever. We'll sort the rest out somehow. I'll deal with it. Or Lucy can; it won't kill her to take on a bit of responsibility."

"What about school?"

"You're not due back till Monday; but I think you could do with some more time. We'll talk to Dr. Cowan about that."

*

We said goodbye. I flicked the phone shut, and held it in my palm. It seemed impossible to move. There was nowhere to go. Not back to the cottage, and face the massed evidence of my failure. Not to the shop, since I was leaving tomorrow, and wouldn't be needing anything now. But soon the car-cleaning man would be out with a chamois leather, to wipe away the beading water on the bonnet, and stare at me. I hauled myself back onto my feet.

I walked slowly back along the verge, where the tarmac crumbled into grass, and little yellow flowers grew, their petals waxy and pointed. I had the word *celandine* in my head, but didn't know where it came from. I reached the cottage. The sky was blue above it, the windows caught the sky and were filmed with shifting blue and white. All it needed was Mum on the front steps to complete the picture. I couldn't go in. I picked a sprig off a low-growing plant on the garden wall, crushed the leaves, sniffed it. Thyme. I stuffed my hands into my pockets and continued on down the village street.

The street ended at the church gate. Daffodils stood in clumps in the churchyard, snowdrops lolled under the weight of seedpods. A dark yew tree stood to the right of the gate. The space was so quiet, and calm, and so old; the surrounding woods were like a filter on the world. I went in. The graves stood blank, their

backs to me, their faces to the east. I followed the path till it
dwindled away among the graves, then I picked my way through
the mounds till I'd reached the far wall, where I slumped down,
and leaned my head back against the rough cool stone. The sky
was overcast and the light was fading. A breeze had blown up:
branches were tangling overhead, creaking against each other
and casting moving shadows. That day in the rain seemed like
an age ago; the gate into the woods must be somewhere nearby.
I didn't look.

Bits of stone dug into my back and the air felt damp on my
skin. I could smell the dark rot of the woods behind me. I could
smell the crushed grass beneath me. I could feel my own pulse,
the way it made my vision throb at the edges, each invisible blood
vessel juddering with its work. I could feel the press of my feet
into the earth, the way my calf muscles bunched and my thighs
stretched. My hand was haunted by the memory of her wrist,
thin as sticks. The failing flutter of her pulse beneath my pressing fingers. The beats of her butterfly heart. I counted her pulse,
conscious of the press of Cate's feet, pushing against the inside
of me. The taut, hard pod of my belly. The smell of coffee and
chrysanthemums and cancer. And the great choking lump that
was in my chest.

And then a shift. So peripheral to the vision that it registered in the flesh. I couldn't help myself. I looked up, casting
around. The worn faces of the gravestones stared back at me,
blotched with damp. The boundary wall stretched out in either
direction, its stones dark and cornerless, tracing an egg-shape
around the dead. The earthwork rose up to my right. The light
was failing fast, colours sliding into grey. The breeze kicked up

again; boughs creaked against each other, branches stirred. I was alone.

I straightened up and pushed away from the wall; coins dug into my thigh, my phone bulged in a back pocket. My legs ached. The breeze stiffened. I scanned the churchyard. Still nothing.

But then movement. In the corner of my vision. I swung around. An old headstone, low and dark; the same as the others. But there had been something there. Just that flicker of movement, like the houses melting, like the blackbird fixing me with its onyx eye. There would be a cat. A fox, perhaps. There would be a blackbird.

I was vividly aware of myself; the way my feet sank into the soft earth, the oily chill of my nose and chin, the tug and twist of my hair in the wind. I shoved my hands into my pockets. I was treading on grave earth; it seemed to give too much underfoot. Grit and cotton fibres pressed under my nails. My skin was bristling with cold.

The trees stirred in the wind, hissing. The shadows flitted over the headstone, making it look as if the stone were crawling with words. I came to the foot of the grave. No sign of a cat, a fox, not even a bird. Nothing but long tangled grass, bleached and dead and sodden. I came close, crouched down and rested a hand on the top of the stone. I read the family name. It was in capitals, across the top of the stone, like a headline. The stone was granular and cool, like sugar.

WILLIAMS

I rubbed at my arms and peered at the smaller lettering underneath. The first burial was in March 1802. Sara Williams and her infant daughter, Mary, buried together. Forty years later, Sara's husband, Isaac, was interred at sixty-three. Death in childbirth, the husband forty years a widower. I found myself welling up, stupidly, at this. I knelt down to peer at the names beneath. Damp pressed up from the earth and through my jeans. The letters became more cramped and narrow the further down the headstone they progressed. Tobias, Isaac's son, and Anne, Tobias's wife. The lettering had been eaten by the damp, algae softening its edges. I pushed aside the long grass at the foot of the grave.

. . also their son, THOMAS

Unease drew itself together, thickened and crept close.

Moss grew up the base of the stone; I pressed at it, feeling the dips and troughs of carving underneath. I dug a nail underneath the edge and peeled the moss away. It came off in a scab, bringing with it a layer of the crumbling stone. In uncovering the words I was eroding them, but I couldn't stop. The stone was darker, damp, the words shallow and indistinct. The name was in capitals. An elongated rectangle of a name.

The breeze gusted stronger, blowing hair across my face; I pushed it back behind my ears. Then I remember a curious feeling of stillness, as if the breeze stopped, as if my heartbeat and breath were suspended for a moment. I did the only thing that I could think to do. I shuffled close. With a fingertip, I followed the loop and curve and rise of the first word. I was like a child again, struggling, tracing letters with a fingertip, forming words with my lips. The long grass brushed at my inner wrist.

and his wife

The stone wore at the pad of my index finger, crumbled softly under pressure.

ELIZABETH

No date, no space for anything more. I was held for a moment in stillness.

Elizabeth.

The beech leaves so new the sun shone right through them. The cool touch of linen to my cheek. The taste of liquorice.

My heart was racing. I shook my head clear. It had been a young woman's voice that I'd thought I'd heard, the sunshine slipping under the door. I had sensed the presence of a young woman in the room, just out of sight. I had thought to see a young woman standing at the pump, catching up on the day's news, waiting her turn for the water. *Elizabeth?*

I was on my feet and stumbling back off the grave, my hand and arm stinging as if from an electric shock. I backed into a headstone. My hands fumbled behind me for the edge of the stone and caught it. I slipped past it, stumbling away. There was a strong smell of sweet rotting grass, of algae and moss and damp; it caught in my throat and dragged nausea up to meet it. I was weaving my way between the grave mounds, just trying to get away, trying not to throw up, dizzied by a vertiginous slide of images like laundry falling from a high shelf: the static in the air; sunshine streaming under the door on a dull day; a voice. A breath on my neck. Someone in the corner of my vision, waiting.

I'd reached the wall and the wired-shut gate into the woods. I glanced back. The Williams grave: I couldn't pick it out. But I felt something. On my skin; on the hollow where jaw and throat meet, just beneath the ear: a breath drawn. Someone about to whisper in my ear.

I ducked away, desperate, scrambling up the gate. Wire sank into the ball of my thumb. I swore and lifted my hand free, the metal pulling from the flesh, the pain jarring all the way up to my shoulder. I dropped down onto the soft earth on the far side, pressing the cut to my mouth, digging in my pockets with my left hand in the hope of a tissue, stumbling on. The woods were dark.

I slithered down the bank. Birds rose cawing overhead. Stumbling downhill, I grabbed one-handed at saplings and tree trunks, tongue hard against the raw metallic harshness of the cut. Brambles tore at my clothes. I was going too fast, almost blind, not thinking. My foot snagged on something and I went headlong. There was a moment before landing, a moment suspended in the fall, both hands flung out in front of me, the darkness blurring, and I was thinking, this could end really badly, this could end stupidly, my neck broken, my head staved in, blood drying in the leaf mould, and no one would know to look for me here, and Mark would be ringing and ringing my mobile, and it would be a really stupid way to die, and Cate would grow up and she wouldn't have a mum, not on any birthday, not on the day her first baby was born, and that just can't happen to her.

My hands landed on the earth and sank into mulch. It was cold. My elbows buckled and my chest, cheek, the length of me hit the ground. I lay on the leaf mould. There was a smell of earth and garlic and sap. My hand was stinging. Something pricked my knee through my jeans. Blood thudded in my ears; beyond that, the woods were silent. I lay there, palms pressed onto the earth. I thought, I'm an idiot. I thought, I need help. I thought, I am going crazy here. Slowly, I picked myself up and brushed off wet flakes of leaf-flesh with my left hand. My right arm ached. I felt deeply shaken. My hand was trembling as I brushed away the dirt.

*

I set the shower going and stripped down to chicken-flesh. I stepped in, my skin flinching at the shift in temperature, at the battering of the spray, as if it were unwilling to believe in the possibility of warmth. I held my hand out to the falling water and let it scald the cut. It had gone pale and thick around the edges. I turned and let the water hurl itself against my back, and the room filled with steam. I breathed a long breath, and closed my eyes, and let my head hang, and watched the red darkness behind my eyes, and felt the gorgeousness of the water on my skin, and the throb of the cut, and the gentle sting of my scar, like a day-old nettle sting, and all of it felt good.

Wrapped in a towel, my hair in wet tangles, I rummaged left-handed in my wash bag for the tea-tree oil that I usually used on spots, and dripped it into the cut. I found a plaster in the bottom of the bag, its paper-casing rubbed around the edges, stained with eyeshadow dust. I peeled it, stuck it on, flexed my hand. It'd last till I got home.

I bundled up my clothes to pack them. When I lifted my jeans, I knew by their weight, its evenness, that the phone wasn't in the pocket. I rifled in all the pockets anyway, uselessly, knowing the phone was gone. It must have slipped out when I fell. It was lying in the woodland earth, beaded with rain; its screen-clock counting out the minutes till the battery ran down. I wasn't going back for it.

I left out underwear for the morning and threw the rest of the clothes into my bag. The house was not packed up; I'd even managed to add to the work with those new books. I switched the lights off as I came downstairs. I would be rational. I would do what needed to be done. In the morning, I would throw my stuff in the car. I would drive home. Five hours down the motorway to an empty flat. Cate and Mark would be back at teatime. The warm weight of her in my arms, the warm vice of his arms around me. The next day, I would go and talk to Dr. Cowan; I'd meet the peeled man's sympathetic gaze.

*

Outside, the breeze blew up into a full-on wind; rain was flung in handfuls at the window. The dark out there was massive, boiling. It had swallowed up the house.

I switched on the TV for the noise. I opened kitchen cupboards and fumbled in an open packet of breadsticks. I crunched a breadstick down, squatting to rifle through the fridge, my stomach sore and tight with hunger: I couldn't remember my last meal. I lifted tomatoes and an avocado from the salad drawer onto the counter above me and dropped a bag of mulching lettuce into the bin. I drew another breadstick from the open packet, crunching on it as I got out a knife and chopping board. The breadsticks were stale. I started on a third. I cut the tomatoes into slices, lifting the first shallow fleshy cup of seeds to my mouth; it was overripe, too sweet, the flesh melting unpleasantly. I peeled the avocado, pared away a slice, slipped it between my lips. The flesh was buttery and giving and smooth. Calories. The sheer instinctive pleasure of calories.

I lifted out a bottle of wine. It had sat there, untouched and forgotten since Mark's visit. It seemed like a last drink: no alcohol with those pills. I sloshed wine into a tumbler, took three quick swallows, sat down at the breakfast bar to eat.

The news came on the television. Bodies lying on a dusty road; blackened, broken, uncovered; pools of dark blood in the dust, like oil dripped from a broken sump. Then a woman spoke urgently, her head cowled in dark cloth, the sky above white with dust and sun. A boy was crying and crushing himself into her dark-draped body. She stroked him, pressed him to her, cupping his head against her side, her other hand pushing tears away across her cheeks. As she spoke, a journalist translated. Her elder son, the market where he waited with others, looking for a day's work; the van that pulled up, the driver who called them over, grinning, not knowing the truth of other people, the agony of martyred flesh. The explosion. The boy lifted his face from his mother's side, and glanced at the camera, his eyes wide and horrified, his face streaked. Then the piece ended. Back to the studio. I switched off the TV and was left with the ache.

Outside, the wind was blowing up against and buffeting the house. Inside, all was perfectly still, weirdly still, with the TV off. No hum. Nothing. I felt suspended, sealed up in a bubble. Far away, down streaming motorways and past dark fields and through cities and at the other end of the country, Mark and Cate were safe in the warm cocoon of our flat. The smell of milk and drying laundry. The smell of his skin, and her skin; the smell of us. And I could be there soon, dazed and floating in blue amniotic warmth. And I wanted to be there now.

A sound. Directly overhead. A floorboard creaked; I lifted my head.

The whooshing buffet of dark air against the house, like wet sheets slapped and snapped against the walls. I strained my ears for indoor noise. The slaty taste of wine in my mouth. A prickle in the air.

Again. A floorboard creaked. Just above me. It must have been pretty much on the threshold to the Reading Room. And as I thought this, it seemed to me that there was an explosion of static: the house fizzing, brimming, overcharged. The wind hit the window. A great woof of air on the panes, pressing them, making them flex.

An old house. A windy night. Creaking was no big deal. But my skin was prickling, the faint hair down my arms standing on end. I did the rational, sane thing. I switched the landing light on and climbed the stairs. The flicker at the corner of vision, the stirring of nerves; it's just the mind filling in the blanks. It's evolutionary twitchiness. Stare at it straight, it disappears.

The door stood open on darkness.

"Hello?"

The word was barely spoken and already I regretted it. It seemed ridiculous; it also seemed to countenance the possibility of a reply. The landing light slipped past me, illuminating a strip of floor, a corner of the bookcase. My bag lay open-mouthed near the dressing table; a book was splayed face down on the bed. Through the window, the moon was low and full; clouds bunched and tumbled. Beyond the shaft of light, the bookcase was laden, swelling, bursting with books, heavy with newspapers, spilling journals, magazines. I glared at it, making it resolve back into a tailing-off half-shelf of books.

Something moved. At the window. I looked straight at the dark panes. I wouldn't let this happen, not again; I wouldn't let my mind fool itself.

A floorboard creaked under my foot. The air seemed to thicken, to condense. The wind tore at the slates, buffeted the glass. The dark was tussling outside; something was reflected on the glass, a pale shape. The pane rattled and the reflection juddered. I moved towards it, and it came clearer and closer: just me. My reflection. That was all. Beyond, the trees were in constant movement, the clouds massing and shredding across the moon.

The image was thin against the dark. A suggestion of pale skin, dark eyes. I blinked, and was vividly conscious of what is normally an instinctive unnoticed act; she was using my eyes; she was watching me. The fizzing in the air changed, grew into a hum, a vibration; the boards were shivering under my feet and a new light glimmered through the room. The air seemed to coalesce into something else, something more dense.

I thought, this is it.

The image grew clearer. Dark eyes in deep shadowed pits, the line deep between her brows. The air was humming, shuddering with sound; light gathered, thickened. Her features were becoming more distinct. All sense of mutedness, of pinned-down restraint was now utterly dispelled. It was happening. She was coming. She was here.

"Elizabeth?" I breathed.

The buzz exploded into a roar. Light swept the room. Everything was thrown into stark brilliance. The reflection stared back at me, blank with shock. The growling rattle of a diesel engine; a tractor spun past the house, its headlights raking through the window, tearing across the room, spattering me, the bed, the almost-empty bookshelves with sudden searching light. The tractor ground on up the village street, some piece of complex farm machinery chinking and clattering behind it. The roar fading out again into a hum, a buzz, a prickle in the air, and then quiet.

I let a breath go. The breath shook. I watched my own faint reflection in the window. I tried to laugh; it didn't come out right. I went downstairs. I plucked the cork out of the top of the bottle. I filled my glass to its brim. No pills to be had: I needed to use what came to hand. I'd switch myself off for the night. Tomorrow. Tomorrow I'd go home. I'd get my pills.

JUST AS MRS. BRIGGS WAS DUE TO DISH UP THE SERVANTS' dinner, I was called for to dust the morning room. The curtains were drawn against the harsh summer sun, and it was dim and pleasant there. I skimmed the little tables, the windowsills and overmantel with a cloth; wiping down vases, ornaments, commonplace books and books of engravings, and whisking my feather duster over the clock, the carved flowers and grapes on the mantelpiece, enjoying the feel of things, the cool of alabaster, the give of carpet, the palm-shaped curve of carved chair backs. I returned to the kitchen with my nails grey, the cracks in my hands lined with grey, and ready for my dinner. As I came down the kitchen steps, into the smell of mutton stew, the morning-room bell jangled overhead. Maggie straightened her cap and trotted up the stairs to answer it, and I continued on to the scullery, put my cleaning things away and washed the dust off my hands. I was scrubbing at my calluses, trying to get the dirt out of the hardened skin, when I heard Maggie's voice in the kitchen. It was pitched high and going fast; I couldn't catch the words. I came through, drying my hands on my apron. Mrs. Briggs, Mr. Fowler, Clem Taylor and Alice were all sitting at their places, their dinner steaming in front of them; there were two places vacant, one for Maggie, who was standing on the kitchen steps and telling her tale, her hands on her hips in delighted scandal, and one for me. Maggie saw me come in, and her mouth snapped shut like a snuffbox. Mrs. Briggs glanced around, her raised eyebrows pushing her forehead into sweaty creases. Maggie pitched her voice at me as a child might pitch a ball: "Madam says, you're to go back, and do it properly this time."

Mr. Fowler took out his handkerchief and blew his nose.

"There's not a dust-mote left," I protested.

"That's not what Madam said."

"But it's as clean as a whistle."

"It doesn't do to defend yourself, lass," said Mrs. Briggs. "Madam wouldn't complain for her own amusement, and if there's fault to be found then it's your fault. Get your things and go and do it again."

I went back to the scullery for clean cloths, troubled and confused. I left them in the kitchen eating their dinner, with mine cooling on the table. I dusted the morning room again; every inch, every single thing, and I couldn't find any fault with what I'd done before. Afterwards, I ate alone, standing with my plate and fork in a corner by the door, out of Mrs. Briggs's way. The stew had gone cold, and clots of fat had gathered in the gravy.

That afternoon, I swept the bedrooms. The rooms were still and sun-warmed, as if sealed like jars. From Madam's dressing-room window, I could see the first reapers up on the high meadow; Blacows' land. They moved together, each body turning in one strong movement, like a salmon's leap, to swing the scythe, each one for safety's sake keeping pace with and distance from his fellows, so that they passed in a steady line across the field. The stubble lay dark and blunt behind them, heaped with glossy mounds of fallen grass. Haytime. I flung open the sash, let the sweet breeze come in. The air was full of the scent of cut grass, linden blossoms, lilac. The sweet smell of high summer.

Haytime meant reprieve.

Only Mrs. Briggs stayed at the vicarage during those weeks. School was suspended; home life paused; no clogs were made, no roofs repaired, no baskets woven. Everyone who was fit for it turned their hand to the hay. It must be cut, and dried, and stored, before the rain could come and ruin the crop. Nothing else mattered, for a time.

It was a holiday feeling, at least at first; the sky wide and blue above, the country stretching wide and softly green around us. For that short space, there would be no scrutiny. Not of mother, father, master, mistress. In the fields, all were equal in the pursuit of the common goal; the bringing in of the hay.

Tossing the grasses into the air, watching their silken rustling fall, heaving the pitchfork under the heaped stems again, lifting the lower levels into the sun, I felt such a pleasure in the warm sun on my cheeks, the fresh open space, in the satin hand-smoothed feel

of the pitchfork's shaft. There was the simple, almost animal satisfaction in the work of my body, in its strength, its staying power.
At dinnertime, we sat in the shade of the hedgerow, and drank tea
from our bottles, ate our bread and cheese and onions, and I was
happy, mute with the sky's dazzle, my body slack, my palms hot
with wear. I closed my eyes. The red glow was patterned with the
shadow of stirring branches.

You can work as hard as you like at other work, but nothing can prepare you for haytiming. My palms blistered, and the
blisters broke, and the loose skin wore into rags and peeled off.
I rolled seed-heads between my palms; they leave behind a soft
purple dust that's good for drying haytiming sores.

*

The stars were out; it was a beautiful clear night. We were walking up from the water meadow along the wash-house lane. My
shoulders burned with fatigue, my brow and cheeks were hot
and tight from the long day's sun. When we got home, Mam and
Dad and the boys would all stream off to their beds like mice into
their holes. I could just lay down on my blankets, and drop into
the deep dark hole of haytiming sleep. The trudge up the hill was
only bearable for this, that at the end of it, I could lie down, and
I could sleep, and not have to think about anything, not have to
think at all.

We reached the gate and waited while someone at the head of
the party unfastened it. We were next to Agnes's house and as I
glanced at her side window I saw a faint light burning inside. A
jar of flowers had been set on the windowsill; a few campions and
Queen Anne's lace screened the room. Beyond, faint in the dim

light of a single rush, softened by the ripples and bulges in the glass, a movement caught my eye. She was in the rocking chair, gently rocking the child. Her skin was shades of shadow-blue and gold in the dim rush-light; her bodice was open to expose her breast and her head was bent to watch the baby feed. She must have been unconscious of almost everything, perhaps even half-asleep; she didn't seem to notice the noise of the passing hay-timers. I felt a warm flush of tenderness and guilt. I missed her.

The workers on the new Hall were not spared to help, even with the Oversbys' hay. They must have lived on short commons those weeks, with their landladies out in the fields. They must have welcomed the end of that time as much as we did, with the last drift of hay shut up tight into the final barn to wait the winter. The farmers sent pies and pastries and cheeses and fruit, and we had our dinner on trestles on the green. I drank Haytime Ale and ate a slice of pork and apple pie, and slipped into the hazy trance of bodily exhaustion. Joe Stott had brought his fiddle, and Thomas asked me to dance, but I shook my head and smiled at him, and told him I was way past dancing, there wasn't a single step left in me that I didn't need to get me home.

Long before the celebrations ended I was making my slow way back along the village street. The moon was pale in the still-blue sky; there were no stars yet; fiddle music drifted from up on the green. There was a candle burning gold in Mr. Moore's room. I ignored it. I slept like a stone.

*

Haytiming done, Dad came back from Storrs and the Williamses' with a faggot of willow-wands on his shoulder, and pale cold foul temper on his brow. I ducked out into the garden and listened to the raised voices from within the house. Greaves was a bastard, my father said. It was lies, all lies, that he could get his baskets better and cheaper elsewhere, because whose baskets were better nor cheaper than ours? Mam made some placating remark, which I couldn't hear, but must have been to do with the fine lot of willow he'd brought back, and how she and I would have it turned into baskets in no time, and we'd sell them at Hornby Market if not at Storrs. Williams was a thief, Dad announced; whatever else might be going on, it had to be said now loud and clear that old man Williams was a swindler and a crook. He'd charged Dad twice as much as usual for the willow.

"Coming to the end of the season, that was his excuse."

"Well, we are, I suppose," Mam answered.

Dad swore; there was a scuffle then a sudden crash. I went back in; the tea canister lay on the floor, dented, the tea all spilt on the flagstones. Mam was crouched beside it, scooping the tea back into the canister. Dad stood flushed, his gaze challenging. I crouched down beside Mam and quickly checked her face. She didn't seem to have been hit, she was just a little pale and contained-looking, a lid firmly pressed down on her feelings. I helped her gather up the tea.

"You're a good girl, Lizzy," she said.

It was meant to annoy Dad as much as please me. He snorted. "Aye, right. The model child."

He turned and thumped up the stairs, and we could hear him for an hour afterwards, debating noisily with Mr. Moore, as we picked grit out of the tea leaves until I suggested that it would probably sink and get left in the pot, and no one would really notice it.

So now Mam and me had another batch of greenwork to do, at twice the cost and expecting half the payment, and with our hands already raw and weeping, our limbs still stiff and aching from the pitchfork and the scythe. The sap stung my sores, and then began to numb them; willow has this virtue, that it can make you numb. My flesh seemed to cure, like bacon, my palms taking on the darkened hardness of dried meat, and the bitter smell of willow. Even at the vicarage, when I scrubbed pewter or polished brass or silver, or waxed the hall boards for the second time that day, even if there was tallow or baking or a roast spitting in the oven, I could smell the bitterness of willow about me. It was worn into my flesh; I could taste it in my mouth, every moment, every day.

Reverend Wolfenden never asked for me, unless it was to clean again something that I had cleaned already, to do something right that I had done perfectly well just moments before.

It was around then, after the hay, before the corn, that I began to notice the change in my father. One night, he and Mr. Moore were sitting downstairs after supper. Mr. Moore was quiet and Dad was talking about the poorness of the season, the late frosts we'd had that spring, the rains he'd expected to ruin the hay, that hadn't come but when they did the ground would be so dry and hard that there would be floods, no doubt about it, floods to rival Noah's, and the corn would all rot. The chill in the air now, even though it was but turning August. What was certainly a hard winter to come. The scandalous cheapening of baskets. The scandalous dearness of bread. The Corn Laws that suited the gentry and the Poor Laws that suited the manufacturers, and no laws that suited the likes of us at all. It was like learning a new word; having seen it once, I noticed tokens of the change in him all the time: a new eagerness, a sharp eye for trouble, a looking-forward to disaster, a keenness to apportion blame. Mr. Moore would sometimes nod, sometimes speak; his words were like dark spaces in the air. I felt a note of caution in his voice, but did my best not to hear the words.

The meetings started up again, after the haytiming. My father went along, and so did Thomas, and so did the other men. There began to be noise, and voices raised. I couldn't make out what was being said, since the words were muffled and obscured by the floorboards and the closed door.

I wanted to ask Thomas if the Reverend had spoken to him, and what he might have said in reply. Whenever I saw Thomas, he was in the company of other men and I never got the opportunity to ask.

*

That August, Sundays, rather than being a looked-for rest, became like a storm cloud hanging over the whole week, as the Reverend's sermons grew more fiery and fierce. I sat in the free-seats, between my mother and the boys, my father wedged glowering at the end of the pew. Hot sun pooled on the flagstones like molten lead. There was no air. The nave was full of shuffling and rustling, of the smell of close-pressed people, of Sunday clothes taken straight from the closet where they'd hung since last week's wearing. As the sermon began, I bent my head, and kept it lowered all the time that the Reverend spoke. I hoped it looked like piety. My eyes swam; tears fell onto my clasped hands as the Reverend spoke of the torments of Hell, and the sinfulness of the human state. I could not pray. I felt so far from God. My soul would not be soothed.

One night as Mam and I sat half-sleeping over our work, the door upstairs was flung open with a bang, making us start awake, and Mr. Gorst came thumping down, and touched his cap to us sitting by the hearth, and we said good evening, and he left the house.

"Isn't Jack Gorst still up there?" I said, meaning his son.

"I think so."

Mam and I both craned our heads to listen. The door was standing open upstairs; I heard Mr. Moore's voice clear as though he were standing beside me; it was raised above the clamour of other voices.

"It seems to me that when all is reckoned together," he said, "the difference between man and man is not so considerable as that one man should therefore set himself up as an authority over another, simply by virtue of the class into which he was born, and claim to himself any benefit to which another may not pretend as well as he."

Recognition made me catch my breath. I could not have said it, in such a way, but I'd felt it, when I was standing in the library while the Reverend had sat rehearsing Martha's tale. Mr. Moore's words went as the crow flies, straight, and I could feel the justice and the truth of them; but I could not let myself listen to him, could not let myself fall into sympathy or agreement with him: if my feelings matched his words then both were wrong. He walked in darkness; he refused the light of Christ.

Then the door above was slammed shut, and the words were

lost, and all I could hear was the sound of his voice, like an emptiness welling overhead.

*

I was unhappy. I was desperately, sickly unhappy, all through
those long late summer days. I was unhappy at work, I was
unhappy at home, and there was nothing else but work and
home. Agnes didn't want me; she was barely there, and I couldn't
be easy in her company. I couldn't read: I couldn't face my books;
I couldn't bear that he was there to watch me trail along their
well-trampled tracks again.

One evening, my mam said I looked like I was ailing, and she
got the tonic down from the dresser, and poured me an eggcup-
ful. The next morning, she got up with me, and saw that I had
something to eat, and another dose of tonic before I left for work.
I welcomed the touch of her hard hand on my chin as she tipped
the treacly mixture into my mouth. It tasted good: rich, sweet, of
aniseed and other herbs; it made me shake my head and shudder,
and it softened the edges of the day, helped me drift into sleep
at night.

I heard them talking one evening, my mother and father. I was
working a basket, turning it in my lap to weave the withy through
the frame. I must have looked as if I were dreaming, or dozing, or
dazed after taking my tonic. They had their heads close together,
closer than they ever usually were, whispering. I heard Mam say,
she, and again, *she*, the hissing sound of it carrying better than the
other words. I kept my eyes on the basket and my hands moving,
pretended not to notice. Mam nodded towards me, still speaking
quietly to my dad.

"Well, the lad needs some encouragement," he said out loud.

Mam shushed him and glanced at me, and we looked at each other a moment, and then she looked away.

The next evening, after tea, Mr. Moore and my dad and Mam were all in the kitchen. It was still light and would be for hours yet. The boys were out playing. Mam and I were at the baskets, Dad read his paper and Mr. Moore a book, which I took care not to let my eyes linger on. There was a knock; the kind that does not expect an answer; the door opened. I could hear the children playing out, and fiddle music from up the street. Thomas came in.

He said a general good evening, and pulled the door shut behind him, cutting off the children's calls, the music and the evening air. He seemed stiff and strange. His eyes skimmed over Mr. Moore, lingered on my dad, and then rested on my mam. He didn't look at me. Mam dipped her head, almost a nod. Thomas's expression seemed to ease for just a moment, then to screw even tighter. He turned to me, and cleared his throat.

"The evening's fine, will you come out walking for a while?"

I noticed Mr. Moore lift his head and look at Thomas, then at me.

I glanced down at the unfinished basket. "I have too much work to do."

"Leave it," Dad said abruptly, making me flinch. "The baskets can wait."

Dad got up from his chair, lifted the basket from my lap and took it over to the stack under the stairs, leaving me without excuse or defence. Mam raised herself from her chair and went to the chest. I stood up to protest. She brought my Sunday bonnet out, and over to me, and set it on my head, and smoothed the ribbons. She tied them under my chin. I could smell the lavender from the chest. She didn't meet my eye.

I was at a loss. Finding myself so conspired against, it was impossible to resist without giving real offence. Mam gave me a little push on the small of the back, and I crossed the room towards Thomas. As he opened the door for me, I glanced back, and caught Mr. Moore's dark gaze. I had a sense that it lingered on me after I had turned away.

Thomas and I walked in silence; I was astonished at what had so easily been managed between them. The evening was a soft one, grey and cool. We walked down to the shilloe beds, side by side, a basket's distance apart. Thomas skimmed stones, and I watched them bounce and ripple across the river. The heron flapped away, legs trailing.

"Will you come to the Harvest Dance with me?" Thomas asked, brushing his hands.

I watched the heron rise above the hornbeam trees, its slow wing-flap dragging it higher and higher into the air, away.

I said, "If you want me to."

*

When I got back, Mr. Moore was still sitting in the kitchen. He glanced up when I came in. Thomas had followed me in, and came to stand by my side. My father regarded us both, somehow differently, as if a change had been effected which was for him a source of pride. For a moment I just stood there, conscious of Mr. Moore's enquiring gaze, as Dad folded his arms and looked fondly on me and Thomas, and Thomas stuffed his hands into his trouser pockets, and grinned.

"Where's Mam?" I asked.

"Evening milking," Mr. Moore replied unexpectedly. Our eyes met. I thought of what he'd said about God and the Bible, and how he must have watched me disputing with the carter and known what was said about husbands and *us* and *we*; how he'd stared at me and laughed when I had curtseyed to him and said I'd mistaken him for a gentleman, and how he'd offered me any book of his to read, and had had the grace never once to question how I might have come to read them before he'd given me permission, which proved he was a gentleman however little he liked to own it, and the way he'd said, *Nineteen and a house-maid*, and shaken his head. And the way he was looking at me now as I was standing by Thomas; his expression was so sharp and thoughtful, it seemed as though he were about to speak. The moment was of vital importance; it was the crux of everything; what he was about to say mattered more than I could understand.

"Had a good night then, my lass?" Dad asked.

The moment broke, our gaze fell away from each other, and I was left with a hint of something wonderful, something I couldn't really believe.

"It's lovely out," I said. "Just beautiful."

"I asked Lizzy," Thomas said, "and she said she would, but I wanted to ask you too; can I take her to the Harvest Dance?"

Dad expanded happily. "Of course you can, son."

Thomas made as if to reach out a hand towards me. I pretended not to notice. Mr. Moore stood up. He turned to lift a book from where he'd left it on the windowsill. I could still feel the place on my arm where he had touched me all those weeks ago; though painless, it was almost as if I'd been branded there; if I were to roll up a sleeve, there would still be his mark upon my skin.

"Goodnight," Mr. Moore said, to no one in particular. The stairs creaked under him.

*

It was still light out when I went to bed. I thought that I might read a while. I padded over to the dresser in my shift and considered the chapbooks, the Martyrs and Saints and Pilgrims, without enthusiasm. And that was when I noticed it, slipped in between the *Progress* and the Bible; the thick red spine of an unknown book. I drew the volume out. The cover was soft cloth, worn about the edges so that the threads were bare, and the grey board beneath showed through.

I could not help myself. No more than Eve. I bit deep.

*

It was a book of natural history; I'd never seen anything like it before. I was enchanted by the engravings. A bramble stem and flower; I gazed at that plate a long while in the evening light, the way the dark fruit glowed, the way the petals had that pale delicacy that they have in life, like the skin beneath the shell of a boiled egg. *Rubus fruticosus*, I read, spelling the words out in my head, and I was nervous, because I knew that this was Latin and Latin was religion, and Catholic at that, and that if this book was religion and Mr. Moore's I should certainly not read it; but I couldn't leave it now.

The bramble was near relative of the rose, with stems that

arch and scramble in hedgerow and scrub. Flowers white or pink, solitary or clustered, petals five, stamens many. I turned the page. Water Avens, I read, Wood Avens, Wild Strawberry. Head of achenes, styles persistent, becoming hooked. The words were strange, but linked to such familiar things, they gained a kind of resonance and poetry. The book was a study and celebration of God's creation: it seemed therefore that it could not be wrong in matters of doctrine. The pictures showed the plants laid out whole and in their parts against a blank background, like skinned and gutted animals. I recognized many from the hedgerows, fields, marshes and fells, and at the same time I felt that I was seeing things for the first time, entirely new. I had picked wild strawberries, and eaten them, relishing the sweet graininess of their flesh, but I had only known the plant as an animal knows it, as being good to eat. This book set each plant apart from all other plants, from all other things, from every other part of creation, and considered it for itself alone, and when that was done, it drew, as it were, a spider's web of relation between it, and all its relatives, and everything else with which it had connection, from the beasts that ate it to the butterflies that laid their eggs on it, to the wet or dryness of the soil in which it flourished. I had never thought that there could be a book like this. I learned that sorrel was a sister to the dock, that what we call Queen Anne's lace, elsewhere others call cow parsley.

The light faded and my eyes were sore. I let the book fall shut. That night, my dreams were tangled and overgrown, and blossomed with white flowers.

*

That day at the vicarage was the bottling of plums. The kitchen was all steam and scalds and burning sugar and bad temper. I didn't care: the book would be there when I got home. I'd slip it into my apron pocket and say I was going over to see Agnes. Then I'd head down to the river, sit on the shilloe, where Thomas and I had gone the night before, and read for an hour or so undetected.

But when I returned the book was gone. There was another in its place; a small blue volume. I turned around to Mr. Moore, my lips parting to challenge and complain. Mam was setting the kettle and Dad was hanging up his jacket. Mr. Moore sat at the fireside, his eyes rigidly set upon his book, his lips pursed tight as if to hold back a smile. I realized I could not risk saying anything.

My dad sat down and started talking to Mr. Moore. Thomas was a good lad, he was saying, but his father was a villain, which is how he'd got to be so prosperous, more prosperous than other folk. Mr. Moore closed his book, keeping his thumb between the pages to mark the place, and set his face in a listening expression. The only thing for it, Dad said, was to make more baskets, and if that meant making them faster and less well, what matter, since as it was no one else seemed to recognize their quality anyway.

Dad occupied with complaining, I took the book down, examined it discreetly. The pages were thick and creamy. It was by Reverend John Milton, and called *Paradise Lost, A Poem in Twelve Books*. I glanced over again at Mr. Moore. It seemed to me that although his eyes were fixed on my father's flushed face, his attention was somehow directed towards me. I watched his profile. I watched the lines around his eyes. They seemed to deepen, even though his lips did not smile. I slid the book into my pocket.

"I'm just popping over to Agnes's for an hour or so," I said; no one seemed to notice.

*

The sand martins skimmed over the river, catching flies. The willows made a screen from passers-by. Those first lines were more difficult than anything in Mr. Lyell's *Geology*, and there were no engravings or plates to admire; but I would not be put off, I would not be beaten. With persistence, I got the pattern of the verse, the way the meaning stretched and twisted and slid through the lines. Since it was written by a clergyman, I read it without qualm, and was soon caught up in the familiar inevitability of the story. I didn't notice the passing of the hours, the dimming of the light, the striking of the bell; it was only when I started to shiver in the evening chill that I realized that it was late, and that I would be in trouble. I had to run most of the way home.

The kitchen was empty. No one had sat up, worried or angry, waiting for me. I made my bed, and lay in the last glow of the fire, and read about Sin, who was beautiful, and lived in Heaven, and whose father was Lucifer himself, and who I hadn't read of before, not as a person, not in the Bible. Sin never had a mother, but was born straight out of her father's head, and he left her to grow up in the company of angels, and when she was grown, Lucifer met her again, and saw how beautiful she was, and wanted her. He had his way with her. When Lucifer was cast out of Heaven, she was cast out too, and fell when all the other rebellious angels fell; but she was alone, outcast from their company, which was a double cruelty, since she had not been so much rebellious, as obedient and abused. Fallen and alone, kept in utter darkness, she was made keeper of the Gate of Hell, entrusted with a key and made to wait there, and forbid passage to anyone who came that way. A baby was born, a son to her father, and the child was Death, and he grew up fast, a demon of a child, and he forced himself on her. She grew hideous and serpent-like in her dark maternity, and bore to Death a swarm of vile creatures, which crawled and clawed all over her and in and out of her, and bit at her and sucked her blood, and she lived there in darkness, loathsome and tormented, till Lucifer came to the Gate of Hell, seeking his escape, radiant with the light of his own beauty. He didn't know her for his daughter and the woman he had ruined, she was so hideously transformed; Lucifer, for all his evil-doing, for all his accursedness, had been allowed to keep his beauty. He told her to open the gate, that he might make his escape from Hell, and since he was her father, she obeyed. My eyes were becoming too tired, and were falling shut, and I let the book drop onto my chest, and closed my eyes, and fell straight asleep, and when I woke the next morning, the book was splayed like a dead bird on top of me. I put the book back on the shelf, but with some anxiety; I had not finished it; what if it went the way of the red one?

I was walking down the village towards the vicarage, the warm early sun in my eyes, my mind still locked up in the darkness of that story, and thinking why God would have made a gate to Hell; He could have dropped the falling angels in from above, filled Hell up with syrup and pressed a lid down tight and sealed it, and kept them there like bottled plums for all eternity, and never let Lucifer and Sin out to torment us. I came up to the servants' door, and went into the dim hallway. Petra stalked through, her tortoise-shell fur sleek with pleasure; for once she had a dead mouse hanging from her jaws. I let her out. I sat down on the bench, untied my laces, and pulled off my clogs. I pushed my feet into my slippers. Wiser minds than mine had almost certainly settled such questions long ago, but I couldn't forget Sin, and what seemed, to me at least, the unfairness of her situation.

The book's ghost followed me all day. The words I spoke seemed to arrange themselves into the patterns of the Reverend Milton's verse. My thoughts were dark with Hell, entangled with Eden's vines, glowing with the light of Lucifer's approach. All day I was on edge that when I got back the book would be gone. When finally Mrs. Briggs released me from work, I flung on my shawl, knotted my clogs and walked as fast as I could up the village street, doing my best not to break into a run that would be noticed and talked about by the women on their doorsteps.

I came up the steps, into the kitchen, and over to the dresser: the book was gone. In its place was a squat black volume.

"Oh!"

I swung around. Dad was in his seat and Mr. Moore was coming down the stairs. Dad's glance was irritable: "What?"

Mr. Moore paused at the stairs' foot, and looked with innocent enquiry at me.

"Nothing," I said. "Sorry."

I lifted the new book down from the shelf, glanced at it swiftly. Mr. Moore crossed the room and took his hat from the peg. Dad said something more, making me start; I turned guiltily towards him, tucking the book behind my back.

"Pardon?"

"It's a fine evening," he said. "You should call for Thomas."

I could feel the flush rise up my throat. "I've been on my feet all day."

"When I was courting your mam, there wasn't an evening went by that I didn't walk the three miles to Capernwray and the three miles back, just to take a cup of tea in the kitchen with her, and with that old hag of a cook glaring at us the whole time. Things were different then. None of this nonsense then. Isn't that right, Moore?"

Mr. Moore pushed his hat onto his head. "I wouldn't know," he said. He nodded to me, said good evening, and went out.

While Dad was in the room, I worked on a basket; he retired to bed early, and in what was left of the long evening, I read the new book. It was a play, by William Shakespeare, about a king called Henry. I didn't much care for it. Mam came home, and went to bed, then the boys came in, and went up to their room. I was vexed with the story. I missed the other book. I didn't believe the ending to the current one, didn't believe he loved her; I didn't see how he could have come to love her, like that, in a moment, so conveniently. It was almost dark in the kitchen when Mr. Moore came home. Outside some of the light still lingered. He caught me there, frowning at the book.

"Not to your liking?" he asked.

I blinked up at him; my very bones ached to speak to him. But I didn't speak; I couldn't name what it was I felt, and if I could, I would not have dared to say it.

"Never mind," he said. He said goodnight, and went upstairs.

The Reverend Milton's blue book had left a mark upon my thoughts, as looking upon a candle flame leaves a scald upon the vision, that drifts across the sight after the flame itself has been snuffed out. When I lay down, it was to think of Sin, tormented in the darkness. It was to think of Eve, blinking and new born, confronted by man and God, a snake always at her heel.

Mr. Moore must have intended this. He must have known what I would do.

*

The next Friday was a washing day. It was all so precariously balanced; work, home, Thomas; at any moment a slight shift could cause all to fall down around me. I kept my thoughts averted. If Mr. Moore was home, I would ask him straight out: can I borrow the *Paradise Lost*? If he was not there, I would borrow it anyway. I had been given permission, after all; and it had not been withdrawn.

The house had that dim cool feel of emptiness: Mam would be down at the wash-house, expecting me. I kicked off my clogs and climbed the stairs, knocking on his door confident that there would be no reply. Silence from within: I pushed the door and it swung open. The room was empty. The bookcase stood solid and huge; it seemed familiar to the room, as though it had softened into place.

I would find the book. I would take it downstairs, hide it in the press, and then go down to the bleaching-fields and help get in the linen. He might notice the book's absence, or he might notice its presence in my hands that evening, when I sat to read. What could he say? What could he do? He was as deep in this as I was; deeper, even: he couldn't accuse me of anything.

I found the Reverend Milton's book; its slim blue spine was

pressed between two bulkier volumes. I teased it out and dropped it into my apron pocket. At the end of a shelf was the stack of newspapers that Mr. Moore collected in packages from the mail coach: *The Northern Star*. I picked the top one up out of curiosity, and was just going to glance at the first page; but when I lifted it, I saw, underneath, the red buckram cover of the ledger. It lay amongst the papers, as if hidden hastily there, as if tucked quickly out of sight.

There would be dry linen on the lines, and the wet linen needing pegging out, and the women already muttering at my tardiness. I should take the book I'd come for and just go. The house was silent. The air was dry and warm and still carried the scent of oak. I heard a curlew's cry from up the back field. There was the deep call of a grown lamb, the deeper reply of the ewe. Mr. Moore wasn't there. I knew he wasn't there. He wouldn't catch me. He would never know.

I lifted the ledger down and replaced the paper on top of the stack. It was a big unwieldy thing. Resting the top edge of the ledger on the shelf, I held the bottom edge in my hands; if I heard someone coming I could push it back in amongst the papers in an instant. I peered at his writing. The letters were small and densely packed. They filled the page like the weft of a dark cloth.

Slavery has numerous phases, but every system which tends to place the labour, life and destinies of man at the disposal of another, deserves to be classed under that odious name. Since the great betrayal, when our hopes were so utterly dashed, every interest has been represented in Legislature save the interest of the People. The Church, the Bar, the

*landed and moneyed interests, all these flourish, and the
People are worse than undefended. We have arrived at
a situation where the wolf legislates for the lamb. What
the wolf desires is not the lamb's welfare, but his own
dinner.*

*The exclusionists said that the People were incapable
of choosing proper representation; the melancholy truth
was that at the time, in many parts, men were receding in
knowledge. If they were not fit then, they have worsened
since; but to set up the People's ignorance as a barrier to
their suffrage is a great injustice. Ignorance is considered
a barrier in no other part of the Legislature; the rich and
propertied may be as ignorant as they like and still keep
their vote. No one seeks to remain ignorant; it is simply
that the remedy for it is kept under lock and key by the
very class of men who accuse us of ignorance and deny us
the vote. I think that we must shift for ourselves, since they
are not about to stir themselves on our behalf. We must
educate ourselves, we must arm ourselves with knowledge,
so when the time comes round again, and we present our
demands, supported by our petition with its thousands
upon thousands of signatures, the justice and intelligence
of our arguments will be unassailable.*

I felt as if I had been struggling with a tangled thread for months,
teasing at this loop and then that, and then suddenly with one
tug in the right place, the whole muddled mess fell into a straight
clear thread. I saw why the Reverend was so interested in Mr.
Moore. I saw that the Reverend was afraid. I felt it too: the force

of this intelligence, this facility with words, this faith, all trained upon the state of things, a state of things that I had only known as I had known the ground I walked upon, as something that was there, God-given, unchanging and unquestionable. I shivered. The world seemed a different place. A darker place. I turned the page.

I found them in such miserable circumstances, six of them crowded into the one room, a damp and stinking cellar. There, all the necessary activities of life took place, in such crowded and miserable conditions that I find it impossible to recall without shuddering. The father was instructing his eldest daughter in the working of the loom; though it had provided him with such meagre support in life, he was unable to offer her better.

Such light as entered the place, from a grille high up in the wall, was frequently obscured by the passing of people in the street. The only furniture was the loom and a heap of straw; when it rained, the room flooded ankle-deep. On wet nights, the mother told me, there could be no rest for anyone, since there was nowhere to lie down.

The youngest was a child of fifteen months, and still at the mother's breast. When I asked why it was not weaned, the mother told me that there was little enough to feed the older children, if she did not feed it herself, she must take something for it from the other portions. She must have considered me to have a physician's brief, for she told me that in the winter past, when she had been brought very low by fever and bad food, that her husband had found her

in a swoon, and the child at her breast, by then a hungry
nine-month-old, had sucked not milk, but blood.

I slammed the book shut. Sunlight poured in through the window; a blackbird was singing in the garden. One of my stockings
needed darning at the heel; a hairpin pressed into the back of my
head. None of it was real, not as real as what I'd just read. I had
to speak to Mr. Moore.

But there was no escape until the washday was done. I had
to go back, and comport myself as if nothing were amiss, until
the last of the linen was dry and hefted back up to the houses to
air, the five o'clock bell was fading from the air, and everyone
was heading for Mrs. Goss's house for tea. Only then could I slip
away, back down the lane, without protest. I knew that it would
not go uncommented on. The women had seen me arrive late, and
they had seen me leave now. I couldn't help that. My mam would
be saying that I was a good girl, but close, terrible close, and that
you wouldn't suspect a thing unless you knew, I kept it that much
to myself, but there would be a wedding there before the year was
out. And the others would agree that Thomas was a fine young
man, and that I would be lucky to have him, with his twenty
pounds a year from the baskets alone. And it was true: Thomas
was, in his way, a fine young man; he just wasn't right for me. I
came down the lane, my feet thumping on the packed-hard mud
and stones, to where the ways part, one path heading across the
shorn meadow towards the Williamses' willow holts, the other
climbing the hill towards Storrs.

The rooks wheeled high above the trees. I crossed the beck by
the wash-house, and climbed the hill. Halfway up the hillside an

oak tree stood, casting a pool of shade. I spread my shawl on the mossy turf underneath and sat down. The path passed close by and from where I sat I could see a good stretch in both directions. Mr. Moore must come that way to return home at the end of his working day. If I waited there, he must pass me too. I waited.

The bells chimed the quarter, then the half-hour. I bit at the dry tag of skin beside my thumbnail. I heard voices from above, from the cusp of the hill. The men's figures were dark against the sky. I started to my feet. They came down the track, and I could see them clearly. Mr. Moore was in company with two men, in shirtsleeves and britches, leather tool bags slung over their shoulders. They were talking; Mr. Moore said something and the others laughed. They were workers on the Hall; I recognized them from the meetings, but they weren't village men. I came forward, to the edge of the shade, and hesitated there. He was almost past: I opened my lips, determined to speak, but before I had to, Mr. Moore's tread faltered, and his dark head turned, and he saw me. He stopped and regarded me with an expression of puzzled concern. I smiled uneasily.

"Is something wrong?" he asked.

I glanced from him to his companions; they'd stopped too, a little way ahead, and were waiting for him. I didn't know what to say. Mr. Moore followed my line of sight and registered my concern.

"Go on, I'll see you there," he called to them.

The men exchanged a glance and went on down the hill; we watched them cross the beck, then begin the slow climb up the hill towards the village. I was glad they were not local men. We were alone: Mr. Moore in sunlight, me in the shade of the tree.

"Is something wrong?" Mr. Moore asked again, and came towards me, into the shade. His face was blued by the shadow; there was a bloom of wood-dust on his skin. I felt an edge of anxiety at what I'd done, putting myself here, alone, with a man. He was studying my face.

"Elizabeth," he said. I could feel the warmth of his body near mine; his shirt was damp with sweat. "You're pale as buttermilk."

He took my elbow and gently steered me towards the bole. I let myself be guided back and sat down on my shawl where it was still spread. He crouched down in front of me and dropped his tool bag onto the grass. There were clear lines, free of dust, at the corners of his eyes. He must have worked in full sun that day, squinting against the glare, at the clouds of dust.

My mouth was dry; the words came out strangely: "Who are you?"

He said, "You know who I am."

"I don't, I really don't. You live in our house, you share our bread, you dole out your books like they were barley sugar, and all the time you keep yourself to yourself, you don't say a word, and no one knows a thing about you, not really."

He tilted his head, his brows raising; he seemed to accept this. He shifted, sat down at the edge of my shawl.

"Was it *Paradise Lost*?" he said. "Did it upset you? It is rather extreme; I shouldn't have started you so soon on that."

I shook my head, looking at the man who had made the bookcase, and who had made those pictures out of words. The wolf that legislates for the lamb. The high grille obscured with passing feet. The loom, the heap of straw. The baby that sucked its mother's blood.

"You said you were a carpenter."

"I am."

I shook my head. "I read your book."

He frowned, puzzled, fumbling for my meaning. "My book?"

"The one you've been writing in. The ledger."

He raised his hands to his face, wiping his fingers across his dust-stuck sweaty skin. He pressed the heels of his hands into his eyes.

"The only book in the entire collection that I forbade you," he said. "When I laid out every other for you, even put out the ones I thought you particularly would enjoy on your own shelf for you to read, you took the one book you were forbidden and you read it?"

I spoke low, ashamed: "Yes."

He looked at me in silence. I was too young, I remember thinking: I was too young for this, far too young to deal with him. He looked tired, hot, and older than I'd thought him, the wood dust smeared into his sweat. Then his face broke into creases and he laughed.

"Good for you," he said. "Good for you."

He took a bottle of beer from his bag and uncorked it. He offered it to me, and I took a sup, and passed it back: the beer was soft and malty on the tongue. He drank, then pinched the dampness from the corners of his lips with thumb and forefinger.

"Reverend was asking me about you," I ventured. I felt lighter for the confession.

"When was this?" he asked.

"The day after the first meeting."

"What did you tell him?"

"Not much. I didn't know anything. But I was wondering, how did he know?"

"Know what?"

"That you're a Chartist," I said, trying out the word, "and an agitator and a democrat and a viper."

"Is that what he told you?" He shook his head, half-laughed again. "D'you think I'm a viper?"

"I could think of better words." He glanced at me, almost smiling. "But the thing is, he seemed to have heard of you already. He knew about you."

"You stick your head above the parapet, and people notice. And take shots at it."

He set the bottle upright between us and leaned back on his hands, stretching his legs out in front of him. I felt strangely at ease, as if this was as it should be: someone seeing us would think we were a courting or a married couple, taking a pause from work together. Someone hearing us would know different.

"I didn't know what the Reverend meant by Chartist and that. Having seen some of your book, I think I begin to understand."

"It's simple enough. Chartists support the Charter; the Charter is the statement of our demands. We want representation: a vote for the working man, and changes to the current system that will allow working men's votes to count, and enable working men to become members of parliament. That's the kernel of it all."

"Because of the hunger? Because of the woman and the baby? How would it help?"

Mr. Moore shifted his position, brushing the scraps of bark and grit from his palms.

"Last week," he said, "in Preston, in this same county palatine of yours, four men were shot dead. Many others were wounded. The men had stopped the works to protest at dangerous working conditions, at their low wages. In striking, and inciting others to strike, they were endangering the mill-owners' profits. So the mill-owners called in the army, and the army shot the workers."

I watched the lines and creases of his face; "No," I said, but I could see that he was telling the truth.

"Men are cheap. There's a glut of them; they're to be had in plenty. But profit and property, they must be defended at all cost."

"No."

He was sitting forward now, leaning towards me, animated, even with the fatigue of the long day. "And this is what we must change. I don't just mean money, I mean opportunity, the opportunity to be more than just a pair of hands, employed at others' work, to be shot for stepping out of line, for insisting that there will be more to your life than work and hunger and death. In this country, privilege and property and opportunity are inherited, passed from parent to child, and poverty's the same; like having blue eyes, a talent for music, or a weak chest. We need the vote. If we are to effect change, we must have the vote."

I felt a strange kind of shyness, speaking of it: "There is Heaven, Mr. Moore. We may trust to that. That there will be consolation in the hereafter."

"What good is consolation?"

"You may not believe," I said, "but I do, I always have, as long as I can remember. A world without God . . ."

He raised his hand, palm turned towards me, asking me to stop; it was creased with grass marks and a fragment of bark was stuck to the ball of this thumb. "Even by your lights, then, it still holds true. This is not the world as God created it. Satan has worked his evil. You'll remember, in Genesis, God created Man and Woman, not Rich and Poor."

Images of Sin, and of Eve and the serpent and the fruit filled my inner sight, and then Agnes, pale as the sheets on which she lay, and the bucket full of bloody cloths, and her eyes closed and her mouth open as she was crushed by the birthing pains.

"I'm sorry," he said, in answer to my quiet. He sank back again, his palms pressed onto the earth, his arms locked. "Perhaps if I felt there was another world, I could rest easier about this one."

We sat in silence. The heat of the sun brought out the scent of the tree, a scent like moss and oatmeal. We looked across the water meadow, across the valley, towards the terraces of cottages at Melling, and beyond. There's a house on the top of the far hills; a lane runs up to it, it stands square against the sky. I always thought I might walk there one day, knock on the door, and find out who lives there. Stand on their doorstep to look back across the valley, to see what the village looks like from there.

"Perhaps it does not help to speak of God," Mr. Moore said after a while. "Think perhaps of the Church; this is what bothers me most, that a man like your Reverend Wolfenden keeps a grand house and a good table and a wife dressed in silk, who is herself a luxury, a fancy toy that plays music and looks pretty and is no use or good to anyone. This is all on your goodwill, paid for by your labour, by your tithes. And what bothers me is, what law did God lay down that you, Elizabeth, must labour to keep

Mrs. Wolfenden in fine clothes? Did Christ insist that his priests have grander houses, better food and clothes than the rest of his flock—did Christ insist that he have *priests*?"

I was picking at a patch of parched moss, watching its fibres come apart. I looked up at him. "They look after us. The Wolfendens do."

"Are you children?"

"They give charity. They have wealth so that they can give charity."

"So you are given treats for being good. Is this any way for grown men and women to live?"

"But he's—" I said.

Mr. Moore finished my thought, "A gentleman?" We were looking at each other. He made a comical face, his eyebrows raised, his lips pressed together, as if the phrase were meant to explain and answer everything, and that we both knew that it was entirely inadequate. I smiled. I couldn't help it.

"That book. The one that you're writing, what kind of a book is it? Is it like *Crusoe*, where everything happened but happened differently to someone else, or is it . . ." I was going to say Gospel Truth, but didn't.

"It really happened. Everything in that book; it really happened, and to me, or in my presence. I was just trying to get it down as coolly as I could."

"Why did you come here?"

"I thought it would be quiet. Oversby had not heard of me, but perhaps, by now, he will have: Wolfenden must have spoken to him." He thought a moment, tilted his head: "It would explain the way Greaves has been working me lately."

He lifted the bottle and drank. I watched the roll of his Adam's apple, the sheen of his sweated skin.

"I've never met anyone like you," I said.

He spluttered, coughed, and beer ran down his chin. He wiped it away. "You really have seen nothing of the world. I'm common as a sparrow. There's a meeting next month, on Caton Moor. We expect at least five hundred there."

Something caught my notice, some movement in the water meadow, over in the far corner. On his way home from the willow holts, with that long-legged lope that you would know a mile off. He crossed the stubble in full sun, his head low, a bundle of green willow on his back: Thomas.

"The meeting is just a step. A show of strength and purpose. Today, we're kept like children, and so, like children, we can only sulk and refuse to do our chores, and be beaten for our disobedience. But when the Charter becomes Law, there'll be a vote for every man. We'll all have a hand in the making of all other laws, in the establishment of taxes, in the conferring of rights and obligations on our fellow men, and we will be treated as children no longer. And then you will see what a fine world we make of this."

I stood up, lifting my shawl. Mr. Moore raised himself on a hand to let it slip out from beneath him.

"So I will have a vote?"

I shook out the shawl.

"Your husband will."

There was silence. I folded the shawl and drew it around me. I saw Mr. Moore's gaze catch on the figure of Thomas.

"Are you going to him?" he asked.

"I have to," I said, meaning that he might have seen us, or

might soon, if I didn't leave. Mr. Moore nodded and looked down, watching his forefinger picking at a crumb of loose bark.

"Goodbye," I said. "Thank you."

He glanced up, shook his head, not understanding.

"For explaining," I said. "For taking the time."

He smiled, his face breaking out into a map of lines, making me smile back at him.

"Pleasure," he said. "A genuine pleasure."

I went out into the sun's glare, and down the path towards the wash-house where the ways meet, and waited there, leaning against the gatepost, my heart hammering against the stone. Thomas approached across the water meadow. Mr. Moore came down the hill, and crossed the beck; I glanced up to watch him pass. He had his hat on; it shaded his eyes.

He touched his hat, and passed me without speaking. He climbed the hill towards the village, leaving me there.

I walked there, through the fields. I went down the track to the point where the ways part, then climbed up past the oak standing in its own quiet shadow. Storrs Hall stood clear among the trees. I climbed up the open hillside to a narrow wooden garden gate; beyond, the path was squeezed between laurels and rhododendrons. The hinges were stiff, the wood soft and damp; it left algae on my hand.

I should have been going home. I should have done what Mark said I should do. Got a good night's sleep and packed my stuff into the car and come straight home and gone and got the pills and forgotten all of this, forgotten everything. The wine had switched me off, but only temporarily. When I woke my hand was

236 · *Jo Baker*

throbbing under the plaster, and my head was sore and there was the sourness of a hangover in my mouth, and the edge of anxiety that came with it infected everything that had gone before and been dismissed: the reflection in the glass last night; the flood of images at the gravestone; the breath drawn as if someone were about to speak. What if I'd held my breath and listened, instead of running away? A woman's voice from an empty room. The static. If I were losing my mind, then it was a very specific madness. I had to find out what happened here; only then could I know what was happening to me.

And if anyone would know, it was Margaret.

The building was sheer and dark, flanked by close-growing shrubberies. I followed the path around the side and came to a broad sweep of gravel, parked with cars. I knew that what I was about to do was almost certainly wrong: procedurally, socially, possibly even ethically wrong. But I didn't have time to follow the proper channels, and wouldn't have been able to explain myself if required to. I didn't mean any harm: I kept telling myself this as I climbed the broad stone steps, as I pressed the intercom. It might not be, strictly speaking, appropriate, but it certainly wasn't malicious. I didn't mean any harm.

The intercom crackled.

"Who is it?" A woman's voice.

I leaned in. "My name's Rachel," I said. "I'm a visitor."

There was a buzz and click; I pushed the heavy wooden door, and was through into the lobby. The room was panelled in dark wood; a flight of stairs curled up the wall; the carpet was old and thick and crimson. I just stood there, staring up at the smooth curve of the staircase; it set off an echo of something I couldn't place.

A vacuum cleaner kicked into life, making me turn. A long corridor opened off the lobby. At the far end, a young man in a green polo-shirt and jeans was swivelling a Dyson around, rearing it back on its wheels and flapping a length of cable out of the way. The corridor carpet was dusted with Shake 'n' Vac, as if there'd been a frost indoors. The place reeked of synthetic peach.

"Who are you here to see?"

It was the woman's voice again. I turned towards it. She leaned through the gap between a door and doorframe, revealing a wedge of nurse's uniform and a cluttered office beyond. She had a pleasant, young, worried face. The Dyson started to drone back and forth.

I smiled. "I'm here to see Margaret."

"Okay." Her intonation left the word open; she needed something more.

"Margaret Hutton? I'm Rachel; I'm from down in the village. I've been meaning to come for ages. You know how things are; always so much else to do."

She glanced back over her shoulder, towards the office; priorities were shifting; she was accepting this. She turned back to me, her expression easy.

"She's in the Day Room. She's in pretty good form today." The young woman gestured down the corridor, towards the cleaner, who was moving back and forth in that leisurely vacuuming dance. "You won't mind finding your own way, will you? I've got a mountain of paperwork to get through, and they're due their meds at ten."

I thanked her, headed up the corridor. The cleaner swept the Dyson back to let me past. I walked white Shake 'n' Vac footprints onto the clean carpet. I turned to look back, to mouth the word "Sorry" at him. He was just a lad, his skin blotched and sore-looking with acne. He shook his head at me, and grinned. His smile was catching: I found myself grinning back at him.

＊

The Day Room was full of armchairs; they were lined up along the walls, circled around coffee tables and spread in an arc in front of the television set. Nets covered the window so the light was filtered and dulled; the TV was on with the volume down low. The ladies occupied almost every chair. Their clothes and hair and skin were the same muted shades as the furnishings. One was sleeping, her head thrown back, her mouth open on dark wet tongue, pastel-pink plastic gums, white teeth. The others were all looking at me.

The room was warm, smelt of old milk, Shake 'n' Vac, and pear drops. The vacuum cleaner hummed in the background. The TV prattled brightly.

The women's collective gaze was mild, interrogative. No one spoke. I swallowed drily.

"I'm looking for Margaret Hutton," I said.

"Margaret."

"Oh, Margaret."

"Margaret Hutton."

Heads turned stiffly, eyes seeking other eyes, summoning consensus. At the back of the room, a bent head raised itself, fingers unlocked.

"Mrs. Hutton?" I asked. The woman nodded carefully. I threaded through the chairs towards her.

She was a tiny person, frail as wood ash. Age had bent her; she was hunched forward protectively around herself, her chest hollow underneath the patterned polyester of her dress. The other women resumed their conversations, their voices soft as crumbled cake. I sat down in the upright wood-framed armchair on Mrs. Hutton's left and the seat sank deeply on its springs.

"Is that you?" she asked.

Her skin hung in swags beneath her eyes and at her jaw, in shades of translucent purple and manila. I felt myself choke up. Stupid, that this would make me miss my mum; she never got to be this old.

"No," I said, and then didn't know what to say, how to frame the question.

Mrs. Hutton studied my face. Her eyes were smudged with age, the whites marked with yellow and fine webs of pink, the irises watery blue. She shook her head. "I thought you were her."

I felt my cheeks redden with guilt. She thought I was a friend or relative; a daughter-in-law, a granddaughter, a niece.

"No. Sorry."

Her attention slipped to my hand curled on my lap; the pink swell at the base of my thumb, the plaster stuck inadequately across the infected cut.

"Been in the wars," she said.

"A bit."

"You have to watch yourself," she said.

I smiled awkwardly. "A friend of yours sent me to see you. Your old neighbour from across the street. Mrs. Davies."

Mrs. Hutton's face cracked with pleasure. "Ah. Jean."

"Yes, Jean." I seized the name. "She sends her love."

"That's nice."

"She said I should ask you about the house."

"The house?"

"She said that you were the one to talk to."

Margaret looked at me a moment, nonplussed. She raised a hand, the knuckles swollen like tree roots. She gestured to the room, frowned deeply. "This place? The Home?"

"No, I mean your cottage. My mum and dad bought it. I'm—"

"No," she said, and frowned deeper still. "No."

"Sorry?"

"I told Jack."

"I'm sorry?"

"I told Jack, I said he mustn't." Her voice was raised in irritation. Other conversations fell away; attention was drawn to us.

I spoke low: "He mustn't what?"

She looked at me sidelong, appraisingly. She seemed extremely lucid, needle-sharp.

"I was sure you were her," she said.

"I'm not, honestly. We've never met. Your neighbour. Jean. She said that I should—"

"You look like her."

I felt a prickling at the nape of my neck. "Who do you mean?"

Mrs. Hutton's hand fixed itself around my wrist. Her touch was cold and dry.

"I got so cross with her," she said. "Getting me up at all hours. Those tricks of sunshine and voices. The kind of smells that get you right here." She tapped her concave chest with a thick fingernail; a shiver of electricity shot through my skin. "The smell of wet linen, and wood shavings, and woodsmoke, and liquorice.

There'd be someone talking downstairs, and I'd think Charlie was there, and I'd think the boys were home, and I'd think it was all back as it used to be, and I was young again, and if I could just find Charlie—"

Mrs. Hutton drew a ragged breath. Her eyes were brimming. She raised a loose-skinned finger to a lower lid.

"I couldn't bear it anymore."

She fumbled in a skirt pocket, raised a bunched tissue to blot at her eyes.

"I'm sorry," I said clumsily.

She shook her head. "Oh, I like it here, I like it here. It's a good place; it's good to have the company—it's just"—she squeezed my wrist, shook her head—"cruel," she said. As she looked at me, her expression softened; her face seemed somehow to slacken. She shook her head again, gently.

"I'm sorry," I said again, my voice thick, colluding with her tears.

"It's never that, he didn't mean—"

"He?"

She said something else; I couldn't make it out.

"Mrs. Hutton?"

She didn't seem to have heard me. Her eyes had clouded; she mumbled something about rain, and something that had to be brought, as if she were trying to convince herself, to set it straight in her own head.

"Are you okay?" I leaned closer. "Do you need anything? Shall I call someone?"

She shook her head, her eyelids sinking.

"Margaret?"

She didn't respond. I lifted her hand from mine and laid it in her lap. Her fingers, with their loose skin, their swollen knuckles, curled upwards like coral.

The boy was still swinging the vacuum cleaner back and forth. He smiled at me again, then saw my expression, and his smile collapsed.

"Where's the nurse?" I asked.

He gestured me on, towards the lobby.

The staircase. The sweep of it like a waterfall, like birdsong, and somehow annoyingly, intangibly, important. A figure crossed the landing above; white tunic, navy trousers: the nurse. She came padding down the stairs, her mind elsewhere, her hand skimming the smooth curve of the banister. She noticed me; her smile went. She clattered down the final steps to join me.

"Problem?"

"She's just—" I tried.

"Margaret?"

"She just. Went blank."

She glanced down the corridor, glanced back at me. "I'll check on her." She touched my arm, gave me a quick smile. "Don't worry. It happens. It's not your fault." She was gone, heading off down the corridor, breaking into a run. I turned, and left: I didn't believe her.

*

I crunched down the driveway. Dark yew trees lined the way; overhead the branches of deciduous trees were heavy with buds. Crocuses sprouted underneath; celandines dotted the grass.

You look like her.

I came out onto the road, turned towards the village. Hands stuffed into pockets, shoulders up, hand throbbing and hot between the press of my leg, the restriction of denim. Just a narrow grass verge and a wire fence between me and fields. Lambs stood in gangs. No cars passed. A rabbit had been smeared into pulp and fluff on the tarmac. A stray hubcap lay on the grass verge. The road swept down towards the village. Beech trees spread fine branches overhead. I was thinking of her wet blue eyes, smudged with age.

Those tricks of sunshine and voices.

There was a bench on the green. I sat down, looked at my hands. At the backs; at the tracery of veins, the fan of tendons beneath the skin. I thought of Cate's newborn rippling water-creature fingers, Mum's darkening claws on white hospital sheets, Margaret Hutton's tree-root swollen hands. The tricks of sunshine and voices. The tricks the mind plays on itself. The misfirings of synapses as the nerves fail, as the neurones decay. The vacancy that settles, clouding the eyes, softening the expression, making speech falter into meaninglessness. Is that what Cate saw? When I'd gone, did her clear eyes watch the blankness of my face? What would that do to her, to see her mother leave like that?

I wasn't having it. I wouldn't let it happen again. I couldn't let it happen to Cate.

*

I stood on Jean Davies' front step, sidelong to the door. Across the street, the windows of Reading Room Cottage looked at me blankly, catching no reflection.

She opened the door. She looked at me. I smiled for her.

"Jesus Christ," she said.

She wanted to give me tea and biscuits; cake, a sandwich, soup, anything at all. I thanked her and shook my head. As she spoke, I was conscious that I was scraping my middle fingernail rapidly back and forth across my thumbnail; I couldn't stop. I was conscious of the throb underneath the plaster in time with my pulse. I was conscious of the fragment of pain underneath my skull, where the hangover still lingered. I was conscious of time dripping away, that I should be doing seventy, my hands wrapped around the steering wheel, my right foot on the accelerator, my mind calculating niceties of speed, of movement in the cars in front and behind, their shifting relationship to my own frail metal box, its slight cargo of flesh. But I was standing in this almost-stranger's hallway, on the blood-and-blue lino squares, just beside the dresser, trying not to glance too often or urgently at the old burgundy Trimphone, the thumb-index address book. I spoke very carefully.

"That local history enthusiast. Could you remind me. What was her name?"

"Pauline, Pauline Boyd."

"I'd love to have a chat with her."

"I'll give you her number."

"Is there any chance you could call her for me? I seem to have lost my mobile."

She pressed a fingernail into the B section of her address book and lifted the receiver. She glanced over at me, smiling slightly. I could hear, through the receiver, the faint ring of the distant telephone. It stopped, answered. She dropped her gaze.

"Hello, Pauline, it's Jean."

*

Normal, I told myself. Be normal, normal, normal.

The house was modern. It was down the street towards the church, with its back oriented towards the street and its face turned towards a wide open view of the valley. I stood on the doormat. It was made of thin strips of metal, laid on edge. They bit through the soles of my Converse, into my feet. Just facts. Just ask for the facts. If she knew who lived there, and when, and anything at all about them. Surnames, first names, a family called Williams, anything. Even in my own mind I refused to use the word *haunted*. The glass was rippled; I could see into a dim parqueted hall; there was a rectangle of light where a doorway opened into a brighter room. I pressed the bell; and it rang a little way off, in the hall, and there was silence, and I waited. Normal. Normal, normal, normal. There was a flurry of denim and navy blue, broken into ripples by the glass panes. The door opened.

Miss Boyd was a small, sturdy woman in her sixties, dressed in jeans and an RSPB sweatshirt. She hustled me through to the living room and asked me to take a seat, offering me coffee, tea. She'd disappeared off to put the kettle on before I could refuse.

Patio windows looked out on smooth lawns, a willow. The room had a precise kind of dryness to it. Spare green furniture, an upright piano backed up against a wall; a music stand and two dark curvaceous violin boxes propped up in a corner. I'd have thought she was giving music lessons to the village children, if the village hadn't been singularly empty of children; empty of everyone but the elderly.

She was clattering about in the kitchen. I couldn't settle. I went over to her bookcase. Music, gardening, handicrafts, history. I recognized one of them; the local history book I'd bought. No use. Nothing specific. Except. Except. The photograph. *Last of the Lune Valley Basket-weavers.* The house had looked like Reading Room Cottage. And the name—Williams. The same family as was in the grave? I twitched the book off the shelf, was whisking through the pages. She bustled in with a tray, looked at me. I felt my cheeks flush up.

"You can borrow it if you like."

"Sorry." I put it back. I came over towards her, standing awkwardly as she put the tray down on the pristine teak coffee table.

"It's really good of you to see me at such short notice."

She wafted the idea away with a weather-tanned hand. "More than happy. Please, have a seat."

I sat down on the edge of the sofa. She collapsed into an ancient green Parker Knoll armchair, sighing in relief.

I leaned in to reach my coffee, took it in my left hand and sipped carefully at it. Everything was difficult: to smile, to drink, to hold anything steady, to make casual conversation. She was picking up sugar lumps and dropping them into her cup. She looked at me, smiled broadly and stirred her coffee.

"So," she asked.

"So." My voice creaked.

"What can I do for you?"

"It's the cottage, Reading Room Cottage; we're going to sell it, but I—" I cleared my throat. "We don't know anything about it, and I wanted to find out about the people who lived there. The family. I was wondering if you could help."

"Well, obviously there will have been lots of different families living there down the years. It was built as a labourers' cottage, part of the Storrs Estate; they were still renting it out till the late seventies, when the estate was split up and sold. A lot of this'll be on your deeds. The Huttons had it next: it was Jack's place when the kids were small, and then the parents—Margaret and Charlie—retired there when Jack took over the farm. And then there were your—" She hesitated, smiled cautiously. "Your parents. Is it a particular family you're interested in?"

She lifted her coffee, drank.

"No, no, it's just—" I felt myself grow hot. "I don't know anything, really, don't know how to go about it. I wanted an overview, a sense of who might have been living there. Just to start with."

"That's easy enough." Miss Boyd set down her cup. "Census records, parish records. That's what you'll need. Mind you, it'll just be the bare bones."

"Bare bones?"

Her expression was easy, open, suggested nothing out of the ordinary.

"Of their lives, I mean; all you'll get is their names, and their date of birth, marriage, death, and their occupation. If you're lucky."

"Right. Of course. And how do you do that?"

"You can get to a couple of the censuses online, but the parish records are held at the local record office at Preston. They house census records too, so you'd be best off heading down there. Get it done in a day. And you've got the archivists on hand if you run into difficulties."

She pushed herself out of the chair, crossed over to the sideboard, opened a drawer, took out a spiral-bound notepad and a steel biro, and the phone book. She flicked through, running her finger down the columns. She opened another drawer, lifted out a train timetable and studied it a moment. She spoke over her shoulder.

"You're better off taking the train," she said. "Parking's a nightmare."

There were precise creases across the backs of her knees. I picked a scrap of loose skin by a thumbnail. My cheeks still burned.

She brought the notepad over to me and I rose from the chair. Her fingers were swollen and distorted with rheumatism. I thought of the violins, their dark clipped-shut cases.

She said, "Direct train from Carnforth. The next one's half past twelve. If you hurry you might just make it. Funny, you asking about Reading Room Cottage."

"Why's that?" I asked; it came out too abruptly. She didn't seem to register.

"When I first came to the village, thirty odd years ago, I had this theory, that with the name surviving like that, the reading room itself must have been recent, that there would have been memories, oral history."

"And there wasn't?"

"Not a thing."

"Can you think," I said carefully, "why would that be? Why there would be no stories?"

She shook her head. "It must have been short-lived. That kind of thing was often set up in a spirit of self-help, to give people a wider education than the church offered. It was sometimes done by groups, sometimes by an individual with strong political motivation. But these institutions, they're relying on subscriptions from working people, so if wages take a slump, then people are faced with a stark choice . . . and if you're a political radical, and there's a crackdown . . . It makes you realize how vulnerable that kind of thing is, how those lives, working-class lives, they're just so—"

"Perishable," I said.

Her eyes were bright, hazel, acute. I was conscious that my own were dry and sore, my cheeks were burning and my hand throbbing hot. I was not managing to do normal, not remotely, not at all.

"And yet the name survives," I added.

"Indeed."

"So it must have mattered to someone."

She looked at me a moment too long. It was a moment of assessment. She ripped off the sheet of notepaper and handed it to me.

"I hope it works out for you," she said.

*

A spider had made its web between the window-seal and the wing-mirror. It was poised there like a hand on piano keys. I cupped it in my fingers and set it down on the garden wall, beside the tiny creeping thyme plant. It picked its way across the stone and slipped into a gap. I slid into the car.

It was as though I were moving through the pre-programmed environment of a computer game, shifting gear, depressing the clutch and accelerator in response to changing constellations of pixels. The road swooped me up the hill, and through the woods, past Storrs Hall, out into open fields. Solitary wind-twisted trees, and sheep clustering with lambs, and cows just standing as if in a trance, and then the farm, and a tractor lazily grinding across a field.

The road brought me down into the blustery, blackened little town. I coasted through and pulled to a halt in the station car park. There was no queue in the ticket office. Seconds later, ticket bought, I was loping down the ramp to the underpass, my stride stretched by the slope, passing beneath the silent railway lines before climbing back into daylight.

Above me, the ceiling was a glass-and-iron canopy. A clock, massive, weighty, was tethered with cables to the cast-iron ribs. Five minutes to wait till my train. I sat down on the edge of a bench. The light gleamed off the rails. There were railway lines in front of me and railway lines behind. A single tick; the minute hand clunked forward. I watched the clock's steady, authoritative care of minutes; seconds were left to shift for themselves. The railways had relied upon time. They'd whisked time from village to village, dragging it along in their slipstream like dandelion down or the fluff of old-man's-beard. Before railways, communication was confined to the speed of a galloping horse. To walking pace. The church clock stood alone, unchallengeable, eccentric as it liked. Ticking away the minutes, the hours and the days. It seemed just minutes ago that my daughter was this starfish thing, her eyes wide, wrenched from the wound, her arms and legs flung out, shocked by existence. Just moments before that, my mother's pulse was fading, her eyes moving under thin eyelids, dreaming morphine dreams.

The clock's hand jolted forward.

Suddenly, an express train punched through the space behind me. I turned to follow its rush. It thundered on and on, heading north, and was gone, dragging its pocket of dust and noise with it, leaving a tear in the day.

A couple climbed the slope from the underpass together. They stood, in matching anoraks, unusually close. The minute hand jumped again. A young woman came up out of the shadows, pushing a pushchair in which a toddler slept, his head flung back, his eyes squeezed tight, as if making a serious and well-considered wish. Cate: I could only see her in fragments; the luminescence of her cheek, a red bulge in a wet gum, a dimpled hand. The smell of her: milk and apple and ammonia and skin. The minute hand clicked. The woman pushed the sleeping child across the platform and stood in a square of sunlight. She took her mobile phone from her bag and cupped it in her palm, tapping buttons with a thumb. A hooped earring caught the light. Her head, bent to peer at the phone, was beautiful. The child slept on. I wanted to go over to them, to crouch at the pushchair's side and run the back of a finger over the child's cheek, just for the memory of how it felt, for the sheer wonder of the reality of a new being.

We were sitting at the traffic lights when I told Mark. I'd just picked him up from the station. He said, You're very quiet, and I said, I'm sorry, and he said, How's your mum, and I said, I'm pregnant. He laughed. A big, happy, laugh. I turned to look at him, pleased, almost puzzled, and he kissed me, his hand on my hand on the gear stick. Then a horn beeped behind us, and

I glanced ahead: the light was green, swimming with the dampness of my eyes. We drove home, the atmosphere odd. Mark kept
starting little streams of talk, to which I tried to contribute. He
was conscious of my quietness, conscious of the reasons for it, but
unable to quite contain his happiness.

The rumble of a train's approach. The tannoy crackled, an
announcement began and was overwhelmed by the judder and
clank of the train, the screech of its brakes. The pushchair was
swivelled towards the noise, the young woman's face serious
with calculation: deceleration, distance between doors, distance
across the platform to be covered. A slight adjustment between
the middle-aged couple; only one of them was travelling. The
woman kissed the man, the coloured panels of their jackets pressing briefly together and parting. The young woman dipped the
pushchair back onto its rear wheels, and I got up from the bench,
and walked over to the slowing train.

*

The train ripped past backyard washing-line views. The brief
grace of rivers and the slow panning shot of wide silver mudflats
and the sea. At times, a canal flanked the railway; a barge moved
at retirement's leisurely pace. It was such ordinary beauty; I
should not have been there to see it. I should have been on the
M6, past Birmingham by now.

How long before Mark started to wonder? He'd have tried the
mobile and been unsuccessful; he'd think I had the phone on silent
while I was driving.

The carriage was half-empty. The anorak woman was sitting across the aisle from me, reading a soft fat paperback, its

cover folded back upon itself. Her jacket was off and bundled onto the luggage rack. Outside, the flat spread of a valley floor, and then moors rising ink-blue to the clouds, sunlight shafting down through cloud gaps to patch the turf with yellow. Then mills; red-brick, monumental, their windows reflecting back the sky. We came into the station. The light was dim. People stood on the platform, some scanning windows for a familiar face, others turning to move towards the carriage doors. I got up.

The wind blew sharp outside the station. Crisp packets and swirling paper coffee cups and fag ends in the gutter. Taxis lined up patiently, their engines burbling fumes out into the air. I was dazed by the travel, by the strangeness of being elsewhere, of being somewhere entirely unforeseen, like when the car broke down on the motorway and Lucy and Mum and me sat on the fence at the top of the embankment among the long grass and teasels, and watched Dad on the hard shoulder, bent into the hot engine, his glasses steaming, unable to wait for the tow truck to arrive.

I have to imagine her moment of knowing, years later, at the mirrored wardrobe door, her jumper and bra on the bed, her arm crooked back over her head, pressing with two fingers at a hard bead of flesh in the side of her breast. I wonder at the timing: whether her sickness had been slowly accumulating for years, a gradual accretion of mutation, or if it were quicker than that, if the cluster of madly splitting cells was the fault of some strange sympathy, as in the dark of my uterus, a faint speck of meticulously dividing cells drifted, settled and dug in, putting down its roots, beginning to grow. The thought always comes tainted with guilt: it was her death, after all, and unknowable as someone else's love, and here I am like a typical child, trying to make it be about me.

There was grit in the air, and the smell of petrol. I made my way through traffic cones and under scaffolding, across a patch of sad municipal grass. I had the instructions in my hand; the breeze caught the paper and ruffled it, pulling at the loose shreds along the top, where it had been torn from the spiral. I rounded a corner and there it was: a concrete cube held aloft by concrete pillars, sealed off and insulated from the grit and clatter of the town. A glass-walled stairwell dipped to touch the grey-slabbed ground below: the Public Record Office. I went up to the glass doors and pushed through, climbing the stairs into the concrete box.

The archivist murmured instructions. I followed her, half a pace behind, past rows of desks where figures hunched over books or leaned in close to illuminated screens. At the end of the room stood a wooden card-file cabinet and beside it, a table. Ring-binders were laid out in rows, each with a label giving the census date. The assistant told me that parishes were listed alphabetically in the folders, and assigned a number. All I had to do was find this same number in the filing cabinet: it would be typed onto an envelope and the census records for the parish, reproduced on microfiche, would be inside. The Parish Records themselves; the baptisms, marriages, burials—she gestured over to the side of the room—were catalogued in much the same way over there. They rarely brought out the actual documents nowadays, she said; it saved on wear and tear. You must only take one at a time, she warned me, and shrugged in a self-deprecating way, tucking her loose blonde hair behind an ear. Otherwise, all hell breaks loose.

"So, what's first?" she asked.

"I'm trying to find out about the occupants of a particular house." I could feel my cheeks begin to flush. I gave her the name of the village. "This would be, I imagine, around the middle of the nineteenth century."

"What diocese?"

"I have no idea. Sorry, is that important?"

She shook her head, already flipping through the file: "It's all right."

She ran a finger across a page, then turned to the cabinet, lifted out an envelope. She held it out to me.

"Is that it?"

"Census records for 1851. Slap bang in the middle of the century." She gestured for me to take it. My hand shook. My arm ached, all the way up to the shoulder, from the cut. "Have you used a microfiche-reader before?"

I shook my head.

She gestured me over to a nearby desk, on which stood one of the screens I'd seen other people using. She leaned over me; I caught her perfume, something fine and sweet and faintly woody. She showed me how the microfiche-reader worked. It was proportioned like an old TV, but simpler, lighter, and more elegant. She shook the envelope and a transparency fell out. About the size of a postcard, it was printed with rows of smaller black rectangles, like miniature X-rays. She slipped it between two sheets of glass, like a microscope slide, at the base of the device. She flicked a switch, a light went on underneath the slide, and the images were projected onto the screen in front of me. I watched her hands, the neat clear-painted nails, the diamond solitaire on her ring finger; I couldn't bring myself to look at the records with her there. She demonstrated how the slide could move in any direction on a plane, bringing different records into view. She showed how a lens could be adjusted to sharpen the focus of the image.

"Got it?"

"Yep. I think so." I smiled up at her. Her skin was creamy, soft and clear. I felt grubby, grey and really tired.

"Any problems, I'll be over at the enquiries desk, okay?"

"Okay. Thank you for your help."

I watched her go. The neat shape of her pencil skirt, the neat hem of her cardigan. A grey-haired gentleman straightened up and turned to catch her eye. She stopped, studied the records he was viewing, and they dropped into muted conversation.

I slipped the slide around in its orbit, murky images rearing up onto the screen. I focused the lens with a twist. It still didn't seem quite real.

The handwriting was fine and regular and careful. The first record for the village was that outlying farm beyond Storrs. The name of the house was not given; it was just listed as number one. Living there was the patriarch (farmer, fifty-five, widowed); a son (farmer, thirty-six, married), daughter-in-law (thirty-five); a grandson (farm worker, fifteen), and a granddaughter (scholar, eleven). I wondered if the official had been brought in and given tea. I wondered if the girl was doing well at school. If they were, more or less, happy.

I shifted the slide across, counting out the house numbers,

noting landmarks: Storrs Hall, Public House, School House. I shunted the slide on: for a moment the screen was just swirling white space, dust-motes the size of cherry-blossom petals, trapped fibres big as millipedes. I glanced down to the mechanism and lined up a dark rectangle beneath the lens. Then I looked back up, at the screen.

It was number 14.

In 1851, the head of the household, the individual who accounted for all the occupants of the house was a man called Thomas Williams; the man whose name appeared on that grave. He lived there with his wife, Elizabeth, whose name had crumbled half away beneath the moss. They lived in that house. To read it here made my throat constrict with unaccountable tears. She was twenty-seven at the time of this census. And then I saw it.

Their son, James. Eight years old. A scholar.

I hadn't considered the possibility of him.

*

Outwardly, it all seemed so normal, so everyday. Afternoon light streamed in through the window, making the hanging strips of the blinds glow and casting a wedge of brightness across the top of the wooden Parish Records cabinet. It seemed to me that there was something wonderful about this human conspiracy of order, that everything should be catalogued and housed and copied and filed, just to serve the possibility of future significance, the idea that this might matter, at some time, to someone.

There was just one envelope: the best part of a hundred years of baptisms, marriages and deaths all recorded on one slip of film.

The parish must have been so small, the population so scant. I drew the transparency out of the envelope and tried to slide it into place between the sheets of glass, but my hands were clumsy, and it juddered and crumpled. I took a breath, straightened it, smoothed it and tried again. It slotted into place.

An image reared up onto the screen; a copy of the Parish Register cover. Flaking leather, heavy gothic type, and a crest of a lion and a unicorn. I pushed the slide away, careening through decades of blessed release, better places gone to, patters of tiny feet and doesn't she look beautifuls, to get to the end of the century. The records were in negative. The dark grey pages were traced across in white ink, like the writing in an old photograph album. It was difficult to read. I hunched forward, squinting to pick out the names, the dates.

Burial
1881   John Ireby   Febry 5th   Jn.º Tatham
         aged   Vicar
         71 yrs

I shunted the slide sideways, the records flicking past.

Burial
1887   Catharine Barns   Febry 6th   Jn.º Tatham
         Infant   Vicar

Deaths clustered at the beginning of the year, as if there were a season for death, as there is for making hay, or buying swimwear. Infants, children, women, men. I shifted the slide again, down a row. A trapped hair slipped across the viewing screen, monstrous, wormlike. And there she was.

Burial

1897	*Elizabeth Williams*	*September 14th*	*Jn.º Tatham*
	Aged 73		*Vicar*

She was seventy-three. She was buried in September, out of season. Her coffin—if she'd have had a coffin—her shrouded body, wrapped in a wedding sheet perhaps, was let down into the Williams family grave. She was laid on top of her husband's bones. The sextons filled in the earth, and someone chipped her name into the remaining clear inches of stone. No space for dates. No space for anything more than the defining phrase, *his wife*. And for the first time I wondered was there more to that phrase than met the eye; was there a hint of defiance to it, an undertone of assertion? Was it her son who had insisted it be carved? Her husband was dead, after all, and couldn't comment.

The son. Conceived when she was nineteen. I flicked back, looking for his birth. The neat accounting for the souls received, united, dispatched. The Reverend Jonathan Tatham's careful double-entry bookkeeping for God. I found myself warming to the man; the unassuming abbreviation of his name, the smooth looping quality of his handwriting.

There was a season for babies too. James Robert Williams was christened in the summer of 1843, between a Stephen Goss, plump son of George and Mary Goss, farmers, and a Dorothy Anne Hollings, bastard daughter of Anne Hollings, domestic, pinkly bawling as the water washes her ill-begotten soul.

June 23rd   *James Robert*   *son of Thomas Williams*
                                      & Elizabeth Williams

There it was, in black and white, though the words were white and the background black, like text on a computer screen, highlighted before deleting.

I was in that moment's stillness before gravity bites. I was looking at the boy's name, the boy who grew up, and died, and was buried somewhere other than the family grave, and was long rotted away to bones. Whose own grandchildren will have been of an age to be ploughed into the mud at Ypres or picked apart by fishes in the Dardanelles. Far worse than the burials, the baptismal records: the freight of heartbreak they carried; the inevitable grief of living. Then I noticed the handwriting; that it was different. It was not so neat, it scrawled and scratched; the signature was practically illegible. Initials R. and G., possibly W. Not Reverend Jonathan Tatham anymore. The clergyman before him.

A baby suspended over the font, water dripped over his head, the muttering of benedictions. A young woman standing in the background, weak, pale, fierce. The vicar's blue-shaven wattles shaking with the words: *In the name of the Father, the Son, and the Holy Ghost. Amen.*

A baby born in June.

I scrabbled at the microfiche in its slide, my hands clumsy with haste. June June June June June. If he was christened late June 1843, he must have been conceived . . .

There was no wedding recorded in September between Thomas Williams and Elizabeth. The year scrolled back through harvest-time and hay and dog roses in the hedgerows, back through May blossom and cherry blossom and bluebells, back through daffodils and snowdrops and wind-chased clouds, and there was no wedding between Thomas Williams and Elizabeth. I shifted the slide again, scrolling back through that same summer again, through other weddings and babies and unseasonable deaths, and the days shortened, and the leaves began to turn, and they fell, and there was frost in the mornings, and my hands were shaking. They married in December.

December the 12th, 1842. Elizabeth was nineteen, must have been two, nearly three months pregnant, and must have known that she was, since there was no blood when there should have been, and there was sickness and fatigue. She would have seen these signs in other women, and have known what they meant.

Elizabeth Parke,
her mark

The X was large, out of proportion, displayed the cautious awkwardness of someone unused to a pen. It shocked me more than anything else. More like a denial than an assertion, it seemed to make a kind of sense.

*

I passed the counter on the way out. The same girl, sweet creamy skin, who looked up to give me a concentrated and concerned look that made me almost love her.

"I—" I tried.

She lifted a box of tissues from underneath the counter, but I shook my head.

"I just wanted to know—" I cleared my throat. "I found this thing. A young woman, mid-nineteenth century, she marked a cross by her name rather than signed. I thought that there was basic education, pretty much, by then. Sunday schools and stuff."

The assistant nodded sympathetically. "It wouldn't have made her illiterate, necessarily. Some church schools, they'd teach the kids to read, but not to write. People often learned to write in later life."

"I don't understand."

The grey-haired man had come up to the counter. He was leaning in to catch her eye, smiling impatiently. Her attention flickered to him, back to me.

"They needed to read, for the scriptures. Writing; that's a different matter. Teach people to write, and before you know it, people are asking questions, constructing arguments, communicating with each other over distances. It wouldn't do."

*

I don't quite know how I got back. I bought a coffee somewhere, drank it on the train, chewed through a scone as dry as lagging, watched the fields and roads unscroll, the houses flick by. At the station, I got into the car and followed the ribboning tarmac back to the village, to pull in in front of the cottage, switch off the lights and the ignition, and slump forward onto the steering wheel, and rest my head on my arms, as if it were just momentum that had kept me moving, had kept me upright all this time.

I closed my eyes.

I'd got what I had gone for, but I hadn't reckoned on how bare the bones would be. A marriage, a birth, a death. This wasn't a life. It was nothing like it. Life's what happens in between. The tease of a flame at a dry twig. Snowflakes melting in upturned palms. The drip of chlorinated water from soaked curls, lips unsticking in a smile, outstretched arms with fingers crooked to coax a child into swimming. The dip of the tongue's tip to the palm of the hand to lift a sweet blue pill from a skin-crease. These tiny things that change the world, minute by minute, and forever. These perishable moments, that are gone completely, if we don't take the trouble of their telling.

WE WALKED OUT, THOMAS AND ME. DOWN TO THE WATER'S edge where he skipped stones and sent silk-ripples across the surface of the water. I sat on the bank and watched, and saw the swallows skim up and down the stretch of water, catching flies, and I wondered if they got their blue sheen from the flies they caught, all the little shiny insects that dart about the surface of the water, and how duck eggs are that fine pale blue, and mallards have the shot-silk heads, and the females flashes of blue amongst their wing-feathers, and how blue seems infused through all these things, all these manifestations, and I opened my mouth to say something, but didn't, because it was Thomas. He sent a good throw out across the river, and watched it curl across the water all the way to the far bank, then turned to me, brushing his hands together, his face flushed with satisfaction.

"Are you going to that meeting?" I asked him.

"What meeting?"

"The one at Caton Moor."

His expression flickered. "How did you hear about it?"

"Something Dad said."

"I might go," he said.

We walked up the coffin lane towards the village; the rabbits were out in the low field, nibbling at the grass. We walked in such complete silence that the rabbits didn't notice us, and continued to feed and lope about. It was getting dark, and the air had a nip in it.

"Did you know," Thomas said out of nowhere, "that paper is made out of rags, and in cities men go about the streets, calling for old rags, and they are shredded and soaked and boiled and dried and pressed and turned into paper, and that in some places they can't get sufficient rags and so are now making paper out of wood, turning whole trees, whole trees imagine, into paper."

I looked at him. I'd never thought about it. "Did Mr. Moore tell you that?"

Thomas shook his head, and was trying not to smile. "No, I read it for myself in the *Penny Journal*."

We walked back up the path to the church, the white gravel crunching underfoot. At the church side-gate, he took me by the hand, and stopped me, and turned me to him, and he grasped my arms, pinning them to my sides, and I didn't really think that he would do it, but he kissed me.

His lips were soft and fat and damp. He stopped, and moved

away from me, still holding me by the arms. I couldn't look at him; he sighed, and put his arms around me, drawing me close to him.

"Ah, Lizzy," he said.

I pulled away and ran from him. He caught up with me, and kept talking all the way, more than I'd ever heard him say in one go before: what had he done wrong, if I was going to the Harvest Dance with him, and walking out with him, then I should expect to be kissed, I should expect to be held, and if I didn't like it then I shouldn't go out walking with him.

We'd reached the house. I wanted to tell him if I had the choice I wouldn't, but that would only lengthen the dispute, so I just said goodnight then ran up the front steps, and in through the door, slamming it behind me, scrabbling at my bonnet strings.

*

Mr. Moore had left a book there for me on the shelf. Plum-coloured leather, fresh as a new glove. It was a collection of plays that a gentleman had translated from another language, from the Greek. The Greeks were heathens, I knew; the Reverend had some books in Greek in his library, filled back to front with a strange, impenetrable script. Now, coming upon the stories in plain English, clear enough for even me to read, I could see why the Reverend preferred to keep them locked up in those mysterious symbols. These were bloody tales, the people passionate and unwavering and cruel. I might have thought them unfit for a girl like me to read, if I had paused to consider the matter, and not rushed headlong into them. And if my thoughts had not begun to shift and alter, and become other than they had been.

*

The Thursday evening, Hornby Market-day, Thomas came to our house with red cheeks and the smell of river from the walk home. He was carrying a parcel tied up in brown paper. He'd made good money on his baskets, he told my mam; he said our dad should take ours to Hornby too; there'd been a lack of them further down the valley, with the building work at Storrs taking up so many. I was sitting at the window, with another of Mr. Moore's books in my lap. *The Odyssey*, it was called; Odysseus's men had been turned to swine; I didn't want to leave the story, but I was worried by the sight of the soft parcel crushed in Thomas's thick fingers. Had he formed no impression, had he taken no hint from the other evening? He was already right in front of me, and was laying his slight burden down on top of my open book. It was light and soft inside its wrapping. I glanced up at Thomas; he seemed at once gleeful and buttoned-down, like a child who knows he has been especially good, but must continue to be good, if he's to get his treat.

"I brought you a present," he said.

Mam bent eagerly to see what I'd been given.

"Go on, Lizzy."

I knew what it was, and I knew what it was for. I picked at the knot and loosened the paper. The fabric was pretty. It was tea-dyed cotton, sprigged, with matching ribbons and braiding and thread.

He said, "You're to make yourself a new dress for the dance."

The cotton smelt of the warehouse and of camphor-wood and spice. My face felt numb and cold. My mam was saying what a good boy he was, bringing me such a beautiful present, and that I'd need to ask Mrs. Wolfenden for a pattern to copy, and I would look lovely in something like the high-waister with the bell-shaped sleeves that Mrs. Wolfenden had worn last spring, and all the time I sat there, frozen, looking down at the beautiful rich colour, the wonderful soft folds of the fresh new fabric, hearing my mam's voice as if through a blanket, and I wanted to fling the parcel away from me, the fabric, ribbons, braid and thread flying out like a fountain of spilled tea, and push past them and get out of the house and just run. Mam was chattering on about Mrs. Wolfenden's old dresses and her generosity with patterns and such, and Thomas was nodding and agreeing as if familiar with the subject. My mouth was dry; I had to lick my lips before I could speak.

"There's no need for this." I said. "My Sunday dress will do quite well enough for the dance."

"Nonsense," Mam said. "What are you thinking? With this beautiful bit of cloth Thomas has so kindly got for you—"

She fingered a fold, and lifted a corner so that the bundle tumbled undone, and she lifted the fabric up to the light, so that tiny squares of sunlight shone through it, and it glowed. She and Thomas exchanged a glance, a little smile, and I was conscious of a fierce and sudden flush across my face and through my whole body. They were not conspirators, I remember thinking; the need for conspiracy was over. They were victors.

*

I didn't ask Mrs. Wolfenden; not for weeks. I couldn't. Not the way things were at the vicarage. Every day when I got home after polishing the hall floor twice, or being scolded for invisible dust, or having fresh linen returned to me for re-laundering, my mam would look me over, seeking out the neat little parcel of patterns that she daily expected, and seeing nothing, would frown and start to scold. I was leaving myself scant time to get the work done, all the pinning and cutting and sewing. I'd end up having to go in my Sunday dress after all, and what would Thomas think of that. Perhaps he'd take the hint, I wanted to say, but instead I'd begin some half-hearted excuse; that just when I was going to ask, Mrs. Wolfenden had gone out on a morning call; my work had kept me from the house and out of the family's company; the lady had been out of sorts and it hadn't seemed right to trouble her; I'd speak to her tomorrow.

"If I were your age, and in your position," Mam said, "I'd have asked her pretty smartish. I'd have the dress nearly finished by now. I'd have thought of little else."

It was September already. There was only one meeting that month, when the moon was full, since it was too dark otherwise for people to find their way home afterwards without ending in a ditch. It was a noisy meeting: voices were raised behind the closed door, and three of the men left before it was ended. Mr. Gorst didn't come, though his eldest boy did; and there were others who had often come before but didn't now. There were newcomers too; Methodists and other non-conformists, people we never met from one season's end to another, walking in miles from the hill-farms and the hamlets above Docker, walking back by moonlight. They arrived with furrowed brows and left in huddles, muttering.

There was a book waiting for me, every evening, squeezed between the *Progress* and the Bible on the dresser shelf. Some books were left for several days, giving me time to become so deeply engrossed in them that I moved in a haze, a dream of them. Some books were there overnight, and disappeared like mist in the daytime, while I was at work. I'd go to the shelf when I got home, and there would be an unknown book waiting. It became almost a joke: Mr. Moore would sit, cool as the September day, and he'd glance up at me with his brown eyes, his gaze level and uncharged, as if he were innocent of everything, and I would take the book, and return his gaze coolly, and sit down to read. All the unfinished stories: they wrapped themselves around me like vapours, trailed after me like mist.

*

"Not much more than a week now," Mam said, jolting me out of my reading. "Till the dance. Sall's coming home for her holiday, and can help with the trimming of the dress, if it's ready for trimming." She was folding linen, her face lined with vexation and bother. "Have you even spoken to Mrs. Wolfenden?"

"It's not easy," I said, my eyes pulled back down to the book.

"It's perfectly easy. You just ask her. You're a good girl. You deserve a treat once in a while."

"It's not my place. Alice is her maid. I'm just a housemaid; it'd be too much of a presumption. I'll do fine in my Sunday dress."

"If you don't ask her tomorrow," Mam said, "I'll march down there and ask her myself."

*

The ewer was warm and heavy in my hands. I walked carefully with it, conscious of each step of the stairs, looking at the pretty flower pattern and the shiny glaze; I tapped on the door, pushed quietly through and put the ewer down on the washstand. Mrs.

Wolfenden sat up from her pillows, all creamy cotton and frills, her hair in braids, and blinked around her.

I spoke softly. "Madam?"

She was startled to see me, and tried to conceal it. "I expected Alice." She held to the sheets as if she were resisting the urge to pull them up over her head and hide, as if I were a penny-dreadful villain come to ravish her, as if I were the big bad wolf. That she could be so nervous of me made me nervous too.

"I was given some cloth, madam," I said, clumsy and reluctant. "To make a dress, but there isn't a pattern to be had that's not been twice around the parish already, and we thought that I might ask you, since you would have something newer, and less seen, that would suit the fabric well." She eyed me uneasily. "Not anything *new*," I added; "last year's, perhaps, or whatever you have that you wouldn't mind me using."

Her voice was dry with nerves. "What cloth have you got?"

"Tea-dyed," I said.

Her eyebrows rose. "Really?"

"Yes, ma'am." The fabric was clearly too fashionable, too much of her world, to be thought appropriate for someone like me.

"Of course, yes." She seemed to shake herself. "I have something that would do you well."

She slipped out of bed, her feet soft in cotton bedsocks. She went over to the far side of her bed, to her workbox. She came back with three fat envelopes, each illustrated with a drawing of an elegant young woman in fashionable dress.

"They are cut to my size," she said, and looked me over as if noticing for the first time that I had a shape, a figure, dimensions. "But then we are not so different after all."

272 · *Jo Baker*

I watched the uneasy flicker of her eyes as she shuffled the parcels around in her hands. She selected one, and offered it to me. "Take this one. It will just suit the fabric, and your figure."

I took hold of the nearest edge of the envelope. She did not let go. I glanced at her face, but her eyes were downcast.

"You'll remember I was good to you?" she said.

"Madam?"

She glanced up. Her cheeks were pale. "Whatever happens, you'll remember I was good to you?"

"Yes," I said, puzzled. "Of course."

She let go of the package. I fumbled it, then clutched it to my chest.

"The Reverend has told me," Mrs. Wolfenden said, "he has told me he will protect me, but, Lizzy, I do not see how I can be protected, or anyone at all can be protected, not while men like Mr. Moore move freely in the world."

I was caught between sympathy and laughter. We were as harvest mice in a corner of a field, I thought, wearing a summer's worth of tracks through the wheat and thinking it a whole world, an eternity. She was afraid. She was afraid of change. I understood that; change is frightening.

*

Mam helped me with laying out the pattern on the kitchen table; Sally arrived as we were pinning the paper to the cloth. My heart skipped to see her; I went to hug her, but she was busy with taking off her smart bonnet, so I helped her off with it, and she took it from me and glanced about for somewhere to lay it. She set it on the dresser, and teased at the feather trim to smooth it, and when she was satisfied with that, she took off her gloves and cloak, and came to kiss us both; and the kiss was not a kiss but the light brush of her cheek against mine. I put my arms around her, but she backed off, cautioning me against crushing her poplin, and I found myself standing there, slightly shy, and not knowing what to say, and glancing to Mam, to see if she were faring any better. She stood back, glowing with admiration at her handsome daughter.

"Don't you look fine, my love? Don't you look fine!"

Sally brushed down her skirts, said "Thank you." She nodded to the cloth and pattern on the table. "Who's that for?"

"Our Lizzy."

A flicker of surprise crossed Sally's countenance. "I thought you were taking in sewing. Mrs. Millard had a tea-dyed dress this summer."

Mam exclaimed warmly at this, then asked, "Who's Mrs. Millard?"

Sally took up a fold of cloth and rubbed it between her finger and thumb, pouting. My cheeks burned. She glanced up at me.

"You can borrow my second set of stays, if you need them."

"Is your box left up at the public house?" Mam asked. "Shall I send the lads for it?"

Sally shook her head. "The Forsters had their man collect my valise. Mrs. Forster has been kind enough to ask me to stay with her."

The glow sank from Mam's face. She smiled, said, "Oh."

"Well, I can hardly sleep on the floor here, can I?"

Sally took herself over to the fireside chairs, arranged her skirts carefully and sat down. "I am parched for a cup of tea."

Mam rushed to set the kettle on. I returned to the work. My mam had had a notion that if we could squeeze the pattern into small enough a space, she could make herself a new bonnet-liner out of the remainder. I unpinned the front panel of the bodice, teased it down a little less than a hand-span, slid the yoke in and stabbed it into place with a pin.

Mam was asking Sally about the milliner's shop as she made the tea, and about Mrs. Millard who was, it turned out, one of the better sort of customers. Sally told Mam about her extraordinary progress, how she had been given silk to work with, how she had feathers such as you wouldn't dream, that came off great big birds from half a world away, and cost more than the silk; and weight for weight cost more, almost certainly, than gold. I took up the scissors and snipped into the cloth. She got up, and smoothed herself down again, and came over to watch me, distractingly. I glanced up at her.

"You're going wrong there," she said.

I looked back down. I had. I retreated with the scissors, then set them down. "Only a snip."

"So, you and Thomas are finally courting."

"We're not courting." There was a faint darkness under her eyes, I noticed, as if she were fatigued, or somehow troubled, but her manner gave nothing away.

"He's been pining after you long enough," she said.

"We are *not* courting."

"What do you think this is, then?" She nodded at the fabric. The pattern was laid and pinned out, and I had already begun to cut the cloth that he had given me. There was, after all, no disputing what she said.

*

The Reverend leaned on the pulpit's edge, his hands gripped around the rim, his knuckles white. He was speaking, his voice level, setting out the argument of his sermon as if he were laying paving stones. I was watching the whiteness of his knuckles, the way the veins stood out on the back of his hands.

I sat between Thomas and my mam. My dad was sat on the far side of her, at the end of the tight-packed pew. All the free-seats were full, the air heavy with the press of warm bodies, the smell of clothes, goose fat and lavender water and bad teeth; a whiff of drink here and there, including off my dad. Michaelmas daisies and marigolds were brilliant on the windowsills; their faint scent was the scent of funerals and did little to sweeten the air. I kept my eyes on the pulpit.

The Reverend's surplice was spotless as the Lamb; spotless as all the linen that we laundered for him. It hung in folds, as if carved out of wood and whitewashed. I watched as his face filled with blood; noticed that his voice was getting shrill, and there was spittle at the corner of his mouth. The words were coming from his lips like ash-flakes lifting from the fire. It was as though I didn't so much hear them, as watch them rise.

> To presume too much, seeking to rise above the station allotted, tempted by Satan to presumption, it is folly, folly, folly of the most abject kind, to look to the things of this life, and so lose the Life to come.

I could hear Thomas breathing, too close. I felt my mam's shoulder press against my own, too close. I could smell the breakfast egg on her breath.

The wise man seeks rather an inheritance incorruptible, undefiled, that fadeth not away. A Crown of Glory, Life Everlasting, garments that shine like the sun. The Righteous Man will heed the word of God, and not the word of Man, or the word of the Devil from man's lips. The Righteous Man knows that to do otherwise is to fall into sin and folly; he knows that there is no wisdom greater than that of the Pure Heart and the Innocent Mind, that there is no worldly consolation for the troubled soul.

I could see the back of Sally's head, the bare nape of her neck underneath her fancy feathered bonnet. She was sitting between Mr. and Mrs. Forster in their pew. And as Reverend Wolfenden said *A Crown of Glory* she reached up, and touched the curl that had escaped on the nape of her neck, and I loved her for it. Dad said something. I didn't quite hear it; he spoke under his breath, and was at the far end of the pew. I saw Mam shushing him; he shook his head, and fell silent.

For the Lord has ordered our estate, and set every man in his situation, from the highest in the land, to the most wretched pauper at his door—

Dad rose from his seat, making me gasp, sending off rustles of movement across the church as people turned to stare. He was standing now, one hand clutching the back of the pew in front, the other clenched in a fist at his side.

"Damn fine luck for some," he said.

Silence filled the whole of the chancel; it was as if the nave, from flags to roof-beams, had been turned into one solid block of ice. Mam scrabbled at his arm, but he pushed her hand away. He stepped out into the aisle, and I lunged across Mam, trying to grab his coat-tails.

"Dad," I said, "please, Dad, don't—" But it was too late, I couldn't catch hold of him, and I doubt it would have done much good if I had.

"Isaiah," he said, far too loud, his voice ringing around the chancel roof like the Reverend's. "The prophet Isaiah. He said you were damned if you took more land than you needed to feed yourself and your family, that you were damned if you added property to property and left nowhere for ordinary men to live. Isaiah said that was devilry, and you'd be damned for it. What would be your thoughts on that, Reverend? On Isaiah's teachings?"

The silence was melting, people began to mutter. Dad raised his voice over the noise.

"And then there's the rulers who make unrighteous decrees and turn aside the needy from justice, and take away the rights from the poor; they were damned too, according to Isaiah. There was a time we had rights. A bit of land to farm. Cattle and fowl on the common. Hogs in the woods. Them rights were taken away, and property was added to property."

"Shut up," someone said, low and urgent.

"God's sake man, sit down," someone else called out. "We'll be here all day."

Dad was moving up the aisle towards the pulpit. His words rang out through all the church, strange and heavy-sounding.

"You're very ready to tell us how it's all God's will, that this is

God's will, and that is God's will, but what I really want to know is if it really is God's will, his own Holy Decree, that you eat meat every day, that you have a house big enough to be home to a hundred men, that your wife wears those pretty frocks of hers, all those silks and satins and what have you. And if it is," he said, "I want to know how you got to be such a great favourite with Our Lord, and what I ever did to annoy him, so that I have to get by on a crust and a paring, and what the poor souls must have done so that He'd arrange a wage-cut just to watch them starve. Maybe you could share the secret of it, Reverend? Maybe you could tell us how you managed to persuade the Lord that you deserve better than the rest of us?"

My father's voice had grown, was strong and harsh and demanding. The Reverend opened his mouth. There was a moment's pause; he gathered breath. His face was greyish-white. A line of spittle joined his upper lip with the lower one.

My dad said, "And while we're at it, d'y'happen to know the Lord's opinion on the fashions, Mrs. Wolfenden? Is He fond of lace?"

Mrs. Wolfenden shrank in her pew.

"See, I only want to know what the Lord is up to, I can only ask them as'd know, them He's set above us to govern and guide us ignorant folk. If I'm assured my tithes are being spent as He would have it, if He's keen on you getting your satin and sirloin and coals, if He's all for luxury and sloth for some and famine and drudgery for others, then good for you, I say. Good for you. Well done. You must be very holy folks indeed."

My father moved up to the chancel step, and stepped up onto it, and then he turned to the congregation.

"Time we did summat, don't y'think?"

Looking at him standing there, scruffy even in his Sunday best, his face shining with a passion that I had not seen before, I felt the whole frail structure of my happiness crack and splinter; the mist of half-read stories burn and shrink away. This was the end; I knew it was the end. This was exactly what the Reverend had been anticipating. Dad would be locked up; Mr. Moore would have to leave. He would take his books and go.

The Reverend's expression had narrowed. "Mr. Aitken," he said, "would you be so kind as to support my wife, and see her safely home?"

Mr. Aitken stood up and left his pew, and went to the vicarage pew, and offered Mrs. Wolfenden his arm, and she reached up and took it, and it looked as if she were being hoisted out of a hole, and Mrs. Aitken joined them both, and took her husband's other arm, and he supported them down the aisle and out of the church, and Mrs. Wolfenden's plump and pretty face looked pale as death; I thought she might be about to faint, and part of me thought I should go after her, assist her, but I knew my attentions would not be welcome. I watched as Mr. Forster stood and gave his wife his arm, and offered Sally the other, and, crushed close together, they made their way down the aisle. Sally passed us, and kept her eyes fixed on the floor, but I could see that she was blushing like a beet, and there was, I thought, a hint of satisfaction in her face, to find herself treated as a lady, as something fragile and prone to harm.

Dad swayed on the chancel step. His face was blurring with the drink. Beside him and above, up in the pulpit, the Reverend still stood, like a schoolmaster, waiting.

"Sit down, man," someone called out. "Sit down. You'll ruin everything."

"They's nothing but a parcel of leeches, they suck us dry; they took the land that had been ours by right since God gave it to Adam, they took it from us, and they lie to us about what it means, they lie and say God wills it, and who are we to know better?"

Mr. Aitken and Mr. Forster came in, and stood just inside the church door. To be back so soon, they must have left all the ladies at the vicarage; it was the nearest suitable dwelling.

"We must join together, we must arm ourselves!" my father cried. "We must take back the land."

No one moved. The church was filled with a strange tension, as if this were somehow familiar to some of those assembled there. Thomas's eyes were narrowed on my father; he half shook his head. The movement seemed involuntary.

"What is this? What is he playing at?" I whispered at him. "Do you know anything about it?"

He glanced at me, and when he replied, his voice was low, distinct and careful, and it did not sound like him.

"Your father is a drunkard and a fool."

I sat back. I looked at Thomas differently.

"Ya bunch of worthless layabouts," Dad spat. "Spineless bastards."

"Idiot," someone muttered.

"Sit down, Frank."

Someone coughed. My mam was slumped and shrunken beside me, her hand to her forehead, shielding her eyes.

Mr. Wolfenden spoke: it seemed as if it were for the first time in an age. "Jack Gorst, Joe Stott, bring this man to the Old Hall, and have him locked in the strongroom there."

Someone coughed again, self-consciously. Nobody shifted. My father staggered off the chancel step, cursed, and came back down the aisle.

"Anyone, any man, you are on your honour," the Reverend asserted, his face pinkening.

No one stirred. Not a finger was lifted.

"On our honour be damned," Joe Stott said.

The impact of the words made Reverend Wolfenden flinch. When he spoke again, his tone was different, colder.

"The man is clearly intoxicated. He is threatening violence, and has terrified the ladies. Any honest man. Stand up."

No one moved. Someone mumbled something; it sounded very like *do it yourseln*. There was anxious laughter, quickly stifled. Dad was making his way down the aisle still; he passed us without acknowledgement. I twisted around to follow his progress to the back of the church, where Mr. Aitken and Mr. Forster still stood guarding the door. He came to a halt there, facing them, drawn up as tall as he could manage, which wasn't particularly tall. No one spoke. Everyone in the church must have heard as he gathered the rheum in his throat, as he hoiked the phlegm from his chest, as he spat it onto the floor at the two men's feet. The silence was terrible. My dad grabbed the handle, swung the door open, and was gone before the men could act. The door slammed shut behind him; the noise echoed through the church.

"I'm sure you know yourselves who is on the cleaning rota for this week. Would you be so good, gentlemen," the Reverend addressed Mr. Aitken and Mr. Forster, "would you be so kind as to summon Mr. Moore?"

They left. The door clanged hollow behind them. Its echo faded, and the silence afterwards seemed threatening. It seemed to throb with my blood. I was very conscious how close Thomas and my mam were to me; I could not let them see that this affected me.

The Reverend stood in the pulpit. He did not speak. His expression was closed and cool. After a while, he shifted on his feet. Someone in the congregation muttered something behind me and to the left; someone gave a reply, and there was a low, restrained laugh. Someone else spoke, and then there was another voice, and soon the congregation was boiling with conversation. I could hear the two men behind me; I didn't turn to look but I knew from earlier that it was George Horsfall and Matthew Williams, Thomas's cousin. George was saying that Frank could never be trusted, the big meeting was only next Sunday, could he not have waited another week? Just another week and then they would have begun to see things done. Frank always had been a fool when he had drink in him, Matthew replied, but then fools sometimes did wise things; all the meetings in the world would have changed nothing. And all the while the Reverend Wolfenden stood there, gripping the railing of the pulpit, his knuckles getting whiter and whiter, and his face becoming more and more flushed, and then his face cracked into pained lines, and he opened his mouth, and he roared:

"Silence!"

A hush fell at once. There was an uneasy shuffling of feet and adjusting of clothes and prayer books. Then the door creaked open. I kept staring straight ahead. There was the sound of three pairs of leather soles on the stone floor; my breath caught in my throat. Mr. Aitken and Mr. Forster stopped at the bottom of the aisle, and I felt Mr. Moore walk up the aisle, and pass me, and then I could see him, the dark shape of his head, his dark jacket worn thin at the cuff and elbow. He was in his everyday clothes; he didn't acknowledge Sunday's distinction in dress. He halted just ahead of me, at some distance from the pulpit; he did not have to crane his head back to meet the Reverend's eye. I watched between the backs of the people in the pews in front. I could see one of Mr. Moore's hands as it clenched into a fist, the knuckles livid, then uncurled. I heard him take a slow thin breath. I wished I could go to him and stand at his side, let him see that he did not stand alone. I loved him. The world expanded in a moment; it seemed vast. I loved him.

"I bring you here today," said Reverend Wolfenden, "to reveal what kind of a man you are, so that you may no longer deceive these good and simple people."

Mr. Moore's voice came out dusty-sounding, as if it had lain long unused. "You didn't bring me. I brought myself."

"Admit you are a Chartist, and an Atheist."

"I have never made a secret of either."

"Admit that you are a criminal; that you have been transported."

His hand clenched again, the dark fingers pressing tight, nails pushing into the flesh of his palm, the white scar stretching livid. "I served my sentence."

"But clearly learned nothing from the experience."

"My wife and child died while I was in Hobart Town."

He stood alone in the centre of the aisle, as if he were part of church ritual, as if this had been going to happen, as if this always happened, like the Eucharist or Benediction. All the time that he had lived with us, every moment that I had known him, when he had laughed at me, when he'd shared his beer with me, when he'd left or retrieved a book; all the time that wound, that loss, had been bleeding in his side. It made me ache for him. It made me reconsider everything that had passed between us.

A man's voice called out from the congregation, "What did you do, then, lad?"

Mr. Moore turned to him. "I injured a policeman."

Matthew Williams called out from behind me, "Why did you do it?"

Mr. Moore turned to answer him. His eyes caught on mine and I smiled; a slight attempt to reassure him, but the smile trembled, and threatened tears. I looked down, at my rough hands still gripping the black prayer book.

"See," said Reverend Wolfenden, "a wolf in sheep's clothing! A violent criminal in our midst, taken into your homes, you see how—"

But no one was listening to him anymore. Mr. Moore was addressing Matthew Williams.

"It was a peaceful meeting," Mr. Moore said. "They had no right to break it up. The police said that they shot over the people's heads, but a girl was wounded in the ankle, and I don't see how you can shoot over people's heads and still wound someone in the ankle, unless you're such a criminally bad shot that you have no business to go armed." He took a breath, and the breath shook, and I realized he was not nearly as calm as he appeared. "She is a cripple now," he said. "She walks with sticks."

"This man," the Reverend said, "this *man*—"

My gaze shifted back to him, to the pulpit. I felt faintly surprised to see that he was still there.

"This man," Mr. Moore said, turning back towards the Reverend, "is just a man, and not a devil. I've committed no deception here, and certainly no crime. I've done nothing but offer my books and my opinions; no one is obliged to accept either; I do not evangelize. I happen to believe that intellect is not commensurate with wealth: that the poor may read, and learn, and think, as well as the finest gentleman in the country, if they're given the opportunity, and that's all I seek to do, to give that opportunity. These are peaceful ends, pursued by peaceful means, and still no crime, even in this day and age. Men of my class have their fill of duties, and precious little in the way of rights; but I believe we still possess the right to be left alone." His voice had grown tired. He said, "I simply wish to be left in peace."

The Reverend's lips moved soundlessly. Then he swept his right arm grandly in front of him, taking in the whole of the congregation. "Cast him from you; cast him from your homes. This man is a criminal."

"He's paid more than amply for it, by the sound of things," said Joe Stott.

"Take him to the Old Hall," the Reverend urged. "Lock him up."

No one moved.

Someone cleared their throat: "I've never really understood; what is an Atheist?"

Someone else tried to silence the speaker, but other voices

broke out again all over, addressing questions to each other, answering them, calling out to Mr. Moore. I heard someone else talking about the Charter, saying that they would sign it soon as look at it. Reverend Wolfenden stood bolt upright in the pulpit, his white surplice like a marble column. Mr. Moore stood in the aisle, addressed from all sides, having his sleeve plucked and more questions thrown at him before he could answer the earlier ones. All sense of ritual was shattered. The Reverend made his way down the pulpit steps, through the chancel, and out through the vestry door. Mr. Aitken and Mr. Forster slipped away through the main door. I don't think anyone else noticed them go. I knew that this could not be forgiven, this could never be got over. The whole church was in commotion. People were talking at the top of their voices, elbowing, pushing to get past each other to get to Mr. Moore. He stood trying to answer someone, trying to lay out an argument, while all around was bedlam. He finished speaking, his questioner nodded, satisfied. The noise did not abate, but for just a moment there was stillness around him; for just a moment everyone was engaged with someone else. He turned his head and looked at me. I managed to form a smile. He gave me only an abrupt upward movement of the head, not quite a nod, as if in agreement, or understanding, but of what, I didn't know, and my expression began to falter, and I saw his change again; a questioning, concerned frown. Then someone laid a hand on his shoulder, dragging his attention away. The aisle swarmed with people heading for the door; he was carried by the swell.

*

The crowd thinned and clumped in the street. The men went ahead and the women followed after. The children fled, glad for their parents' distraction and the opportunity for play; as we trudged up the dusty street their shouts and laughter rang out from the fields. I didn't know where we were going: I don't think anybody really did. We were just leaving church, and following whoever went before. Up ahead, I saw my father leaning against the wall in front of the Old Hall. He was half slumped, scuffing the gravel, making a trough with his toe. His head went up as the first group approached; he pushed away from the wall and moved out into the street, attaching himself to Mr. Moore. He received only the slightest of acknowledgements. A nod from Mr. Moore and a word from one or two of the men. My dad muttered something back.

I looked around for my mam. She was just behind me, her face pale and lined and somehow fallen-looking. I offered her my arm, but she shook her head.

"As if things weren't hard enough every day without this," she protested. "What has he done? What has he gone and done?"

I saw the same look on every woman's face. They had fed these men, and washed their clothes, and mopped up their crumbs and slops of tea; they'd borne their children, they'd nursed their colds, they'd sat yawning across the fire from them night after night, and year upon year, and never once in all that time had one of them done anything that could have presaged this. Church was broken up, and Sunday was all out of kilter, and there was no knowing what would follow next.

"What's got into your Frank?" Aunty Sue demanded. Mam just shook her head, her face pinched with shame. I peered ahead, trying to catch sight of Mr. Moore's tall dark shape between the moving bodies.

"He's over that side," Mam said. My cheeks flushed and I glanced at her, and then at where she was looking, and I realized that she meant my dad.

We passed over Brunt Hill and came down the slope towards home. The men were stopping there, gathering at the foot of our steps, as if of one accord, as if it were the obvious and natural thing to do. My Mam stiffened at my side; we slowed, and stopped a little way off from the crowd, a little way up the hill.

"Oh Lord," she said. "Oh Lord, preserve us."

"Let's have him then," a voice called.

"Aye, let's hear from Moore; proper-like."

Mr. Moore moved through to the front. He climbed the steps; his expression was resolved, but he was pale. I offered Mam my arm again, and this time she took it. She was glancing around her, scanning the faces of the women. She turned to me and whispered, "Where's our Sally?"

"She went with the Forsters, remember?"

Mam nodded at this, her chin dimpling as she pressed her lips together.

"For the best," she said. "She'll be all right."

Mr. Moore spoke. His voice was faint from where we stood.

"Haste is the hallmark of the shoddy workman; everyone knows that. To overcome that impatience is the first lesson of a youth's apprenticeship. This wood will not work unseasoned; it will crack and splinter. When it is ready, it will be stronger than iron, but we must give it time. We must be patient."

There was silence for a moment, then a blackbird sang in the horse chestnut tree.

"We should each of us go to our homes," Mr. Moore said. "We *must* each of us go to our homes, and weather out this storm, and hope that it passes over without harm, perhaps leaving us even a little better seasoned for the work."

He came down the steps; a hand was placed on his arm; he was instantly folded into the debate.

Some men were already trailing away and women were skittering off to catch up with their husbands. A crowd remained on the street, locked in argument. Mrs. Bibby approached her husband, put her hand on his arm, and was shrugged off. Her failure was conspicuous. Women started to drift home alone. Men remained.

We couldn't get indoors without passing through the crowd. My father was among them, his arms raised in angry gestures. Mr. Moore was talking to him in low, placatory tones. My mam and I pressed through the throng, my mam's face as pale as china clay.

Inside, she fell into a chair. I bustled about to make her tea; she sat there mute as a fish. The quietness in the house made me feel sick and empty. The commotion in the street was awful. Mr. Moore came in a little later. There was still noise outside. His skin was grey, his face haggard-looking. He took the teacup I offered him.

"Thank you, Elizabeth," he said, and sank down in my father's chair, and drank the tea, and did not speak.

My brothers did not come home, nor did my father. There was no talk of a meal. Work was not even picked up. Books stood unread on the shelf. The street fell silent as it grew late, and dark.

At about nine o'clock, Mam got up and fetched a batch-cake from the pantry and cut lumps off it, and told me to get the kettle on again.

She addressed Mr. Moore with more than usual carefulness. She blamed him, it was clear to me she did.

"What will come of it?" she asked.

Mr. Moore glanced first at me, then at her. "Let us hope that nothing comes of it at all."

Mam looked at him narrowly. "Hope isn't good enough."

Mr. Moore nodded. "I agree."

The boys tumbled over the threshold around quarter-to-ten: they were flushed and happy, smelling of outdoors and woodsmoke: they must have had a bonfire, as if it were a holiday. They were hardly in the room before Mam started scolding. They dived onto the remainder of the batch-cake, broke it in half and started stuffing it into their mouths; Mam went for her wooden spoon. They hammered up the stairs, giggling and choking and spraying crumbs, and she went after them. There was laughter and shouting from up there, and then talk, and then silence; she can't have beaten them. When I went up later, she was lying between them on their bed, their fair heads resting close to hers, and they were sleeping, all three of them, cuddled together, stuck with cake crumbs, worn out by the strangeness of the day.

So I was left alone with Mr. Moore. He was sat by the dimly glowing hearth, still as a monument, his face turned from me. No one had thought to light a candle or to tend the fire. I was leaning against the kitchen table, chewing on a thumbnail, not looking at anything, feeling sick and hungry and impatient, as if there were, somehow, something I could do, could I but think what.

"I am so sorry, Elizabeth."

My name again on his lips; I took my hand from my mouth, looked around at him; in the dim light I could not make his expression out.

"It's not your fault," I said.

"If I hadn't . . . your father . . ."

"He's been spoiling for a fight for years."

I think I caught the ghost of a smile, but it didn't linger.

"They will read the Riot Act," he said. "If this doesn't resolve itself swiftly, they will read the Riot Act and they will send for troops. There's a company of Militia at Skipton; they'll ask for a detachment to be sent."

"For my dad?"

"Maybe."

"For you?"

He inclined his head.

"But you've done nothing." I was indignant, and then flushed with shame: I hadn't been able to feel indignant on Dad's behalf.

"The state of the country," Mr. Moore said. "A tiny percentage of the population owns the vast majority of the country's wealth. That suits them, but at the same time it's terrifying; they are so outnumbered and have so much to lose. The idea that we might act in concert is appalling, that we might work towards something grander and more permanent than the filling of our bellies—they will crush this; they are too terrified to do otherwise."

He raised a hand to his eyes, pressing them with his fingertips; the white line of the scar down his thumb moved with the movement of sinew and muscle.

"I should have had more sense," he said. "I should have seen where this was tending."

"No."

I came over to the fireplace and sat down opposite him. He didn't speak. Half his face was lit from the embers, the other half in shadow. He looked worn and tired. He looked unloved.

"That scar," I asked. "How did you do it?"

He shook his head, not understanding.

"On your thumb; that white scar running the length of your thumb."

He glanced down at it. "I've had it since I was a lad. I did it with a chisel; I was holding it wrong. My master let me find out for myself."

"That's cruel. To do that to a boy. How were you to know?"

"He didn't have to tell me twice."

We both looked at his scarred hand. It was a moment before I could raise my eyes to meet his.

"You said there would be troops. What will happen to you if—"

He shook his head. "The other side of the world. Tasmania. It's beautiful, but it's hard. The winters are cold; people get sick, and I'm not a young man anymore."

"But you said so yourself, to Wolfenden, you haven't committed any crime."

"You'd be surprised how circumstances can conspire against you, how things can be construed. This place was quiet as the grave till I arrived. If someone gets hurt, someone gets killed, then—with my reputation—"

I had to say it. The words were freighted with misery, but they had to be said. "You must leave now. Before anything can happen, before there is any charge to lay against you. You must get away from here."

He looked at me. "I've been telling myself that all day, telling myself that for weeks. It's suicide to stay here, in this house, your father's house, of all places." He shrugged. "Yet here I am."

I could feel my face warming as I spoke, but it didn't matter in the near darkness: "Your wife, having supported you through everything, would she have wanted—"

He gave an abrupt laugh. "If there is a heaven, and Jane is there, she'll be splitting her sides laughing at me now."

"No," I said. "No, I don't believe that."

"I wouldn't blame her. I'm not an easy man—I was not a good father."

"You—" I said. "I am sure you—"

He interrupted me again. "They died, Elizabeth. They died in misery and squalor. Had I been there to look after them—"

"But you were *transported*."

His eyes fixed on mine; they caught the fire's glow, and glittered. "And for what? That poor girl still walks with a limp; my wife and child are dead; that policeman is probably all the keener to strike the first blow. I am a very stupid man, and the older I get the more stupid I become; it took far too long for me to—"

The door crashed open and my father tumbled in, his cap pushed back and his shirt-tail hanging out, his face blank with drink. He started to say something, but the words were slurred. He staggered. Mr. Moore stood up to help him, and was brushed off. He tried again, taking my father under the arms and speaking mildly. He helped him upstairs to bed, a slow dragging shuffle, way-marked with outbursts from my dad. Afterwards, I heard

Mr. Moore's careful tread through to his room. He did not come down again. I went up and checked on my mother and the boys, and listened for a moment outside his door. He'd left a light burning; there was no sound from within, so I hoped he'd managed to lose himself in reading, or in his writing, in something that would give him peace and satisfaction. I went back down, and made my bed, and tried to sleep, but my mind would not be calmed; it raced through everything, revisiting every moment from his arrival back in Lent to the meeting of our eyes across the church this morning. I flinched at the recollection of scolding him about religion when his faith had had so many challenges, and mine had had almost none. I'd asked him about his travels, when he had been *transported*. I remembered the way he'd looked at me under the oak that day, when I had left him to go to Thomas simply because it was easier than staying and risking being seen. He should wear a sign, I thought; a paper pinned to his lapel, listing his wounds, the damage done, the raw places that must not be touched. It was the only way to give fair warning. I wished I had been kinder to him.

Evening. The light dim in the Reading Room. The give of the mattress and quilt beneath my weight. The dry smell of dust and the quiet of the street beyond. Eyes unfocused, head bent, I was aware of blurred floorboards, the peripheral pulse of blood. I was looking at nothing, concentrating on nothing. I had this feeling that what happened here was like a puzzle-picture, meaningless dots until someone lost focus, stopped looking directly, and the image swam into clarity.

Perhaps it took me being there to make this happen. To catalyze the air into a fizz, to elicit shapes from the shadows. The house didn't have a reputation. Mum and Dad had noticed nothing odd. In all their excited talk about the place, there wasn't a shade, not even a moment of unease. There had been no mention of the air's electric charge, voices, unaccountable scents. And Margaret; she'd lived a life here; it was only when things began to spiral apart into dementia that she started to notice the scents of wet linen, wood shavings, liquorice. So *us* being here made this happen. Me and Margaret. Each of us with our own particular condition. Our blank spaces. Our lapses.

I lifted my head, mentally addressed the empty room: does our absence somehow allow you to be present? Do you slip into the gap we leave when we depart?

My ears strained for sound. There was no noise from outside: not a bird, not a sheep, not distant traffic. Indoors, the faintest suggestion of a hum, which might just have been the sea-shell sound of the inner ear.

Charlie died, and Margaret went looking for him in her nightdress. Mum died, and I saw her in the bookshop. I saw her in Cate's concentrating frown. I saw my hands becoming her hands. I caught myself laughing with her laugh.

My vision clicked sharp on the bookcase, a knot in the back panel. The room was still, its breath held. The bookcase stood tall and dark; the knot stared back at me.

Loss. It had stopped both of us in our tracks. The world continued, the clock ticked on; snowdrops broke the soil, daffodil blooms burst from their paper-casing and shivered in the wind; roses budded, unfurled, and dropped their petals to the ground. But we were caught in the moment before change, unable to move forward with the clock's tick; still waiting, still expecting a return.

The hum built; I could feel it gathering in the air.

This room. The name of the cottage. The bookcase. Is that

what happened here? Is she caught in that moment, in this place, in that year, still waiting, still expecting someone to come back?

"Who was it, Elizabeth?" I asked out loud. "Who did you lose?"

I got up from the bed and crossed over to the bookcase. I rested my hand on an empty shelf. The electricity prickled my arms, made the faint hair on the nape of my neck stand on end. I could have sworn that she was there, just out of sight, just beyond the edge of my vision. I didn't look.

"I lost my mum," I said. "She was fifty-seven." My voice sounded strange and dusty in the silent, attentive room. I hadn't expected to speak.

"They never had much money, but when her mum died they sold her little house in Clapham and had enough to buy this place. They were here a couple of times, but they didn't live here, they never got the chance."

My nose was prickling. I rubbed at it with the back of a hand.

"She found out that she had cancer. I found out that I was pregnant just after she got the news. For a while, after the first operation, we were hopeful, and I was going to tell her about the baby, but then they found secondaries. She had to have chemotherapy. Medicine so strong it makes you ill. We both got thin: I had morning sickness. We both had scans. On hers, there were these grey-white beads; they looked like a broken string of pearls. On mine, we'd seen tiny bones glowing translucent grey, a skull like an eggshell. I could see her on the screen, flipping around like a caught fish, though I couldn't feel anything inside me yet. And I didn't tell her."

Instinctively, my hand descended to my belly and rested on the scar. My throat and palate ached with the threat of tears.

298 · *Jo Baker*

"The nurse gave her wristbands, tight grey cuffs with plastic beads sewn onto the inside: they pressed between the bones of her wrists, and wore red marks there; they looked like stigmata. They were supposed to help with the nausea. I asked her if they did any good, and she said, I kind of hope not; if they're working I can't imagine how shit I'd be feeling without them."

My vision swam with the wetness of my eyes. And still the words kept coming, hard lumps of words, retching out of me, hurting.

"She got so thin: she didn't want anything; the flesh just fell off her, her hair came away in clumps. Her skin went grey; you could count the bones in her hands. She faded. And I got better. I bloomed, like you're supposed to. It felt obscene. There was never going to be a good time to tell her. There was never going to be an all-clear. She was back at home. She was resting on the bed, propped up with pillows, a blanket over her legs. We'd been talking for a while, and I was too nervous really to remember what was said, until I said, I have something to show you, and I took out the print-out and held it out to her, and the paper was trembling in my hand. Her hand looked so mechanical, you could see every shift and movement of the tendons—"

The words seemed somehow to slice through into the dark; it was an agony to speak them. They grasped hold of my grief, wrenched it out into the air. It was raw, skinless, bloody; it didn't want to be born; it had tried so hard not to be.

"It was ages while she looked at it. The whites of her eyes were yellow. Then she asked, When are you due? I told her, End of January. I watched her register the fact that I was halfway gone, and had left it till then to tell her, and there was a flicker of something. I couldn't quite see what it was. Anger, or frustration, or resentment, I don't know. I don't know that it was directed at me, but I could have been sick there and then, I really could. She laid the picture down, her lips peeled back from her gums; she smiled at me."

There was a faint tickling sensation on my cheek. I pressed a hand to it; my fingers came away wet.

"Sweetheart, she said. Sweetheart. She lifted up her thin arms for me to hug her. I laid myself against her gently, afraid of my own weight. I pressed my face half into the pillow, half into her throat and hair. I was afraid. I wanted to be forgiven. She smelt sour. She stroked my back. Then, after a moment, she said, Is this okay for the baby? And I asked, What? and she said, All the chemicals in me. I nodded and sat down, and she held my hand— hers was so cold—and she smiled at me again, and started to talk about the baby, and I joined in, but all the time I knew that part of her was sealed up, was somehow contained in her disease, and that she just could not be reached.

"And I've been stuck too. Stuck in that year, when she was dying and I was pregnant, and if things could have been different—I—"

Outside, in the street, a car drew up; the engine cut off, the door slammed. I pressed my eyes then glanced around the room; whatever had been there, if anything had been there, was now gone. I rushed over to the window, glanced out.

Mark.

*

"You're here."

"Yes." He came up the front steps to me.

"Where's Cate?"

"She's with my mum." He stopped short, a step down. His voice was tight. "You didn't come, Rache. You didn't come. I waited, and I waited, and you didn't come. I rang you. A million times. I checked with the AA in case there'd been a motorway pile-up. I drove five hours and didn't even know if you'd be here."

"I'm sorry."

"You said you were coming back. You said you would get help."

He stepped up, and I moved back into the house. He took my arm and looked at me closely. His eyes were tired, his skin soft with fatigue. I wiped my free hand across my face, wondered what he could see there. I'd rinsed my skin quickly with cold water, taken deep shaky breaths to calm myself, but my face still felt sore and exposed. I willed him not to notice.

Because it all seemed different now. The air was softly thrumming, my head was swimming; everything seemed charged, every molecule of the place vibrating on a new frequency. I was thinking of the records reproduced on microfiche like tiny X-rays, the microfiche stuffed into envelopes and crowded into card-files. I was thinking what mine and Mark's would come to show eventually, if someone encountered them in a hundred years; how it wouldn't add up to anything like our lives. How we could have decades or a week or minutes left, but one day it would all be over, and irretrievable, all those moments unrecorded and gone forever. And I knew there was just this. Just the moment, the fragile, vulnerable moment.

I put my arms around him. I remember lifting my face to kiss him, and the way his face softened into tenderness. The feel of his cropped hair. Eyes closed on the darkness of tongue, and lip, and coursing blood.

He broke away. "I missed you."

"I'm sorry."

"I missed you. Jesus, Rache; I've missed you."

The smell of him: coffee, *Eau Par Kenzo*, mint. The taking of hands and the climbing of the stairs, each tread marking a deepening conspiracy between us. The smile that he caught from me, and offered me back. The peeling off of clothes. Skin, and the press of his mouth on mine. I remember my stomach muscles contracting, my breath caught. The warm silk of his skin. It could have been before; before all of it, before Mum and before Cate, when there was just us. And now, for a moment, there was nothing else but us.

Afterwards, I lay looking up through the uncurtained window, at the sky as it darkened to deep night, as the stars pricked out. I felt grateful for this. He lay next to me, his hand on my belly, just above the scar, his head on my arm. He slept. I watched him sleep. He was so beautiful.

*

In the morning I dressed without waking him, made coffee and brought it up to him. I put the tray on the floor and sat down on the edge of the bed. I skimmed my hand over his hair, kissed his cheek with dry lips. He stirred; I reached down and lifted his coffee cup. He leaned up on an elbow. The covers rumpled. He looked gorgeously soft with sleep. He took the cup, rubbed his face and smiled at me.

"Thanks," he said.

I got back into bed fully clothed. We drank coffee. The distant sounds of livestock, birds.

"Odd," he said, "waking up without a radio."

"I like the quiet."

He was quiet for a moment, as if listening. "So," he said after a while, "what's the plan?"

"You go back today," I said carefully. "I'll follow soon as I'm done."

"But—" He sat up, slopped coffee over his hand and onto the sheets. "Shit. Shit."

I reached to take the cup from him, but he moved away, set it down on the windowsill.

"You need to run that under the tap. It'll hurt." I reached for his hand. He pulled it away.

"I thought you were coming with me. I thought, last night—"

I heard the certainty in my own voice. "Soon as I get this sorted out."

"What about Cate? Jesus, Rache, what about your daughter? Don't you think you've left her long enough?"

My voice edged itself with guilt. "It won't take much longer."

"She needs you."

"She doesn't need me doped up on tranks."

"Do you think I want that?"

I considered this for half a second too long: he narrowed his eyes at me.

"Sometimes I think you just want me to be okay," I said.

"*Just?*"

"I mean—"

"If that's what you think—"

He swung his legs out of bed and grabbed his T-shirt off the floor. He pulled it on, the fabric tensing drum-tight as he pushed his arms through, softening to ripples as he tugged it down over his belly.

"I mean, it's not something that can just be fixed," I said. "There's no magic pill that'll make it all better."

"I know," he said. He sat there, half-covered, half-naked, and rubbed a hand over his hair. He shook his head, and his speech came falteringly, as if he didn't know what he thought, and was waiting for the words to tell him.

"Sometimes I just feel that you're disappearing," he said. "That you're making yourself fainter and fainter and more and more distant and then one day you'll just be—gone."

I took his arm. He shook me off, reached down and grabbed his boxers off the floor.

*

Standing at the bookcase, I listened to the car pull away. Underneath jeans and jumper, my body was still conscious of his, still tender from the night before. The coffee in his cup gave off a faint curl of steam. I felt the air soften and settle around me. For the last two years my mind had turned in a loop: if only, if only, if only. If only the scar would melt away, if only the beads would fade to pinpricks and dissolve, if only her breath would come easier, her pulse steady, the morphine surge back into the syringe, her eyes flicker and open, and she'd be back with me, and we'd move from there down a different track, towards recovery and health and years of each other's company, decades of loving and being loved. But the clock ticks on. There is just now, and that's all that anyone could ever hope to have.

"I am sorry, you know," I said. "I'm so sorry for your loss."

I held myself quite still, listening, my nerves alert. But there was nothing. The air was soft and cool; the room was empty, and gave nothing back.

I WENT TO WORK; I DIDN'T KNOW WHAT ELSE TO DO; IT was what I always did. The village was stirring. Women were mending fires: smoke drifted from chimney pots, curtains were drawn back. The world had been turned upside down on Sunday, and it seemed that no one knew what to do about it, but to carry on as if the sky were still clear above our heads, and the ground still firm under our feet. That there could be troops sent for, or the Riot Act read, or that a man might challenge the vicar in mid-sermon and spit on the church floor; none of it seemed to belong to the same world as this morning, when Agnes's mam was shaking last night's crumbs from the tablecloth out of the front door, and chaffinches and sparrows hopped and fluttered after them.

The vicarage windows were dark and blank. I crunched up the gravel driveway, and in through the servants' door, and I felt my skin tighten at the chill.

I had died for them on Sunday, and now I was a ghost. Mrs. Briggs was elbow-deep in a goose and didn't even look up. Maggie's gaze skimmed over me, and didn't settle, and she left the kitchen without seeming to notice me. I went about my usual tasks. When I lit the bedroom fire the Reverend and his wife were still sleeping: when I came back with the water he was gone, the blankets lying neat and flat where he had lain. I set the ewer down on the washstand. Mrs. Wolfenden slept prettily, her breathing gentle; I was thinking about how she'd said the Reverend would protect her. Then he bustled back into the room from his dressing-room door, still in his nightshirt and dressing gown, looking as if he'd forgotten something. He started when he saw me.

"What—" he said, and then he faltered and looked away. He went over to his side of the bed, and picked up a book from the bedside cabinet, then he returned to his dressing room, the skirts of his dressing gown rustling.

*

I was chopping onions. My eyes stung with the vapours, but I was happy to be at the task. After all that had been asked of me lately, it seemed beautifully simple to be chopping onions. I was so reluctant to be done with them that I'd reduced them to almost a paste when the bell rang. I was wanted in the morning room. Mrs. Briggs's plump face was pink and she didn't meet my eye. She stripped leaves from rhubarb stems, sliced the stems briskly into quarter-lengths. "Go on then, girl," she said. I think she knew what was coming; I think she might have been feeling sorry for me.

Mrs. Wolfenden was sitting in her chair. I clasped my hands behind my back, could smell the onions even then. Alice was nearby, perched on an upright chair at a sewing table, an abundance of soft brown merino heaped in front of her. An autumn dress for Mrs. Wolfenden; the fabric was beautiful, but I wasn't sure that it would suit her light colouring. Mrs. Wolfenden herself was at some smaller work; a piece of crisp white linen in her hands; she was trimming it with white silk ribbon. She barely raised her eyes from this work when I came in; just a flicker of a glance, though her cheeks and throat flushed red. When I came to stand in front of her, she spoke without looking up, and it was in a kind of breathless rush, as if she had it all committed to memory, and must not pause for risk of losing the pattern, of finding herself interrupted. She said that they had hardly thought to see me there that day, after the disturbances on Sunday.

"It was my father, madam, not me, who caused the furore."

Her cheeks pinkened deeper; I could see the choice of word had piqued her.

"Well," she said, and looked up, delivering her reasons in a list, "it's nonetheless clear that you cannot be trusted, that you have become unreliable, and are clearly not the kind of girl that we could possibly keep on staff, not coming from a family like that; the Reverend Wolfenden expressed his doubts to me some time ago, but I had suggested generosity, and restraint, and watchfulness, and how have I been rewarded?"

"Perfectly adequately," I said. "You have nothing to complain of. I've done my work, and done it well, even though it has suited you often enough to pretend otherwise."

She shook her head. "The Reverend said to expect insolence. I am sorry that things have come to such a pass, but we will have to let you go."

She set her sewing down and lifted a clutch of coins from a nearby table: my pay. I looked at it a moment. It would have been a great satisfaction to tell her to put it in the poor box, but prudence got the better of me. I held out my hand; she slid the coins into it, not letting our hands touch. Her hand was tugged back as if by a jerked cord and rested on her belly; and then I noticed. The cut of her dress did much to disguise it, but there was the unmistakable swelling, the filling out of breasts, and when I looked again into her face I saw the glowing plumpness of the lineaments, the softness of the jaw. She saw me notice, and blushed deeper still. I jangled the coins in my hand. I smiled at her. I padded out of the room in my felt slippers. Things were about as bad as I could imagine them, but nothing in the world would have persuaded me to exchange my place for hers.

*

I took off my slippers and put on my clogs. I left my cap and apron there. Going out through the scullery door, into daylight and onto the doorstep, I was surprised to find that my heart was lightened at the loss of my place, even though I had no notion of what I would do to find another one. I'd never have to wear those felt slippers again; I'd never have to curtsey again, not unless I chose to. I stepped down onto the gravel path just as someone came briskly around the corner; we nearly collided. Thomas; he blushed right to his ears.

"I was just delivering—"

I nodded and began to turn away. I didn't have the goodwill in me at that moment to hear another story of his success, his accumulating profits.

He followed me, skipping a step to keep up.

"What's up, where are you off to?"

"Nowhere."

"What do you mean nowhere? It's the middle of the day."

"I've been dismissed."

He grabbed my arm, and stopped me, and turned me to him, and I just looked at him blankly. He put his arm around my shoulder, and tried to pull me close, but I pushed him away.

"Times will be hard," he said.

"I know."

I turned again, heading for the vicarage gate, and he followed me, the sound of our paired feet noisy in the morning quiet. We passed Mr. Fowler, who was raking the gravel. He looked at us askance.

"If you need help, I can help," Thomas was saying. "Give you work, whatever you want."

"Yes," I said. "Thank you."

I clutched the coins tightly, the metal edges pressing into my palm. As we strode down the drive, my mind was turning on the possibilities: farm work and domestic work and leaving for the mills; what I could get without a good word from my former employer, who also happened to be the vicar. The future did not look rosy. And whatever work I managed to secure, whatever else happened, Mr. Moore would be gone. He must leave; he must be made to see that he must leave, before it was too late. I flung the gate wide, and it crashed back on its hinges, and I set off up the village street; Thomas stayed to fasten it, and then dashed after me. When Mr. Moore goes, I was thinking, I will have nothing. I will have nothing left at all.

The crowd almost blocked the road where it crested Brunt Hill. Irebys and Robinsons, and some of the Gorst boys, and Thomas's cousins, and men down from the hill-farms, almost strangers; it was uneasy to see them gathered there; another clear indication that the changes of Sunday were leaching into the weekday world. I made to slip through them, but Jack Gorst stopped me, and said, "You'd best know we've called a strike."

I'd thought things were as bad as they could be. I'd been wrong. "A what?"

"A strike," Richard Moss said. "No one's to have any dealings with the gentry or the clergy."

"Who says so?"

"We took a vote. We're all agreed on it."

"No one asked me," I said. Jack Gorst and Richard Moss just looked at me blankly a moment. "To what end?" I asked. "What are you striking for?"

"The land. We want the land back."

"Do you think this'll help?"

"See how they get along without us."

"Does Mr. Moore know?"

Jack shrugged. I shouldered past them. They fell into conversation with Thomas. He asked how they were getting on; the strike was not news to him. And yet he had been at the vicarage, delivering, as he put it. It puzzled me how he could be on such easy and familiar terms with both sides in the dispute. I wondered if the strikers knew where he had been.

There was a new book on the dresser. It was a play about a man called Hamlet who found it hard to screw up his courage to the point where he must kill his uncle, which seemed quite reasonable to me. Mam came home and found me reading. Although the house was spotless, it sealed her bad mood for the evening.

She'd been stopped in the street and told about the strike: there seemed no need to tell her about my dismissal; at least not yet, since nobody would be working. She couldn't be still; she was fretting that her cows would suffer unmilked, and she went out to talk to the men, and a crowd of them went up and did the evening milking. I stayed at home, and waited for Mr. Moore, but he did not come back. I finished the play, but at every sound from the street, at the faintest voice in the distance, I was up and at the window, or peering around the edge of the open front door, into the evening street.

The men brought pails back down from the Oversbys', slopping with milk. They went around all the houses with them. Mam filled a quart pot. She looked grim.

"They said I had to take it. They said everybody had to have some."

The boys had a mug of milk apiece, and Mam made a custard, and we sat and ate custard, my mam and me and the boys, and though it was sweet and good and the boys slobbered it down like puppies, when I caught Mam's worried expression, things felt very far from good. She told me that there had been a fight up at Oversbys'. The women of the family had already fled to town, Mr.

Oversby had stayed, they believed, but nobody had seen him. He'd left Sammy Tate to guard the dairy. Mam wouldn't have minded leaving the milk behind; it was only the cows she was concerned about; but the men were saying that the village was to have it, because the village needed it, and why should they pay for it, and Sammy had tried to stop them, and had got his head broken, and the milk was stolen, and that was why we all had to have some, so that everyone shared in that guilt. *If someone gets hurt*, Mr. Moore had said. *If someone gets killed, then—with my reputation—*

"Was Mr. Moore there?" I asked.

She shook her head. "I don't know where he's got to; or your dad."

They were out till after I fell asleep, and I didn't hear them come in. I don't know if they came separately or together, or if Mr. Moore had paused to look at me sleeping there on the kitchen floor. I remember thinking that despite everything, despite the danger and the trouble, and the worry, Mr. Moore had thought to leave a book for me. It made me strangely happy, even in all that confusion.

*

The next day stretched out ahead of me like a flooded field, calm and flat, with the usual paths across it hidden. Little to do but the chores of the house, which got done in no time at all, by my mam and me together. We started to consider daft ideas; that we would take down the curtains for cleaning; that we might drag bedding outside to let it air. In the end we didn't accomplish any of it. Mam remembered my half-finished dress, and set me to sewing, and set herself to help me with it.

"We'll hardly have the dance now," I said, "with all this going on."

"I don't see why not. And there's no good in leaving a thing half done."

The day started chilly, and then grew overcast. The boys were out of the house, though whether they'd actually gone to their work, I didn't know. Neither the smith nor the cordwainer could be considered gentry, much less clergy; but I doubted the boys would care for such nice distinctions.

Mr. Moore stayed alone upstairs all morning; I could hear him moving around. He only came down a little after dinner-time, though we hadn't actually thought to prepare a meal. He went straight over to the dresser and took the book and replaced it with another. Until then, the books had appeared and disappeared mysteriously, covertly. To see him do this, quite openly, made me feel even more uneasy. Things were different now; some things that had seemed to matter no longer mattered at all. There was no time to waste. The way he did it also seemed so simple; as artlessly thoughtful as the lighting of a candle to save my eyes. It made my throat ache.

He drank tea with my mam and me, and he tried to talk of ordinary things, but Mam was stiff with him, and I was awkward and over-full of feeling. I tidied away the tea things, and glanced towards the new book, but I had to sit back down to my sewing. Mam acted as if neither of us were really there; she barely spoke, barely looked at either of us. She mentioned Sally's absence as if it were an inexplicable thing. I heard horses approach, and looked up to see the Wolfendens' carriage pass the front window. I glimpsed Mrs. Wolfenden's face, pale; she was staring bolt ahead.

Around four, my father banged into the house, a paper clamped in his fist, and I saw it was a *Northern Star*.

"So much for shoddy workmanship," he yelled at Mr. Moore. "So much for hastiness. There are strikes all over the region, in Colne, and Preston, and Skipton, and Lancaster. You should have stood with us, you should have stood with us. This is the dawn of a new age, a better one."

"I hope you're right." He gave my father a thin smile.

I knew that none of it was news to him, and that it didn't change a thing.

The new book that he had left me was another of those Greek ones; it ended badly, with a deal of blood. I lay reading it in the firelight after everyone had gone to bed. I left it on the dresser when I went up to speak to him.

He stood in the doorway, in his shirt and britches, and did not offer me to come in. His eyes were tired, and there were deep creases in his brow. We spoke in whispers.

"How long before the troops arrive, do you think?"

"I don't know."

"Go. Pack up tonight and go."

"I am an old man—" He seemed about to say something more, but shook his head. "Go downstairs, and go to sleep."

He closed the door on me, and my throat felt thick, and I was clumsy and stupid. I made my way blindly down the stairs, and lay down in my blankets, and could not sleep. I could hear the noise from the public house, all the way from the top of the village. Shouting and calling, and then music, and the jollity of it made me feel even more miserable, made me feel sick.

The next day I learned that the Reverend Wolfenden had been

seen out on horseback, heading away from the village towards
Storrs; it seemed no one had spoken to him. Mrs. Briggs, who was
from outside the village and lived in, and Mr. Fowler, were the
only servants kept on at the house. The other servants had said
that they were striking; I think many of them had been dismissed
as I had, because of their families' connections to the trouble; they
just didn't like to own it. Thomas told me all this, passing on the
news in the cool of the morning, as he stood on our bottom step
and leaned against the handrail.

"I don't mean to be peddling scandal," he said, "just to let you
know how the wind blows, so that you needn't feel so bad about
your own circumstances." He smiled at me. I was grateful to him
for the kindness.

The Harvest Dance was to take place that evening. There was
a strange holiday air about the village. The women had been
out putting up decorations, pinning corn dollies and wreaths of
autumn flowers, of fern and bay and ribbons to their doors. It
seemed there was no getting out of it.

"Did you finish your dress?" Thomas asked.

I lied and said I had. He nodded, looking satisfied. I leaned
there, on the handrail, a couple of steps up from him. Mr. Gorst
passed on his strait-cart; it was tied with streamers, a rosette nodded on Poppy's forelock. Agnes came out of her front door with
the baby at her shoulder; I waved to her and she crossed the street
to join us. That so much had happened, so much had changed,
and that I still had to go to the dance with Thomas; it seemed
unjust, it seemed ridiculous, it seemed almost funny.

Agnes stood with us a while, and the baby, swaddled tightly,
its head hidden in a white cotton cap, butted at her shoulder.

"He's hungry," she said. "I'm trying to keep him hungry for a little while, so that then I can fill him up completely, otherwise all I ever do is feed him day and night, little dribs and drabs."

Thomas flushed up. "I'd best be gone," he said, and he went off down the village street towards his mam's house with that long-legged lope of his.

"How are you now?" I asked Agnes. She shook her head, and looked puzzled, and was almost laughing.

"Every day he changes," she said. "It's as though he becomes more like himself. It's stupid, but I already miss him, the tiny little him, I miss yesterday's him, and tomorrow I will miss today's."

Mam opened the door behind me, and I pressed back against the handrail to let her pass. Her right arm was weighted with a covered basket. She greeted Agnes and commented on the baby's size. She was at the bottom of the steps when she turned back to me.

"When your dress is finished, will you pick the damsons, and bring them with you when you come up to the green? I haven't had a minute, but they're good and ripe and sweet as anything." Then she went off up the street.

"Well, I must go and feed the little man then," Agnes said. I stepped down onto the street and kissed her, and said that I would call for her soon.

"I'll be at the dance," she said, "though I doubt that I'll be doing much dancing."

*

The damsons were warm and soft and bluish-bloomed. They came away easy from their stalks. I was thinking of the last spate of books that Mr. Moore had left me, of the bewitched Medea sailing off with Jason, her dismembered brother's body drifting in their wake. I was thinking of the smell of crackling fat, the skin stretched crisp and golden, a roast child on a platter carried into a wedding feast. These things of such horror and gravity and darkness, that had, at the same time, a kind of conviction and certainty that seemed wonderful to me. A poet lost in a forest and confronted by wild beasts; Ulysses lashing together tree trunks on Calypso's island; Ophelia adrift in the water, trailing flowers, because there was really nothing left for her to do but die.

Once I had picked the damsons, I would have to finish the dress. There was only the hem left to turn. Then I would wash and dress and pin up my hair and go to the dance, and I would dance with Thomas. And Mr. Moore would leave, if not today then very soon; he had to leave; he had to be made to go. I would stay, and Thomas and I would marry, unless I could think of some way out of it, and I was beginning to see that I could think of no way out of it at all. I felt angry with Dad, and with Thomas, and with Mam, and with Mr. Moore, but most of all, I felt angry with myself. Other hands may have cut out the pieces, but I had sewn every stitch of my situation.

I was standing underneath the drooping damson branches, my bowl not yet half full. I had stood there I don't know how long, without picking a single fruit. I closed my eyes and took a long slow breath. The gentry were fled. The clergy were gone. The strike continued. The troops were on their way, no doubt of it. However little I wished him to be gone, he had to be made to see that he must go. He had stayed too long already. I had to make him leave; I had to know that he was safe, even if that meant I

could never see him again. He could not be sent half a world away
to die. I would not let it happen.

*

He'd left the door open. He was sitting on his bed with his legs
stretched out over the counterpane and his patched boots dangling over the edge. He was leaning back against the wall, so that
he could look up the village street, at the passers-by, the flower
garlands, the corn dollies, the streamers. I watched him in silence
for a moment, then he turned from the window to look at me.
His face was drawn; it seemed to be in strange contrast to the
childlike way that he was sitting.

"There you are," he said.

I nodded. He had been thinking of me: the realization made
other thought difficult.

"Did you get your dress finished?"

The question was even more unsettling. I watched his right
thumb stroke the back of the left, following the length of the
white scar.

"I haven't done the hem yet."

Then the band started up on the green. It was faint enough due
to the distance, but the music seemed to buzz around me, and I
wanted to bat it away, like a wasp. An annoying tune, bright and
cheerful.

"You'd better get it finished then," he said.

"It doesn't matter."

"Your mother will have your hide."

"I know."

His fingers interlocked, separated. Nails pinched at a scrap of skin, pushed back cuticles; just like that first night, his hands were restless, never still.

"That boy will be lucky to get a look in."

I shook my head, vexed by the distance between his thoughts and mine.

"With you in your new dress," he said, "every man there will want to dance with you."

"I wouldn't," I said. "Anyway, they won't. It doesn't matter."

His eyes were so clear and direct that although I was colouring I could not look away. I was still holding the bowl of damsons; I hadn't thought to put it down. I knew I must look bad-tempered and ridiculous; it didn't matter. I took a step towards him, into the room.

"You must go, Mr. Moore." The subject finally broached, words kept tumbling out. "There was a boy hurt last night, up at Storrs; Sammy Tate."

"Sammy? Is he all right? What happened?"

"I don't know, I don't know. But you must leave now, as quickly as you can, you must get out of here before they blame you for it."

He blinked. "I can't leave you."

And though everything was just as it had been, the bookcase, the bed, the table and chair, and him sitting there looking pale and tired and like a child, it was as though the sun had come through clouds and lit everything differently, and everything seemed transformed. He shifted himself to the edge of the bed and got up. The wooden frame creaked just like it used to.

"I know you hate to sew," he said. "I know you have no patience for it. Every time you've picked up that dress to work on it, your face has been a picture of vexation, and you don't know it but you look so—your skin, and the cotton in a heap in your lap, it's the perfect colour for you, that boy isn't entirely witless. And the light catches in your hair, and maybe you don't know that there's a tint of red there, and you sit there squinting at your work, and your forehead's all furrowed and you're muttering under your breath." He took a breath then and let it go thinly, between narrowed lips. "It's been breaking my heart every day, watching you, knowing that you'll wear the dress for another man. For him."

I felt that I was standing in openness and sunshine and air, the sky great above me, the prospect limitless. He came closer.

"Not even a man; a youth, a *boy*. I have to ask you, I'm sorry, but I have to know. Are you going to marry him?"

Up on the green, the band lost their timing, the individual instruments stumbling to their separate halts. For a moment there was peace.

"My parents think I should."

"And so you will?"

"I have to do something, I can't go on living here forever. It's been far too crowded since they let out my room."

His face went as grey as ash. "You can't resign yourself to this, to being a beast of burden, a brood mare—"

"Do you have a better idea?"

I couldn't help but smile. He caught my smile and answered it. "Yes."

I didn't know why there were tears. I moved towards him, and his arms were open to receive me, and there was a moment's space between us, and my eyes were on a level with the open neck of his shirt, the brown skin and soft curls of hair. Then he put his arms around me and drew me to him, and I reached my arms around him, and his body was warm; I felt the warmth of him, and rested my head against his shirt, and pressed myself tightly to him, and I could hear the thud of his heart, and feel his breath press against me, and I could hardly breathe for happiness.

Each type of wood has its own particular scent. Where woodlands are old and mixed it is not always easily determined, but where only one type of tree is planted for timber or coppiced for charcoal or basketwork, or where one tree stands alone, distinct and separate from all others, the individual scents are unmistakable. In sunshine, after rain, sycamore has a greenish sappy scent, beech trees smell sweet and nutty. Shelter under an oak from a shower, and you will become conscious of the fragrance all around you, a wholesome smell like moss and oatmeal. Willow, on the other hand, retains through all processes a bitter yellow taint: it seems to linger on the senses, remain a sourness in the throat.

Robert Moore smelt of oak.

I know I smell of willow, it is worn into my skin.

*

We ate the damsons, sucked the melting toffee flesh from the stones. We lay there without speaking, lying on the bed, on my old bed, on my old patchwork quilt, me in nothing but my shift and loosened stays, him in nothing but his shirt. I felt shy of him, very conscious of the sounds of my eating, and of the places where our limbs still touched. I turned a damson stone around on my tongue, and picked it from my lips, and held it warming in my hand with the other ones, not knowing what else to do with them. The street was quiet below, and there was distant gentle music from the green.

He touched the cool flesh of my arm with his scarred hand. I glanced around at him. He smiled an awkward, shy smile.

"Now you have to marry me."

My future had seemed set in stone, but we had thrown that stone into the air, and it had landed with a smash and shattered, scattering into a thousand little pieces, and the pieces had rolled and tumbled, and were settling into a new pattern; a beautiful new pattern, any pattern at all: I could arrange it as I wished.

"Do you remember how you told me about that shrew?" he asked.

He lifted the empty damson bowl and held it to me: I dropped the fleshless stones into it; he tumbled his palmful in after.

"I remember."

"And you said, *We flicker into life, and out again, like candle flames.* Do you remember that?"

He put the bowl down beside the bed; I closed my hand, feeling the fruit-juice film of stickiness.

"I think so."

He turned back to me. "And you said about fishes turning into stones, and everyone going about from day to day ignorant of the fact?"

"Yes."

"I always thought that you were pretty. But since that day, the idea of you with that boy—" He shook his head.

A thought blossomed in my head, making me smile: "Is that why you kept lending me the books, to keep me from my sewing?"

He smiled back at me. "My motives there were purely schol-
arly."

The clock struck the half-hour, and he asked what o'clock it
was, but I didn't know. He said that we should get dressed and
I agreed, but neither of us moved. We lay in silence for a while.
My shyness had melted entirely. He reached out an arm, and I
pressed myself to him; his arm under my head, my cheek on his
chest, a knee curled onto his leg, an arm around his waist. His
hand touched my hair.

"It'll be unsettled, Elizabeth. Our life together; it's bound
to be."

"I don't care."

"It'll be difficult."

"I don't care."

And I really didn't. No obstacle was insurmountable; anything
could be achieved.

"I've been thinking about America. Could you fancy America?"

America. The boy had sailed there in the ballad. In a ship with
sails that bellied out like linen on the line.

"I think I could."

The three-quarter bell struck, and he stirred, slid his arm out
from underneath my head, and he got to his feet, and then took
my hand and I stood up with him, and he took a step back from
me, and just stood looking at me as I stood there, and he was so
serious and sober in manner, that I didn't feel ashamed, and I
knew that this was a time more real than any other, and unchanging, permanent. He pulled me to him and held me again, the
length of his body pressed against mine.

"Did you know, before Eve, Adam had another wife? God made her out of clay, just like Adam."

I smiled against the soft linen of his shirt, the warmth of his chest. "Nonsense."

"No, it's just not in our Bible. They left it out."

A moment passed while I considered this. "What happened to her?"

"They didn't get along so well."

"That's a shame."

"Adam was a fool. I love you."

*

He helped me with my stays. He drew them just tight enough, making me breathe high and shallow, but not pinching too much. I found myself wanting to ask about his wife, about the child, but I knew that it was not the time. He bent close to peer at the tiny hooks and eyes of my new dress.

He would leave that evening and walk to Lancaster, taking the footpath along the riverbank, avoiding the main roads. He could go unobserved that way, he said. The most he'd be likely to come across would be a poacher or a gamekeeper, and the lack of interest would be mutual. When he got to town, he would make arrangements and send for me, and for his books. We would be married in Lancaster, he said, that is, if I consented, since I hadn't actually given him an answer yet.

"But you haven't actually asked."

"Didn't I?"

"No, you instructed."

"Well then, that must be remedied." He took my hands,

looked into my face, half smiling, half serious. "Would you do me the honour of consenting to be my wife?"

It was dizzying, the way things had changed, the way we'd changed towards each other. I was so conscious of my own happiness that it made me shy again.

"Yes," I said.

He touched a hand to my cheek. I still remember the feeling of it, the cool hard dryness of his palm, as if the flesh there is somehow haunted by his touch. "Just to do that; to touch you—" He shook his head.

He said he'd a friend who had a packet boat at Glasson Dock, it would take us down to London. There, he had other friends, and we could stay with them while he found work, since there was always work in London. And it was easy to go unnoticed there. He would keep his head down, stay quiet for a time. If that did not fall out well for us, we would go to America. He knew people who had gone there, and been prosperous. They'd help him find work and establish himself. Whatever happened, we would be together, and therefore happy.

I was so giddy with everything that if he'd just suggested emigration to the moon I wouldn't have raised a single objection. He loved me. His happiness depended on my company. We would be together. Anything seemed possible now.

He found paper, and folded it, and wrote a direction on it. He fixed a stamp to it.

"If anything goes wrong, if something happens and you find you need me urgently, write to me. You know how this works, don't you. All you need do is write your message, seal it, and leave it in the box, and it will be collected and brought to me at this address. If I can't come for you myself for whatever reason, I'll send for you."

I took the paper and tucked it inside my bodice. I reached up and combed my fingers through my fallen hair. I divided it into three and began to twist it into a plait.

"You must be patient," he said. "It will take a while to find lodgings, to make arrangements and send for you, it might take days. But I will send for you as soon as I can."

"I know." I felt a new kind of calm. All would be well. The certainty must have shone from me like light from a candle flame.

"Enjoy yourself," he said. "Dance yourself giddy. Behave as though nothing is out of the ordinary."

I lifted the plait, coiled it around with a ribbon and pinned it into place. "Everything is out of the ordinary."

He touched the nape of my neck. "I used to have to try so hard not to hate him, and now I haven't even a shred of guilt regarding him. I don't even feel sorry for him. I really must be a wicked man."

"You're irredeemable," I said.

"And yet uniquely blessed." He paused for a moment, suddenly grave. "You don't mind leaving all this? You won't miss your family, your friends?"

I found myself thinking about this a moment longer than was comfortable. His expression clouded with concern.

"Not second thoughts?" he asked.

"Not second thoughts," I said, fumbling for the right words. "The opposite, perhaps. I feel like I've been missing people for a long time now; that they're already gone." I smiled to show it didn't matter. His looks clouded deeper. He touched my face, kissed my lips.

The piece of paper, that I had tucked so carefully inside my bodice; I knew it would not be needed. It would be my talisman, my charm. Nothing would stand between us, not Thomas, not my father, not the whole of Her Majesty's Militia. To me, at that moment, it didn't matter whether we were married in Lancaster or London or not at all. This had been my wedding, this was my wedding dress. Though I hadn't had the chance to finish it: the hem was still held up with pins.

*

There was a smell of woodsmoke, the peppery scent of fern, and sweet straw and late roses. I could hear music from up on the green, and as I got closer, laughter, and talking. It seemed as though the houses were decorated in honour of my passing, the music was playing for me, everyone was gathered on the green to wait for my arrival. I was the heart and purpose of it all, and at the same time set apart, observing and appraising like a queen. The skirts were soft and rustling around my ankles; only now and then did the point of a pin snag my stocking or prick my skin. Everything was beautiful and strange and familiar, and none of it mattered at all.

The road was almost blocked with gigs and traps and wagons; horses were cropping the grass banks. The green swarmed with people like ants in a broken anthill. From the elevation of a wagon's tail, the musicians gave out a vigorous rendition of "Grimstock," and on the ground in front of them the dance was in full swing. Children raced about in packs or sat in conference over a posy or a ribbon. Older folk were ranged on benches and clusters of stools, rehearsing ancient gossip. It was the same as last year, the same as the year before and the year before that. The same people, bar a few losses and additions; the same decorations, the same tunes, the same dances. The same smell of horses, sweat, ferns, flowers and smoke. It was the same as every year that I could remember since I was a little girl, except that now I was changed and was no longer part of it.

I walked out onto the green. I caught Mrs. Forster's eye quite by chance; she was standing with her husband, who was in conversation with Mr. Aitken; seeing me, she turned uneasily, and I saw that Sally was with her, on her other side. It was unexpected to see them there, after everything. Perhaps, I thought as I went over to them, things were not quite as bad as I had feared. I greeted them, and ducked in to kiss Sally, and she straightened her bonnet. I hadn't seen it or her dress before. They were both remarkably pretty.

"You're looking well, Lizzy," she said. I thanked her. "It was considered important that we be here."

I nodded; I didn't register then the significance of her words, or her look, which was much older than her years. I was thinking that this might be the last time I ever saw her, and that I loved her, and that she was a perfect little madam but I'd miss her.

"Sally?"

She was scanning the dancers, her sharp face at once aloof and curious.

"Yes?"

I chose the words carefully so as to fit with her new way of speaking.

"Have you seen our mother?"

"She was helping with the dinner, but I think she's watching the dancers now."

I wanted to hug her, shake her, remind her of the times she'd wet the bed on us. "Thank you."

I took her hand; she gave me a sharp little glance. I went to find my mam.

*

She was perched on the end of a bench, watching the dance. She glanced up as I approached, got up straight away, and took my arm, and walked with me away from the dance, to where there was space to stand comfortably and talk.

"Did you bring the damsons?"

I nodded. "They're eaten already."

"That tree's a good fruiter." She kept hold of my arm, and glanced down at my hem. "And you got that done."

She looked up at me and raised her fingertips towards the ribbon in my hair, and the ghost of Mr. Moore's touch grazed my skin again. I blushed, and seeing the blush, and misunderstanding it, she smiled, and said, "You look lovely, Lizzy; Thomas is over there."

I didn't mean to; I glanced over. He was standing with David Airey, and they were both staring at me, and Thomas had a faint smile on his face that I didn't like. I looked away, asked Mam if she'd seen my dad. She shook her head. There was something odd about her manner; I couldn't place it for a moment, and then I realized. She was peaceful. She was content. She wasn't worried.

"What's happened?"

"All is well."

"What do you mean?"

She smiled and tugged my bodice straight.

"What about Dad? Mr. Moore said there would be troops; that the Riot Act would be read and there would be troops. And now the Aitkens and the Forsters are here as if nothing's happened, and there's no sign of Dad."

"The Riot Act's been read. We are quiet now. You're father is in the public house if he is anywhere; and he'd better enjoy it because it's his last chance: after this I'm cracking down."

"I don't understand."

"The troops are on their way."

"But then—" Panic seized me. I turned from her. She took my arm again, speaking calmly, as if delivering a dull but necessary lesson.

"Mr. Aitken read the Riot Act this afternoon, and then the Reverend spoke to the men; you'll have missed all this, staying home to finish your dress. Without Mr. Moore there to lead them on, the men have seen sense, it's all cleared up, so you needn't worry about your father. Or no more than usual, anyway. The worst he's going to get today is drunk."

"But what about Mr. Moore?"

My mam shrugged. "We'll be rid of him." She let go of my arm. She looked quietly happy. "It was only Sammy actually got hurt; a crack to the head was all; he's never been the sharpest stick in the woodpile anyway; there's no real damage done. It's all forgotten. Or it will be soon."

I was lifting my hem to go, to rush back the way I'd come, to get to Mr. Moore, but then Thomas was there; he took my other arm, and said, "You'll dance with me, Lizzy," and he drew me off into the dance.

They were lined up for Strip the Willow; the band were playing the opening phrases of the new tune.

"I can't," I said, "I have to go."

Thomas didn't seem to hear me. He was marching over, trailing me behind. He deposited me at the top of the line of women. It all happened so fast. Feet thumped the grass to the music: it lurched towards the cue, and Thomas grabbed my arm with his, clamped me to his side, and spun me down the lines of dancers. I was dragged along, dizzy and whirling, flung from Thomas to be spun by the other men, then grabbed hold of again by him, and spun some more. My toes barely touched the ground. We came to a dead stop, and Thomas let go of my arm. We stood, gasping, facing each other. Down the vacant strip of grass between us, the next couple whirled in the dance. Thomas stood there, his cheeks flushed, grinning at me.

"Were you there when they read the Riot Act?" I asked.

His smile faltered and he looked away, towards the dancers.

"What's going to happen? What did they say?"

"It doesn't matter."

"What did they say?" I asked more urgently, stepping towards him, suspicious of his uneasy smile. The dancers reached us; Michael Robinson slipped his arm under mine, and he spun me around and around, and I was almost flying, desperate to be set down, to be let alone, to get my head clear. He dropped me down again, facing Thomas, who was stamping his foot on the crushed grass, slightly out of time, and was gazing up the line of dancers as the next whirling couple bore down on us.

"What did they say?" I asked again.

Thomas pretended not to hear.

"What's going to happen, Thomas?" I could hear the irritation and impatience in my voice. "*What did they say?*"

Thomas looked directly at me. His eyes were clear and cold and knowing. "The Reverend said we could repent, and be forgiven, but there are some that are irredeemable."

And then Richard Moss grabbed my arm, and spun me. And as I whirled around, ribbons flying, dress tangling around my feet, the pins pricking at my ankles, I saw them. The vision blurred, and then my back was turned, and then again, I saw the blur of red, the light glinting on metal, the dust rising from the dry road as they came. And through the beat of the music, and the clapping, and the dancers' stamping, there was, beneath it all, and through everything, the beat of their marching feet. I was dropped, I staggered, sick and winded. My head seemed to catch up with me, and I saw them for the first time clearly. Foot soldiers; half a dozen of them; an officer on horseback. They were turning down the village street. Six men and an officer, and there was only one of him.

I stepped out of the line. Thomas caught my arm. The music seemed to falter, slow.

"They are coming for him—"

"Stay in your place," Thomas said.

The music picked up again; the next couple had taken hold of each other's hands, and were spinning down the lines towards us. I pulled against his grip.

"Stay in your place," he said again.

I dug my nails into his fingers, twisted my arm out of his grip; he cursed and let go. I took one last look at the red coats, the glossy sheen of the horse's flank. I knew a shortcut. I ran.

I bundled up my skirt to scramble over the stile into Gosses' field. I raced through the stubble, not caring who saw me, not caring about anything but getting to him in time. My hair was falling loose; I was running faster than I'd run since I was a girl and we used to race each other over the hay meadow stubble, leaping over drifts of drying hay.

I could hear Thomas's heavy footfalls behind me. I didn't care; he wouldn't stop me; I'd get there before he could reach me. Down the road came the thudding march of the soldiers, the creak of their leather and jangle of tackle, and hoofbeats of the horse. My way was just a little shorter than theirs; they had the advantage of a start on me, but then they didn't know that it was a race. My hair was streaming, my eyes wet, my breath caught high in my chest, my ribs crushing themselves against my stays. They couldn't have him; I wouldn't let them. I would get to him in time.

I came flying up to the back wall of our garden and crashed into it. I was too late. They were there. Two soldiers in red coats were trampling the garden, pushing the currant canes aside, crushing the leeks and kale. I saw others through the side windows, already in the house. One stood sentry at the back door. Another stood near the bottom of the front steps. The officer sat poker-straight on his horse. Thomas thundered up and landed against the wall beside me. His breath was noisy; mine had already calmed. I remember that slow strange feeling of certainty as I watched a soldier come out of our house and approach the officer, and the officer lean down in the saddle to hear him.

They had not found him. I knew they had not found him. Mr. Moore was gone.

The officer straightened up, nodded, and dismissed the man. His voice carried clear across the battered garden.

"Burn them."

I couldn't watch, but neither could I leave. I turned my back and sank down in the blunt stubble. I put my head on my knees. Thomas slumped down beside me. For a while, there was just the noise of the soldiers moving around, and orders barked at each other, and the flutter and thump of books flung in armfuls from the window and landing on the ground beneath. Then there were other voices. I heard Reverend Wolfenden. I heard others too, volunteering details of the local paths and byways, the greenlanes he might have taken. The crackle of kindling; a taint of smoke in the air. Orders were shouted from horseback: three men sent down the coffin lane towards the river crossing, another three to accompany the officer along the wash-house lane and sweep up the river paths towards Lancaster.

I got to my feet and turned to look. The clatter of running footsteps and hoofbeats was receding, and my father stood there, with the Reverend, and Mr. Aitken and Mr. Forster, and other men; they were just standing there, not looking at each other, not looking anywhere, not speaking. The Reverend turned and walked away down the village street, towards the vicarage, and the men drifted off up the village, and as they walked they fell into pairs or threes, but still I didn't hear a single word spoken. No one fell in to walk beside my father. He walked up the street alone.

Mr. Moore would hear them coming a mile off with the noise they were making. He'd slip off the path, dodge down a bank or behind a tree. They had no dogs to scent him out. His eyes would glitter like the river, but he would go unseen. Maybe he hadn't even gone yet. Perhaps he'd seen them coming, had slipped out the back way and hidden in the fields behind the house. I pressed the tears off my face and turned around to look. Across the sweep of field, the stubble stood brittle and upright in the evening cool. One trampled pathway crossed it, where Thomas and I had crushed it flat. No one else had come this way tonight.

Thomas stood up beside me. In silence, he put his hand on my shoulder. It was hot and heavy. I did not shake it off.

*

We trailed back to the dance. We walked up through the middle of the field, retracing our own footsteps. Thomas went ahead, and I followed, my skirt caught up in my hand. The pins had fallen out, and now the hem trailed, the edge thready and raw. Underneath, my stockings were snagged and bloodied. When we reached the stile, Thomas offered me his hand to help me over. We stood like that for what seemed an age, looking at each other, his hand raised to take mine and help me over and down, back onto the green, back among the people, back into the dance. I could have asked him then what part he'd had in this, what had passed between him and the Reverend, what he had been doing at the vicarage that day; but I was worn out, preoccupied, and I still hoped that things would be well; in truth, I didn't want to know. After all, it was Thomas, only Thomas, with his kind broad face, and his ears that stuck out a little, and he was looking at me with such fierce attention, that I felt something like tenderness for him. I took his hand, and he helped me over, and the moment for asking him was gone.

"Your hair is all fallen," he said.

I stood, and began to gather it, divide it, twist it and pin it up. Thomas watched, and he touched the ribbon there, his fingers rough-skinned but gentle, and nodded to show when it was done. We were walking side by side towards the dance, towards the music and people. There were nudges and smiles. I touched at my hair uneasily. There was no remedy for the fallen hem.

My mam didn't say anything. I told her that I wanted to go home, and she gave me a long assessing look, and her face softened.

"Come on then."

The bonfire was visible from the turn of the street; a dark bloody red, smoke that seemed to hang in a pool around the house. Indoors, the rooms reeked of strange smoke; of burning leather and paper and buckram and glue. Mam moved about, tutting, setting things to rights. I sat at the window in the dimming light, and watched the fire grow deeper red, and the plants and fruit canes wither and scorch, felt the vapours and mists of the unfinished stories burn away, and disperse with the smoke into the evening air.

Mam brought me tea, and I blinked away tears. She dragged over a chair to sit with me at the window, and we drank our tea from the cups she was given when she was seventeen and left service to marry Dad, and we sat in silence while outside the books burned orange and green and blue, and cracked and spat, and the words peeled away into black ash, and tiny fragments of paper were caught by the wind. A word here, a phrase there, lifted to the sky and scattered.

"Would the Wolfendens take you back, do you think?" she said. "The Reverend was saying a lot about forgiveness today."

"I doubt it."

There was silence. Then she said, "Did he touch you?"

I looked at her; her dark lined skin, her apple cheeks.

She said, "Sweetheart?"

There was just the soft sound of my lips unsticking, but I couldn't speak.

"I saw the state of you when you got back to the dance," she said. "Everyone did."

She meant Thomas.

"There's nothing you need to tell me about?"

"No," I said, half-choked.

She nodded. After a while, she said, "You're tired, you should go to bed."

I rose, went to get the bedding from the chest.

"No, honey," she said.

I let the blanket fall back into the chest, let the lid fall shut. Upstairs, she meant; in my old bed, in Mr. Moore's bed. My face flushed with feeling: to hide it, and to show that there was nothing out of the ordinary, I went over to the dresser to get a book, as I had done every night since I was a little girl. There, pressed tightly between the black spines of the Bible and the *Pilgrim's Progress*, was that little blue-backed volume of John Milton's verse. Mr. Moore had left it for me. In those last hurried moments before departure, he had risked himself, and his liberty, to leave me this. I slipped it off the shelf, and wrapped my arms over it, pressing it close to me. I went straight up to the room. The room bore the marks of the soldiers' presence: the rucked-up rug, the empty shelves, the smell of burning. He had gone, but there were traces of him still: his empty box, the compression of the pillow, the bookcase. I stood in the middle of the room and opened the book that he had left me. On the flyleaf he had written, in his neat, practical hand,

> *For Elizabeth*
> *a loan,*
> *until I see you again*
> *Robert James Moore.*

I lay down. I buried my face in the pillow, breathed deep the scent of him. Oak. Still in that dress, my ankles pricked and bleeding, my face tangling in my hair, worn out with crying, I fell asleep.

*

I had been as a salmon hatched and grown in a backwater, its flesh muddy and soft from the stillness of its pond. With Mr. Moore's arrival, a flood had thundered through my life, joining the backwater to the river's flow, washing away the murk, bringing life and possibility, bringing evidence of a better life beyond, of an element that seemed my natural home. Having felt it, having tasted it, I knew it would be a joy to be alive in it. I could never settle again in the backwater, and be content. I knew now that I had never really been content before.

Weeks passed, and I heard nothing. I stayed at home to nurse Dad, who had been laid low with a chill from staying out all night after the dance, carousing with his friends. With scant distraction, it was hard to keep the images of Mr. Moore's capture and imprisonment at bay: I saw him shivering with fever in a gaol cell. I saw him lying in a ditch, a sabre wound in his side, flies buzzing in his open eyes. Every passing cart or wagon or walker made my heart race with possibility, but it was never him. It was a torment to remain at home when any moment might bring a message from him, but never did. When Thomas called, I walked out with him.

And a month had gone.

Mam got the tonic bottle down, started dosing me with it again. It smelt particularly foul; worse than before; I could barely keep it down. She had something else for my father, another bottle that she'd got Thomas to fetch from the apothecary in Hornby. She took it up to him in the evenings and would sit with him a while to give me some relief. The house seemed terribly quiet. The boys stayed long hours at their masters' and now mostly took their meals there. We worked on baskets; little whitework ladies' baskets that Thomas had asked us to make for him to sell on Hornby Market.

*

"Have you come to an agreement with him?"

Mam was turning the edge of the basket lid. We had been sitting in silence for a half-hour; I'd been lost in reverie. The sudden words made me start, and I didn't catch her meaning.

"Pardon?"

"Thomas. When are you going to marry him?"

"Mam, no, don't—"

"Don't you *don't* me!" she snapped, suddenly cross. "It's too late for *don't*, miss. If you didn't want to marry him you should have said that to *him*."

"Said what?"

"*Don't*." She just looked at me, her lips compressed, her cheeks flushed. Then she put down the basket, and touched my arm, and said that we could make it right. They could get the banns read, there would be plenty of time, and no one thought much of a baby born seven or eight months after a wedding, it happened all the time, and it would put an end to all the talk, I must know there had been talk, even I couldn't have missed noticing it.

There had been no blood that month. I knew that she was right. I went up to my room, and I took the folded paper that Mr. Moore had given me out from where I kept it, tucked between my stays and my shift. I read the direction he had written. A house on Fell Lane, Lancaster. The ink was already smudged and soft; the stamp was black and beautiful, with a young girl's head on it, her hair ringleted and pretty. I'd been so happy. I'd never thought I'd need it. So I hadn't told him—I'd been too ashamed to tell him— that I couldn't write. I'd thought that he would come to teach me. I'd thought that there'd be years.

*

I left that night, following the way he was to have gone, along the river path to Lancaster. It was still and clear, the ground hard with frost. There were boys out setting snares for rabbits down near Thrush Gill. I thought I saw Ted's pale thatch of hair in the moon- light, but wasn't sure, and they didn't notice me, and I hoped the keeper didn't notice them. I tried not to think of my dad, the way the flesh had fallen from his bones, the yellow tint to his skin. If I saw any of them again, it would not be for many years.

I followed the silver glimmer of the river, the thick shadow of the riverbank. I climbed the rise up through the trees. Birds twittered in the undergrowth; something passed through the long grass; I glimpsed it in the corner of my eye; the trailing brush of a dog fox. I came out of the trees to the parish marker, where we'd sat at Easter, and had our dinner spread on blankets. Below, the river rattled over shilloe; ahead, the arched stonework of Loyn Bridge caught the moonlight then lost itself in the woods on the far bank. Soon, I was beyond the bridge, skirting open meadow; keeping to hedgerows, copses. The light grew. The sun was rising over the hills to my left as I passed Caton; it flooded the valley with lilac and lavender light; birds were breaking out into song. Halton was just waking as I passed through. I came to a vast bridge, spanning the entire valley, pillars studding the meadow and river like petrified giants. I was dizzied just with looking up at it. The path turned to the hillside; steps rose up the flank of the bridge. I climbed up, thinking to find the road into town, but it was the navigation, a great weight of water suspended in the sky. A heavy skewbald mare came clopping slowly along, towing a barge, hundreds of feet above the valley floor. There was a man at her head, leading her.

"Pardon me," I called, "is this the right way into town?"

"Aye," he said. "It is." His voice was strangely accented, his face weather-tanned and pocked. "D'you want a lift? Hop on."

I thanked him. He held the horse, and a second man came out of the long low cabin and helped me on board. There was a bench built into the front of the boat; I sat there, and wrapped my shawl around me, and the horse began to walk on, and the barge to move, and suddenly the weight of all that had happened, and what I had done, and the fatigue of my journey, descended on me together, and I leaned my head against the side of the cabin, and I closed my eyes. I heard the gentle thump of the horse's hooves, the wash of the water against the prow, a clink and clatter from within the cabin. It was a relief to be borne along.

I may have dozed a little; the next thing I remember was being offered a cup of steaming tea.

"It's a bit stewed," he said. "I've just heated it through. We were going to get new supplies at Atkinsons."

The tea was black and sour, but I was in need of it, and was grateful for it. He sat with me and asked where I was heading for, and I told him the street, and lied, saying that I was going to stay with friends and look for work, and he said he knew the street, it crossed the canal; he could let me off at the bridge. I thanked him, and he said it was no trouble, and he smiled.

The canal continued through open, marshy-looking fields, studded with sheep and cows. We passed a farm, then the canal was flanked with hawthorn and hazel hedgerows, heavy with berries and nuts, and it wasn't easy to see beyond them. There were high buildings ahead, built of golden stone. I could hear a strange humming, clattering sound, and was just about to ask the bargeman if he knew what it might be, but then we cleared a bend and were between the buildings; the air was filthy with smoke and damp; it was dark. Walls rose up on either side of the canal like cliffs, but full of bright-lit windows. Men scrambled to unload cargo from the barges onto the banks; others shifted the loads and hooked them to ropes hanging slack from winches and pulleys; others hoisted them up into the air, others leaned out to grab at the bundles and guide them into the buildings. All the time insults and instructions were flung back and forth and up and down. The noise was terrible. The air was vile. The clattering and burring were too loud almost to talk over.

"What's the noise?" I asked.

"Spinning," he said. "And weaving. They've got power looms now. They're the worst of it."

We'd passed the first mill and were approaching a bridge. He called out to the man at the horse's head, who spoke to her, slowed her to a halt. He lifted a pole from the roof of the cabin, and lowered it into the water, and pushed against it, moving the boat into the bank. They helped me off the barge.

"Up yon," the bargeman said. "That's Fell Lane."

I could see nothing but a flight of stone steps up the bridge, the slab-fronts of mills on either bank, the buildings beyond blanking out the sky.

"Thank you: thank you very much."

He shrugged. "Nay bother. Take care of yourself."

The horse walked placidly into the shadows of the bridge, and the first man went with her, and then the barge slipped into the darkness, and the bargeman waved at me, and they were gone. I climbed the steps up to the street; I felt faint now that I was nearing the journey's end; I couldn't catch my breath. I came out through a narrow gap; below me the street swept down through mills and warehouses and shops; above, there were flat-fronted terraced houses built in stone.

I checked the number on my slip of folded paper. 108. I made my way up hill, the paper clutched in my hand. The sound of the mills grew a little fainter. I'd never been to a house with a number before. It was new-looking, as if it hadn't yet settled onto its foundations, but was already streaked with damp. The front door opened straight onto the street. I knocked.

I waited, listening. A baby's cries, sharp and demanding. I felt something inside me cleave towards it, an urgency to comfort it, to stop it crying. I heard footsteps, and a murmuring consoling voice. The door was opened by a woman; she was carrying the baby. Too old to be the baby's mother, she was broad-hipped and broad-shouldered, with neat features; she had probably once been pretty. The baby was pressed to her shoulder, and as we spoke she shifted her weight from one foot to the other, swaying slightly back and forth. We pitched our voices over its cries.

"I'm here to see Mr. Moore."

She looked at me, tilting her head a little to one side.

"Mr. Moore. Is he in?"

I glanced past her into the dark, distempered hallway. A child came out of a back room; two years old perhaps; his head was a mop of straw-coloured hair.

"You've got the wrong house," she said.

I held out the folded paper for her to look at. "I don't think so. 108. That's what it says here."

She didn't even glance at it, just shook her head. I felt oddly cool and disconnected. All I had to do was find the right form of words and she would understand, all would suddenly come clear. She would smile and step aside and usher me through to him.

"I've come a long way; I do need to see him."

The baby's crying intensified. "I'm sure you do," she said.

"His friends, they live here, he gave me this address."

She just shook her head and shifted the baby. "There's just us. Family. I've never heard of your Mr. Moore. But then, we're not that long moved in." She laid the baby face down along her arm, its head in the crook. She stroked its back. It still squalled. I felt the first prickling possibility of alarm.

"My daughter's at the mill," she continued. "So's her husband. Shift's not long started, and the babby's already starved."

The baby's face was turned outwards, away from the woman's body. It was puce, outraged, the mouth a dark red gummy hole. My body wanted him; I wanted to take him, to soothe him somehow, his need seemed so overwhelming. "What'll you give him?"

"Sugared water, till she gets in."

I nodded. My own need pressed his aside: "The people here before you, do you know where they went?"

She shrugged. "There were chairs broken, the door kicked in, all sorts. Our Davey had to fix the lot."

And that was when I knew. He was not here, he would not be here. He couldn't be. He had stayed with me too long. When I spoke again my voice sounded strange to me, half whisper, half croak.

"Was it the Militia?"

She shook her head and shrugged, and the baby let out a howl, and she glanced down at him, and back at me.

"Sorry," she said. "I've got to try and get him settled. Good luck."

"Good luck," I murmured back.

She stepped back into the hall, and closed the door. I noticed then that the wood had been recently patched: cheap boards had been hammered across the timber, at the bottom and top, where the night-time bolts would fasten. The door kicked in in the middle of the night; men dragged from their beds. I turned away. Cobbles rose up steeply to my left, cobbles sloped down steeply to my right. The buzz and clatter of the mills, the rough air full of smoke. I had no strength, no will for anything. I thought of the baby, starving and furious and unfed. I thought of the baby's mother at the whirring bobbins, her breasts filling with milk, soaking wadded cloths so that her frock was patched with damp, and at dinner break she would have to wring out the cloths into the privy. Back home the baby wailing and wailing and wailing with hunger, until it was at last too tired to cry.

I was back home by the middle of the afternoon. My father was sleeping. I went to my room and lay down, and slept, a cold black sleep, a void. I was too heartsick for dreams. I woke towards evening, to the sound of Mam coming in, and I brought myself downstairs to her, expecting a fury and bowing my head before it. But she was calm, and tired, and didn't ask where I had been, and I realized that she hadn't known that I had even gone. She must have left in the morning without looking in on me, and had got back after I'd returned. She hadn't noticed my absence, and yet it had seemed ages-long to me.

The next time I walked out with Thomas, I took him to the hay barn, where we had sat a lifetime ago, when I had helped him learn his lesson for school. He kissed me, and I lay down with him, and let him coax my skirts up. He must have taken my awkwardness for innocence; he didn't seem to know enough to know that he was not my first. Afterwards, he said that we would be married in December, and that he would not take no for an answer. I did not say no.

*

Having seen Agnes in her throes, I thought I knew how bad it could be, and that I could get through it, but it is always different, and there is no way to know. Agnes was telling me it would be all right, that it would be all right, and she should have known that it was far beyond all right already, and could never be all right again. I wanted to say his name. I just wanted to say his name. I had to bite my lips from speaking it out loud, from shouting out his name with each dark hard squeeze of pain. I wanted him. But I could not say a word. The cowed, shambling, painful steps up to the room, where my mam had spread an old blanket on the floor, and the strange silence of the house, since Dad had died in the winter, and the boys were gone to their masters'. I knelt at the side of the bed, the bookcase looming dark and empty beside me, my brow pressed into the quilt, and I said it to myself, my lips moving where Mam and Agnes and Mrs. Skelton couldn't see them, pressed into the coverlet. Robert James. Robert James. Robert James Moore. Then there was the need to push, a need more overwhelming even than the pain, and the slow burning tear, and then the child was there.

They wrapped him up, and gave him to me, and he was so odd-looking, his face purple-blue and his head squashed, and I looked at him, the poor ugly little scrap of humanity that he was, and thought, I am going to have to love you, little boy. I am going to have to love you so very much.

The photographs were all in one bag, wrapped loosely. Some of the frames were newly bought, and held pictures culled out of photograph albums. Most were old and familiar, had been lifted from Mum and Dad's sideboard, dresser or bedroom wall. The images were etched deep into me from years' exposure. Dad, Mum, Lucy and me in a rowing boat on a day out at the seaside; I'm about four, Lucy's two, she's in navy blue dungarees; Dad's squinting in the sun, heavily moustached; Mum's hair is dark as treacle, her skin still smooth and pale, she's smiling carefully, waiting for the shutter's click. Lucy and me in school photographs: disastrous fringes and adult teeth too big for the rest of our faces. Nana in the back garden at home, in the sunshine, her hair still salt-and-pepper grey, smiling a perfect false-teeth smile, holding a tiny baby in her liver-spotted arms. The photographs that Mum had selected, the moments of her life that she had wanted to keep, to return to, to experience again. I laid them out on the carpet around me, an array of family images. There were just two pictures left in the bag, their backs turned to me. The first was in an old battered frame, the cardboard backing stuck down with crystalline-brown Sellotape. I lifted it out, half-knowing what it would be. She can't be more than twenty-four. She's wearing the coat; the empire-line, double-breasted, slate-grey woollen coat. It's snowing; she's laughing; shoulders up, hands raised to cup the falling flakes. She's beautiful. I found myself smiling back at her. I leaned the picture up against a box, was still smiling at it when I reached in for the last one. I took it out, glanced down at the back of a newish-looking clip frame, its brown hardboard and silver clips still unscuffed and shiny. I realized then that she must have brought the photos here quite recently, perhaps the last time that they came, in a break between treatments. She must have hoped, even then. She must have hoped there would be other times, that there could yet be years to come. I turned the clip frame around in my hands. I saw the picture. Black and white. A frail eggshell skull. Tiny translucent grey bones. The twelve-week scan. The scan of Cate.

I crushed the picture to me, leaning forward over it, cramming it into me; I couldn't breathe. Winded, choking, my lungs heaved out all their air, till I was empty and perfectly still, as if for a moment my heart ceased to beat, my lungs stopped their fluttering. Then, somehow, I drew a breath, a deep ragged breath, full of the smell of old carpet and dust, and curled around upon myself, curled around on the hard-edged picture frame, I began to cry.

*

It may have been hours later, I don't know. The day was brilliant, the sky hard blue. I carried the pewter jug out into the garden, blinking, set it down on the low stone wall. My eyes felt raw against the light. I was as exhausted as after labour, my limbs limp and soft as sponge. My movements were slow and careful, but my mind felt fresh, as if filled with cool clear water. Across the lawn, the grass was long and tangling, unkempt. I waded through it, getting my Converse soaked. Details caught and held me. A twist of pink and green, tiny entrails that a cat had left after a kill; the fat digestive progress of a slug across a leaf. I lifted drooping shrubbery out of the way, and there were a dozen skeins of flowerbuds hanging underneath; all they'd need was time and bees and sunshine and water to make them fatten and swell and darken into blackcurrants. I picked daffodils. A great heavy sappy bunch of them, each stem snapping with a satisfying puck. I lifted the pewter jug and walked down to the churchyard, my feet squelching.

I tore away the long grass, so that the name showed. I set the jug down, with the daffodils, on the flat earth. In the absence of any other ritual, I said her name, her maiden name, her nineteen-year-old name, out loud; there was no one there but me to hear it. No flicker of movement, no sense of someone hovering at the edges of my sight. The air was cool and soft; there would soon be rain.

I tidied up after, took the torn grass to the edge of the grave-yard and lobbed it over the wall onto the heap. The sight of the wired-up gate made me glance down at my hand, at the dark scab on the ball of my thumb; it itched, but the flare of infection was gone and it was beginning to heal. I climbed over the gate, into the woods, and headed on, eyes on the dark earth, looking for my phone. I finally found it under the skirts of a holly bush, its battery completely flat, damp beading the surface. I wiped it dry and slipped it into my pocket.

Back at the cottage, I plugged the phone in to charge. It beeped with missed calls. Forty-three calls from Mark, others from Lucy, Dad, and from friends. I left them all unanswered, for the time being. I had to talk to Mark first, and a phone call to him seemed utterly inadequate. I made other, practical calls: I made arrangements with the estate agents, that furniture charity.

I took a last walk around the house, moving from room to room, following the grey tracks in the carpet, running my hand up the rough timber of the banister. I paused by the bookcase, stroking the grain of the wood as if it were skin or fur. The house felt serene, and empty. As if a charge had been earthed, somehow; as if a tension had been released.

I left a set of keys with Mrs. Davies. We agreed that it was better for houses to be lived in, and that a young family would be nice; she kissed me goodbye.

*

The front of the car was still cluttered from the drive up: Dad's directions, half a packet of chewing gum squeezed flat at one end, a muddle of cassette tapes.

I drove for five hours, stopping only for coffee, sandwiches and petrol, the car rattling as I nudged it up to seventy-five, to eighty, to eighty-five. I swigged coffee through a plastic lid, eyes sharp for speed cameras, alert for a change in engine tone, for a hint of approaching breakdown. I was passed continually by bigger, sleeker cars. I wished I'd called Mark. At least then I would know what I was coming home to; I'd know if I could come home at all.

I elbowed my way through London traffic, sneaking through on ambers, nudging across carriageways, almost bouncing on my seat with frustration as I watched the traffic streaming past at junctions, thinking *come on come on come on come on come on*. I veered into Kirkside Road, and there was just one free space, right down at the far end. I had the car parked in one brisk and careless move. I'd slammed the door and was already heading for home, and then had to turn back and lock the car. I almost ran down the length of the street; a kind of hobbled run, eager and apprehensive, sick with nerves. I climbed the steps two at a time and got the key in the lock and was into the communal hall, and then I stalled at our front door.

I saw her. Through the textured glass, her figure was smudged and bleary. She was standing looking up at the table; there was something on it, something out of reach, something fascinating. Belly round in front of her, the soft bulge of her nappied behind. I turned my key, pushed open the door. Warmth; the smell of cooking, drying laundry. Cate turned towards the sound, away from the bowl of grapes that had been holding her attention. There was a moment. She looked at me, I looked at her. She pushed a finger into her mouth and chewed on it. My heart was still with anxiety and love. I crouched down.

"Sweetheart?"

Then her face broke into a wet smile, and she wobbled towards me, and put her arms up and around my neck, and I squeezed her tightly, teeth gritted, burying my face in her neck. The milky, musky scent of skin; the apple of her hair, my heart full, my eyes filling. I looked up, and there was Mark. He was standing in the kitchen doorway, a blue and white checked tea-cloth hanging from his hand. The cloth was stained with tomato sauce. His eyes were tired. I stayed there, holding Cate, looking up at him. We didn't speak for a long moment. Then he broke the silence.

"You're back."

"Yes."

"How are you?"

"Okay," I said.

"Really?"

I nodded.

"You look—" he said. He didn't finish the sentence.

"Is it okay?" I asked. "That I came back?"

His reply was out before I'd even really finished speaking: "Yes."

"I'm sorry."

He shook his head, his lips compressing, his chin dimpling. He blinked and pressed his eyes. When he spoke again, his voice was clotted with emotion: "Are you really okay?"

"Yes," I said. "Getting there, yes. I got the house sorted."

He nodded again. He just stood there, the tea towel still in his hand, his T-shirt dotted with sauce, looking at me.

"I'm sorry," I said. "I am really sorry."

"Bad timing," he said.

"Awful timing," I agreed.

"Come here," he said, with the first hint of a smile. I swung Cate up onto my hip, held her close. I went to him.

Historical Note

Despite massive popular support, the Chartist movement came to an end in 1854 without securing any of the aims set out in the Charter. Government repression of the movement had been harsh. The Chartists suffered mass arrests, show trials, transportation and imprisonment with hard labour. Submission of the Petition to Parliament was met with stonewalling: signatures were dismissed as either fakes, or as women's, both of which were considered equally valueless. Following the rejection of their petitions, the various factions within the Chartist movement found it difficult to agree on what strategy to adopt, and these internal tensions contributed to the movement's decline. Although the Chartists didn't see their goals achieved, their ideas eventually triumphed: their main demands (with the exception of annual parliaments) now form the basis of our democratic system.

Though Robert Moore is a fictional creation, his biography and experiences owe a great deal to two real characters: Robert Gammage, Chartist leader and the author of *History of the Chartist Movement*, and Robert Marsden, a handloom weaver, autodidact and key member of the Preston Chartists.

Acknowledgements

Key to the writing of this novel was an encounter with R. G. Gammage's *History of the Chartist Movement*. This uncovered to me a dark period in history of which I had been almost entirely ignorant. As a member of the Chartist movement himself, Gammage gives an account of its inception, struggles, and eventual dissolution that is compellingly vivid and intriguingly partial.

A number of other books have been helpful to the writing of this story, in particular William Graham's 1891 publication *Socialism New and Old*, Josephine Kamm's *Hope Deferred: Girls' Education in English History*, J. E. King's *Richard Marsden and the Preston Chartists*, Jonathan Rose's excellent *The Intellectual*

Life of the English Working Class, and E. P. Thompson's *The Making of the English Working Class*.

I'm extremely grateful to Dr. Mike Sanders for his invaluable insight into the Chartist movement and the events of 1842. His patience and erudition in answering my many queries, and his generosity in allowing me access to his own ongoing research, are greatly appreciated. Thanks are also due to Valerie Baker, Robert Baker, and Daragh and Daniel Carville, who have all helped in their various and much-valued ways. A good deal of the early work on this book was undertaken at the St. John Cavalier Centre for Creativity in Valetta, Malta; my thanks are due to the staff there, and to the British Council and Arts Council of Northern Ireland for funding my stay.

Very grateful thanks are due to Laura Barber for her care and extraordinary editorial insight in bringing the book to completion. And finally, to Clare Alexander: thank you.